TRUSTING YOU, TRUSTING ME

Tylor Paige

This book is dedicated to Sabrina.
You told me "Good luck making Derek likable."
Well, here's hoping I figured it out.

Chapter One

SHE

DITA

I WAS NEVER KNOWN for making good decisions. In fact, I always seemed to purposely choose the wrong one. From the time I could walk I was running away from everything that even slightly inconvenienced me. It was easier to avoid the problem altogether than deal with it head on.

Hence my current situation. For the first time in my 28 years, I was being held accountable for my actions; and it sucked.

For almost a year and a half I had been having a secret affair with my ex-boyfriend Adrian's best friend, Derek. I would have kept it private forever if Derek hadn't opened his mouth. It was easy to pretend it wasn't wrong when no one knew about it.

When Adrian found out the truth, he launched his fists and harsh words at Derek. Understandably. Those two were as close as friends could be. Them and their other two band members,

Mark and Cleo, were inseparable. Now, it looked like my mistakes could ruin everything.

That night Derek came over to my apartment with his face covered in blood. He told me that Adrian knew and had kicked his ass for it. Me, being the runner, I panicked and left.

Derek didn't seem nearly as concerned as I was.

"We can finally be open and honest about us. It was bound to happen eventually," he told me as I packed my bag.

"I don't want to do this Derek. Why did you tell him?" I demanded. He shrugged his shoulders.

"I don't know. I was pissed, a little buzzed. It just came out. What are you doing?"

I swung my backpack over my shoulder and went to the front door. I turned one last time before I opened the door.

"Remember to lock it when you leave," I said as I hurried out the door. I didn't know where I was going, I just needed to get out of there. The space was suffocating me.

As I pulled out of the parking lot my phone went off. I glanced down and saw Adrian's name on my screen. I ignored it and decided maybe it was time to really leave. But where could I go?

"Do you understand Miss Fox?"

I looked at my ancient, bible-thumping asshole of a boss, Mr. Faust. I took a deep breath before answering him. This was not the first meeting I'd been pulled in for, but it had been a long night and I was ready to go home.

"Yes sir. I will make sure to keep my tattoos fully covered from now on. Is there anything else?" I asked in my politest, fakest voice. His scowl turned into a bright smile. I swear he kept me around just because he loved yelling at me on a regular basis.

"Actually, yes. Some of your coworkers have expressed concern over some things they have seen lately- on the television."

I rolled my eyes and sat back in the chair. I wonder who it was that came to him. Amanda, or maybe it was Audrey. They were the office mean girls. It was probably both of them.

"What's on the television?" I asked innocently, although it was safe to assume what had been mentioned.

"Apparently they saw you and a man. A *musician*." He shuddered at the word, as if it tasted gross in his mouth.

"Yes. That is my boyfriend, Derek. Why is this an issue?" I asked, my patience dwindling quickly.

"Dita," he sighed and shook his head, as if he were explaining a basic math problem to a child for the millionth time. "I opened this veterinary clinic forty years ago with a promise to myself and my patients that they were being cared for by wholesome, good people with good values. Image is everything here and you are not the image I want my patients seeing. They are used to a certain kind of people and services. I will not have you causing a stir and causing distress to the people coming to us or your coworkers!" He slammed his hand on the desk causing me to jump. What in the hell? I swear this old man was going senile. I sat up straight and looked him dead in the eye.

"Are you punishing me or not? I've had a long night and would like to go home and get some rest for tonight's shift."

He huffed and glared back at me.

"Dita, I am afraid that I am officially putting you on warning. If you embarrass this office anymore, then I am going to have to let you go. You're a damn good veterinarian, but I can't have clients coming in and asking if we have a groupie working here. I don't care if you like being passed around from band member to band member like a bag of jelly beans, but I can't have that here. Do you understand?"

I clenched my jaw and took a few deep breaths, trying to calm myself before smiling and nodding.

"Yes sir. I'll be on my best behavior. Thank you," I said before standing up and quickly leaving his office. I passed by a snickering Audrey and giggling Amanda. I didn't give them the satisfaction of causing a scene. I left quickly, before I turned back and said something to them I'd regret later.

In the car I pulled out my phone and clicked on my web browser, typing in Derek's name with his band name added.

Derek Turtle Maria Maria

Clicking the search button, I closed my eyes tightly and did a silent prayer that it wasn't too bad. I took a deep breath and looked down at my screen. My stomach dropped. The first article was titled: Rock Band Members of Maria Maria Share Girlfriend.

I clicked on it and read the horribly researched article. There was a picture of me with Adrian from three years ago. I cringed at our forced smiles. We weren't really that happy. We were fighting more often than not.

The first few paragraphs were about how Adrian and I dated publicly for about a year and then we broke up and he started dating and then married Chase Wilson.

Underneath that was a picture of Derek and I leaving a club. We didn't look particularly happy. Not that we weren't. They just snapped the picture at a bad moment. We had been there all night and we were both exhausted. I remember falling asleep in the cab that night.

The following paragraphs were about how Derek and I were spotted around L.A. doing this or that without any of his band members. Considering his band members did every-thing together, whoever wrote this article was hinting that maybe there was trouble in paradise. *Is Dita Fox the Yoko Ono of our time?* I had to laugh at the last line on the page. Yeah right.

I had to admit, when Adrian called me that night to tell me he knew the truth and that Derek better run, I was terrified. I had been purposely avoiding that moment for months. Well, longer than that. If Derek had had it his way, we would have told everyone about us a long time ago. I admit it wasn't the greatest decision on my part, but I wasn't known for making great choices.

Putting my phone away I turned my car on and left that hell hole that paid great. If my salary wasn't fantastic, I would have left a long time ago.

Pulling into the parking lot of my apartment complex I saw the mailman walking back to his truck. I grabbed my mail as I walked to my apartment. Bill, spam, and a letter from the complex office. I ripped it open and read it as I walked. *Oh, come on.* I sighed as I scanned it.

This was my final letter informing me that if I didn't come and sign a new lease for the next year then they would be expecting me to move out in 30 days so they can give my apartment away. They had denied my request to continue paying month to month. New management decided that the leases were one year minimum now.

A full year. Twelve months. I gulped. The idea of promising that I'd stay here for that long made me nervous. Staying anywhere permanently wasn't my thing. I unlocked my door and tossed the mail on my end table, deciding to make that decision later. I was too tired to think properly. I would end up making a rash decision. Quickly showering to get the smell of the clinic off me, I was asleep before my head hit the pillows.

I woke up to my alarm, set for the afternoon. I reached for my phone and saw that Derek had sent me a good morning text. I wouldn't be surprised if he'd just woken up as well. I called him but it went straight to his voicemail.

I tried to think of what he was doing today. They had just finished recording their newest album. They were all super excited for it. Apparently, their label was as well. They were putting a lot of money into promoting it.

I got out of bed and dressed for the day. I was just about to leave the house to go to the office and see about a 3-month lease when Derek called me back.

"Sorry babe, we're doing the music video for "Maria" today. I just stepped out for a smoke. I've only got a few minutes."

"Aw, and you used them to call me," I teased him. I could hear the smile in his voice when he spoke next.

"I wouldn't want to talk to anyone else. You want to stop by the set? I can get your name on the list. We've got a few more hours I think."

"No thanks, I've actually got some things to do today. Are you doing anything afterwards?"

"Party at Cleo's, maybe taking it to a bar or something after. You in?" He asked eagerly.

"I'll stop by before work. I could go for a beer and you can tell me all about the shoot."

"Sounds great, I can't wait to see you," his voice lowered.

"You haven't gotten sick of me yet?" I joked. Ever since we'd been outed, he has been a bit clingy. I wasn't sure how I felt about it. I was used to the casual dating thing. I was fine with our on again off again thing we had before his friends found out. When I suggested we end things when he told them, he begged me to reconsider.

"I've never wanted to be with someone more than I want to be with you. Come home," he asked me when I ran back to Michigan. I finally agreed to try the relationship thing, and I found I didn't mind it. It was a first for me too. I told him that and of course it led to more questions about my previous relationship with his best friend.

He was surprised to hear that although I liked him a lot, I

hadn't loved Adrian. We were too similar. Derek seemed to be satisfied by my answer and decided to dive right in with being a boyfriend. My boyfriend. I was actually surprised he wasn't sleeping in my bed when I got home from work today.

"I don't think that's possible. Ope, they are calling us in. Gotta go. I love you," he said. I hesitated and he repeated his last words, they were almost pleading.

"Dita? You still there? I love you."

"Yeah I'm here. I love you too, see you later."

I could hear him sigh heavily before I hung up.

Love wasn't a word I was used to using regarding men. Why should I love them when none of them ever loved me back?

But when Derek said it, it was different. I didn't feel like he was saying it to make me feel better. To get me to stay. He meant it. That was terrifying.

Speaking of scary, I went into the apartment complex office and begged again to do a lease less than a year. The greasy little woman behind the desk smirked and repeated that there would be no exceptions. I sign the lease or give them a 30-day moving notice.

"How long do I have to decide?" I snapped at her. She rolled her eyes and looked me up in her computer.

"The end of the week." She grinned, her eyes shining with amusement. I stormed out and went to find the newest apartment listings. I wanted to move out of spite now. I would be damned if I would be forced to stay somewhere. I found some listings on a cork board at a nearby cafe. As I grabbed the flyers, I frowned. I kind of liked my apartment. It was a great location and the neighbors weren't terrible. They minded their own business and never asked when Derek came by. Plus, the rent was reasonable for L.A.

I frowned. I might end up signing their lease after all. At least I had a few days to think on it. I grabbed a coffee and pulled out the book I had brought in my purse to attempt to relax my nerves. There was something about a good book that made all my problems go away, if just for a little while. I stayed there reading until Derek called me and asked me to meet him at Cleo's.

When I got there, I found all of his bandmates and their spouses sitting in Ethan's man cave pouring drinks. I came into the room and looked around. Suddenly I was being thrown to the floor! I screamed as the body around me held on tight as we fell. I giggled when I sat up and saw an adorably sexy, curly blonde grinning ear to ear.

"Hey babe!"

I gently punched Derek and then hugged him tightly.

"I take it the shoot went well?"

Everyone let out various hoots and cheers.

"Hell yeah it did. I can't wait for you to see it." Helping me up, he grabbed my hand and pulled me over to his friends at the bar. Mark asked if I wanted a drink and I nodded. He started to pull out a half dozen liquor bottles, but I stopped him.

"Just a beer please. I've got work tonight." He nodded and pulled one out of the fridge behind him. He popped the cap and handed it to me.

"To Maria Maria!" Chase, Adrian's husband shouted. Everyone repeated him and we clinked our glasses together as we drank.

Suddenly music started playing all around the room. We turned to see Cleo playing with her tablet, setting up her playlist. We all relaxed and moved to sit down as the band started telling us all about their day.

"It was insane. About as big as the "Better Off Missing You" video. There were like a hundred people there," Mark exclaimed. He was the band's drummer and newest father of the group. Him and his wife Renee had Lola, a little girl that was just like her dad. A noise maker.

"It's going to be our first single. There were even a few of the big wig CEO's there watching us," Adrian added.

"But we rocked it. I think it's gonna be amazing!" Cleo exclaimed.

"I think they were a little pissed about the whole kiss thing, but other than that the director seemed happy about it," Mark said. I turned to look at Derek, who was avoiding my gaze.

"What kiss thing?" I asked and all eyes went my way.

"The director wanted me to kiss all of the guys for different parts of the video. All of us said no."

"Derek and I volunteered to make out for the whole video, but they said they'd pass," Adrian said, breaking the tension.

"We argued a bit back and forth and we agreed to almost kiss, but we pull away. I honestly think it works better this way," Cleo explained, looking at her bandmates. They all readily agreed.

I don't know why, but it made me uncomfortable. I felt like I was the last one to be told this. I didn't really care so much about the almost kiss as much as I hadn't been in the loop. Was he purposely not telling me?

The mood shifted back to happy as they continued talking about their day and their upcoming plans for more videos, the tour, and the parties. Eventually the alarm on my phone went off, alerting me that I had to get to work. I squeezed Derek's hand and he turned to me in understanding. I said goodbye to the group and he walked me to my car.

"Do you really have to go? Mark, Adrian, and I were thinking about going to the bar. Come with us. It's always more fun when you're there. We'll go to Chase's pub and close it down. Please," he begged. Those gorgeous brown eyes grew big and he puffed out his lower lip as he pleaded. I groaned. That sounded like so much fun, but I was on my final warning with Mr. Faust. I had to look away from his face to be able to say no.

"I can't. Not tonight. Maybe this weekend. I'm sure you'll have some party energy left." I grinned and kissed him quickly as I opened my car door. He frowned for a millisecond before smiling again.

"Hell yeah I will. We'll go crazy Saturday. All of us. Or just me and you if you'd prefer." He stared at me cautiously, remembering my hesitance to hang out with all of them when we first went public.

"A night out with everyone sounds great. I've got to go. I can't be late." I climbed into my car and shut the door. I turned it on and pulled it out of park. As I started to go, I stopped and rolled the window down. He leaned forward and gave me one last kiss.

"Be safe, will ya?"

He stood up straight and saluted me, his blonde curls bouncing.

"Scout's honor. Doc said if I break my legs one more time, I won't be able to walk straight," he laughed. I rolled my eyes and left. I really had to get out of here. If I was late, I was fired.

Thankfully I made it just in time to grab my spare scrubs from my locker and throw them on before my shift started. My assistant Wendy gave me the biggest fake smile when I came to the front and reached for my first folder. By the way her beady eyes followed me as I walked, I knew that she was also my new babysitter. I'm sure Amanda and Audrey filled her in on all the juicy details of my supposed crazy life outside of here, and Mr. Faust's final warning. She was older than me by about thirty years and had the same attitude as our old as dirt boss. I wasn't quite convinced that she didn't come with the building when he bought it.

"You know Halloween is over, right?" She smirked, eyeing

me up and down. I glanced at my scrubs. Dark purple with spiderwebs and lime green spiders. I bit my tongue. All of my scrubs were spooky themed. They had skulls, Frankenstein's, creepy cute things. She knew this and was just trying to egg me on. I glanced at her outfit. She was wearing bright pink scrubs with yellow daisies. I wanted to reply back with a snarky comment about her clothes but chose to skip past it and open my folder to see my first patient.

"Baltimore?" I asked, even though there was only one person with their dog in the lobby. The pair stood up and followed me into the room. We had a standard case of pup eating the wrong thing. In this case, their owner had come home from a late shift to find their Pitbull puppy eating a lightbulb. Thankfully, little Baltimore was going to be okay. Once they were gone, I had no other patients waiting. Night shifts were pretty tame. I was usually just an emergency trip. Animals that ate something they shouldn't, hit by vehicles, or other various accidents. We were lucky if we got one or two a night. That's why only Wendy and I worked the shift.

When we didn't have patients, we were filing paperwork. Even then we quickly finished it and then we just sat around and relaxed. My previous assistant Callie was really cool. We'd watch movies and play card games just to pass the time. It had only been two weeks since Wendy had been switched to night shift to rat on me for every little thing and I already missed Callie. I was sure Wendy was the one complaining about my tattoos. No one in this day and age gave a crap that their college educated doctor had a little ink.

She confirmed my suspicions when she asked about them a little while later.

"Are you going to cover your tattoos up permanently or just start wearing those covers down to your wrists?"

I turned my chair around to look her square in the eye.

"No, I think I'm actually going to go get more."

Her eyes went wide and for a moment she didn't have anything to say. Finally, she smirked and began to turn away.

"You look ridiculous you know."

I looked down at my arms. They were both covered in colorful, permanent ink. I lost count, but I probably had over twenty on both of them.

"They don't determine how well I do my job, so why does it matter?"

"You think people will want you to treat their animals looking like that?" She spat.

"No, I'm sure they'd rather let them die in the lobby instead of letting me save their lives," I shot back. That shut her up for awhile. We went back to filing our separate paperwork.

After two solid hours of typing away, my personal phone rang. I glanced over at Wendy who was already switching her laptop on to watch a movie. She couldn't really talk about my work performance. Looking at the screen in my own hands my stomach flipped.

"I'm going to take this. I'll be in the break room. Come get me if you need me," I told her as I left quickly.

"Hello?" I said into the phone as soon as the break room door was shut.

"Hey sis!" The familiar voice of my younger brother Griffin filled my ear.

"Griff, how's it going little brother?" I teased. I could almost hear the eye roll. He was barely a year younger than me. My parents didn't seem to take a break. Four kids in four years.

"Not bad over here. Mom, Dad, and Graham send their love."

I smiled, thinking about them all. Happy memories of life on the farm filled my thoughts. I made a constant effort to not think about the unpleasant times. What was the point? No need to hold grudges.

"Aw, tell them I miss them all. Why the late-night call?" It was past midnight here, which made it around 9:30 in Michigan. That was late for Griffin.

"Actually, I have some news. I met someone. Someone serious."

I sat up straight in my chair.

"Oh? Do I know her?"

"No, well, I doubt it. Her name is Cherie, but everyone calls her Cherry. I really like her. I'd like to think I could have a future with her."

"That's amazing Griff. I'm so happy for you. Tell me everything, how did you meet?"

We spent the next hour talking about his girlfriend and life back on the farm. Not much has changed since I left almost nine years ago. My oldest, younger brother was a mechanic now, and Graham, our next brother in line worked the farm with our Dad.

"Ma has taken up scrapbooking. I'm not entirely sure what it is, but she has books and pictures scattered all over."

"You're still living at home?" I questioned. There was a slight pause.

"I did move out for a while. But then Dad needed some extra help with the hogs and it was just easier for me to come home. If Cherry accepts my proposal than I plan on buying us a house nearby."

I choked on the sip of water I had just taken.

"Proposal? You're proposing? You didn't say it was that serious."

"Oh, sorry. I don't know. I'm kind of nervous. Sometimes it feels like she doesn't feel the same as I do. Graham says it's just in my head. I plan on asking her soon though."

"Did you get a ring already?"

"Yep. Cost me a pretty penny. Ma would have offered me hers since I'm the oldest man of the family, but you know,

Grey…" his voice trailed off. My happy mood sank. Of course. Grey, our youngest brother.

"Have you heard from him lately?" I asked, treading carefully. Grey was a very sensitive subject. I didn't really blame everyone for turning their backs on him. What he did was kind of unforgivable. I had only wished I had been there to understand what really happened.

"Not since he left." Griffin's voice was tight, anger hiding just under the surface. My stomach dropped. So, five years.

"Nothing? Are you sure? Not even a phone call?"

"Gretchen, I know you guys had this special bond but what he did to us was something we can't just forget. He's too stubborn to call, if he's even alive. Who knows? He was always reckless. I'm sure he'd find you before he comes back to see any of us."

I let his anger simmer down before I changed subjects. I knew he wouldn't understand. I didn't blame him for his hatred of our youngest brother, but it still stung. Just like the betrayal Grey had done to them had.

"How is life in L.A? You too good for us yet?" He teased.

"It's great. I love it here."

He asked about my job and I gave him a half-assed lie. I told him how happy I was here and that I was looking at a promotion soon. I didn't have the heart to tell him the truth. I didn't want him or any of the family to be disappointed in me. Or use the information about my current job situation against me. Nine years of being shamed for my life choices was enough. I now only told them good things, even if they were lies. I refused to let word get out that I was failing here.

"How about Derek? Are you two still a thing?"

"Yes, and better than ever. Thanks for asking," I lied, thinking about the earlier phone call where I hesitated to tell him I loved him.

"You think you're gonna settle down with him? You know,

maybe get hitched too? I'd fly out to see that wedding," he teased. Even the *thought* of marriage made my stomach churn uncomfortably.

"Not any time soon. Enough with the interrogation about my relationship. Let's talk more about you."

I deflected and we spent the next hour chatting about anything and everything we could think of until Wendy came to tell me that we had an animal. I hung up, with promises that I'd call more. Both of us knowing that I was lying. The only time I talked to my family anymore was when they contacted me. I tossed my phone into my purse and hurried out.

I grabbed the folder off the counter and hurried into the patient's room. We had a golden retriever with a cut on his paw. When I returned to the lobby Wendy sighed and motioned to my purse under the desk.

"Your phone has been ringing since you took them back. You know, one personal call is pushing it. You shouldn't be on your phone the entire shift," she reprimanded.

"What Scarecrow Fever movie are you on now, 4, 5? You've been burning through them like crazy since you came to night shift," I said as I reached for my phone. Just as I picked it up the front door opened and a woman with her gagging cat came in. I dropped my phone and hurried over to help her.

Once we got the rather large hair ball out and made sure he got some water and food I discharged them and walked out with them to the lobby.

"Those are some cool tattoos. I want to look like you," the woman chuckled, eying my arms. I laughed and thanked her, reminding her to make sure her cat was eating well over the next few days.

Once she was gone and we were alone again Wendy stood up and laid into me.

"It's bad enough that you flaunt them for our more wholesome, less accepting patients, but now you're influencing others to get tattoos? You can't do that!" She screeched. I turned around and stared at her. Did we just hear two different conversations?

"What the hell are you talking about?"

"Don't you swear at me! You think just because you're younger and prettier than me that you can come in and boss me around like that?"

"No, I think I can tell you what to do because I'm your boss. You are my assistant. Do you have your degree?"

She slammed her mouth shut quickly and glared.

"You are ruining this establishment. Mr. Faust has spent many years growing his reputation as a great clinic and you come in with your black clothes, tattoos, and open legs and ruin this place."

"Excuse me?" I interrupted. She crossed her arms and raised an eyebrow.

"What, you think no one's heard about you passing yourself around between dirty musicians just to get that fifteen minutes of fame? Honey, those looks are not going to last forever and those men will drop you like a hot potato. What are you going to do then?"

"Probably turn into a nasty crone like you."

She opened and shut her mouth. She was completely shocked that I said that. I groaned. That was definitely getting passed to Mr. Faust. Perhaps I could explain what led up to it. I doubted he'd listen to me. I apologized to Wendy.

"Wendy, I'm sorry. I was just heated. I didn't mean what I said," I tried to explain. She gave me the dirtiest look before plopping down in her seat and began typing something on the work computer.

My phone ringing broke the icy silence between us. I went around the counter and picked my phone back out of my purse. It was Mark. I looked at the clock and saw that it was barely 4 a.m. Why was he calling me at this time?

"Hello?"

"Renee? No, Dita. Dita! Hey, Adrian, she answered!"

"Mark? Why are you calling me? You sound drunk."

"I am! We closed down the bar! But then the cops came."

"Oh my God. Are you calling me from jail?"

"No, no. The parking lot. Derek's the one in jail," he told me very matter of factly.

"Derek's in jail? What happened?"

"Renee? No, Dita. We called Dita. Derek's in jail!" He repeated. In the background I could hear Adrian squealing with laughter as he repeated Mark.

"Derek's in jail! Derek's in jail!"

"Are you going to get him?"

"We can't go in there. They'll get us too!" Mark laughed.

"He's fucked," Adrian murmured, or thought he murmured. He was still loud enough for me to hear clearly.

"Is it serious? Is he okay?"

"I don't know. You should probably come though," Mark said, and then hiccuped. Jesus.

"Okay, I'll see what I can do." I hung up and looked down at my desk, weighing my options. Would this count as a personal emergency?

"Your delinquent boyfriend's in jail?" Wendy smirked. I grabbed my purse and stood up.

"I've got to go. Family emergency." I started walking towards my locker to grab my day clothes.

"I heard everything. If you leave this building, you are fired."

I turned back to see her standing with her arms crossed.

"What?"

"I'll call Dr. Faust right now. He told me that you're on your last chance. If you go, don't bother coming back. We don't want you here. You will no longer be welcome at this clinic."

I stared at her, my eyes slowly unfocusing to stare past her.

Was this really happening? I was about to lose my job because of my boyfriend. No, it was more than that. They had been trying to fire me for months now. Was I going to let them berate me in the morning for an hour before they told me what I knew was coming? Would Wendy be in the room, watching smugly as they canned me? I could picture it now. All three of those bitter women watching me do the walk of shame as I was escorted out.

Finally, I snapped back to reality. I turned back around and emptied out my locker. I went back into the lobby and as I passed the front desk, I flipped Wendy off and smiled back at her.

"Have a great day Wendy!"

I didn't bother to look back because I wasn't going to step another foot in that building ever again. I officially quit.

Chapter Two

LAST NIGHT

DEREK

I sat in the iron cage attempting to sober up. Where were Adrian and Mark? The last time I saw them they were right behind me. I tossed my head back and closed my eyes. Bastards. They probably called Dita. She was going to kill me.

An officer came and whacked on the bars. I rolled my head to look at him. He was smirking.

"They aren't pressing charges. We'll let you go when you're sober. We don't need a repeat of tonight."

Fine with me. I curled up on the bench and closed my eyes again. I couldn't really remember why I was in here. I mean, kind of. I definitely didn't remember the drive to the animal shelter. One moment we were at the bar, then suddenly alarms were going off and I was holding a fucking cat.

The cat. I shot up and stumbled to the bars. I held them for support. I looked for the cop from before. He was sitting behind a desk, clearly unamused.

"I didn't hurt anything, did I?" I asked quickly. I don't know what I'd do if I squished a kitten or something. He chuckled.

"No, Mr. Turtle. The animals are fine. Sounds like you they found you sitting on the floor just petting them. Go to sleep."

I sighed with relief and returned to my bed for the night. It wasn't the worst drunk tank I'd been in; and I was sure it probably wouldn't be the last.

I was woken up by the same officer unlocking the doors and shaking me. I groaned.

"Your friends are outside waiting for you. Come on," he told me. I rubbed my face; a headache was already forming. The lights were horrible in here.

As I was heading towards the front doors, I wondered who was here. Adrian and Mark better have waited for me. I'd kill them if they completely ditched me. I prayed it was only them. Maybe Cleo max. I really hoped they hadn't called Dita.

I swore out loud when I saw my drinking buddies from last night and my girl. I bet Adrian was the one who called her. He loved throwing it in my face that I was a piece of shit and not good enough for her. The smirk on his face when I reached her car told me that my thoughts were right.

I ignored my friends obnoxious cheering and went straight to Dita. I tried to hug her, but she crossed her arms and moved away. *Ouch.* I heard Adrian snicker. I clenched my fist tightly but didn't move towards him. I couldn't tell you how many times I'd wanted to clock him since I told him the truth.

"The woman who runs the shelter said that since you agreed to pay for any and all damages and make a donation, she's not going to press charges," Dita said softly. Her green eyes were filled with disappointment. It absolutely killed me. I gave her my best apologetic smile.

"I did? Okay."

She shot me a death glare, but I raised my shoulders. How

was I supposed to remember? I can't even remember going there. Or how much I drank, for that matter. Or what I drank.

"Oh, and she made you promise to only come back when they are open from now on," Mark added. I whipped my head around. They were laughing. Oh, I couldn't wait until they got arrested next. Tired of standing in the county jail parking lot I opened the passenger side door and got in Dita's car without another word.

They joined me and we were on the highway in no time. I closed my eyes and pressed my forehead against the cool window. I needed some water and aspirin.

"You wanna see your mugshot?" Adrian asked from behind me. When I didn't answer right away, he kicked my seat. I groaned as he shoved his phone towards me.

Despite my desire to remain in this grouchy mood I started laughing. This was one of my better ones. I almost wanted to post this on my social media profiles. *I looked good.* My blonde hair was extra curly and I was smiling wide, like it was the funniest thing in the world. Which at that time, it probably was. The icing on the cake though, was that I was giving the cop taking the photo a thumbs up.

I had absolutely no memory of this, but that just made it all the better. I turned to Dita who was trying her hardest not to smile. She looked over and I gave her a look of 'come on, you know it's good.' And she broke.

"You are obnoxious," she said with a smile. I leaned over and snuggled my head into her shoulder.

"I know. But you love it."

She sighed almost wistfully. "I do."

I glanced back in the rear-view mirror and saw Adrian glaring at me and Mark laughing. I looked back at Adrian and snuggled closer to her. I hated acting like this, but he really irritated me sometimes.

"I can only imagine the headlines for this one," I chuckled.

The mood shifted in the car and we all started trying to guess what the magazines would say about it, especially if I did share it with the world before anyone else could.

"Where am I taking you two?" Dita asked my friends. Adrian groaned loudly.

"Chase will give me a lecture on wasting police time."

His husband is a police officer. Or was. I don't think he had gone back to work yet. He stayed home with their little boy Rocky. Adorable little punk. It was always so weird seeing my friends with their kids. Things had changed since our times in my garage trying to figure out how to do this whole music thing.

"Renee's cool. Just take us home," Mark ordered. As Dita drove us to his place we started to try to piece together last night. It had been crazy. We were celebrating, so why not go all out?

Adrian gagged and mentioned that he wasn't feeling so great. I guess I wasn't the only one still slightly drunk.

"You can't throw up when we get to my place. She'll kill me if another one of my friends gets sick on her floor."

"Hey, it's your floor too man. Take charge of your household!" Adrian tried to get him going but Mark shook his head.

"Nah man, I ain't trying that shit. This is Renee and Lola's house. I just stay there."

Adrian made a whip cracking sound, but Mark just let it roll off of him. He didn't care, he was very happily whipped. I couldn't really make fun of him. I knew that I was slowly starting to get there myself. Dita was my everything.

Just as we pulled through the gate to his house, someone's phone rang. Adrian answered it and then eagerly began telling whoever it was on the other side what had happened to me. He then explained to us in the car that Cleo had finally called him back.

I could hear her say, "What a fucking moron!" Which made me choke and the entire car burst into laughter.

"Alright, we'll stop by later. Bye." He hung up and they got out of the car, thanking Dita for the ride. I cringed when they shut the door, knowing the lecture was coming.

"What were you thinking?" Dita said sharply as we left the premises.

"I have no clue," I lied. I kind of remembered why I wanted to go there. Well, I knew why I needed to go there during regular hours.

"Did they say why I was the only one arrested?" I asked. She rolled her eyes.

"They were smart enough to stay outside when you climbed through that tiny window. Good thing too, or else I wouldn't have been able to come get you."

What good friends they were, I smirked. I couldn't really complain about it. We've all done it to each other at some point or another. Memories of collecting each of them from various drunk tanks and the likes. Good times.

"How was work?" I asked. Her eyes flickered to me, but she didn't reply. Since she wasn't in the mood to talk, I decided to close my eyes and wait for the ride to be over. Although I had slept for a few hours, I desperately needed a nap.

We got back to her place and I stumbled to the bathroom for some headache relief. She was still in the living room when I shouted that I was going to lay down. She didn't argue and left me to it.

I woke up sometime in the afternoon feeling as refreshed as I could be. The hangover seemed to be gone, although I was desperately craving water. I walked out into the kitchen and called her name. There was no answer. She must have taken off to do something. I hoped she didn't take too long, I wanted to get to the animal shelter today and get everything settled.

I poured myself a tall, cold glass of water from the tap and downed it quickly, getting myself another. As I drank that one at a slower pace, I noticed a notepad on the counter. I reached for it and scanned it quickly. What was this?

It was a note, but more of a list of things to do written by Dita. I knew her handwriting well. I read it over and over, trying to figure out how to take it.

Rent storage unit. Pack. Rent motel until things settle.

Was she leaving? Was it because of me? That couldn't be. I had done a lot of stupid things over the past few years. Me being tossed in the drunk tank could not possibly be the straw that broke the camel's back. There was no way.

Why did she leave this out, knowing I could wake up and see it? Was this her weird way of breaking up with me? Dita was notorious for not handling confrontation well. Hell, the only reason I hadn't told Adrian right away was because she insisted I keep my mouth shut.

I pulled my phone out of my pocket and flicked it on. Her gorgeous face filled the screen. I loved everything about this face, and the person behind it. Her bright grass green eyes and stunning smile made my stomach flip. I remembered taking the photo. We had been taking a walk and I had found a white flower to put behind her ear. It looked perfect against the soft waves of dark blonde hair. This whole thing had to be a misunderstanding. It couldn't. She wouldn't do this to me, not like this.

My eyes were watering despite me trying to get ahold of myself. Where was this coming from? I had never cried over a girl. I mean, not one that wasn't family. I wiped them away quickly. I was the only one here, but I still was embarrassed. I didn't do crying.

I shoved the notepad away from me and went to take a shower. I hoped she was back by the time I got out. She was.

When she stepped into the bedroom where I was changing, I paused. She had put her nose and septum jewelry back in. Something about her looked different. She looked... happy.

She had put on more makeup than usual too, and was her hair different? I couldn't tell, but something about her had changed. I liked it. It was a glow, an energy that she had brought into the room that instantly lifted me out of my dark thoughts.

She came over and wrapped her arms around me. She fit perfectly in my arms. I inhaled deeply, the familiar scent comforting me. She pulled away and I realized she was wearing a dress I hadn't seen her wear in a while as well. I had gotten so accustomed to her scrubs and work get up that I really missed this Dita. This was the girl I had fallen head over heels for, despite her belonging to someone else.

"What are you staring at?" She giggled, knowing damn well where my thoughts were at. I winked at her as I finished buttoning my pants and slipping a band tee on. I wanted to do dirty, dirty things to her, but it could wait. I had some things to do first.

"Why Dita Fox, welcome back," I said. She giggled and I embraced her again. She held me tighter and longer. I kissed the top of her head and pulled away first.

"You want to head over to Cleo's for a bit and then the animal shelter?"

She took my hand and led me out of the apartment.

"Sounds great," she told me.

By the time we arrived all of my friends were there and ready to roast me.

"He lives!" Cleo laughed as I walked into the living room. Everyone and their kids were relaxing and eating lunch. I noticed some papers on the coffee table that looked like possible costumes for our upcoming shows. I reached for them, but Cleo smacked my hand away. I opted for a few slices of the sub and some chips they had placed on a large platter beside them.

"We'll talk shop later. You're not getting off the hook just yet," she laughed. I plopped down next to Mark and with an eye roll that almost hurt my brain, I motioned for them to bring it on.

"Alright. Now that everyone is here to hear this stupidity, tell us what happened," Cleo demanded. I looked up from my plate piled high with food. I was like a deer caught in headlights, with my mouth full like a chipmunk. I swallowed quickly and cleared my throat. Sitting back on the couch, I shrugged.

"I wanted to pet some kittens," I said simply.

There was a brief moment of silence before everyone began calling bullshit on my explanation. There was definitely more to the story, but I couldn't say much more with Dita sitting next to me.

"Fine, fine. Okay, so we were at the bar. Drinks were flowing, the good times rolling. We were talking about the next few months. The video, the upcoming tour, how different it's going to be from previous tours."

"What do you mean?" Chase asked, pausing in feeding his son Rocky a slice of banana.

"Well now we are all settled down. We've got families waiting for us back home. It's gonna be weird being away from them for so long," Adrian explained to his husband. Rocky slapped his other dad's arm and Adrian fed him the slice Chase hadn't.

"It is going to be weird. Lola is so young, I wonder if she'll even realize you're gone," Renee added, looking at Mark. He scowled.

"Of course, she'll remember me. I'll be video calling all the time. It's not like I won't see her."

"Anyways," I interrupted loudly. "We then started talking

about things we wanted to get done before we left and I remembered what I had wanted to do."

"You wanted to break into an animal shelter and pet some cats?" Ethan asked, amused. Everyone chuckled but I just rolled his eyes again.

"No. But what I wanted was in there. I just didn't get that far before security and the police came. They took me in cuffs out of there. I was completely smashed, so I know things are a little blurry, but there is one thing I can't figure out."

I turned my head to stare at Adrian and then Mark. Both of them looked away guiltily. I knew it.

"I distinctly remember you guys telling me that you'd be following me in as soon as I was on the floor. Where were you?"

Silence followed for a moment before Mark sucked in some breath.

"Yeah, we were all pretty drunk but even I could figure out that breaking and entering was a bad idea."

"We decided to keep watch," Adrian added. I opened and shut my mouth quickly before flipping them off.

"Watch? Well you two are some worthless fucking guards!"

The room erupted in laughter as I steamed for a moment before relaxing again.

"That's cold. I am offended," I said, pressing my hand to my chest. I gave the room my best hurt puppy face.

"You'll get over it. I can remember a time or two you screwed us over," Mark smirked. I saw Adrian's eyes flicker to me, but it was so brief I was sure only I had seen it. Wow, would we ever get past this awkwardness?

Dita sat next to me the entire time holding my hand and laughing with the others as we recalled all of our times in the clink. We ranked mugshots from best to worst. My newest one was in the top three. It was really hard to beat Cleo's first arrest.

"Remember that time Cleo fell out of the back of that truck and got picked up?"

"Yeah, on Halloween. We were in full costume. They made me take my picture with the makeup on. It was mortifying!" Cleo laughed.

"What were you dressed as?" Dita asked.

"Kiss. I got to take my mugshot lookinglike Gene Simmons. The makeup wasn't as embarrassing as the hair was." She had her tablet in her hands and flicked through the collection of mug shots we had been looking at, found the right one and passed it to my girlfriend.

Dita couldn't stop laughing for a whole minute, which of course made the rest of us erupt in laughter with her. Cleo wasn't exaggerating at how bad the picture was. She was furious in the picture, which made it just that much better.

"What did you get arrested for?" Renee asked.

"Well, someone had called the police because some teenagers were taking a bat to mailboxes all over town. Since I was the only one they caught, I was the only one arrested even though I hadn't even done any yet." She crossed her arms and sat back in a pout.

"You had the bat in your hands," Adrian smirked.

"So? You sound just like the cop who handcuffed me. At least I wasn't arrested completely naked."

All of us who knew the story leaned forward to look at the offender. Mark's face turned beet red from the sudden spotlight. Renee gasped and playfully slapped his shoulder. Mark beamed.

"That was a fun night. Ten out of ten would do again."

Eventually we ran out of jokes to make and the conversation shifted to other things. I looked over at Dita and lifted her hand to my lips, kissing her knuckles.

"Are you mad about it?" I asked, the note on the kitchen

counter still hung in the back of my mind. She shook her head and gave me a halfhearted smile.

"No, just disappointed."

The room went silent, and suddenly Mark screamed. "Burn!"

Everyone began laughing at my expense one last time.

"That's even worse!" Adrian laughed.

"Aww, you two are adorable," Cleo added, and I saw Renee nod in agreement with her.

"It's cool that they aren't pressing charges," Ethan said from beside his wife.

"I know, rad right?" I said and saw the dirty look Dita shot my way. I flinched.

"Sorry. I didn't mean to get that drunk. I was just really excited about the video."

"It's fine, really. I get that. Let's not test their kindness again though. Next time they might not be so nice," she reminded me.

"You got off. That's all that matters. When are you going over to give your donation?" Cleo interrupted.

"Today. You guys wanna come?" I asked, eager to get over there. I couldn't wait to get my surprise. Everyone gave lame excuses, so I shrugged. Their loss. I turned to Dita and wiggled my eyebrows.

"What about you, chick?"

"Sure. I'm curious to see how big of a check you're going to sign," she teased.

"Yeah, me and you both," I said, not hiding my slight bitterness. It wasn't the loss of money that bothered me as much as I couldn't remember what I had promised.

Shortly after lunch we left the party. As she drove to the animal shelter my worries started creeping back to the forefront of my mind. That damn list was burned into my skull.

Rent storage unit. Pack. Rent motel until things settle.

"You know my house is going to be ready soon," I said suddenly. She nearly jumped in her seat, as if I had startled her. Was she in her own deep thoughts? Were they also about her list?

"What?" She asked me, her face looked like I had literally scared her. That was not a great sign.

"My house. I got a call from the real estate agent a few days ago. Everything's almost ready. I'll be able to move in soon. Why don't you ditch your place and come join me?" I tried reaching for her hand on the clutch, but she pulled away putting it on the wheel.

"Don't you think that's a little too soon?" She squeaked. I sighed, and here she was. The same old future fearing Dita. Even the idea of commitment sent her running.

"What? No. We've been together for like two years."

"Not really. We weren't serious that entire time," she said quickly.

"Were you dating other people while we were sleeping together?" I shot back. I knew it was a low blow but this constant state of are we or aren't we was so old.

Her face darkened and she shook her head quickly.

"Of course not. I'm just- I'm not ready for that. I like having my own space."

"You can have that at my place. Have you even been inside it? Emile Dahl's place was obnoxiously huge. It has wings. It's bigger than Mark and Cleo's houses, easily. You can have your own wing if you want."

She drove into the parking lot of the shelter and parked. She turned to look at me and I reached for her hand again. I was pleading with her. Just give me something, anything.

"Why did you buy such a big place?" She asked, avoiding my request. I shrugged.

"The guy was selling it for a steal. He hasn't really lived in it for years and I guess his wife did some damage to some of the rooms before she died. He probably wasn't trying to go back and wanted to wash his hands of it. One man's trash is another's treasure."

"I don't know. Can I think about it?" She finally gave me.

"Of course. But please, really think about it." I kissed her and released her hand to get out of the car. It felt like a dirty move pressuring her like that. I decided not to push it anymore, at least for awhile.

"I didn't know Emile was married. Or that she died. Wait, did she die in the house?" She asked as we laced our hands together to walk inside the building. That was a valid question. That would be why the house was so cheap. Thankfully that wasn't the case.

"From my understanding the marriage was brief. It happened before he did his little three-year disappearing act. She wasn't exactly mourning after him. She was into drugs pretty bad. One day she was on a boat partying and somehow she went overboard. By the time they could get her back she was long gone. Completely blue in the face. According to some friends. I don't know how true it is. But I do know she did not die on the property. I already asked," I assured her.

She simply shook her head, which is exactly what I did when I was told the story. It's bizarre, but so is every story I've ever heard of Emile Dahl.

We were greeted with smiles when we entered the building. I was a little confused considering what I had done the night before. My promise of a donation must have wiped away any anger they had towards me. I gave the lady at the desk my best smile and I swear she turned a little pink.

"Well hello Mr. Turtle. I was starting to worry that you backed out of our deal," she said. I chuckled and leaned against the counter. I glanced at the name plate on the counter. Sally Manchester.

"I assure you Ms. Manchester, that I am a man of my word. Now how much does this place need?" I pulled a checkbook out of my back pocket and flashed my smile again. She giggled and her face flushed noticeably.

"Oh, I don't know. Whatever you want to give I know the animals will be grateful."

"Oh, don't be coy. Tell me. Is there something you've been wanting to add to this place? Perhaps better security?" I laughed.

"Well, we were wanting to get a website going. Somewhere we could advertise the animals to help get them homes quicker."

I tilted my head back and forth, pretending to think about it. I had already known what I was going to donate when I walked in, unless they had a number they could give me. My hair flopped around my face. I pushed the ridiculous curls back and gave her a wink before filling out the check for $15,000. Sally and Dita both gasped. I pretended I hadn't heard. I finished the check and ripped it out swiftly, turning it over to the woman behind the desk.

"This should help. If you ever find yourself struggling, please do not hesitate to contact me. I would love to help." I dug a business card out of my wallet and gave it to her as well. I meant it. She held it up to her face in shock. Her eyes were glazed over as she nodded. I glanced at Dita, who was staring at me strangely.

"What?" I said.

"I didn't know you had business cards."

Why wouldn't I? I mean, why would I, I guess. It doesn't say much, just my name, my occupation as a professional musi-cian, and my contact info. I returned my attention back to Sally.

"Now, the real reason I stopped by. A few weeks ago I called over and asked about something. I was informed that it wouldn't be available until this week. Can I pick it up now?" I asked. They both looked at me curiously. I cleared my throat, helping the middle-aged woman behind the counter snap back to reality.

"Oh, yes. Let me go check the computer and see what exactly you are here for. Just a moment please." She practically fled to the room labeled 'Office'.

I took Dita's hand and led us to the chairs near the door. We sat and waited.

"That was very generous of you," she complimented me. I flashed a proud smile.

"I was happy to do it. I have more money than I need. There's no reason I can't help people who need it. I'll earn that money back just as quickly as I gave it away," I explained. Her eyes widened.

"Really?"

"Well not literally. But the money has been flowing in very well since our last album. That was what, three years ago? That's why the label has backed this new album so much. We are the money makers."

Comfortable silence fell over the room as we waited. After a few moments I leaned towards her and wiggled my shoulder against hers.

"Now that you know I'm loaded will you come live with me? You won't have to work at that stupid clinic. You can be the trophy wife you very clearly should be," I teased, and attempted to kiss her neck. She pulled away, shooting me a dirty look. I flinched.

Why am I like this? I chastised myself. I had just got done telling myself I wasn't going to bring it up and then not even twenty minutes later it was spilling out of my mouth like the vomit from last night.

"I like working," she defended. I sighed and sat up straight.

"Fine. I'm sorry I brought it up. I'm just excited. I've never owned a house before. It's gonna be nice to have something to call my own."

"Yes, and that thing doesn't have to be me," she spat. I dropped her hand quickly. Why was she being like this? Guilt flooded her face and she softened. "You know what I mean. I just like my freedom. I've never been this serious with anyone."

"I know, me too. I never thought I would, but I can't wait to start my life with you. I want what everyone else has," I told her.

"And what's that?"

"To come home after a long day of rehearsal or a gig and find my wife waiting for me."

She stood up suddenly and put her hands up to stop me.

"Derek, stop. I can't. No. You need to stop."

I jumped up and immediately apologized.

"Okay, I'm sorry. Am I blowing this? I don't mean now. I don't want to marry you now. I just mean…" I sighed and paused. How did I fix this? "I really like you. Love you. You are the first person I've ever seen a future with. It's new to me. Ignore all that stuff I just said. You can move in with me when you are ready, and I absolutely insist you keep working."

She stared at me for a long time warily before sighing and moving towards me for a quick hug.

"Thank you. I love you too," she told me. Someone clearing their throat pulled us away from each other. I glanced at the counter where Ms. Manchester was grinning ear to ear.

"Thank you so much for your donation Mr. Turtle. The animals and our staff very much appreciate it. Now, as for your pick-up. Stanley is coming now. Considering the circumstances, we are going to wave the fee," she chuckled.

"Oh no, I insist. How much is it?"

"Twenty dollars."

I pulled the bill out of my wallet and handed it to her. She thanked me once more. Dita asked where the bathroom was and quickly went that way. I had a feeling she hadn't needed to pee, but she was fleeing from me. I really freaked her out with the moving in talk. I was kicking myself in the ass. I knew better than to push her.

Any other person would have jumped on the offer. Cleo, Adrian, and Mark all were quick to move in with their spouses. It wasn't like I was talking kids. Screw that. That was the one thing Dita and I agreed on. Hard pass. But was asking her to move in with me that unreasonable?

I stood there awkwardly with Sally, praying that my girl-friend wasn't pulling a runaway bride thing and climbing out the window. I watched the bathroom door nervously waiting for it to open. A few minutes felt like an hour, but finally she returned. However, her eyes were drawn into suspicious slits. I gave her my best smile and looked away quickly.

An older black man with a bald top and salt and pepper hair on the sides of his head popped out from a door behind the counter.

"Orange, white, or black?" He asked me.

"Oh black, for sure," I told him and he disappeared. Dita returned to my side. Her eyes were wide with realization. I couldn't believe it took her this long to put the pieces together, but it made me start laughing. She glared at me.

"What did you do?" She asked sharply. I smiled wide and said nothing. The door behind the counter opened again and the man from before came out with a wide smile on his face. He was holding the tiniest, fluffiest, blackest kitten I had ever seen.

Chapter Three

SHIVER

DITA

"I JUST DIDN'T WANT you to be lonely when I'm gone," he argued his case to me as we walked to my car, kitten cupped in my hands.

"You don't just buy other people pets, Derek!" I gently scolded. Looking at his face I knew he meant well, but that wasn't the point. I didn't need an animal to take care of added to my list of things to worry about.

"Plus, I won't be lonely," I lied. "I can keep myself busy." Thoughts of packing, filling out applications, and moving filled my mind. Guilt made me shut my mouth.

"I thought you'd like him. Him?" He asked. I lifted the kitten to eye level and as it wiggled and meowed I pushed the fur away to reveal that it was indeed a he.

"Him," I confirmed. Thankfully I kept a litter box and food at my place for when he brought his cat, Big D, over.

"It's the same breed as her. I thought you'd prefer a black

cat over white. I wonder if Big D will like him." He spoke quickly and excitedly all the way home. I remained silent, the stress of the upcoming weeks was beginning to weigh on me.

"You don't like him." His statement interrupted my thoughts. I glanced over and his face revealed his disappointment at my reaction to his well-meant gift. I shook the dark thoughts out of my head and forced a smile.

"No, I love him. Really. Although, you still shouldn't gift people pets. Just because I'm a veterinarian doesn't mean I want a kitten every time you leave," I gently chastised. I gave him a quick peck on the cheek to let him know I wasn't that angry at him. It was hard to be when both the gift and the gifter were adorable.

"Do you not want him then?" He followed me into my apartment continuing to explain his intentions. As usual, although he meant well, he still missed the mark slightly.

"Of course, I'll keep him. Just maybe a little heads up next time. Is he litter trained?"

"The volunteers said yes, but I'm going to keep working with him over the next week or so to make sure."

As soon as I put my keys down, I went into the kitchen and pulled out the bowls for food and water I stored in the cupboards. Derek set the little guy down and showed him to the food. This would work until I could get kitten food. We watched him for a moment in silence. He was kind of cute. Almost a perfect sphere of black fur.

"I really do love the chic goth look on you. It's hot."

I looked up and despite my best efforts to sulk, I couldn't help but smile.

"Thank you. I think it's time I wear more than scrubs."

We moved towards the living room, where he plopped on my couch and closed his eyes.

"I love how all of your work clothes are creepy. Skulls, pumpkins, zombies. It's cool."

"Not all. I have ones with cute little pigs on it," I defended and came to sit with him. He lifted his legs and then promptly set them on my lap.

"Oh yeah. To remind you of home?"

I rolled my eyes and shot him a smirk. I should never have mentioned that I grew up on a hog farm. He rather enjoyed teasing me.

"Do you want to name him? I can go tomorrow while you're sleeping and get a collar and name tag."

I looked away from him quickly. I didn't really need to sleep during the day anymore. Instead I focused on the little guy who was currently stepping out of the kitchen tentatively, looking around with curiosity. I scrunched up my face, considering names.

"What about Hank?" The inky black mass spotted us and hurried over. I scooped him up in my hands and rubbed him against my cheek. I hated it to admit he would be a nice companion. He arched his neck to push back against me.

"Hank? Not something spooky? What about nightmare, or midnight, or anything else. Hank?" Derek eyed me skeptically. I nodded.

"Yeah. I like it. It's dignified."

Derek shook his head.

"Only in this group would we name all of our kids weird, offbeat names and our pets human names," he chuckled. I laughed with him, considering it. He was right. His band members were rather creative with naming their children. Cleo had two sons Dallas and Blue, and a daughter she named Jimmy. Adrian named his son Rocky, and Mark's daughter was named Lovelace, but Lola for short. Hank the cat would fit in just fine.

"Do you have any plans for today?" I asked. Normally I loved his days off. They were rare these days. But honestly, I really wanted him gone. I had things to do, and none of them I wanted help with. He sat up and wiggled his eyebrows.

"Day off. Why? Do you want to get out of that dress and spend the rest of the day in bed? I could go for that."

I rolled my eyes. Any other time I would jump on that offer.

"I can't. I actually have some things to do. Why don't you relax here with Hank? Make sure he really is litter trained." I gave him a stern look. He grimaced.

"Fine. I guess a day of vegging out would be nice. Are you sure you can't put off whatever you're doing?"

I shook my head. The faster I got the unit and called some listings the better. Maybe I could even make some calls about other veterinary clinics. I brushed his feet off of me and stood up, handing him Hank.

"I'll be back in a few hours."

"Wait, have you slept yet? Don't you need to get some sleep before work tonight?"

My body and mind froze for a moment. Suddenly exhaustion hit me like a hard wave. I had been up for about 20 hours now.

"I'll be back soon. Maybe I'll call in or something."

"They won't be mad?"

Not any more than they already were. I shrugged, trying to play it off.

"I've got personal days I can take. I'd much rather spend tonight with you," I leaned down and kissed him longer than necessary. It wasn't a complete lie. When I pulled away, he was grinning.

"Alright. Was that a sneak peak of later?" He teased. I winked at him and left quickly before the truth about my situation came out. Not right now. I'd tell him in my own time. Forcing me to do something has never worked out. For either party.

I was lucky that the first storage place I called had a space available. I went and put a deposit plus two months rent on it. Next, I called some of the apartments I had jotted down from the coffee shop yesterday. None of them had any openings any time soon. I swore when I hung up after each call. Those listings must have been old. Only when I had done everything I could possibly do did I decide to go back home.

Derek was asleep when I entered. Little Hank was curled up right under his neck, purring in his own slumber. The image melted my heart. I pulled out my phone and took a silent photo. God, I'd miss him when he was on tour.

Being as quiet as possible I went to my room and slipped out of my shoes and dress. I pulled a red nightgown out of a drawer and crawled into my bed. I desperately needed some uninterrupted sleep.

I didn't even remember going to sleep. Suddenly I was being woken up to the smell of warm food. I groaned and sat up, removing the blankets. I must have been more tired than I realized. I looked over at the clock on my nightstand and saw that it was almost 10 p.m.

I drowsily got up and followed the smell. My stomach rumbled. The smell was coming from the kitchen. I went in to find my boyfriend opening containers of what looked like Chinese.

"Yum," I said. He looked up and smiled. My heart fluttered at his gorgeous face. His dimples on his cheeks and chin made me swoon. Paired with his crooked grin, fantastic cheekbones, and eyes the color of melting chocolate, he was easily the most handsome man I'd ever had the pleasure of knowing intimately. Oh, and the curls. I couldn't forget about those. How did I get so lucky?

"Hungry? I figured you would be. You know there were two earthquakes and a fire while you were sleeping?" He teased.

I smirked and reached for a container of sweet and sour chicken. He handed me a fork.

"I didn't realize how tired I was. I didn't sleep after I left work early."

He paused in taking a bite to look at me curiously.

"You left work because of the jail thing?"

"Mark called me," I nodded in confirmation. He frowned.

"Are you sure they won't care about you taking a personal day tonight?"

No, I don't think they will.

I sighed. This is like the one time Derek is able to piece things together. I put my food down and went to the fridge, pulling out two beers. Handing one to him I waited until he had a sip to speak.

"They can kiss my ass. I am good at my job. If they don't see that, that's on them."

He eyed me warily but shrugged and went back to his food.

"So, anything good happen while I was asleep?" I asked, changing subjects. He instantly brightened.

"Yeah, actually. Adrian called me. The label is having a party to reveal the music video and the album. It's going to be this whole big thing." His face lit up as he went into detail about the video and tour information. I loved how passionate he was about his job. I wish I felt the same about mine.

"We go back tomorrow to start another video. I think we're doing "Bring It Home". I can't tell you how loud I screamed when I found out they green-lighted us to do the video for that song."

"That's the one where you sampled Hedwig and The Angry Inch, right?" I tried to remember all the songs on his new album. He'd played it for me at least three dozen times, but I couldn't remember still. He nodded.

"Yep. "Sugar Daddy". That's the one where Mark sings. I

think we're gonna be in drag. I'm pumped. I guess it's gonna be a two-day shoot."

"That's awesome. How many videos are they doing?"

He held up four fingers as his mouth was full of noodles. When he swallowed he continued.

"Let me see, "Maria Maria", "Bring It Home", "Nothing", and "Say"," he finished, listing off their song titles.

I tried to remember the musical each song was inspired by. I loved the concept for this album. It wasn't as heavy as most of their music. Although I loved their old stuff, it was just an interesting new sound. The first time I heard the entire album from start to finish I knew that they had something amazing on their hands. The label did too, hence the giant party, all the videos, and the massive tour coming up.

"So, West Side Story, Hedwig, Sweeney Todd, and The Phantom of the Opera?" I asked, fairly confident I had it correct. He beamed a goofy smile my way.

"Nice job. I wish you had more time off so you could come to the shoots. They are always so much fun. Long hours, and it is hard, but its a blast."

I did have the time, but I needed to use it to start packing and finding a place to live.

"Sorry, my schedule is kind of packed right now."

He set his food down and walked over to embrace me. He gave me a quick peck on the lips.

"Well, you will just have to see them for the first time at the reveal party."

"Really?"

"Of course. I refuse to go without a hot date. I've been going stag to stuff for far too long."

Guilt once again turned my stomach, thinking of all the times I insisted on him going to things without me. I had been so afraid of Adrian and the others finding out about us. About what we.. what I.. had done. I replied with a soft, tender kiss.

"I can't wait," I told him, honestly.

"Good, because it's in four weeks, and you'll need to get a dress to match my suit."

A limousine picked me up from the hotel I was staying at for the time being. I had officially moved out earlier that week. Thankfully, Derek and the rest of the band had been working day and night for the last month. I barely saw him. When he did have time, I was usually able to make an excuse as to why he couldn't come over. But as I stepped into the sleek limo, I knew the jig was up. I would have to tell him. Not tonight of course. But tomorrow.

A loud clamor of voices greeted me when I sat down. Once my eyes adjusted to the dim lights, I looked around to see all four band members and their spouses. The gang was all here.

"That dress is gorgeous!" Cleo called from across the limo. I glanced down at my navy gown.

"You look like you should be on the cover of a romance novel," Renee added. I laughed. I had shopped for hours for a new dress but ended up pulling something from my closet. I had bought this dress years ago, but I never had anywhere to wear it to. It had a a navy blue lace bodice with a slick, silk skirt. Very revealing, very sexy, very me. Derek, being the immature goof he was, stuck a finger down my cleavage quickly and gave me a kiss.

"You look great babe."

I took a look at everyone else's clothing. All of the men were wearing slick suits, matching their partners. Cleo was wearing a bright red corset ball gown, while Renee chose an olive dress that reminded me of something Rose would wear on the Titanic. They were both absolutely stunning.

Champagne was being passed around like candy, so I gladly

took a glass to calm my nerves. I would tell him everything tomorrow, I repeated in my head. The job, the apartment, all of it. Tonight would be his night.

Everyone was talking excitedly and soon my worries started slipping away. I started to become excited for the party. Before I could overthink it, we were stopping and the door was opened. I heard a voice say from outside of the vehicle that Cleo needed to get out last. We all looked her way and she shrugged innocently. She was the leader of the band, it came with the job.

Adrian and Chase were the closest to the door, so they went first. The screams that followed made my heart race frantically. Could I go out there? After that reaction? I could hear the clicks of furious cameras and their crazy owners. The driver's hand motioned for Derek and I to come out next. I gulped and only moved when Derek took my hand and helped me get to the exit.

We stepped out and were greeted by screams just as loud and terrifying as the ones before us. Derek nudged me. I looked up into his handsome face and instantly relaxed a little. He offered me the crook of his arm and I took it gratefully. We began to walk down the red carpet towards the large building.

People were screaming our names and begging us to stop and look this way or that. Derek did as requested and signed a handful of autographs. People complimented me on my dress and my hair. I thanked them but kept rather quiet next to my rockstar boyfriend. I didn't want to give any impression of trying to steal his spotlight.

We stopped at the entrance and waited for the remaining couples to reach us. Adrian and Chase were standing proudly next to each other letting people take pictures, so Derek and I did the same. When everyone was together the band members moved away from their dates and took group photos. It was weird. Separate they were mature, very quiet, and professional.

They walked the red carpet with elegance and grace. They smiled perfectly and didn't take a step out of place.

However, when put together they turned into the kids they were when they started the band. The three men lifted Cleo together and she squealed, thrusting her hands wide in the air with a look of pure glee. Then they put her down and started giving the cameras the silliest poses. They gave each other bunny ears and made goofy faces. They were giggling and talking excitedly the entire time. They were having the times of their lives. All of the stress about what I had to say later melted away. Their smiles were contagious.

A few moments later they called it good and we headed into the building. I gasped when I saw the inside. Every inch of this place was decorated in theme with the album. We hadn't even reached the ballroom, but it was as if we had stepped into an entirely new world.

Giant pillars were draped with black and red curtains. Large, dramatic candle holders with tall, white, melting candles lined the walls as we went further into the building towards the party. We reached the ballroom and were greeted by two large men with masks that reminded me of the phantom from The Phantom of the Opera. In synchronization they opened the doors for us, revealing the party.

It was magical. The room was full of people dancing to what sounded like the new album. We walked in and were bombarded with applause and people coming up to congratulate the band. I was just beginning to panic when I felt Derek's hand being ripped away and quickly replaced with a soft, much smaller one. I whipped my head around to see Renee pulling me out of the pile of people. We didn't stop until we were across the room at the bar. I thanked her and she laughed.

"I don't see Chase or Ethan anywhere, I'm sure they found a place to hide too." She called the bartender over and he asked us if we were interested in one of the themed cocktails of the evening.

"Ooh, what are they?" She asked eagerly. It was clear that she was becoming used to events like these. I felt so out of place here with all of these rich and famous people. By the side looks I caught, I wondered if they all recognized me as the girl who slept with two of the band members. God, why was I such a mess?

"We have the Maria Maria, a cherry rum and coke. Or the Say, which has pear vodka, pineapple juice and cranberry juice. Or if you are interested in something a little more fun, we have Bring It Home gelatin shots. They are topped with various candies. Our final specialty drink for tonight is the Nothing; it's a bloody mary."

Each drink was a play on each of the music videos they would be revealing tonight.

"I'll try the Maria Maria. Dita, what do you think? Wanna get something fun?"

I considered my options for a moment. I wasn't in the mood for shots and bloody mary's disgusted me.

"I'll take the Phantom of the Opera themed one," I decided. He nodded eagerly.

"That would be the Say. You're gonna love it." He hurried away to go make us our drinks. While we waited, I turned and looked around the room, admiring the effort it must have taken.

It looked like a very seamless mix of The Phantom of the Opera and West Side Story. There were candles and swooping curtains that draped tall metal stairs. The ones that one would find attached to New York apartments. On a slightly elevated platform circling the entire room were dancers, dressed like they just came from a 1950's prom. Only they were all in black, and not a one was smiling. They all looked as if they were dancing for a funeral, rather than a party. It was a beautifully depressing scene.

On the far end of the room sat a stage with instruments I recognized. They must be having the guests of honor play a little tonight. I wondered how Cleo would move in her dress on stage. The empty platform made me realize that the music must be coming from a DJ somewhere. I looked around and saw him up on another level above everyone else.

The bartender returned with our drinks and I took a sip of mine. He was right, this was really good. I thanked him and turned to Renee to toast to the wonderful night. We turned away from the bar to people watch and that's when I noticed that all the staff members, men and women, were wearing phantom masks.

Just as the clump of people began to disperse, a man walked onto the stage and took the microphone. He introduced himself as head of the label and thanked everyone for coming out tonight. He then thanked the band for allowing him to show these videos for us tonight. Yeah right, I rolled my eyes. They had no say in the matter. They did as they were told.

"Without further ado, I present you Maria Maria's first single on their fourth studio album "Has, Had, Has", "Maria Maria"."

With a wave of his hand a projector screen came down behind him and the lights dimmed. Derek's voice came first, then Adrian's, then Mark's. Soon, all of them singing in unison. "Maria, Maria, say it loud and there's music playing. Say it soft and it's almost like praying."

Derek was the first to appear on screen. He looked absolutely, drop dead gorgeous. He was wearing a slick black suit, much like the vintage navy one he wore tonight. His curls were slicked back like a greasers. Adrian and Mark appeared shortly after, dressed the same.

The camera zoomed out and they were on a stage in the middle of nowhere. Dust was coming up from the dirt all around them. Tumbleweeds moved across the screen as they sang in a line with no instruments to assist them. It was acapella and eerily beautiful. Suddenly we hear an acoustic guitar and the camera cuts to Cleo in an all black lace wedding gown. Its train has to be at least twenty feet. She's wearing ballet flats that are fully laced up her tattoo'd legs. Her face is serious as she slowly walks towards them, guitar in hand. They continue singing in harmony, their faces unchanging, as if Cleo isn't even there.

She stops moving and their mouths close at the exact same time. There is a moment of complete silence, and I realize that the entire room around me is silent as well, watching the masterpiece that is this video.

Suddenly Cleo opens her mouth and a single word comes out in a chilly, yet heavenly sound. "Maria."

Then in an eruption of sound and dramatic flare the song comes to life. Cleo lets go of the guitar and spreads her arms. Suddenly all around her, hundreds of ghosts appear and began dancing. It was as if her voice raised the dead.

I jumped when a warm hand wrapped around my waist. I looked up to find one of the stars of the video smiling down at me. The most important one, in my opinion. I leaned against him for a moment before straightening to continue watching.

The rest of the video was shots of them performing their hearts out for their ghost audience. It ended with them all collapsing in a graceful yet blunt fashion. As if the song was the only thing keeping them alive, and once it was over, so were they.

There was a long moment of silence and then an eruption of screams and applause rained down on the room. Spotlights moved around the room, looking for the stars. They found

Derek and I moved away so he could bow and accept the well deserved applause.

The head of the label returned and gave a little speech that I didn't bother listening to. He promised they'd show the other three videos later in the evening, but in the meantime why not hear the song played live for the first time? He called for the band to join him on stage. Derek squeezed my hand and kissed my cheek quickly before hurrying to join his friends.

The screams were beginning to give me a headache. I finished my drink and requested a second one. Renee laughed and did the same. Suddenly we were joined by Ethan and Chase. We turned back to the stage when we heard Cleo's voice through the microphone.

"It's gonna be kind of hard to top that one, huh?" She laughed. The room let out a collective chuckle. Once the screen had returned to its home in the ceiling, they took their place at their instruments. All of them looked high on life. Derek was almost bouncing in his dress shoes.

"Why don't we play all of the songs we'll be debuting videos for tonight?" She turned to her bandmates who all shrugged and agreed. She lowered her mic to talk to them in semi-private before turning back to us. She grinned and stretched, her arms raising like in the video. Suddenly Derek's voice rang out, then Adrian's, then Mark's.

The song performed live was phenomenal. I was so proud of Derek. He had done vocal training specifically for this song. They all put their hearts and souls into this.

Cleo moved surprisingly well in her dress. She wasn't doing any head banging or jumps, but she could walk around quickly without tripping. Their first song "Maria Maria" turned into "Say", and then "Nothing". The anthem, followed by two ballads. The first of those, a love song, while the second was more about loyalty to each other. They then ended their small set with their high energy song, "Bring It Home". It brought the house down.

They bowed and hurried down the stage to the guests crowding them again. All of us around the bar turned away and began to talk amongst ourselves. When it appeared that our dates were not close to coming back yet, I decided to use the restroom. I excused myself and hurried away.

The bathrooms were just as elaborately decorated as the ballroom. I stepped out of the stall and stepped up to the sink when a young woman joined me. By her dress and hair, I knew she was one of the dancers from the platforms. I smiled kindly at her from the mirror, but she didn't smile back.

"Are you having fun?" She asked me suddenly. I almost jumped. The room had been so quiet, it was almost out of place.

"Yes. They really went all out. How about you? It must be thrilling to be a dancer tonight."

She scoffed and crossed her arms after she dried them. She was rather pretty, despite the sour expression.

"Is it ever fun being on the clock?" Her face softened into a small smile. "I saw you talking to the bassist. Do you know him?"

I blinked, not really knowing how to respond to that. Before I could answer she answered herself.

"You were with Mark's wife too, with the purple hair. Were you Derek's date tonight?" She said it with an accusing tone. I wanted to get out of the bathroom now. I tried to move past her, but she caught my arm. I ripped it away and glared at her.

"He's my boyfriend. We're dating," I shot at her before leaving. The confusion and hurt on her face haunted me. Did she know something I didn't? I hurried back to my group to find that our dates still had yet to make it back. I asked what everyone was talking about to catch up.

"We're discussing what our plans are while they are gone,"

Chase explained, then pointed to himself. "I'm going back to Louisiana to spend some time with my folks. Let them get to know Rocky."

Ethan raised his ice water to cut in.

"And I'll be at work with Evan's place. Plus, full time dad. That's gonna be fun," he chuckled, rolling his eyes.

"How about you? Saving animals in the middle of the night?" Renee giggled. I noticed she was sipping a new drink. "You're like Batman for pets!"

The bartender brought me another drink and I took a large gulp. I don't know if it was the alcohol, the stress of holding it in, or that dancers painful look in the restroom that caused me to reveal the truth.

"I quit a month ago."

Everyone's smiles melted off their faces and were replaced with looks of surprise. I gave them a shrug.

"They told me if I left to get Derek from jail I was fired, so I quit."

"Does he know?" Renee asked. Before I could speak, I was interrupted by our dates reappearing.

"Know what?" Adrian said, popping his head in.

"Dita quit her job over a month ago," Renee blurted. My eyes bulged at her big mouth. My head then swiveled around, looking for my boyfriend. He was still talking to someone. I shook my head, but Adrian didn't see me. He was drunk. I knew that face. I couldn't tell if it was alcohol or adrenaline; probably a mix of both.

Just then Derek caught my eyes and smiled. He patted the man he was talking to on his back and came over to me. I gulped and just as I was going to tell everyone not to say anything, he wrapped his arms around me.

"Why don't you try out to be a dancer for the tour? They are doing auditions next week," Adrian said cheerfully. I closed my eyes, silently wishing to go home. If only I could click my heels three times and disappear.

"Dancer? Dita can't dance. I've never seen her… she's told me before she can't dance. Babe, can you dance?" Derek questioned me quickly. Oh my God. My eyes flew open and I raised my hands for Adrian to shut the hell up. This wasn't happening. It was as if time had slowed down. There was nothing I could do but watch the disaster happen.

"Well stripping is basically the same thing," Adrian smirked.

"What did you just say?" Derek squeezed me tighter, defensively. It was the opposite of where I wanted to be right now. I wanted to be as far away as I could from here. Adrian looked down at me. I pleaded with my eyes for him to shut his mouth. My reaction only fueled his amusement. My ex-boyfriend looked back up to my current boyfriend and smiled as if he finally had caught the mouse he had been tracking for years. As innocently as he could muster, he revealed what I had hoped to never talk about again.

"How do you think Dita and I met?"

Chapter Four

COMMON MISTAKE

DEREK

"Did you have a signature song?"

She sighed, hating that I kept asking questions, but knowing that she would have to answer them. She really screwed the pooch this time.

"I guess "Human Nature" by Madonna was a popular one."

"Ooh, can I play it right now?" I reached for my phone connected to the car stereo. A quick search and the song was blasting through the speakers. I glanced over and saw her cringing. I turned the volume down a few pegs. I had gotten a little too eager.

The rest of that night was a mess. I wouldn't say the night was ruined, because it wasn't. It was kind of chaotic and it felt like the moments after Adrian's comment went in slow motion.

Dita was frozen to the spot. So was I, actually. How did I not know this? Surely she had told me at some point in our relationship. I racked my brain trying to remember, but nope. There was nothing. She had kept something from me, and by the look on her face, she had never planned to tell me.

I wasn't really upset by her past career choices. Your body, your choice. However, I was pretty pissed by Adrian's smug face when once again he was able to throw a kick at me. I really wished Dita had told me just so he wouldn't have had the pleasure.

I did feel guilty that she lost her job because of me. She assured me over and over that she wasn't upset and that it was a blessing in disguise, but it still sucked. It felt like just another reminder of how bad I was for her. We were way too different for this to be easy.

My friends made relationships look easy. Everyone matched so perfectly it only made sense that they were together. When people looked at Dita and I, they were just plain confused.

Despite the sudden revelation, the party went on without another hitch far into the next morning. When we left, the sun was beginning to rise. That had been two days ago, and to make up for her massive lie, Dita took me to a hotel and we didn't leave until an hour ago. Can't beat that.

"Did you have a signature move?" I asked, continuing my questions. She gave me a disgusted look and I just laughed.

"What do you mean?"

My eyes lit up and I sat up straighter.

"You know, like some girls do stuff with ping pong balls or can tie cherry knots." I wiggled my eyebrows at her suggestively.

"You are disgusting. No. I did not have a *signature move.*"

"What about a costume, or did you guys just share everything?"

She grimaced and her eyes glossed over for a moment. Perhaps she was thinking of a specific memory. Guilt started to get to me. I frowned and decided to stop pestering her. She glanced over and saw my deflated mood and decided to throw me a bone.

"We mostly wore lingerie, but sometimes I wore a patriotic set with cowboy boots and hat," she offered. I whistled.

"You're really not mad I didn't tell you?" She asked again for the tenth time. I shrugged.

"Not mad as much as embarrassed. Adrian loved throwing that in my face. We try to pretend things aren't still weird, but they are. I just wish he wasn't the one to tell me." There was a moment of tense silence before I brightened again.

"What was your stripper name?"

She chuckled.

"Dita Fox."

I frowned. "You used your real name?"

There was a long pause, which was starting to put me on edge. I knew her well enough to tell that she was trying to figure out how to avoid the question.

"You'd be surprised at how common that is."

"That kind of ruins the illusion a bit. Talking to you about this isn't so much fun anymore," I pouted, turning my head towards the window.

"Maybe I'll show you a routine sometime," she offered, and I perked right up.

"Well I'm sure you'll use some of your moves today at your audition. Are you ready?"

She chewed on her lip. She gulped as we pulled into the parking lot of the building where the auditions were being held. We parked and she clicked her seatbelt off, turning her body to me. I gave her my best reassuring smile which seemed to ease a bit of the worry off her face. I wanted badly to tell her that she didn't have anything to worry about, but she'd kill me if she knew what I had done.

When the air had cleared a bit on her past, the idea of her being a backup dancer for us made sense. She could dance, we needed dancers. So, I made some calls; mostly to Sam, the band's manager, but still. I got her the audition. It only took a little prodding to convince them to make it happen. Sam said people weren't happy, but as long as she wasn't a total screw up, the job was hers.

I had every intention of telling her the truth right away, but when I started to tell her she got so excited. She was absolutely over the moon about getting to audition. I didn't have the heart to tell her that she had a leg up over everyone. She'd refuse to go.

"I appreciate you getting me the audition, but are you sure it's a good idea you come in with me? I don't want people to think I'm here because my boyfriend is in the band," she said, repeating my exact thoughts. I got a small chill. That was eery. Maybe we were a good match for each other. I blinked at her.

"But you *do* have a boyfriend in the band," I told her. Maybe this is the opportunity I needed to come clean. I was just about to tell her when she sighed.

"I know, but I don't want everyone to hate me. Please. You can take my car and go get ice cream or something," she pleaded with me. I gave her my best over the top grimace but still took her keys from her hand. Ice cream sounded kind of good.

"Fine, but I'm not bringing you back any."

She kissed me hard and quick as she grabbed her bag from the back. I could barely give her one last 'break a leg' before she was jumping out of the car and hurrying inside. I waited until she was all the way inside before I got out and went to the driver's side.

I sent her a quick text wishing her the best of luck, knowing she probably wouldn't see it for a while. I turned the car on and started out of the parking lot. She'd be busy almost all day, so, what now?

I sent a quick message to the band group chat to see who

was available to hang. I said a silent prayer that Mark wasn't the one to answer. Thankfully, his face was the first to show up in in the replies. He was taking Lola to the park. His idea of hanging out was rehearsing, and I wasn't in the mood to sit inside all damn day. I wanted to enjoy the nice weather.

I sat in Dita's car in a random parking lot smoking a cigarette while I waited for my other friends to respond. She would kill me if she knew I was smoking in the car, but the windows were all down. No harm no foul, right?

Adrian replied that he was going to join Mark at the park with Rocky. Lame. I was just about to give up on my friends when Cleo chimed in.

Twins are at school and Tabatha's got Blue. I could use some fresh air. Let's go.

Yes! Someone who wasn't going to talk about babies all day. We went back and forth and decided to start at a cafe for coffee and go from there. Surprisingly, she was already sitting at a table sipping her drink when I got there. I noticed she had two tall cups on the table. I sat down across from her and she passed me my drink. I thanked her and took a sip. Mm.. warm, sugary goodness.

We shot the shit while we drank our coffees. I got up and bought us some muffins, and once we finished them, we were ready to get up to do something else. Just as I was picking up our things to throw away my phone rang. I glanced at it and saw it was Kim, one of the people running the auditions. Sam had given her my number and told me that she would update me on how things were going. Glancing guiltily at Cleo, I took the call.

"Hello?"

"Mr. Turtle?"

"This is. How are things going?"

There was a pause and then when she spoke next it sounded like she was whispering.

"Ms. Fox is fine. She has a very good partner who will carry her through the steps she misses, if any. Her number is a high one, so we won't see her perform for a few hours, but I think it will all work out."

"Thank you. I appreciate your discretion."

I hung up and looked back up at a very suspicious Cleo. I looked away from her scrutinizing gaze.

"What?" I shot at her and she crossed her arms as she rocked in her chair.

"You didn't tell her, did you?"

I didn't answer right away, which was an answer in itself.

"Derek Lawrence Turtle, what were you thinking?"

I flinched.

"She wouldn't have gone if I had told her. She's insisting on getting the spot on her own."

"Well why didn't you let her? Sam said it was nothing to get her into the auditions. You should have left it at that."

"Yeah, but..." I hesitated. Taking a deep breath, I voiced my worries out loud for the first time. "I don't want her here alone while I go on tour."

"Why?" She said and then her eyes grew wide. I gave a weak smile and she shook her head.

"Because she cheated on her last boyfriend when he went on tour."

"Derek that's not fair."

"I know. It's not fair and she's never really given me any reason to not trust her, but I mean, come on. It's Adrian. How could you step out on that guy? He's a freaking model."

Cleo rolled her eyes.

"You are just as attractive as Adrian. Stop it."

"Yeah? Well why did you only sleep with him then?" I said, smirking. Her frustration shifted and she started laughing.

"Okay, that's not fair either. Derek, I love you and I am telling you that you have nothing to worry about. What you and Dita have is way deeper than what her and Adrian had. All they ever did was fight and have sex."

"Not helping."

She laughed and reached across the table for my hand. She squeezed it tightly.

"You know I'm right. If she doesn't want to go with us, don't force her. Touring isn't for everyone."

I took in her words. She was right. I didn't want to hear it, but she was right. We stood up and I glanced at my watch. I still had a whole afternoon to burn. I told her so and she tilted her head side to side, thinking.

"Well, what do you want to do? Movies, live theatre, skating, arcade. Ooh we could go do one of those painting classes! Ethan refuses to do them with me."

I grimaced. I didn't blame him. I thought about her suggestions and then an idea hit me.

"Laser tag?" I offered, she shrugged.

"Do you know a place?"

"I'm sure we can find one."

Sure enough, a quick internet search lead us to a bowling alley super fun center. It advertised bowling, bumper cars, an arcade, a full bar, and of course, laser tag. We hurried inside and I almost jumped with excitement when I discovered that they served alcohol and pizza too. Cleo rolled her eyes, but when I suggested we get drunk then play tag she was all for it.

Cleo didn't get too many opportunities to drink anymore. Her husband was a recovering addict. Alcohol and cocaine. In respect for him, she didn't drink most of the time. He never once told her she couldn't. She's just that type of person. But Ethan wasn't here right now.

We ordered a few shots of rum with ginger ale to chase it. It went down like cream soda. Once we both felt sufficiently drunk, we went and paid for a few rounds of tag. It was then that we were directed to the second floor. The first floor was for kids, while the next floor was strictly for adults wanting to play. Hell yeah. Like little kids we ran to the elevator and hurried to the better area.

It was the middle of the day on a Monday, so we were the only ones playing. They handed us two vests, red and blue. I offered them both to Cleo. She took the red one and gave me a smirk, as if it was even a question.

"I'm always red. Reds never lose."

"Yeah yeah. Talk all you want, let's see how you fare on the field. Suit up Rosa."

We got ourselves fitted and armed and were lit up. They gave us 30 seconds to get inside the giant room that was lighted purely by black light. Drunk, I stumbled over large foam blocks and even ran into a wall face first more than once. This place was massive.

Most of it was a large maze with random blocks and ramps tossed around the room but a set of stairs caught my eye. There were stairs and what looked like a giant foam pit on one side of the room. On the top of the stairs was a diving board. Oh, hell yeah. I needed to get on that. I crouched down behind a large wall and waited for the buzzer to go off, activating our vests, and effectively starting the first game.

It went off and then the room was completely silent. Suddenly I heard a clicking sound and then Cleo's voice rang out from the other side of the room.

"Tur....tllleeee. Tuuuurrrttllleee, where are you?" She teased. I peeked out from my wall and saw her crouched and walking around, swinging her gun wildly. She repeated herself and when she got a little closer, I darted out. She screamed and I heard her shooting, but she missed. I turned around and began walking backwards.

"Ha!" I said back at her and just as I aimed to shoot, she

dropped to the ground and rolled. I stormed after her, firing aimlessly. I lost track of her and as I was looking around my chest let out a loud buzzer sound and it began vibrating. I whipped around to see a very smug Cleo. She made a gun with her fingers and blew it.

"Gotcha."

I had to wait for my gun and chest to reactivate before I could chase after her, but she was long gone. I was storming around the room with no luck when I noticed the diving pit again. I started up the stairs on my hands and feet like an animal. I reached the top and looked around, noticing her flashing lights inside the maze. Bingo.

"I see you," I shouted. Her lights froze and I watched her head swivel around, searching for me. "You can't hide now."

That last little comment helped her to find me. Damn, I got too cocky. She looked up at me and aimed her gun. She shot and missed. I stood still as she made her way out of the maze and into the open area towards me. She was making this way too easy.

However, the moment she stepped out of the maze she started darting left and right wildly. I couldn't get a good aim on her. I shot and shot but missed her every time. She was getting close to the stairs. I bounced on the diving board and realized that she was now right near the foam pit. I wouldn't be able to shoot her from here. I guess this is it then.

I let out a scream as I bounced on the diving board and jumped off. I started firing rapidly as I fell and just as I hit the foam, I heard her cry out in anguish. Score!

I popped back up to see her laughing as she rolled around on the floor.

"I've been shot!" She repeated over and over again.

We played a few more rounds but between her lack of bladder from motherhood and my horrible lung capacity from a decade of smoking we had to call it quits. We fist bumped and agreed to finish the day off with ice cream.

We had just gotten our waffle cones and sat down when my phone chirped with a message from Dita. I opened it and saw a selfie of her with the number 27 pinned to her chest. Like always, she looked gorgeous.

I replied with a quick selfie of my own, complete with giant mint chip ice cream in the picture. I captioned it, "Jealous?"

Her reply made me blush a little. I glanced at Cleo, but her attention was on her cone of butter pecan. I glanced back at the message.

I wish I was that cone.

I told her that it could be arranged and another good luck. She shot me a kissy face emoji and I put my phone away. After our day of fun Cleo told me she wanted to get back home. Ethan was making her dinner tonight. With a few hours left I went back to Dita's hotel room and took a nap.

A few hours later I was just getting out of bed when she called me. She was finished and I could come pick her back up. Thank God. I was beyond bored. I hurried to the audition site. My stomach flipped when I saw her standing with a guy that looked way better than me. He was making her laugh. That was my thing.

I pulled up and rolled the window down. She brightened and moved away from him.

"Looking for a ride?" I winked at her. She giggled and turned to the guy who looked even more ridiculously good looking up close.

"Grant, this is my boyfriend Derek. Derek, this is my new dancing partner Grant."

I gave a tight smile. It wasn't that I didn't like him. I didn't know the guy. I just really didn't want to stand next to him. It would be horrible for my confidence. He did a wave and then told her that he'd see her tomorrow. She jumped in and we took off.

"There were 50 pairs here today, and they whittled it down to 16 couples. We made it!" She said excitedly.

"That's great babe!"

"I'm still in shock to be honest. I was all by myself until Grant came over and took me under his wing. He's great."

I tried my hardest not to be a jerk. Cleo's words from this afternoon rang out in my head. I needed to reign in my jealousy.

"He seems nice," I said lamely.

"He really is, and don't worry, he never once hit on me. He was friendly and nothing else."

I wanted to call bullshit, but I knew that I would have to believe her. It wasn't fair.

"How long did you rent the room?" I said, changing lanes and heading back to the hotel. She didn't answer for a long moment.

"Eh, who cares. I bet that hot tub will feel amazing on your sore muscles. How about we get you in the water and I'll order room service?"

Maybe it was the guilt over keeping her rigged audition a secret or just the desire to get laid, but we got back to her room and I spent the evening rubbing her calves, ankles, and feet. We talked animatedly about the tour. She was finally starting to get on board with it.

"I didn't really want the job before I went in, but now that I'm in the top 16 I really hope I get it."

I squeezed the pads on her feet.

"You're going to get it," I smiled and she rolled her eyes. Guilt hit my stomach again. I technically told her the truth. She just took it as me talking her up. I changed subjects quickly.

"Today was our only off day. We're doing interviews tomorrow at some radio station and a photoshoot for Polygraph magazine Wednesday. Maybe on Thursday I can get some time away and we can go shopping for tour essentials. Shampoo, soap, socks."

"Your confidence is comforting," she said as she closed her eyes and relaxed into my massage. After a long, soapy bath, she promptly fell asleep. I was grateful, because I don't think if she wanted to get in some sexy time if I could perform properly. I was too focused on other things.

The next day she dropped me off at Cleo's and drove herself to the auditions. She said she felt like a teenager waiting for her dad to come pick her up last night. I was glad to be dropped off rather than be even a minute late and one of the male dancers jump to offer her a ride.

I sent her one last good luck text before agreeing to rehearse some songs with the band. I was pretty confident that our music was solid, but Mark and Cleo wanted to work on a few songs. In between songs I found myself checking my phone constantly, even though I knew Dita was busy. Eventually I was called out on it.

"What's so damn important Turtle?" Mark asked as he returned from a bathroom break.

"Yeah, I mean she's already got the gig. Did she even need to show up to the audition?" Adrian added. I didn't say anything and my quick glance to Cleo wasn't missed by my other friends.

"She doesn't know?" Adrian asked, his tone accusatory.

"Why is this such a big deal? Everyone's freaking out over nothing. She wanted to earn the spot."

"But she didn't. She got the job because of her connections. You know that, her fellow dancers are going to know it, and when she finds out she's going to flip."

I clenched my jaw. I was so sick of Adrian's opinion on everything.

"Why do you keep butting into my relationship?" I stood up from the chair I had been relaxing in. Adrian set down his guitar and stepped away from the equipment.

"You had no issue butting into mine."

Cleo and Mark protested our fighting but we both ignored them. Adrian pounded his chest quickly, daring me to come after him. Before I could control myself I was stalking over and I shoved him into the wall.

Adrian pushed back and I swung my fist blindly. I didn't care what I hit as long as it was him. After a few more shoves and punches I was tossed onto the floor. When my back connected with the hard floor all the air in my lungs whooshed out. I was gasping as Adrian plopped down on my stomach, fist raised and fire in his eyes. Cleo screamed.

"Do you want me to break your fuckin' legs again?" He shouted. I was struggling to catch my breath as I glared at him. Suddenly Mark hurried over and ripped him off me. I rolled quickly and jumped up, ready to take him again. Cleo's dainty hands on my forearm caused me to hesitate.

Adrian and I glared at each other from across the room as our friends held us in place.

"I thought this was squashed. What the hell is going on?" Mark demanded, looking at me like this was all my fault. What in the hell? I motioned to Adrian with my entire arm dramatically.

"Ask him. He's the one who keeps making snide comments all the time. Every little thing I do he's judging me. What is your problem?"

Adrian gulped but said nothing. Cleo came to my aide.

"He's right. Adrian you have been harsh on him. I thought it didn't bother you. Why should it? Chase and you are perfect together."

"And Rocky." Mark dropped his hold on Adrian. "For real dude, what's up?"

Adrian didn't take his eyes off me. He was still fully ready and able to beat my ass. I don't know why I decided to pick a fight with him. I worked out and maintained my abs and muscle tone, but Adrian was more built than I was. His punch hurt way more than mine did. I was still wincing, and he didn't even blink at my blows. His glare despite our friends calm interrogations began to piss me off.

They repeated themselves and I got a little cocky. They were back on my side. He was the jerk, not me. I raised an eyebrow and opened my mouth.

"I don't think it has anything to do with Chase, but everything to do with the fact he lost a fine piece of ass to me. Does it hurt that you couldn't satisfy a woman, but I could?"

I heard Cleo gasp, Mark swear, and Adrian growl. It happened so fast I couldn't fully comprehend what was happening. Cleo took a step back. Mark wasn't fast enough to grab Adrian before he lunged at me. I felt him grab my shirt and I saw his fist raise to my face and then one last crunching sound before everything went black.

When I came to, I was lying on Cleo's couch with her sitting beside me. It was dark, but I could see lights from the hallway and kitchen. I groaned when I tried to sit up. Everything hurt. My chest, shoulders, gut, and more than anything, my face.

Cleo whispered for me to take it easy as she offered me a glass of water. I took it and drank until I emptied the cup. My throat was killing me. She then handed me an ice pack and motioned to my nose. I set it on there and closed my eyes. She urged me to lay back down.

"What happened?" I moaned.

"You opened your mouth and stupid came out," she smirked. I sighed. She wasn't wrong.

"You two obviously haven't gotten over it. We can't go on tour with you guys like this."

"Tell him!" I tried sitting up, but she lightly pushed me back down.

"Nuh uh. I'm not getting involved in it anymore. You were wrong to sleep with Dita, and then hide it for so long. But Adrian said he was over it and he can't keep bringing it up every chance he gets. It's not fair."

"Where is the bastard?" I asked.

"He's in the kitchen with Mark. You guys need to have a long talk. I'm serious. Mark and I will not get on that bus with you two. You guys need to sort this out for good. All for one, remember?" She said, her voice almost fragile.

I raised my arm to flash my matching tattoo at her. Whether we liked it or not, we were in this for life. She was right, Adrian and I needed to talk. I sat up slowly and removed the ice pack from my face. I could barely open my left eye. It was swollen shut.

"Did he break my nose?" I asked, trying to feel for a fracture. It was swollen just like everything else, so I couldn't tell. Cleo shook her head.

"No, Tabatha looked you over. She's got some medical training. She said a few days of ice and pain meds and you'll be good as new."

I thanked her and stood up. I let out a yelp of pain. Holy crap. How long did it take for them to get him off of me after he knocked me unconscious? I steadied myself on Cleo and then straightened. I couldn't keep using her as a crutch. Metaphorically and literally.

Inching my way out of the room I found Mark and Adrian sitting around the island in the kitchen. They were talking low, both looking angry. They lifted their heads when I came in. I looked at Mark first and his anger quickly turn into sadness. When I shifted to Adrian, he still looked irritated. However, he didn't look like he was going to murder me anymore, so baby steps.

Mark turned back to Adrian and slapped the counter.

"Well, I'm going to head out. You two sort this out."

"Why don't you guys go outside? No one will bother you," Cleo suggested. Adrian sighed deeply and motioned for me to follow him out. Begrudgingly I did, stepping out into the cool evening air. How long had I been unconscious? What time was it? Dita was probably out and waiting for me. I patted my pockets for my phone.

"Cleo called her and told her we were rehearsing late tonight. She's home, and she got the job," he told me through gritted teeth, answering my unspoken question.

We went to the glass table and plopped down in the chairs. Neither of us were ready to look at each other. Silence followed for what felt like an hour. Both of us were too stubborn to start this conversation. Finally, Adrian reached into his pocket and pulled out a smoke. He lit it silently and only after his first drag did he speak.

"That was fucked up man."

The smell of his cigarette made my lips tingle. I wasn't even sure if I could handle smoking right now, but I reached for my own metal case in my pocket and pulled one out. I stuck the unlit cigarette in between my lips and glanced at him. He was staring out into the yard.

"Yeah, I know. I shouldn't have gone there. I'm sorry."

We smoked our cigarettes and nothing else was said for a long time. I didn't know what to say. We'd been through this time and time again. I apologize, he pretends to forgive me, and then it's shoved under the rug again. This cycle had to come to an end now. The future of the band depended on it.

"How did it start?" He asked suddenly. I jerked my head up from the grass I had been staring at.

"What?"

"Who initiated it? Come on, I need to know. I won't be able to move on if I keep wondering about this stuff."

I gulped. Really not wanting to go down this road. I lucked out with a swollen face and no broken bones. *This time.* I wasn't interested in testing my luck again tonight. I glanced back up at him and saw him staring at me, waiting. Fine, I guess we're really doing this.

"Her," I revealed.

"How?" He demanded quickly.

"She was commenting on all of my social media pictures."

"So? That doesn't mean she likes you," he snarled, his anger rising to the surface.

"No, but her sending me messages at 2 a.m. while on tour about how much she missed everyone and especially me does."

There was a pause in the interrogation. Adrian stared hard at me, trying to figure something out. I stared back, exhausted and regretful.

"Why didn't you direct her to me? Tell her to message or call me?"

I scoffed.

"You don't think I did? I told her in that first message that this was wrong and to call you. And you know what, she did. I heard your phone vibrate from the bunk above mine. You pulled your phone out, mumbled that she was so annoying, and I heard you swipe ignore. You ignored and avoided her all the time."

"That's not true. I…"

I stopped him, putting my hand up.

"No dude. Before shows, Mark was on the phone with Renee, Cleo was hanging with the kids and Ethan, and what were you doing? You weren't cheating but you sure as hell weren't turning away any groupies that wanted to hang around."

"Oh, so you told her, and she decided it was okay then?"

I tried to roll my eyes but winced.

"No. I had no obligation to tell her that her boyfriend was close to stepping out on her. She saw it in some fan video. A meet and greet. She sent the video to me. You had your hands around some chick's waist and looked about to kiss her."

"I'm a flirt. That's my whole stage personality!"

I shook my head.

"No dude. The video was focused on me. I was waving to the camera and talking to whoever they wanted me to. You were in the background, completely unaware that you were being filmed. I had nothing to do with her seeing that video."

He took in my words. He was the one who screwed up. Sure, he hadn't actually cheated. Not to my knowledge anyways. But he was flirting with that line and his girlfriend back home found out. He couldn't blame me for that. Finally, he spoke again.

"What happened next?"

"I consoled her. She wanted to break up with you. I tried assuring her that you loved her still and it was a mistake. She seemed to calm down and agreed that she would wait until the tour was over and see how your relationship went. Our nightly conversations turned from me listening to her rant to purely friendly. You know, funny pictures, jokes, stories. Completely innocent."

"Okay, so how did I come to catch you two in the act then?" He said, accusingly. He was treating me like he didn't believe a single word I said. It was starting to irritate me.

"We came home for Cleo to give birth to Blue. We were all partying. Everyone was drunk. You had disappeared and Dita came over to thank me for being a good friend the last few months. I told her it was no problem and that's when she started hitting on me."

"How so?"

"Jesus man, do you want every little detail?"

"No! I mean, I don't know." He sighed and lit another cigarette. I joined him and continued this horrible story.

"She told me that I was hot, and my personality made me even better. We realized that we were alone and she kissed me. Again, both of us were very drunk. I kissed her back and then before either of us could process what we were doing we were heading into a room. That's where you caught us."

"Unknowingly. I just thought it was her and some random guy. Not my best friend."

I said nothing in response. His words were a punch in the gut. He sighed.

"That was the first time?" He asked.

"I swear."

I let him take in everything in peace. I wouldn't add any more details than necessary. No salt on the wound or whatever.

"Why didn't you tell me?" He said finally, sighing deeply.

"I wanted to. All the time. She was the one who wanted to keep it quiet. She didn't want to be judged and the longer it went on the worse it got."

"Why did you let me get that tattoo?"

I smiled or tried to. My mouth protested. Finally, we were making progress. He was calming down. I let out a small laugh and groan as my stomach tightened in pain. That tattoo was gold.

When Ethan's crazy ex tried to run over Chase, I pushed him out of the way and took the hit. When Adrian told me that he would do anything for me I had every intention of telling him about Dita. It was the perfect timing. But Cleo's reaction in the hospital when she found out beforehand made me cringe away from the idea. Instead, I told Adrian he could pay me back by getting a tattoo of my face. On his ass cheek. And, to my surprise, he did it.

"It was funny?" I offered and Adrian started laughing. I relaxed and sat back in my chair.

"Chase wanted to kill me. Still does sometimes."

"I know I've said it before, but I really am sorry man. I shouldn't have kept it a secret for so long."

"It's all good man. I think I was angry for so long because I felt like my best friend betrayed me for a chick. It was gnawing at me. How could he so quickly turn on me? Knowing the truth makes it so much more palatable. For the first time since I found out, I feel okay with it."

"Are you sure? Do you hate Dita now?"

"Meh. You're right. I wasn't fully committed and that's not fair. Plus, I'm happy. She deserves to be too."

"Do you think I can make her happy?" I asked, a little bit of seriousness coming out of me. He raised an eyebrow at me.

"Seems like it. Although you both need to stop keeping secrets from each other. That's no way to have a healthy relationship."

I nodded. He was right. My thoughts returned to her audition. I'd have to tell her the truth. We couldn't have any secrets between us anymore.

"She's the only woman I've ever wanted a future with," I revealed.

"Future?"

"Yeah," I dug into my pockets and pulled out a slip of paper. A receipt. I slid it across the table at him. He took it and read it. He blinked rapidly. I nodded when he looked back at me.

"I'm going to propose after the tour."

Chapter Five

RABBIT DOWN THE HOLE

DITA

THE NEXT FOUR weeks passed in a blur. I saw my fellow dancers way more than I saw my boyfriend and his friends. Finally, the launch day was upon us. I was exhausted already.

When I wasn't rehearsing, I was arguing with Derek. Shortly after I got the job, the truth about my living situation came out. Of course, he was furious with me for lying to him about the apartment. I tried to feel bad, but my anger over his meddling overshadowed any guilt I had.

Our first show was also the first time I got to see him in full costume and makeup. Despite my constant irritation at him, I had to admit he looked amazing. All of the guys had colorful vintage suits, while Cleo had a dozen or so old dresses in a variety of styles.

Our costumes were similar, only all black. Since our bus was packed full, we were only given one dress and one suit. Thankfully, most of us women were the same size, so we could trade dresses. We were limited to one carry-on. Even then, the bus was extremely crowded.

I thought about asking if I could stay on the band's bus. I knew for a fact that it had way more room. However, days before the tour began, we were handed a list of do's and don'ts.

We were to keep with the dancing crew. We had a curfew and given a strict diet regime. But what shocked me the most was that we were to have little to no contact with any of the musicians or crew members. If we had any concerns or needs, we had to talk to our director.

I mentioned my concerns to the other dancers but was met with indifference. Apparently, the pay and exposure was well worth it. This was a part of the job. It was only new information to me.

Our first show went perfectly. I could do all the dances in my sleep. Despite the rules, when Derek waved at me, I waved back. He tried to come over, but I was shoved onto my bus before he could come any closer. I had told him about the rules, but he still tried to get me to break them. Honestly, if I could, I would. It seemed like there was always something blocking my path from him.

The days began to blur, each show felt exactly the same, despite Derek's long text messages telling me otherwise. He bragged about how much fun he was having, and how happy he was that he got to see me everyday. I lied and told him I felt the same. In reality, I just wanted to go home.

A solid month of draining shows and cramped quarters passed and I had never felt so happy. Finally the director announced we were going to be allowed a full evening to spend unsupervised. We didn't have to be back until morning. Everyone eagerly exited the bus without even a glance back.

"I'm going to sleep under the stars. Soak up the moon's energy," Lyric told us, flipping her long hippy hair over her shoulder.

"I think I'm going to go to a movie. Or maybe bowling. I don't know. I just want to have some real fun." Gwen sighed, leaning against her dance partner, Freddy. I suspected they were dating.

"You want to join us?" She asked me. I shook my head.

"Nah, I think I'm going to spend some time alone," I lied. She rolled her eyes and giggled.

"Sure. You go have fun, alone." She winked at me. Despite our director insisting on keeping strict to the rules, no one else cared. We all cheated with our diets, curfew, or other things when we could. My only vice seemed to be Derek.

I walked away from the bus and looked around for my waiting prince. I was on the sidewalk, walking quickly when someone jumped out from behind a tree and shouted. I screamed and jumped back. Derek burst into laughter as I gave him a dirty look.

"Hey you!" He wrapped his arms around me. I inhaled his scent. I had missed him so much, despite seeing him from afar every day. It wasn't the same. We pulled apart and he took my hand as we began walking away towards a strip of buildings.

This was the first time since the tour had started that we had time together. I hadn't realized how truly I had missed him until now. He was the treasure that was just out of reach. I could admire from a distance, but never touch. Until now.

We walked until we found a restaurant. Derek begged me to stop so we could eat. I didn't mention my strict diet to him, but instead agreed to go inside. It was a simple midwest diner. We were greeted by a pleasant older woman who told us the specials were meatloaf and all you can eat fish fry. Looking at the menu, I couldn't find anything that I could eat.

"Do you serve breakfast all day?" I asked.

"Sure do. Would you like an omelet?"

"Oh no. Just a fried egg please."

"One?" Her and Derek both looked at me skeptically. I

nodded. Derek ordered the meatloaf with extra mashed pota-toes. I was jealous.

"Are you not feeling okay? You didn't even get toast." He reached for my hand over the table. I forced a smile.

"I'm fine. Just not that hungry. I'm just happy we get to spend some time together. I feel like I barely get to see you."

He frowned but said nothing. Guilt started churning my stomach, so I changed the conversation.

"But at least we're here now. Tell me all the gossip," I said.

Over the course of our meal he caught me up on our friends back home. Chase had gone to Louisiana to spend time with his parents, while Renee was keeping down the fort at her and Mark's house. Not only did she have their daughter Lola and their two dogs, she was also caring for our cats, Big D and Hank.

"When the tour is finally over Renee is going to fly down to Louisiana and we are all going to meet there. Have you ever been there?"

I shook my head and let him go on and on about life after the tour. It sounded like a lifetime away. When we finished our food and were waiting for the check, I stepped away to use the restroom. When I returned, I stopped in my tracks when I saw a woman in my seat.

Derek was facing me, he was smiling and holding some-thing in his hands. He saw me and waved. The woman in ques-tion turned and gave me a scowl. She stood up as I began walking back to the table.

"It was nice meeting you. Just think about it." She glanced at me again and then left quickly. She was rather pretty. Jeal-ousy flared in me for a brief moment.

"What was that?" I asked, trying to keep my tone steady. He handed me a business card and stood up.

"Just a fan. Bills paid, let's go." I read the card and then looked back up at him curiously. She was an exotic dancer at some place called MERMAIDS.

"You got a stripper's business card?" I asked, confused and irritated. His eyes widened with innocence.

"She came over, introduced herself, and invited me to amateur night."

"Are you going to go?" I demanded. He looked away quickly.

"No. I mean, she said there was a prize to whoever gets the most money, but no. Not if you don't want to." He looked back at me, an innocent expression on his face. He stuck his tongue out at me and my angry heart melted. We left the restaurant and continued down the strip.

"You think you can win the prize?" I asked him as he reached for my hand.

"You think I can't? It's not like stripping is hard. The instructions are in the job title. I can take my shirt off and wiggle around. Easy."

"Easy? Being an exotic dancer is not easy," I defended. He scoffed.

"Okay. With your background in the art, why don't we go and we'll sort it out then?" He smirked. I stopped walking and thought about it, then shrugged. I'll call his bluff.

"Sure. If you're okay with men seeing me naked then I can be too. Let's make this bet more interesting though."

The smile fell off his face. He gulped and then nodded.

"Fine. What do I get when I win?"

"I'll do that thing you keep asking to do," I wiggled my eyebrows. He bit his knuckle and hissed.

"Oh, you play dirty. Alright. I'll have to up my game. I got us a room at the hotel here. You're staying with me." His eyes were determined and full of lust. It was hot. I could fully understand his desire. It had been over a month since we had the opportunity to spend the night together.

"And if I win?" I asked, reaching for his hand again. We started walking again, only now we had a destination in mind. He thought about it for a moment before speaking.

"If you win, I will stop asking you to move in with me."

"I can work with that," I smiled and he frowned. Ever since I revealed that I had left my apartment he was really pushing for me to move in with him more than ever.

"You know I don't like being dependent on anyone," I said softly for the hundredth time. He nodded and sighed loudly.

"Yeah I know. But it's not like that."

We saw the signs for the strip club and turned to head that way.

"I'm a bird, I have to be able to fly when I need to."

"Do you need to?"

I gulped. That was a weighted question. No, but I needed to have the option. Why couldn't he understand that?

"Can we talk about it when the tour is over? I love spending time with you, and love where our relationship is at right now. When I'm ready, I'll consider it. But you have to let me decide on my own." The more he asked, the more I wanted to run. Old habits die hard.

I was surprised that the strip club was right in town. Most business like this tended to be on the outskirts of the city. The music was blaring. We could hear it from a hundred feet away.

A giant sign blinked with the words, "Ladies and gentleman amateur night. Come one come all!"

"Are you sure about this?" I asked one last time. It was one thing to know about my past, it was another thing to see it in action. He bit his lip and then nodded.

"Yeah. I think so. Let's go."

Upon entering I squinted, the dark lighting hurt my eyes. A bouncer greeted us and we paid our cover. He let us through and tentatively we stepped into the lounge.

It looked exactly like I had pictured it. I swore that there had to be a strip club furniture magazine. It was furnished and decorated very close to my old palace, JASMINE'S. Everything was red and purple velvet. It was tacky and reeked of old sweat and an over abundance of perfume. My stomach turned slightly. Now I wasn't the one so sure of this.

I looked up at my boyfriend who was gripping my hand tightly. The room was packed with both men and women. Throughout the room women in skimpy lingerie carried trays of drinks to patrons. On stage was a dark-skinned brunette, topless and twerking against the pole. She must have been a popular one. The stage was full of dollar bills.

I giggled when Derek met my eyes. He looked panicked, like he didn't know if it was okay to look.

"Do you want to go to the ATM and pull out some money for the dancers?" I asked.

"Is that okay? Sorry, I've never done this with a girl before."

"Don't apologize, come on. Let's get you a drink and have some fun."

While he went to the ATM, I ordered him a beer and a vodka tonic for myself.

"Where do you sign up for the contest?" I asked the bartender. The woman behind the bar smiled kindly and pointed to the clipboard at the other end.

"Twenty dollar entry fee. Write your stage name and song preference if you have one. Did you bring something to wear?" She eyed my street clothes. They weren't exactly sexy. But I was wearing my cutest bra and had grabbed a thong to wear today. I must have known I would be need them. I shrugged.

"We're just passing through. Thought it'd be fun." I reached for the clipboard and pulled out forty dollars for her from my wallet. I signed my name first and paused at the song choice. I thought back to what songs I preferred in the past. I could go for the slow seduction with R&B, or something hot and fast with a rock song. I wanted to surprise him.

I glanced up and saw him focusing hard on the machine. He would be expecting something fast and crazy. I wrote down my old favorite song to dance to and then wrote his name down. I crossed it out after a moment. He needed a stage name. I couldn't help but giggle as I decided on his name and quickly his song. A laundry list of songs I had seen men perform to ran through my head.

I looked back up to see him coming my way. His cocky grin made me rethink my choices. His words about how easy it is made me feel less guilty about giving him a surprise song.

I gave the clipboard to the bartender. "Can you guys play those songs?" She eyed them and then gave me a confused look.

"These are some oldies. Sure."

Derek finally reached me, holding what looked like at least five hundred dollars. I gasped and playfully slapped his chest.

"Are you trying to get some lap dances? Jesus Derek," I laughed. His smile fell and was replaced with fear.

"Should I have grabbed less? I don't know, maybe this was a bad idea babe. I don't think we should do this."

"I already signed us up. We're numbers three and four."

"I'm not wearing anything... sexy." He looked down at his clothes. I gave him his beer and told him to drink up. I ordered another one and after his third he began to relax.

"Look, this room is full of more women than men. You already have the advantage. All you have to do is be flirty and let them touch your abs. Like Adrian does on stage."

I regretted my words immediately. He hated being compared to Adrian. Even if it wasn't even remotely sexual, it was still a sore spot with him that we had been together.

"We can go if you want. I will never force you to do something you aren't comfortable doing. This isn't for everyone."

"It was for you."

I flinched. I didn't do it for fun. I had college to pay for and was completely on my own. I did what I had to do. He slammed another beer and set it on the bar. He furrowed a determined brow.

"If you can do it, then so can I."

Suddenly the woman from the diner appeared in front of us. She was wearing a strappy leather ensemble. She let out a small shriek and hugged Derek, pressing her large chest against him. Her outfit barely covered her nipples. I gritted my teeth, reminding myself that this was her job, and I had once been in her shoes.

"You came! Are you here for the show or to perform?" She asked when Derek kindly pushed her off of him. He reached for my hand and raised it.

"I think we are going to try getting on stage. Just need a little liquid courage," he tilted his head towards the bar we were still sitting at. She gave me a tight smile then returned her attention to my boyfriend.

"Well, when your done, if you want a private lap dance come see me." She winked and hurried away, with a bounce in her step to make her ass jiggle. Derek watched her go with an amused grin. I rolled my eyes but had to laugh. I couldn't really get mad.

The lights flashed and the DJ started announcing that amateur night was starting.

"Can we have Miss Peaches to the stage please?"

A group of girls in the corner started screaming as one of their friends jumped up and strutted to the stage in six-inch heels. She was wearing a sexy police officer costume, complete with hat and handcuffs. She came to play. Climbing the stairs slowly, she made her way to the pole. The DJ announced her again and her song began. Nelly Furtado. She pulled out her handcuffs and slowly bent down, keeping her back and legs completely straight. Snapping back up she went into her routine.

I had to admit, she was really good. This couldn't be her first time. I glanced over and saw Derek bobbing his head as he watched her remove her shirt.

"She's good," he commented.

"You wanna go give her a few bucks?" I asked while he was taking a drink. His eyes bulged and started to choke. Beer spilled from the corners of his mouth.

"No! I mean, that's weird. Right?"

I shrugged. "We are at a strip club, that's what you're supposed to do. I don't care if you grab a boob or something, as long as she lets you and you're not using more than your hands."

He considered my words for a moment and then nodded.

"Alright. I can get on board with that. Same to you, wait, no. I can't watch you touch a guy's junk."

I rolled my eyes. "Okay, babe. Scout's honor. You realize the girls may try to grab you there, right?"

His eyes went big again and gulped. He leaned closer to whisper in my ear.

"What if I get hard?"

I burst into laughter. He scowled.

"The harder the better. That's what they want. If they get too handsy, move on to another person. That's a pro tip right there." I tilted my drink at him.

Miss Peaches' song ended and the DJ announced that Chamella was next. Miss Peaches grabbed all of her money and hurried to the bar to get it counted. Chamella took her place on stage with cowboy boots, hat, and overalls. She was dressed like a sexy farmer. A country song I didn't recognize began playing, and she started her dance. It was much rougher than Peaches' performance. This girl was clearly nervous and drunk. I turned away just as the bartender was handing her the money she had earned back, minus the club's cut.

"A hundred and five. That's pretty good for amateur hour!" She said, writing her total on her little paper behind the counter. I glanced back at Derek, who was watching the show. He looked nervous.

"Excuse me," I called to the bartender. With a smile she came back over to us. "Could you switch numbers three and four please." She nodded and I saw her text what I assumed was the DJ.

It was very obvious that Chamella did not earn as much as Peaches. Her song ended and my heart began beating furiously.

"Alright, we have a new face on the stage tonight. For one night only, Raphael! Come on down."

I nudged Derek and he jumped.

"That's me?"

I laughed. "Yeah, you know, Ninja Turtles, you're Derek Turtle? Clever, huh?"

He rolled his eyes. I stood up and helped him off his stool. He stumbled, but I held him tight as he walked to the stage. When people saw us coming the women started screaming obnoxiously. Derek suddenly perked up and started grinning. He loosened his grip on me, so I let go completely and let him climb on the stage, which made the screams louder.

The DJ welcomed him, and I suddenly regretted the song I had chosen for him. I wanted him to enjoy it. Maybe he could understand better. I practically sprinted to the DJ booth.

"Please don't play that song. I picked it for him. Can I pick another one?" I begged. The guy looked annoyed but told me to pick it quick.

"Can you play "Word Up" by Korn if you have it." He nodded and quickly found it in his computer. The song started blasting through the speakers all around the room. Derek stood there like a deer in headlights for a moment. I cringed. *Do something. Please.* Suddenly we heard some girls screaming for him to dance. It seemed to break his trance. With a nervous smile he began moving, doing a little awkward jig. It was stiff, but it was movement and it was a step in the right direction.

Someone screamed for him to take his shirt off and in one quick movement he did so, revealing a very tight white muscle shirt. His tattoos and large muscles made the screams and dollars fly through the air. Finally, he loosened up and began playing with his belt to his jeans. I cupped my hands to my mouth and screamed.

He dropped to the ground on his knees and lifted his shirt. Girls leaned forward and began helping him take it off. They rubbed his very defined ab muscles. One reached for his belt and he let her pull it out of the loops. Looking dead at the woman he undid his pants and stood back up, moving on to the next eager woman.

Eventually the jeans were pulled down and I had never been so grateful that he was wearing clean underwear. By the time the song ended he was in just his boxers and shoes and had gotten his package groped at least six times. There was so much money on the stage even I was shocked.

One of the dancers came to help him gather his clothes from the spectators and money from the stage. When he finally stepped down, I greeted him at the bar. He was holding his clothes, blushing. Even in the dark light I could see how red his face was. Before I could ask him about his experience I was called to the stage for my own turn.

"Alrighty, do we have a Dita Fox in the house?"

I gave him a quick kiss and slipped my sneakers off, setting them on the stool next to him. He was attempting to get dressed as quickly as possible. I hurried away before the DJ grew impatient. I slid onto the stage and looked out into the crowd.

I put my hands on my hips and took a deep breath. This felt too familiar and not in a good way. I suddenly didn't want to be up here. The strobe lights made my stomach churn. I looked towards the bar. Derek smiled at me and gave me two thumbs up. He was still reeling from his own performance.

I pursed my lips together and nodded to the DJ. He started my song and I closed my eyes, forcing myself to forget Gretchen, the simple farm girl, and let myself be Dita Fox. Just like the first time I stepped up to the pole almost ten years ago. I reached up and pulled on the hair tie holding my hair, letting it cascade down.

The ladies in the audience had fallen back, only to be replaced with a dozen eager men with sickeningly sweet smiles. I glanced back towards the bar and saw Derek coming towards the stage. Aaliyah began singing the song that started her career. The song that also started mine. "Age Ain't Nothing But a Number". Back then, it was quite fitting. I was barely eighteen.

I knew I was already at a disadvantage at winning this contest. I was wearing a baggy black t-shirt and jean shorts. I decided to use the pole to my advantage. I had noticed that Miss Peaches and Chamella both had avoided it. However, I knew how to use it. I twirled around it spreading my legs out. A saw a few dollars fall onto the stage as I dipped. I wondered if any of them were from my boyfriend.

With a large gulp I played with the bottom of my shirt and finally removed it, revealing the white lacy bra hugging me tightly. The all too familiar cheers and vulgar phrases invaded my ears as I hugged the bar. I closed my eyes and removed myself from this vile place. Focusing on the music and nothing else.

Remembering the old steps, I removed my shorts and kicked them out into the audience. Someone must have caught them, because a flurry of cash came towards me. I then left the comfort of the pole to crawl near the edge of the stage.

Hands reached for me, pulling on my underwear. I ignored them, moving on quickly. I sat up and with shaky hands I unclipped my bra, letting it fall to the stage. The shouts grew loud and I had to move away or go deaf. The numbness that always came with the compliments washed over me.

Looking out into the floor I finally caught eyes with Derek. I paused for only a millisecond. His mouth had fallen open as he watched me with greedy eyes. I was surprised. I had expected him to get upset, not aroused. I had to turn away from his stare. It didn't sit right with me. Is this what he wanted from me? Did he like other men gawking, touching, and pulling on me?

I stood up and walked around, then on the last thirty seconds I dropped back down, letting my head fall off the front of the stage.

I closed my eyes, and suddenly I was being kissed! My eyes flung open to stare right into eyes I knew better than my own. I softened and embraced the kiss as his hands wandered up to my exposed chest. He pinched my nipples quickly before I turned my head and sat up. This was beyond wrong. Not him, but the stage. This wasn't me. Not anymore.

The song ended and I quickly got up and gathered my things. I didn't care if I won or lost. I just wanted to get away from there as fast as possible.

Derek helped me down and brushed hands away. I threw on my clothes as fast as I could as I hurried to the bar. I could feel myself shaking. I felt like I was going to be sick. He helped me sit on the stool and without me asking he bent down and slipped my socks and shoes back on.

"Wow. You're good. That was hot, girl," the bartender commented. I looked up from the floor. She had pity in her eyes as she looked at me. Normally I'd have no problem telling her to screw off, but I was too lost at the moment. The memory of Derek's face seemed burned into my mind.

"Do you want to know how much you brought in?"

Derek wrapped his warm hands around me tightly. I flinched but let him hold me. After an eternity I finally nodded.

"One hundred and eighty. You're in second place right now. We've still got this last chick, but I think you're gonna stay there." She offered another smile and then slid a glass of water my way. I took it and gulped it down. I watched as the last girl took the stage.

"You ready to get out of here?" Derek asked me tenderly. He refused to let me go. He held me tightly, despite people bumping into us to get to the bar. I couldn't look at him. I knew he meant well, but I felt disgusting. *Ashamed.*

"Let's see who won," I said, trying to force a smile but failing. He sighed but stayed put.

The girl came down with a stack of ones that couldn't be more than fifty. It was quickly counted and with a wide grin the bartender came towards us.

"What size shirts do you guys want?"

"Both of us?" Derek asked. She raised her shoulders.

"You were the winner, but she came in second. If we didn't have a man tonight, she would have won. Congrats." She handed us two black shirts and left us to tend to her other customers. Derek took mine from me and reached for my hand.

Hurrying out into the darkness of the evening I let out a long breath. The cold air was refreshing and just what I needed. Derek clung to my hand as I tried to get a grip. We walked a few steps and then suddenly I lurched forward and emptied my stomach all over the sidewalk.

Derek hurried to pull my hair away and hold my center as I heaved. When I stood back up, I swayed a bit and he quickly picked me up. I wanted to fight it, but I was too mentally exhausted to argue. I closed my eyes and moved my head closer to his chest, letting myself be carried. He walked until he found a bench. Setting me down carefully he took out his phone and called someone.

Ten minutes later a car pulled up in front of us and we got in.

"We're just gonna go to the hotel," he told me and the driver. I closed my eyes and rested against his shoulder. I felt numb. Dita Fox was still on the stage, and this was just a shell of a person. Who was I now? I wasn't Gretchen. I could never be that innocent farmer's daughter again, but I didn't feel like Dita either.

I let him help me out of the car and up to his room. I walked in on my own and without hesitation went to the bathroom and stepped into the shower. I heard Derek swear as he hurried in and began taking my clothes off.

"Shit Dita! You didn't bring any extra clothes." I heard him say.

Once my clothes were gone, he removed his and joined me in the shower. His movements were tender as he washed my hair and lathered up his hands to wash my skin of that place. He wasn't trying to take advantage of me, but instead chose to take care of me. I still could barely stand to look him in the eye.

He shut the water off and wrapped a towel around me. Only then did I glance up into the mirror. I looked like a ghost. I was still pale and my face showed no emotion whatsoever. Seeing my face finally made something inside of me break. I watched as my lower lip began to tremble and my eyes began to go shiny with tears. I heard Derek swear again and he dropped his own towel to grab me and pull me out of the bathroom and into the room. He lifted me again and brought me to the bed where he laid down beside me. He held me as my sobs started. I let it all out and only when I stopped sniffling did he move.

I stared blankly at the pale yellow wall. I felt so unbelievably exhausted. I never thought being back on stage like that would shock my system the way it did. I must have blocked out all the bad memories I had of that time in my life.

"You won't ever step another foot in a place like that. I promise you that," he said. His words seemed to finally reach me. I squeezed the hand that was entwined with mine.

"Do you still love me? After seeing me like that?" I asked him, my voice sounding distant and cold. Suddenly he pulled away, sitting up. He rolled me over and forced me to sit up with him. I looked down, but he reached forward, grabbing my chin and tilting it up to look into his eyes. They were hard, determined, yet filled with pain for me. That man I had seen at the strip club was completely gone.

"I will always love you, no matter what you do. You are everything to me. This doesn't change anything."

"Are you sure?" I asked, giving him the chance to run. Many a men before him had. He reached his hand out and stroked my cheek tenderly. He leaned forward and placed the softest kiss on my lips.

"More sure than I have ever been."

Chapter Six

COME CLEAN

DEREK

I HELD her in my arms until the sun came up. It had been so long since we could spend time like this. I missed her so much. I didn't want to leave the room.

"Should I throw these out?" I asked, waving the shirts at her as we started preparing to take off. She looked at them like she wanted to vomit. I didn't care about her response. I stuffed them in the trash before she started crying again. She would never have to think about those days ever again. She seemed to relax after that, returning to the Dita I knew and loved.

After our shower she began to get anxious about getting back to her bus on time. Her eyes showed genuine fear and it crushed me. I hated that I had gotten her into this mess. If I had known how intense this tour would be, I wouldn't have pushed her to come.

This whole tour felt different. Too much security for my

liking. Everywhere I turned I saw someone new watching over us. I understood the need, but still.

I held onto my girl as long as I could before we parted ways to return to our separate busses. I watched her go back to her own, her shoulders slumped in defeat. It killed me.

Hopping back on my own bus I tried not to stress about how she was doing. I couldn't constantly worry about her. She was a big girl, and I had to let her deal with some things on her own.

Days turned into weeks with barely any time to spend with her privately. I was constantly being ushered to interviews, photoshoots, and meet and greets during the day. Then the shows at night. My only escape was the bus, and she wasn't allowed to leave hers. I wanted to sneak her on to ours and give the rules the middle finger, but her fear of the repercussions kept me back. We would simply have to love each other from afar.

One day when I was sulking on the couch Cleo came over and asked what was wrong. I told her that I simply missed my girl.

"She doesn't seem happy either."

"I know. I feel horrible. I did this to her. She looks miserable."

"They say you should never pick the flowers. Picking them and stuffing them in some pretty vase for you to look at causes them to wilt."

I turned away from the window and shook my head.

"I swear to God if you are working on a song based on my pain, I'm going to smother you with a pillow right here right now."

She laughed and held up her hands.

"Okay, you kind of got me. You guys are just so sad. It's beautiful. Is there any way for her to quit the tour?"

"I have no idea. I'll see if I can find out. Thanks."

Despite our inability to communicate in public, that didn't stop me from sending her long texts filled with declarations of my love. I didn't want her to wilt anymore. I needed to shower her with as much love as I could.

I sent her messages about anything and everything. I wanted her to feel like she wasn't missing out on things. I was starting to pretend that she was right here beside me. I missed her that much.

We had made it to El Paso, Texas. The heat was almost unbearable. Since I couldn't see Dita before the show I chose to nap on the bus rather than endure the heat.

Tonight's show was going to be one of our bigger shows. Every gig we had performed so far was sold out, but the venues ranged in size. This one even Dita was excited about. Apparently, she had been promised that they would have lots of space to move.

I had gotten a chance to see the stage during sound-check. They had delivered on their promise. The dancers would be on one large semi-circle platform behind the band. They were raised slightly above us, so they could move around with ease. I spotted her dancing behind us as we played and my heart sped up every time she spun into view. She looked heavenly.

Despite not being professionally trained she kept up with the others just fine. She didn't look out of place on the stage. In fact, I thought she was the best one up there, but maybe I was a little biased. Cleo was right; Dita was my wilting rose. I needed to get her off this tour before it killed her soul.

Standing behind the curtains before the actual show, I looked around for her. I spotted her standing with the other dancers in line. Her coworkers were all talking animatedly around her, but she was standing still, her face deep in thought.

I noticed then that her cheeks looked thinner, as did the

rest of her. Was she losing weight? She looked almost sickly. There was such a thing as too thin. I knew they had her on a special diet, but maybe it was too much for her. She wasn't used to the stress of performing night after night like everyone else was. I saw her close her eyes and take a deep breath before forcing a giant smile on her face. It relaxed me a little. She could do this. For me. God, what a woman.

I tried to wave to her, but she didn't see me, and I ended up awkwardly waving to one of the other dancers. It was the one Dita complained about the most. Carly? Yikes. She had mentioned to me once about an odd conversation with her at the release party. The unfamiliar girl waved back excitedly, and I turned quickly.

Thankfully they were ready for us. With Cleo in the front and Mark at the back of the line we marched onto the stage and were greeted by the screams we craved so much.

Jumping right into the show made it easy to forget about my troubles off stage. I threw myself into the stage personality the fans loved. I sang my heart out and played like my life depended on it.

Dita and the others dancing behind us paired with Cleo's eerily alluring voice and our fantastic music made for one hell of a show. These were the biggest shows we'd ever played, and the audience was showering us with the affection we needed to know that we had earned this.

They screamed our lyrics, danced to the hooks, and head banged to the beats. This was the dream. Everything we had done was for these moments. The high I got when I was performing for the masses was way better than any high a drug could give me.

As I played, I moved around the stage, bopping my head and interacting with my bandmates when able. I turned completely around to see my girl. She wasn't looking my way. She was focused on her dance partner. It didn't make me jealous though. They were told to not focus on us. They were supposed to be ghosts, like in the music video.

It almost felt like we were in two totally different worlds. While we performed a rock opera in the front, they danced an elegant waltz behind us. Cleo bumping my shoulder caused me to turn back to the crowd. Whoops.

We were right in the middle of our West Side Story number and I heard a sharp cry from behind me. I flipped my head to see Dita's body crumpled on the platform. Before I could react, her partner pulled her up quickly and they were dancing again, as if nothing had happened. Was she okay?

I tried to sneak glances at her from time to time but it was difficult to focus on her and the songs we were playing. After a while I decided that she was still dancing, so she must be fine.

I let myself relax back into the groove as we continued the show. Once it ended, I turned around just in time to see the dancers hurrying off and Dita's eyes roll into the back of her head as she collapsed.

While we waited for the EMT's to get there, I questioned Grant. We had people trying to wake her up, but she was only moaning. Her foot was swollen and purple. I was sure it was broken.

"I saw her fall, what happened?" I demanded. Grant shook his head.

"Some dude in the crowd got her attention and she fell. I don't know, man. I pulled her up and I let her put all of her weight on me. I asked her if she wanted to go off stage, but she said no. I told her we'd get her seen by a doctor when we were done, and she was fine with that."

"Is she always easily distracted?"

"No not at all. That's the weird thing. He shouted at her, she looked like she had seen a ghost, and she tripped."

"What did he shout?"

Grant paused, unsure of if he was going to tell me. "He

called her Gretchen."

I didn't tell anyone about my conversation with Grant. I was still confused about it all. If she was in so much pain, then why didn't she leave?

I rode in the ambulance with her while the band took a cab to the hospital. They took her into a room and quickly shoved an IV in her. They began pumping fluids and pain meds in. She stopped sweating, and now looked rather peaceful in her unconsciousness.

She hit her head when she fell, so the doctors wanted to take her to some testing to see what the damage was in her head and foot. Cleo text me that they were almost there, so I went down to the lobby. I stepped out of the elevator and saw a guy at the desk yelling at the clerk.

"Her name is Gretchen Fox. I know she's here. Please, let me see her."

"Sir, I have looked. There is no one here by that name."

"I watched them bring her in. She hurt her leg."

I paused. *Gretchen?* Was this the guy that made her fall? What was this bastard doing here? I stormed over and pulled on his jacket, turning him around. I gasped.

The resemblance was uncanny. He had the same eyes and nose. His hair was the same dirty blonde as Dita's. Eyes the same shade of green. What the hell?

"Who are you?" I demanded. He pushed my hand away and glared at me. Yep, same glare as hers.

"Who are you?" He shot back.

"What are you doing here?" I ignored his question. He gulped and motioned to the clerk with an eye roll.

"My sister was just brought in here, and they won't let me see her."

"Who is your sister?"

"Gretchen Fox."

"And you are?"

"Grey Fox." He turned back to the clerk. "Can you please look again?"

I let his information sink in. Dita never told me she had any siblings. Or did she? I couldn't remember. She never talked about her childhood or her family. Was it possible that Dita and Gretchen were the same person? I decided to take a chance on this guy. I sighed.

"Come with me. I know where she is."

By the time I took him back upstairs the nurse informed me that the pain meds they had her on were keeping her asleep for a bit. They were putting a cast on her foot as we spoke. She had a broken ankle. I sat outside her room with Grey and started grilling him.

"The dancer from your show is my sister. We were close growing up, but she took off when she was 18, same as me. We've got two brothers in between us, Griffin and Graham. She's the oldest and I'm the youngest."

"Why did she leave?"

"I don't really know. Gretch and I were the black sheep of the family. When she left no one was allowed to talk about it. I didn't even know where she was until I saw her at the concert."

"How do you know it was your sister?"

"She heard me, looked up, and recognized me instantly. Dude, I know my sister."

Obviously, he didn't; but apparently neither did I. My friends finally made it and I gave them a quick rundown of her condition and then who the guy standing next to me was. He gave a quick awkward handshake to everyone but kept quiet. I needed a cigarette. The security guard that came with the band scowled but let me go. I told him to stay with them and not let anyone other than us in. Grey followed me outside.

"You call her Dita?" He asked as we smoked. I nodded.

"Ever since I've known her. She never mentioned the name Gretchen," I said bitterly. The more and more I thought about it the more it pissed me off. It was lie after lie with her. Her job, her apartment, and now even her name. When would this end?

"She seems to be doing well for herself. She always said she wanted to do something with animals. I never would have expected her to be dancing for one of the biggest bands out there right now."

"She does work with animals, normally. She was in between jobs and I asked her to come with me."

"Are you and her...?"

"Yeah. We've been together for a few years now."

He whistled.

"Never would have guessed. Looks like at least one of us did something worth telling."

I wasn't in the mood for small talk, so I finished my cigarette and went back upstairs. Devin, the security guard was the only one by the door. He told us everyone else was inside visiting.

"Sam called. You guys can't be gone much longer. An hour max. The bus needs to leave."

"What about her? She's in a cast, how is she going to dance?"

Devin shrugged and with a scowl I turned away to call Sam.

"I can't just leave her here. She's in a leg cast. What are they going to do?"

He hung up and called me back shortly after.

"They are pulling her from the tour. They are going to send her bags to the hospital with someone. I already called and bought her a ticket to head back to L.A. There isn't much we can do Derek."

I swore, but I knew he was right. She couldn't join us on the bus, and I had an obligation to stay on the tour. She wasn't my wife. It wasn't life threatening. I couldn't get out of this. I'd have to send her alone. My bandmates came out, all looking sad. Cleo looked close to tears.

"She did confirm that he is who he said he is." She glanced at Grey who rolled his eyes. I didn't blame him. They really did look a lot alike. I motioned for him to join me as I stepped into her room. My girl was awake and looking towards the door. She saw my face and instant guilt flooded her beautiful eyes. I stepped aside to let Grey in. I waved at him dramatically.

"Care to explain?"

"He's my brother. That's really all there is to it," she said, as if I was the crazy one. I walked over to her, not amused.

"How have we been together for two years and you never thought to bring up the fact that you have a brother, and your name isn't really your name?"

She put her finger up to stop me.

"My name is Dita. I had it legally changed a few years ago," she defended, but it was flimsy. She wasn't winning this battle. I came and sat on her bed, taking her hands in mine. My anger quickly started melting. It transformed into pain.

"Dita, Gretchen, hell I don't know. Why didn't you tell me?" I said softly.

"There was no reason to. It's in the past. I don't like dwelling on my problems." Her voice was whiny and desperate for me to drop it, but I couldn't yet. I glanced at her brother.

"He's a problem? Is that why you haven't seen him in what—eight years?" I raised an eyebrow at the guy. He backed up with his hands up, shaking his head.

"No! I didn't mean him. He's probably the only family member I do like. Derek, there's just a lot to this that I didn't want to bring you into. You don't need the drama."

"Dita. You can't keep doing this. The job, the apartment,

now this? Why are you so afraid of telling me things? It shouldn't be this hard," I sighed. I was suddenly exhausted. I was so sick of fighting over this stupid stuff. Why were simple things such as a name so hard for her to tell me? Her eyes grew wide and wet. I watched her chin began to tremble. Grey coughed and stepped out.

"Is this it then? Are you done with me?" She asked, her voice cracking. I threw my head back with the biggest eye roll I could handle.

"No! Dita, is that why you refuse to let me in? You're afraid I'm going to leave?"

"No."

I knew she was lying, but I didn't have the energy to continue fighting. My body was craving rest. If I wasn't still in my stage clothes, I would have all but forgotten about the concert I had just been at. So much had changed in the last couple of hours.

I glanced at the clock on the wall. It was past midnight. Sam was going to skin me if I held up the bus. Turning back to Dita, I saw that she had started crying. Oh no. She tried to wipe them away, but I stopped her, leaning down to tenderly kiss her lips. I pushed the hair away from her face and stared down into those entrancing eyes.

"We can't keep doing this. I want to be in your life. All of it, good or bad. Now, you want to introduce me to this guy properly?" I gave her my best smile and her face lit up like she had won the lottery. My heart soared. I wished she'd always look at me like that. She called for her brother and he popped right back in.

"Derek, this is Grey Fox. My youngest brother. Grey, this is Derek Turtle, my boyfriend."

I shook his hand again and turned to her, pretending to be surprised.

"Youngest? You have more siblings?"

She nodded.

"I have three brothers. Griffin, Graham, and Grey. I'm the oldest. My other brothers live in Michigan back on the family farm. I left when I was eighteen, and from what I heard, Grey did the same. I haven't seen any of them since I left home."

"Why did you leave?" I asked. She glanced at her brother and I could tell it was something she didn't want him to hear.

"Can we cover that one a different day? Today has been enough of a mess."

I nodded and came back to sit by her again.

"Sure. We have a lifetime to talk about it. How are you feeling? I forgot to ask, my bad." I knocked on her cast. She looked down at it mournfully.

"I'm not in pain, if that's what you're asking. Am I fired?" She asked. I didn't answer right away, confirming what she had suspected.

"It's hard to dance while lugging that thing around," I offered.

"Do I have to go get my things then?" She looked like she was dreading that. I didn't blame her. After all the stories I had heard about the dancer drama, it would almost be like a walk of shame. Thankfully, her stuff was probably already here. I told her so and a wave of relief washed over her.

"All of your medical bills are covered. You don't have to pay a cent," I said in an attempt to cheer her up, but she was back to looking defeated. She stared at her cast and her lips began to tremble again. I squeezed her hand, causing her to look back at me.

"I'm sorry. I feel like this was all my fault."

She shook my head.

"It's fine. I do these things to myself. I'll figure it out. I always do." Her words came out flat and cold. Something about the way she said them made me think about her past. Unease settled inside me.

"You don't have to figure out a way home. I had Sam get you a plane ticket. As soon as you are released, we will get you back to California."

She blinked and adjusted herself, sitting up better.

"What?" It was as if she was finally understanding that she wasn't on the tour anymore. Guilt hit me again, but my hands were tied.

"I can't just drop out of the tour. There's nothing wrong with me. I wish I could, I really do. I'm going to miss you." I lifted her hand to my lips and kissed her fingers. Tears began sliding down her cheeks again, but she nodded.

"Okay," was all she could say.

"Renee will be on the other side to pick you up. We already called her." I lied, but it was a little one that I knew could easily be fixed. Renee would pick her up. She may not like me, but she was close to Dita.

"Are you coming to the airport with me?"

When I didn't answer, her face flooded with disappointment, only making me feel worse. I was already pushing it for time.

"I actually have to get back to the band soon. They were mad enough we all came to see you. You'll be fine. Like you said, you always figure it out." I tried to sound optimistic, but it came out snarky.

"I can go with her."

We both looked up at the voice in the corner of the room. I had almost forgotten about her brother. I eyed him cautiously, then looked back at her.

"Do you want me to get him an extra ticket?"

She nodded quickly. I pulled out my phone and sent a message to Sam.

"Done."

I wasn't too keen on the idea, but whatever Dita needed to feel better I'd do. I just hoped that he was sane and genuinely wanted to be here for her, and not a crazy fan. She reached for my face and when I came close, she kissed me. It was soft, almost like a whisper.

"You're amazing," she told me, just as soft as the kiss.

I gave her my award winning smile.

"Always."

A deep cough from behind us alerted us that Grey was going to step out again to give us space. When he was gone, I chuckled.

"He looks just like you."

She rolled her eyes, but a giggle did escape her lips. The sound relaxed me some.

"He showed up right after we did. I had gone down to see the guys and he was at the front desk demanding to see Gretchen Fox. The nurse tried to explain that no one by that name was admitted, but he was adamant. When he started describing you, I realized that Gretchen and Dita were one in the same."

"I should have told you. I'm sorry."

"Where did you get Dita from?" My fingers traced light circles on the tops of her hands. She closed her eyes and relaxed.

"I told you, that was my dancer name."

"And you just decided to change it? I would have thought you'd want to forget that life."

"The life Gretchen was running from was way worse," she said bitterly.

"Another time, remember?" I offered and she nodded a small smile. "Are you really okay going with him?"

"Yeah. He always was my favorite. You'll like him too, if he's still around when you come home."

"Home. I like the sound of that. I would absolutely love to come home to you."

"Derek," she started but I cut her off.

"I haven't brought it up in a long time. Now is the perfect time. You can see the place for yourself on your own. You can move in at your own pace. Hell, take my credit cards and decorate it however you want it. Just be there when I get back. Dita, that house will never be a home if you're not there with me," I pleaded with her. I didn't want anything else in the world more than I wanted her. Why couldn't she see that?

Her eyes took on a far-off look and when she returned her eyebrows furrowed.

"What's wrong?" I asked.

"Did you want me on this tour to watch me? So that I wouldn't cheat on you?" She accused. My eyes went wide with surprise. I opened my mouth but shut it quickly. Where was this coming from? Hadn't we already talked about this? I never used the words 'cheat' but still. Her face contorted with anger.

"Where did this come from?" I asked instead of answering her.

"Why aren't you answering me? It's true, isn't it. Everyone was laughing at me this entire tour and now I know why. God, I'm so embarrassed!" She covered her face with her hands. She choked back a sob. I reached my calloused hands out and gently pulled her hands away from her face. She lifted her head and glared at me.

"Look, yes, that's true to an extent. I wasn't going around telling people that. People must have just assumed. But yes, some small part of me was worried. These last few months I've felt like you've been pulling away from me, and I didn't want to lose you just because we weren't seeing each other every day. I thought if I got you on the tour, you'd be happy."

"Yeah well I wasn't," she snapped at me. It was as if she had slapped me right across the face. I pulled away and sat up straight.

"I was miserable for almost the entire time. We weren't allowed to eat, relax, or talk to anybody but other dancers.

Everyone hated me because I was dating you. We had curfews and were practically watched every second of the day. How could anyone be happy like that?"

"Am. Not was." I said firmly. She stared at me in confusion.

"What?"

"You said everyone hated you because of who you were dating. Past tense."

"Jesus Derek, are you that insecure about my feelings for you that you are nitpicking everything I say?"

"Can you blame me? Dita- Gretchen- whatever your name is, all you ever do is lie to me. How can I feel confident that you'll be there for me when I get home?" I threw back at her. The room fell silent.

"I don't know," she answered in what I felt was the first true honest answer I had been given in a long time. It was as if all the air had been removed from the room. A deafening silence fell over us as we took in what she had just said. Finally, I blinked and licked my lips.

"Move in with me." I reached for her hand and she took it, squeezing it gently. Her eyes were swimming with tears. They seemed to shift back and forth with her brain, as if she was trying to figure out something. Each second that ticked by with no response was agonizing. I didn't know if we could move forward if she wasn't willing to do this one thing for me. Was it too big a question? Was I jumping the gun? Finally, she nodded and I almost jumped off the bed. I stood up straight and looked down at her.

"Really?"

"Yeah. I'll do it. Let's move in together."

I embraced her tightly once more.

"I can't wait to get home. I can't tell you how happy this makes me. Dita, thank you," I gushed. I laughed, and before we could speak more a knock on the door made us pause. A man in a white lab coat came and introduced himself as the doctor who had put the cast on.

"We were just waiting on you to come to. You were severely dehydrated and in need of some nutrients. We have a prescription for you for the pain. The nurse will give it to you with your discharge papers. Obviously, no more dancing. At least for six weeks. You'll have to follow up with a local doctor to get the cast removed, but other than that you are good to go Ms. Fox." He left just as suddenly as he had come.

Dita and I spent the next half hour shooting the breeze until the nurse came to remove the IV and put her in a wheelchair. I talked excitedly about the house. I couldn't wait for her to really see it. She had full creative reign on the decor, I told her. She only smiled and let me go on and on about it.

The nurse handed me her crutches and we left the hospital. Grey was waiting outside smoking a cigarette and holding her duffel bag from the bus. All of a sudden, two cabs pulled up in front of us.

I saw the disappointment drip from her face when she realized that one was for me, and the other for her. I hated it too, but this was part of the gig. I knew this when I signed up for this life, and she knew it when we got involved. I helped her into her cab and hugged her for as long as I could. Devin had been waiting for me and tapped my back. I knew without looking at a clock that I was well past the time Sam had told me to be back.

"You know I love you. If I could go I would," I repeated.

"I know. I'll be there when you get back," she promised. We kissed one last time before I stood up straight.

"I'll hold you to that." I winked as I shut the door and hurried to my own cab.

I called Mark and asked if he'd get his wife to grab them from the airport. Before I knew it, we were back on the bus and heading to a different city. I missed her already. My bandmates and the others greeted me and offered their support, but I told them I didn't need it.

"Dita agreed to move in with me," I revealed. The bus erupted with congratulations of all sorts. Hugs, high fives, hoots and hollers. I was feeling good. My girl would be there when I got back. In my new home, our new home. I could not wait.

Sadness over her leg came and went throughout the night. I felt terrible that she was probably in pain. I knew my legs hurt like hell both times I broke them. However, I decided it really was a blessing in disguise. She needed off this tour. She was losing weight, she looked miserable, and the only benefit was having her close. Even that wasn't really a benefit. What was the point when I couldn't even talk to her in public?

It was the best case scenario, Sam explained to me. She didn't do anything wrong to get her contract revoked. It was an accidental injury. Sure, she'd have a cast for a few weeks, but her mental health was better for it.

A few hours later I received a message from Renee telling me she picked them up. I thanked her and made a mental note to do something nice for her. Maybe send her some flowers or something. Despite me being a complete ass to her, she still treated me decent.

We were still shooting the breeze way into the early morning. We didn't have a show the next day, so everyone was enjoying the break. We had all had more than our fair share of alcohol and had the music turned all the way up.

Adrian was dancing with Mark while Cleo clapped them on in a systematic rhythm. I felt at peace. This was my happy place. Sure, I wished Dita could be here, but she wouldn't understand. None of them would. Ethan, Renee, Chase. They were all part of the big Maria Maria family, but we were the solid gold oldies.

Memories of us starting out on our first tour in my old

minivan ran through my head. Practicing in my parent's garage. Way before we knew this music thing would make us rich. We were just four stupid kids who wanted to rebel a little bit. If only they could see us now.

Cleo and Mark plopped onto the couches beside us.

"What are you thinking so hard about over there, Turtle?" Mark asked. I told him and they all agreed.

"It's definitely weird to think about. I'm glad the four of us have still stuck it out through the years, despite everything," Cleo said.

"Like it was ever really an option," Adrian scoffed.

"You guys could have started a new band without me," she argued. "I really thought you would. I didn't think I'd ever get back to music again."

"That, or we almost didn't even make it to this tour," Mark said, pointing at Adrian and me.

We looked at each other and shrugged. Adrian pulled my head into his armpit and began giving me a noogie. I laughed as I fought him off.

"We're gonna be playing together for the rest of our lives. Even if we don't have an audience anymore. We'll make our kids and their friends watch us," Mark laughed.

I pulled away from Adrian's grasp and stood up to grab another beer.

"What's this?" He said and I turned to look. My eyes widened with recognition. Oh crap. He was holding my keys up and jangling them. I swiped them and stared at them in irritation. I was supposed to have given them to Dita.

"Those are my new house keys. You know, to the house my girlfriend is going to move into later this week."

There was a pause before everyone erupted in laughter. Glad to see they all thought this was hilarious. I did not. How was I supposed to get them to her?

Chapter Seven

FREE TO DECIDE

DITA

I AWOKE to my phone ringing like crazy with notifications. Groaning, I debated not looking at them. I could only imagine I was being bombarded with my former co-workers laughing at me and telling me how much I deserved the broken leg. Carly probably had a party last night. However, that wasn't what was causing my phone to go crazy.

Apparently, the world of social media was abuzz about a video Derek had made. I sighed. I could only imagine what it was. With a large gulp I went to his profile and clicked on his grinning face behind the play button. It was loud in the background, but you could see that he was back on his tour bus. He was grinning ear to ear.

"I'm sure some news site will probably mention it, but today my girlfriend had a minor accident during our show. She's gonna be fine, but that's not why I'm making this video. I'm here to say that I finally convinced her to move in with me! When I get back to L.A. she'll be there waiting for me."

There was a pause and you could see and hear all of his bandmates waving and cheering for him. He then held up a set of keys.

"The only thing is, I forgot to give you the keys babe. I'm shipping them express the second the bus stops, so you'll be getting them soon. I love you and can not wait to see you. You have seriously made me the happiest guy on this tour. I'll see you soon."

He was wiping invisible tears from his cheeks as he continued to grin like an idiot and shut the camera off. He was adorable. I almost wanted to cry seeing him so happy. I spent the morning perusing the comments. Since he posted it 12 hours ago, there had been about 5,000 of them.

Most were positive. Some were full of hate for me or him. That was usual though. The hashtag #rockstarwivesrock was trending again. Renee would be happy about that. A writer started that last year when people attacked her on the internet. It was nice that people remembered that and continued to be supportive of the people behind the celebrities.

Using my crutches, I eventually got up and rather awkwardly walked into the kitchen. I found Grey eating breakfast with Renee and Lola. She quickly made me a plate and I picked nervously at my eggs. Despite Derek's video and his fans kind words, the fact that I was alone again depressed me. Maybe this was a blessing in disguise.

"So how was it? Being a dancer in the background? Was it hard to concentrate?" Renee asked, trying to cheer me up.

"You got used to it pretty quickly but, to be honest, I kind of hated it," I revealed. It felt good to finally say it aloud. I let out a large sigh of relief and a short chuckle followed.

"I hated it so much. The other dancers were nothing but drama, we couldn't talk to anyone, and we had a ridiculous diet." With that last memory I took a giant bite of my buttered toast. I groaned with delight. It was so satisfying. She laughed.

"Well maybe this was a good thing? Sounds like it wasn't as great an idea as it seemed. Did Derek know?"

I shook my head.

"No, I didn't want him to say something and get me in trouble or make the other dancers hate me more. It doesn't matter now. I wouldn't go back if they paid me," I smirked. If only I knew breaking my ankle would get me kicked out, I might have done it earlier.

"Well, you won't have much time to dwell on it. Derek called me and said to expect the keys sometime today. Your car is still here, although you can't really drive it." She glanced from me to Grey.

"I've never actually been to L.A., but I think I can handle driving around. I'll get you to wherever you need to go," he offered. I thanked him. Not long after we finished eating, the doorbell rang. Renee hurried out of the room and returned with a small yellow envelope. She handed it to me with a huge smile.

"I've never seen him act like this. Derek isn't the mushy type," she giggled as I opened it and dumped the keys into my hand. They were heavy with more than just keys. This was it. I was really doing this. With a gulp I forced a smile at her and then my brother.

"Well we should get a move on then. Get as much done as we can today." I thanked Renee for her hospitality and had Grey put our things in my car and pull it around. Once we were on the road, I directed him to the moving van place I used when I had moved out of my apartment. We rented a van and then headed over to the storage unit.

I felt guilty that I couldn't really do much with my crutches but Grey continued to tell me it wasn't a problem.

"That's what siblings are for. Plus, you are letting me chill with you while you get better so I can't complain."

"You don't have a place? No apartment or house?" I raised an eyebrow. What had he been doing all this time? He hesitated, holding a large box. I motioned for him to put it in the van. He turned to answer.

"No, I kind of like to drift. I'm not ready to settle on anything permanent yet."

I nodded, fully understanding. Moving in with Derek was a huge step for me, and I still wasn't sure if it was the right move.

"The company will be nice. Derek's new place is ridiculously huge. I don't know why he bought such a big place."

"I've only met him once, but based on last night I think I might know why," he laughed. "He wants to show off."

An hour or so later the unit was empty and we returned the keys to the office. I had to text Derek to confirm the address. He called me right away. His voice was so eager and full of happiness, it made me feel guilty for my hesitance.

"Oh, but the place is gated. You need the code. 062001. Punch that in and it should let you right in. I'll call you tonight after the show and see what you think of the place. I love you. It means so much to me that you are doing this," he told me again. I hung up when we reached the house. Grey whistled as he typed in the code. The machine beeped its approval and began opening the gates.

"This place is overkill. Who owned this before him?"

"Emile Dahl," I revealed.

"Oh, wow," Grey's reaction was more of shock than excitement. I glanced at him, but he gave me a forced smile and turned away from my scrutinizing gaze. I made a mental note to ask later.

We drove up the long driveway and parked in front of the massive house. Grey turned the car off and went up the stairs to the door. I took a moment to take the place in. This was straight out of a magazine. It was two large stories tall, with two small verandas on each side. I lost count of all the trees and bushes. He'd have to have a gardener for all of this. It was gorgeous. The house itself was a peach color, with large white columns from the ground all the way to the roof. The doors and windows were white with a deep brown wood accent. It truly was beautiful, and it was my new home, I realized.

With the front door unlocked and opened Grey came back to me and helped me out of the van, up the few steps, and into the house. Inside was just as impressive as the outside. It was large and open.

"Hello!" He shouted into the room, and we laughed when it echoed back to us.

"Why don't you explore a little while I unpack that van. The faster I get everything inside the quicker we can return it, get back here, and order some pizza while we unpack." He wiggled his eyebrows at the idea of pizza. I rolled my eyes but nodded.

"Sure. I'll look for the kitchen."

"Look for the bathroom too please!" He shouted from outside.

I struggled with my crutches around the large house. There were three bathrooms on the ground floor, and a kitchen that Renee would be jealous of. She loved cooking. This was a chef's dream. I wondered if the previous owner had a full staff to help maintain everything. He would almost have to in order to keep up with this place. A gardener, chef, butler, maid, a pool guy. There was no way Emile Dahl did all of that himself.

I made it to the back yard and my jaw dropped. It was like

I had stepped into an early 2000's rap video. This set up was insane. The pool was at least three times bigger than an average pool. It was way bigger than necessary. There was a hot tub to the side that could fit a dozen people easy. The foliage was just as impressive and gorgeous as the front yard. I was frozen in my spot, staring out at the yard until my brother came up behind me.

"Holy crap. This place is ridonkulous."

I laughed and followed him back into the main entryway. He was moving fast. I watched him for a time in awe. It was odd. In personality, he was the little brother I remembered. However, he didn't look the same anymore. His face had slimmed some, but the most dramatic change was his height and muscle. I remembered a much scrawnier boy. The young man in front of me had grown about a foot and clearly worked out. He reminded me of our other brother, Griffin.

He dropped some boxes in front of me and eyed me cautiously.

"What are you staring at?"

I tried to lean over and ruffle his hair but struggled to keep the crutch under my arm, so I dropped my hand.

"Nothing. It's just crazy how much you've changed since the last time I saw you. You remind me of Griff."

He snorted.

"That pretty boy? Please. What about you? Has mom seen you with all those tattoos? She'd have a heart attack." I noticed that his midwestern twang returned to his voice at the mention of our mother. I laughed, but the thought of my parents dampened the mood.

"I'm surprised we didn't give them heart attacks yet, to be truthful. I don't think they were upset when I left," I revealed sadly. Not once had my parents asked me to return. My mom would only say half-heartedly that I should visit sometime; and the rare times I did catch my dad on the phone he would tell me I needed to get my life together. Looking around, I didn't feel like I was doing too bad. I wasn't the same girl that left the farm in the middle of the night.

"Do they know you changed your name?"

I shook my head.

"Nah. I doubt they'd call me Dita anyways. They are too stubborn. I don't talk to them enough for it to matter."

Silence fell over us and after an awkward moment Grey forced a smile.

"Well, I'm going to finish getting this stuff in, then we'll lock up and take the van back. I'm starving."

Turning back to keep exploring, I found the spiral staircase that would take me to the second floor. It was carpeted, but still loomed over me. Could I make it back up and down with these damn crutches?

It took forever, but I managed to do it on my own. I could feel bruises forming under my arms already just from one day's activities. I took my time exploring the upstairs rooms. There were so many of them. I found another guest bathroom and four full sized suites, two with full bathrooms in them. I noted also that while the ground floor had a huge room for Derek to practice in, the second floor had a large, empty library. Although I had only met Emile Dahl once, and it wasn't really something he'd find memorable, I hadn't thought of him as a big reader. I wondered if he had used this room for its purpose, or if it had been empty while he was here as well.

By the time I made my way back downstairs Grey was dropping the last box onto the floor. The clear exhaustion on his face made me feel a twinge of guilt. He wiped the sweat from his face and smiled.

"You ready? Let's go."

We returned that evening with pizza and beer. The only furniture in the house was my bed, so we sat on the floor in the living room to eat. Grey set up my TV and found a box of old movies and the player to match.

"First thing tomorrow we'll go get some furniture," I promised him. I had given all of my other furniture from my apartment to my neighbor. I got a good price for it all and didn't have to move it. It was a win win at the time.

"Where are we sleeping tonight?" He eyed me skeptically. I shrugged.

"I'll call Renee. I don't think she'll care. It's just one more night."

I was right. She didn't care. We headed back over to her place after we ate and locked things up. We spent some time relaxing with Renee, shooting the breeze and catching up. Grey didn't seem too uncomfortable, in fact, he seemed to fit right in with most of the conversation. It was nice. When I finally got into bed my phone rang. Derek's face popped up and I answered it quickly.

"Hey Babe! So, what do you think?" He asked me quickly before I could speak. I giggled and thought for a moment.

"The house is very much like its brand new owner: obnoxious. Derek, why did you buy something so big?" I exclaimed. He let out a loud belly laugh. I loved his high energy. He must have had a good show.

"I got it for a steal. Dahl didn't care how much he got for it. You like it then?"

"It's gorgeous. I'm still a little star struck by it. I'm staying another night at Renee's. Tomorrow we're going to get a few pieces of furniture."

"You should do the whole house. Furnish it all. Make it look however you want. I give you total control over it."

I rolled my eyes.

"Why don't I just get a few things and we'll go shopping when you get home? It'll be our first major couple thing," I suggested.

"Okay. How are you dealing with your leg?" He asked. That moved the conversation forward to other things. We laughed about how much casts sucked. Then we talked about the concert he had today. Cleo made a shout out to me and Derek. Congratulating us and teasing Derek about growing up. I yawned and he told me he would let me get some sleep.

"Hey, before I go, why don't you pick one room in the house that is just for you and decorate it however you want. Paint the walls, get new carpet, make everything completely you. Pull out all the stops. I want you to have a place that you can call yours. I know you. You need something to do while I'm gone."

I wanted to roll my eyes, but the idea wasn't bad. He was right.

"That sounds perfect. I'm going to do that." We said our goodbye's and hung up for the night.

Although I had been fully prepared to pay for today's furniture, another envelope came to Renee's the next morning. It had Derek's credit card with a note to charge everything to it, and to not argue about it. I had to laugh. I could hear his voice as I read his note. I missed him already.

Grey drove us to the furniture store. I picked out a simple green couch and the tables, lamps, and recliner that matched. My brother made sure to test it out before purchase.

"I just want to make sure it's comfy enough to sleep on for a few weeks," he laughed. I rolled my eyes as we gave them the delivery address.

Despite my hesitancy to make this my home, I was getting used to the place fairly quickly. Grey set up my bed that night and we started staying there. A few days later I brought Big D and Hank from Renee's to let them see their new home. Hank had gotten so big since we had left for the tour. I hadn't realized I would miss so much when I went on tour. Having him cuddled up to me that night made me glad I was back. That I was home.

I had taken Derek's advice and picked a room just for me. It was on the second floor and far away from the library and our bedroom. Since I had limited mobility my brother painted the room for me. I knew right away that I wanted to make the room reflect my personality. I had spent hours combing over the proper colors and when Grey finally opened the first can and stirred it, he stared up at me in confusion.

"Pink?"

I nodded, staring at the color in admiration.

"Did you know that in the original Addams family show the entire set was actually pink? Since it aired in black and white having the dark colors wouldn't work on screen."

He shook his head and laughed as he started working on the walls. Once the main color had been coated on the walls, we added curtains and furniture that was a faded yellow, just like in the show.

Over the next few weeks I would go shopping in thrift stores looking for creepy and weird things to put in the room. It was quickly becoming my favorite hobby.

Six weeks had passed in the blink of an eye and I was ready to get my cast off. I had been having a blast catching up with my brother and making this giant place more homey, but it was time to start my life back up. Although, I didn't really know where to start.

Grey and I sat in the living room eating burgers and fries while watching some trashy reality TV on my last night with my cast. We hadn't really talked about my plans going forward, but it was time.

"So now what are you gonna do?" He asked me. I shrugged.

"I don't know. I should probably start looking for a new job."

"Are vets in demand out here?"

"The world can always use more veterinarians. I just have to find someone willing to take someone who doesn't have any good recommendations and has only been practicing for less than two years. I don't know, maybe I should take a break. I love working with animals, but I hated the clinic."

"Why don't you do something else then? Just because you have the degree doesn't mean you're stuck for life."

I snorted.

"It kind of does. I can't even tell you how much school cost me."

"You probably pay out the ass in student loans each month. That's why I didn't go to college."

I rolled my eyes. Student loans were not the reason he chose not to pursue higher education. I smiled to myself. I was actually debt free. Working at the club really had its merits. I didn't owe a dime; but I wasn't about to explain to my brother why.

"I had full rides every year. Lots of essays and volunteering," I lied.

Grey put his plate down and reached over to the side table where my camera was sitting. We had spent the afternoon going through old photos I had brought with me from the farm.

"Don't get burger grease on that, that's a professional level camera."

"Why don't you become a photographer? You know, babies, weddings. You could make your own schedule, set your own rates. You've always liked taking photos," he said, his eyes darting to the box on the floor. He had a point. I had loved being behind the camera since I was little. I used to buy disposable ones at the drug store once a week and by that next Sunday I would have it filled and ready to be turned in for printing.

I thought about his idea. I liked the idea of setting my own schedule. Especially with Derek's career. It would be good to have a flexible job. I didn't want to take photos of babies though. Or weddings for that matter. I loved candid pictures. Photographs taken when people are living their lives, not posing with fake smiles. I mentioned that and the idea quickly fell flat.

"What are you going to do? Head back to Texas?"

He shrugged, setting my camera back down carefully.

"I don't know. I was just passing through when I found you. I might just hitch a ride somewhere and keep traveling. I don't like to think too far into the future."

I frowned. The idea of my baby brother being a homeless hitchhiker was less than appealing. I brightened, a sliver of an idea started forming in my head.

"What if you stayed and helped me start up a photography business? You could help carry equipment and be like an assistant. I'll pay you half of what I make."

He looked skeptical.

"Okay, but what are you going to take photos of?"

I chewed on my lip, trying to think.

"What do people take photos of?"

"Sports, celebrities, art, animals, scenery, events," Grey listed off with his fingers. "Oh! Animals. Why don't you do animal photography? I can get on board with that," he laughed.

I held up a hand. "Hold on, back up. Events. Like concerts?" I asked.

"Yeah, you could do concerts. Wait," he sat up and stared at me. The idea came to us seemingly at the same time.

"I could take photos at Derek's concerts. Like- in the crowd. I could take photos of the crowd. Of the fans. Oh my God." My mind was quickly filling up with ideas it was hard to articulate.

"We could follow them on tour in our own van; and he can get us VIP passes to get into places to take exclusive photos. This could be so much fun!" Grey added.

I shook my head, trying to process all of my thoughts.

"No, I don't know if I want him to know. What if this was surprise? A project. I could get immersed in the fandom. Be just a random person in the crowd. We could get photos and mini interviews and stories from real people experiencing the tour. Am I making any sense right now?" I pressed my my fingers to my temples. I was beginning to get a headache from all the thoughts rushing through my head so fast.

"No, it does. I like it. Let's do it. We could be like these anonymous people. We'll set up social media accounts with a fake name."

"Yes! So Derek and the rest of the band won't know it's us. Derek is going to love this. We can reveal ourselves after the tour. It'll be my present to him, since he does so much for me." I glanced around the room. Up until now I had always had a sliver of guilt over all of the secrets and hesitance about truly committing to our relationship. This idea, however, felt right. I knew Derek would love this. Especially when he discovers that I had been with him all along. I could finally show him how much I cared.

Before Grey and I could continue discussing details my phone started ringing. I reached for it off the table and saw that it was a number I didn't recognize. I hesitated in answering it, but finally pushed the green button to talk.

"Hello?" I asked, glancing over at my brother.

"Hello, is this Dita Fox?" A young man's voice replied. I jolted in my seat.

"Who is this?" I demanded.

"Don't hang up. My name is Emile Dahl, Derek Turtle gave me your number. He said you moved into my old house."

For a moment my words were caught in my throat. Emile Dahl is on the other line. *Holy shit.*

"Uh, yes," I stammered. "He bought it. Is there a problem?" I could hear my voice raising an octave. He laughed loudly.

"No, not at all. I hope you are enjoying it. It's a nice place. I actually am calling because I forgot something there. Are you at home right now?"

Grey gave me a look and mouthed, "Who is it?".

I just shook my head at him.

"Yeah, we're here."

"We?"

"Oh, my brother and I."

"Brother? Fox? I thought that name was familiar. Do you know a Grey Fox?"

I shot a hard glance at my brother. Why would a huge A-list celebrity know and remember my brother? Grey gulped and refused to meet my eyes.

"Yes. That's him. Why?"

"Just someone I met once. Weird coincidence, I guess. Anyways, can you help me out with something?"

Something about the look on my brother's face and the sharp tone in Emile's voice when he said his name made me absolutely sure that he was lying. It wasn't something casual. There was something they were both hiding.

"I guess?"

"I need you to go up to the master bedroom on the second floor."

I reached for my crutches and told Grey to help me up the stairs. It would take forever on my own with a phone pressed against my ear. Despite my protests Grey grabbed me quickly and lifted me into his arms like I weighed nothing. He practically ran me up the stairs and set me down gently in my room. He went back for my crutches.

"Are you still there?" Emile asked.

"I'm in my room. I didn't find anything while we were moving things in."

"I know. That's the point. It's hidden. If I had been there to move things out, I wouldn't have left this. I really appreciate you helping me out. Okay, now go into the bathroom. Open the medicine cabinet and look in the bottom right corner. Do you see that it's actually two pieces of metal, not one?"

I did as told and did in fact notice that it appeared so.

"Okay, push on the smaller piece. It should open right up." I did and then gasped as the tiny unmarked door swung open.

"What in the world?" I murmured and he chuckled. I reached inside the tiny hole and pulled out a key.

"Did you grab the key?"

I nodded as I stared at it in wonder. Then, realizing he couldn't see me, I confirmed that I had the key he wanted.

"Do you want me to mail it to you or something?"

"Oh no, well not exactly. I kind of need another favor. Or maybe three. I don't know yet. That key is to a storage unit. I'm going to need you to go to it, open it up, and grab something for me. That, you can mail to me."

He was rather bossy, I thought. Did he expect me to just jump when he asked?

"What's in it for me?" I said suddenly. He grew quiet for a moment. Probably not used to people talking back to him.

"I'll pay you. I've got money. I've got tons of money."

"I don't need money."

There was a pause on his side and then his tone changed.

"Let me talk to Grey."

I looked at my brother who had heard him. He shook his head and his eyes grew big, which only prompted me to thrust the phone at him. He took it but stared at it for a moment before putting it to his ear. All the blood in his face had drained and he looked scared. What was going on?

I couldn't hear what Emile was saying to him but Grey nodded and looked more and more nervous.

"Okay. Sure. You got it." Grey shoved the phone back at me and fled the room before I could protest. I raised it to my ear again.

"What did you just say to my brother?" I demanded.

"Your brother owes me. I'm just cashing in."

"Fine, but we're not going tonight. We'll go tomorrow afternoon. I have things to do in the morning."

"Perfect. You've got my number. Call me when you get to the storage unit. I'll tell you what to grab and where to mail it then. Thank you. I really do appreciate the help," he said cheerfully. His moods switched so quickly, like a child getting his way.

"This is really weird, I'm not gonna lie," I told him and he laughed again.

"That's not the first time someone's said that to me. It always pays off I promise."

He hung up. I examined the key in my bedroom. I called for Grey. He was nowhere to be found. Finally, I demanded he come back to help me down the stairs and he returned rather begrudgingly.

"What was that? How do you know Emile Dahl?"

"I don't. Not really. I knew his wife. We were good friends."

"Wife? The one that died?"

He nodded somberly.

"We were kind of close before they met and he swept her away to get married."

"I'm so confused."

"Do you remember when he was all over the news because he just disappeared for like three years?"

I nodded. Adrian had actually taken me to the party Emile's friends had thrown for him when he reappeared.

"Well she died shortly after he ran off. He put her through a lot, and they weren't even married very long."

"If he's the bad guy then why do you owe him?" I asked. Grey looked away guiltily.

"I may have told her that I had seen him with another woman. They were separated when he disappeared, but still legally married when she died. If I hadn't told her..." he sniffled. "I sometimes wonder if things would be different. Maybe she wouldn't have..."

Silence fell over the room as I ingested that information. How awful. On both sides of that situation. The guilt both men must feel.

"What was her name?" I asked, realizing he had never told me.

"Dara," he whispered sadly. "I'm tired. Can we go to bed and if you really need to know more, I'll tell you tomorrow?"

I gave him a halfhearted smile. I knew full well how hard it was to reveal a dark past.

"Sure. No problem."

I handed him the key I found behind the mirror and he examined it, commenting that it was the same storage unit I had used.

"Well we already know where this is. I guess we'll go tomorrow after your leg appointment."

That next morning I was finally out of my cast. My leg looked and smelled disgusting. Before we went anywhere, I insisted we go back home so I could shower and shave it.

I nearly fell flat on my face a few times while adjusting to the cast-less leg. It felt like I had lost some muscle mass. If it wasn't for Grey's pestering me about Emile's storage unit, I would have spent the day at home relaxing and getting used to it.

Eventually I got tired of hearing his complaints, so I agreed to go. We pulled in and drove down the rows of units until we found the one with the number matching the key. I examined the outside quickly. It didn't look special, but that was probably the point.

As my brother started fiddling with the locks, I called Emile back. He answered on the first ring.

"Hello, Dita?"

"Emile? We are at the unit. What are we looking for?"

"Awesome! I just need a very small black velvet box. Easy peasy. Just grab it and I'll text you my mailing address." We said goodbye and I got out of the car, relaying the details to Grey. Just then he got the door open and pulled it up, revealing the contents.

"Holy shit."

"Are you kidding me?" I said under my breath. Emile had made it sound like this would be an in and out kind of situation. This garage was filled top to bottom with dozens, no, a hundred or so boxes. All unlabeled and of random sizes. How did he expect us to find it?

Chapter Eight

COLLAR FULL

DEREK

I WENT through the pictures Dita had sent me of the house. She had been a decorating fiend over the last couple months. Once she got her cast off, she went crazy painting and hanging things on the walls.

She had grabbed all of my things from Adrian's, Cleo's, and Mark's places and brought them all to the house to unpack. It all looked great. My photos and the band's awards had been hung on the walls. Old guitars and band merch were everywhere. I loved it. It made me miss her so much more.

We were about four months into the tour with seemingly no end in sight. They were already talking about adding dates. I groaned every time Sam brought it up. I needed a break. I wanted to go home. It meant so much more now that I actually had one.

The others had similar thoughts. They all missed their families. We were missing holidays, birthdays, and other milestones.

Cleo suggested a few months break and then head back out on the bus, but Sam didn't seem too happy about the idea. The head honchos were in his ear nagging him to get us on board. I hoped it wouldn't turn into a fight.

I mentioned it to Mark in private one day and he assured me it wouldn't.

"We are in a much different position than we once were. From what Sam has told me, we are the top dogs right now. We are making the label the most money. We even passed Cruel Distraction. All we have to do is threaten to not re-up our contract next year and walk. Or buy ourselves out now. They'll have no choice but to give us what we want. Or you know, drop us. But we'll be picked up in no time. Sam said he's had offers. Tons of them."

I took in his words and prayed he was right. I really couldn't take touring for a full year or two. There needed to be some off time.

Now that Dita was healed and more mobile, I begged her to come to a show. She was still hanging out with her brother, but I told her to bring him too. I didn't care, I just wanted to see her.

At first, I thought she was going to start looking for a new job in her field, but she surprised me when she said she wanted to pursue another passion of hers. She had bought some photography equipment and was working on starting a small business. I offered my full support and told her I couldn't wait to see some of her work.

Most of what she had sent me was some standard stuff. She did photoshoots of all the kids for my friends. They loved them. Each of them had them printed out and hung in their bunks.

I was just about to call her and see what she was up to when Cleo walked over to me and handed me her tablet.

"Have you seen this?"

It was a video, titled "MARIA MARIA INDIANAPOLIS SHOW FAN TALK"

I eyed my friend curiously, but she rolled her eyes and told me to click play on the video. I did and began watching.

The video started with us on stage we were playing "End it With a Love Song". One of our hits. Then they switched cameras, and we were watching the fans sing along and dance. The sound of our performance lowered and a man started talking over a quick montage of the show and some fans.

"Maria Maria has been around for over a decade. We've seen them through their pop punk phase, then their emo years. We've watched them bleed on the stage for their fans. We've laughed with them, we've cried with them, and continue to buy their albums and go to their over the top concerts. So, we want to show you guys who you are playing for. You're playing for the new fans and the old ones. You're playing for those whose lives were saved by Cleo De La Rosa's lyrics, Adrian and Derek's devotion to the music, and Mark's familiar yet fresh beats. This is our way of showing you what you mean to us. This is Fan Talk."

I looked up and Saw Cleo smiling. Okay, they had piqued my curiosity. I guess I'll watch this all the way through.

Suddenly we were on the ground again and a chick with short black hair and a mask over her eyes appeared on screen. The mask reminded me of a spiderweb. It was enough to hide her identity, but you could tell she was attractive underneath. Her blood red lips paired with her tight black dress had me intrigued. She was holding a microphone and smiling.

"Hello, I am Trigger Finger and I'm at the Maria Maria concert in Indianapolis, Indiana. Me and my partner Death Wish are here to talk to fans. We want to see what they have to say about the band. So, let's go find some!"

The camera flew through the crowd, they threw in more

shots of us, our opening bands, some of the more interesting fans, and then stopped on a guy and a girl.

Trigger Finger's partner stepped up beside them and began talking to them. He had a similar but more masculine mask and was wearing a black dress shirt and pants with a blood red tie. He gave the pair with our logo on their shirts his microphone and asked them to talk to us.

"What would you tell the band if you had the chance?"

They seemed to think for a moment and the girl started speaking.

"I was able to get out of a really bad relationship because of you. I got your album and was looking at the album art in the CD. You guys had put tons of information on how to get help if you were in a bad place and after a few months of reading it over and over and listening to the album a million times I finally called the numbers on it. You saved my life."

Cleo gasped and I looked up at her. She was smiling and laughing.

"I've already seen this video, but I still get shivers hearing her talk. Keep going."

The two masked figures continued going through and highlighting fans and what they wanted to say to us. Some had stories, others had compliments. One guy told us that he was a bartender and that he had made drinks in our honor for when we came to his town. It was awesome. The video ended with the pair coming on and doing the whole share, subscribe thing and then the guy added one last thing at the end.

"Hello to everyone who lasted this long. Just a friendly reminder to look for us at the next show. We are following them for the rest of the tour. We have our tickets and we're ready. We want to see and hear from you. If you see us, feel free to buy us a drink and have a chat with us. You might just make it onto an episode. See you soon!"

I passed the tablet to Mark who had come over to see what we were watching.

"Is this for real?" I asked Cleo. She shrugged.

"I think it's pretty rad. I can't wait to see the next episode."

"We should give them a shout out or something. Show them that they've caught our attention," Adrian added. That wasn't a bad idea.

I pulled out my phone and went to my camera. I motioned for my friends to crowd in so we could start this. When everyone was ready, I pushed record.

"Hello world!" I shouted and everyone followed with their own greetings. Cleo waved. Mark stuck his tongue out.

"So, we uh, saw a pretty cool video today. Fan Talk," I started, but Mark cut in.

"It's actually hella cool. I loved it. You guys rock!" He threw up the devil horns and the tongue out again.

"I cried, not gonna lie. It's sweet. I've watched it five times already," Cleo added in a much sweeter tone.

"It's alright," Adrian said nonchalantly and we all turned and glared at him. He raised his eyebrows and conceded. "Alright, it's more than that. It's pretty badass. I liked it."

"Just ignore him, he's missing his hubs like crazy right now. Anyways, we just wanted to give them a shout out and we can't wait to see the next episode. See you guys soon in... where are we headed to next?" I asked behind me. Cleo rolled her eyes.

"Chicago."

"Chicago! Be there or be square," I finished and shut the video off. I rewatched it quickly to make sure there wasn't anything we couldn't share and determined it was good to go.

"Should I post it on the band's page?" I asked.

"Yeah. That way more people will see it," Cleo said. I did so and then quickly shut off notifications on my phone. I knew it was going to blow up, and I was not in the mood to hear it go off like crazy. My friends or Sam could have fun with that. I just wanted to call my girl.

She answered on the first ring. She sounded out of breath and far away.

"Sorry, I'm jogging. What's up?"

"Nothing, just wanted to see what you were up to. Sounds like you're staying busy."

"Trying. I'm going to finish my jog and then go take out an ad in the paper for my photography thing."

"Thing? You gotta call it a business if that's what you want it to be," I laughed. I had missed her voice. I missed all of her actually.

"It just doesn't feel like one. Not yet. The only clients I've had are your friends."

"Yeah but they loved them. Your pictures are hanging all over the bus."

Her breathing slowed and she informed me that she was going to walk the rest of the way. I told her it wasn't necessary, but she wanted to keep talking.

"When are you going to come to a show?" I asked.

"When is your next one?"

"Tonight. In Chicago."

"What about the one after that?"

"I think I have a few days off. We're staying in a hotel tonight and then traveling for two days. So, four? Or three? I don't know. Just come to one. Preferably sooner rather than later."

"I'll think about it. Maybe tonight."

"Yeah okay. Are you really going to get on a plane and make it here in time?"

"I might. Who knows?"

She was trying to be playful, but it only irritated me. I hadn't seen her since I sent her to the airport. It had been way too long.

She sighed. "Okay. I'll look at your schedule and find one I can make it to."

"Just let me know so I can put you on the list. I'll make sure you get good seats."

"Sounds great."

We said our goodbyes and then Cleo came to inform me that we were pulling in soon. We'd have sound check almost as soon as we stopped.

I went through the motions, not really interested in things. I couldn't get my mind off of Dita. Maybe I could find a few days to fly back to L.A. Even if it was just for 24 hours. I'd make it count. I could surprise her with flowers and other romantic stuff. I'd have to look up what else would be romantic, but I could make it work. I mentioned the idea to Sam after we stepped off stage and he frowned.

"I'll see what I can do. Don't get your hopes up," he warned, and I nodded. I knew that already, but I had to try. Cleo came up behind me and gave me a hug.

"You are so adorable."

"What do you mean?" I shrugged out of her hug. She crossed her arms and stared at me with a smirk.

"You. Missing Dita. You've been sulking for days now and I think it's absolutely adorable. You've never been like this before."

"I know. It sucks. I hate it."

"Join the club. Sometimes I miss Ethan and the kids so much I want to cry."

We started walking to the dressing rooms to let the other bands get their sound checks done.

"What do you do about it?"

"The same thing you do. Calls, video chats. I send them presents. Online shopping has changed the game."

"What about Ethan? How does he cope?"

I couldn't imagine how he dealt with his wife being on tour

with a bunch of guys while he was stuck at home with three kids. He didn't drink and when he wasn't making new music or touring, he worked a 9-5 job. Bummer.

"I don't know. I'll have to ask him."

With only a few hours left we started to get ready for the show. We didn't have to do much. Just toss on our suits and style our hair. We had been wearing them so much they were beginning to show wear. We had a few different shirts but only two sets of jackets and pants. They reeked of sweat and pounds of cologne.

I tossed mine on and noticed that my shirt was ripped at the bottom. Oh well, I guess. The more I played with it the more I decided I liked it. I could leave it untucked and maybe it'd breathe a little better.

Cleo had five different dresses to choose from. All black and red. Most were tight on the bust and poofy on the waist so she could move around easily. Honestly, I couldn't really tell them apart but she insisted each one was different.

We got dressed and Cleo helped us with our hair. When we started the tour, they had provided us with a stylist every night. Once they figured out that we could do it ourselves and Cleo her own makeup they sent the girl packing. It was one less person they had to deal with. This tour was big enough. We had so many people involved it was hard to keep track.

Sam's assistant came in and asked if we wanted anything. We all requested beer and he left, returning with a 24 pack. We were down to the last four when we were given the ten-minute warning. We stood up and I suggested we shot gun our last cans. Mark pulled out a pocket knife and dug holes in each of our drinks. We toasted and quickly popped the tops, drinking from the puncture wound in the can. I finished mine first and crunched the can in my hand.

"Whoo! Let's do this!" I shouted. We left to head to the stage and moments later we were given our cue.

The concert was going off without a hitch. It was fun and after all the beer I was relaxed and in a fantastic mood. I closed my eyes and let the music take over.

Suddenly Cleo stopped singing and she was nudging me.

"Looks like you have a big fan Derek," I popped my eyes open and looked out into the crowd where she was pointing. I squinted and after a moment I realized who I was looking at. My heart stopped completely. *She was here.*

Dita was sitting on top of her brother's shoulders. She was holding a poster with my face on it with some writing. I squinted to read the sign and then laughed.

Derek show me your tits!

I guess I should oblige.

I was still stunned. Even as she walked towards me backstage. She was really here. In the flesh. For me. She came. I was star struck.

When I finally snapped out of the trance her sudden surprise presence had over me, I ran over to her and picked her up. I held her tight and inhaled her perfume. I got a mixture of sweat and amber. It was intoxicating.

I kissed her everywhere I could. She giggled and insisted I set her down. I did but refused to let her go. I ignored everyone around me as I pulled her into our dressing room. I noticed she had ditched her sign. Everyone greeted her happily. I told her that I just needed to change and we'd take off.

"Where are we going?" She asked.

"I don't know. Anywhere but here. I want to see you. Just you."

"Are you sure? You won't get in trouble?"

"No. We've got hotel rooms, remember?"

My friends made some suggestive noises and lewd comments, but I ignored them. I practically ripped off my suit and tossed on my t-shirt and jeans. I reached for her hand again and smiled.

"Ready?"

She nodded and we left without another word. We walked into the open air using the back doors of the venue. No sooner were the doors closed did I turn and push her against the brick building. I pressed my lips to hers. *Finally.*

Her body relaxed into mine as she kissed me back. My hands explored her body above her clothes. I couldn't wait to get her back to the room to play with what was under them. Dita's thoughts seemed to be on the same wavelength.

"Should we go back to your hotel?" She said in between kisses. I pulled away and calmed myself. I wanted to, God how I wanted to. With a groan I forced myself to stop thinking with my lower head. I gave her one last quick kiss and took her hand instead.

"Later. Definitely. I want to spend some actual time with you first. We'll have plenty of time for that." I winked and she giggled. Walking around to the front of the building I was disappointed to see stragglers still hanging around.

I pulled the hood of my jacket up and hurried her along. I wasn't in the mood for cameras and people screaming in my face. I got to the street and and started looking for a cab. Thankfully one picked us up only a few moments later. I pulled her inside and told the lady to just drive around for a bit.

"Got it."

"Where are we going?" Dita asked. I pulled her into my chest as I tried to think. I had no idea.

"What is there to do for a couple this late? I was thinking something quiet."

"A hotel room is what I usually recommend," the driver

teased. My aching groin did not appreciate the joke. I rolled my eyes and she scrunched up her face in thought as she drove.

"Okay, so you want something intimate. Maybe a movie? Or ooh! I know a place that does those wine and paint things. They stay open way late because it's in the back of a bar. They do classes until closing. Do you want me to take you there?"

I looked down at Dita who shrugged.

"Sounds great, let's go."

It took another twenty minutes but eventually we were in front of a small bar with a sign that said "Bristol's Bar".

"Just go inside and ask the bartender about the paint parties. They'll let you know if they have any open spots left."

I paid her and gave her a quick thank you before we stepped out and did as she directed. Dita clung to my side, making my heart swell. Life was so much better with her here.

The bartender, a young woman with ridiculously curly hair signed us up for the next round which was starting in half an hour. In the meantime, we sat down and ordered two beers.

"You look super familiar," she said to me as she served us. I gave her a tight smile and set mine and Dita's entwined hands on the counter.

"I just have one of those faces."

She looked like she didn't believe me but didn't question it. I turned away from the counter and looked around the room. I perked up when I saw a claw machine filled with cheap stuffed animals. I grabbed my beer and slid off my chair. Dita joined me and we

and walked over to the money thief.

"You want one?" I asked, eyeing the stuffed animals. Easy enough. I'd played claw machines just like this one. Each play was two bucks, and it wasn't even a guaranteed prize every time. What a rip off.

"Sure. Can you try for that guy?" She pointed to a pink

elephant. I scoffed. Can I? Of course I can. Returning to the bar I pulled out a twenty and asked for change.

"Have fun," she smirked as she handed me twenty ones. I gave her my best smile and returned to my girl. Slipping the first couple of bills in, I eyed the pink elephant. It was tucked under a lion and a bear. I guess I'd have to get those too.

Maneuvering the claw, I brought the lion to the door and dropped it. Dita gasped and giggled as she grabbed it out of the slot. I put in my next few bills and snagged the bear. Okay, now for the elephant.

"Wow, you're really good at this. How did I not know this about you?" She laughed with her arms filled with cute, plush animals.

"It's good to have some surprises." I winked at her as I paid to play again. I wanted them all. I handed her another bear and she sighed, struggling to carry them. I chewed on my lip, trying to think. I went back to the counter and gave her a much larger bill.

"Can I have change and a large trash bag please?"

She took the bill and lifted it to the light, eyeing it suspiciously. Once she deemed it legal, she went to the register. She was probably hating me right now for having to break a one hundred dollar bill for the dusty claw machine. She handed me the stack and pulled a large black bag from a roll under her counter.

"Go crazy," she muttered.

I opened the bag and let Dita drop in her prizes. Handing it to her, I cracked my fingers dramatically.

"Step back and watch this," I said. I was now on a mission. She giggled again, which gave my stomach flutters. It was a heavenly sound, especially when I was the one causing it.

After another five or six wins I noticed that people had begun drifting over to watch me. I knew this was potentially bad for us, but I was determined to empty this machine. I needed all the plushy beings.

I had to give the bartender another twenty to completely empty the glass case, but I did it. The bag Dita was holding was completely stuffed. She could barely tie it closed. When that last small animal dropped into the release gate the people around us cheered and clapped. I felt like a hero. I turned around and lifted my fists up like I had just won a boxing match.

Dita and I went back to the counter and were handed two new beers, on the house.

"What are you going to do with these?" Dita asked, motioning to the bulging bag at her side.

"I don't know, you take them." I shrugged. She shook her head.

"No, nope. I am not taking them on the plane with me."

Before I could make a decision, an older woman came out from a door behind us and announced that the next paint party was starting.

Dita and I exchanged smiles as we got up and followed about ten other people into the room. The woman told us to pick our own easels and we'd get started soon. I brought the bag in and set it next to our seats.

"I wonder what picture she's gonna have us paint," Dita said excitedly. The teacher walked around the room, greeting us all. Once everyone was in front of a canvas and she asked if we wanted to grab something from the bar, she pulled out two fully painted pictures from behind a table. One had a guy's foot with tennis shoes, and the other a woman's leg with red heels. When you set them together, they looked like they were probably hugging or something.

"Tonight we are going to be doing a bar favorite. The couple's feet. Here at Bristol's we encourage creativity, so feel free to personalize your painting as much or as little as you want. Now, your paint and brushes are next to your canvas. If you pick up the biggest brush and pick your background color, we'll start."

I grabbed my paint palette and brush and looked over at Dita. She was considering the colors.

"We should match backgrounds," I suggested and she agreed.

"Red?"

"Perfect."

To my surprise, painting was actually pretty fun. I wasn't any good, but the instructor came over from time to time and helped me tighten some of the lines and shade stuff in properly.

"I see your leg is wearing shorts. Interesting," she commented.

"Yep, gonna give this bad boy some tattoos."

"Oh fun!"

When I looked over and saw Dita giving her picture's leg ink too I accused her of stealing my idea.

"I did not! I'm painting my tattoos on it. See, the stitches are the same as mine."

I looked and was surprised at how good she was at painting. Just like her, the painting had fake stocking's going up her leg. It made me think of how high her real tattoos actually went up and I had to divert my thoughts; reminding myself that we had plenty of time.

"Can you help me paint a guitar on mine?" I asked and she leaned over and kissed me on the nose.

"Of course."

I watched as she whipped up a kick ass bass guitar on the canvas just like the one on my real leg. I moved my hand to brush her hair out of her face, but I had totally forgotten about the paint brush in my hand and I swiped a large streak of red across her face! From nose to ear. She squealed and pulled away quickly.

"Derek!"

"Ssshhh!" I said quickly through my laughter. She was furious but it was cute. She glared at me before poking my nose with the brush.

"Hey! That's not cool! Mine was an accident," I laughed. She smirked and then grimaced as she touched her red, wet cheek.

"I could try to fix it for you. Maybe even up the other side? Make you into some cute doll or something?" I offered and she shot daggers at me.

"Only if I can paint your face."

"Deal." Surprised, she lifted her brush and I leaned forward and closed my eyes. "Do your worst Dita Fox."

I could feel the brush strokes on my cheeks and recognized that she was making me some kind of animal. When she announced she was done I opened my eyes and asked her how I looked. She giggled.

"Perfect. Now me?"

I shook my head and dipped my paper towel in the little water cup. I wiped the paint from her face.

"You're already perfect." I said, looking into her stunning eyes. She smiled and just then the teacher saw us and shouted loudly that the paint was for the canvases only. We laughed and finished up our paintings. When everyone was done and they were dried she asked us to stand together as a group to take a picture for her social media page. Dita hesitated.

"Do you want to be in it? People will know where we are?"

I shrugged. "We're leaving in a bit. I'm not worried. Let's hop in."

I looked at everyone else's pictures and saw that most of them stuck to the model painting the instructor had painted.

Ours was the only one who had taken any real level of liberties. Lame.

We gave our best smiles and I asked the instructor if she could use my phone to take a photo of Dita and I alone. She took two, one of us smiling at the camera, and the second one I snuck in a kiss over the paintings.

We went to the bar and I paid our tab. The bartender waved her finger at me with a coy smile as she handed me my receipt.

"I knew I recognized you. I love the new album."

I pointed back at her with a wink.

"Thanks."

We left the bar quickly before she started spreading her news about meeting a celebrity. Thankfully, luck was on my side today and we hailed another cab just as quickly as we had before.

Dita set our paintings and bag of toy animals beside her. We barely had room to sit. She put her hands in my lap. I jumped out of my seat in surprise. She leaned over and whispered in my ear.

"I think it's time to go to your room."

"Aye aye Captain," I said and told the driver what hotel I was staying at.

I held her hand tightly at my side. I wasn't trying to get kicked out of the vehicle. She laughed at my nerves. When we got to the hotel, I grabbed the key to my room and we stepped into the elevator.

"I don't think I've ever seen you embarrassed," she giggled. I laughed and hugged her against the wall, playfully kissing her neck.

"Yeah, well don't get used to it."

The bell dinged and the doors opened. I heard an all too familiar squeal. I groaned and turned around. Cleo was standing there with her hands covering her face. Her eyes sparkled with amusement.

"What are you screaming about?" I heard Adrian say from a few paces behind her. I took Dita's hand and pulled her out of the elevator as all three of my bandmates took our place.

"Oh! You guys painted pictures? I have been begging Ethan to do one of those with me. Ugh, I am so jealous," Cleo pouted. She crossed her arms, and stuck out her lower lip, furrowing her brow. Dita lifted the pictures quickly to show her. Cleo perked right back up and complimented us on them. I tugged gently on my girl's arm. We could talk to them later. She laughed and took a step towards me.

"What's in the bag?" Adrian asked. I ignored him and kept moving.

Mark smirked.

"Nice face paint. Go get em Tiger, or Turtle. Whatever works for you."

I gave him the middle finger.

"Definitely a tiger," I shouted as the doors began to close. Dita nodded beside me.

"Definitely."

Quickly I found my room and forced my friends from my mind. I needed a night completely away from them. I swore I'd kill them if they ruined this for me.

No sooner were we in the room did Dita attack me. Her hands were everywhere. I could barely keep up. I had to gently push her away with a laugh.

"Hey, we have time. I want to do this right. I don't know when we'll be able to do this again. I want to savor this time. What's the rush?"

She groaned and began to pout.

I took off my shirt and unbuttoned my pants, heading to the bathroom. I turned the shower on and tossed my socks and boxers. Dita followed me inside and eyed my ready for war soldier hungrily. I covered myself with my hands.

"Stop. I'm starting to feel like a piece of meat," I teased. She rolled her eyes. "Look, let's both shower and get the paint and sweat off. That way I can enjoy every last bit of you."

Her cheeks flushed with heat and she nodded, quickly undressing as well. I came over and embraced her. Our bare skin together felt phenomenal. I couldn't wait.

Our shower was not even a little sexy and more practical. We were both way more eager to take this party to the bed rather than the awkward shower. I scrubbed her scalp making the shampoo all bubbly while she ran soap all over my body. It was a different kind of affection that I loved almost more than what was going to happen after.

Her fingers were tender on my stage bruises and she made sure to scrub every last spot. Except my bum. I assured her I had that handled. I offered to do hers, but she scolded me. Couldn't blame a guy for trying.

Once we were both clean, I tried to take her to the other room, but she insisted on blow drying our hair.

"Really?"

"Yes. Otherwise the pillows will be all wet and both of our heads will be total messes tomorrow."

I was annoyed but she made it up to me by placing kisses all over my neck while she dried my head. I was quickly getting my groove back.

After what felt like an eternity, she took my hand and led me to the bed. She tried to push me onto the bed, but I shook my head and picked her up, placing her on the bed. I moved to the wall and dimmed the lights before returning to her.

She gave me a seductive pose that had me at full mast. I was so beyond ready to be one with her. I had dreamt of this moment for months. I was an addict who needed his fix. I joined her on the bed and climbed in between her legs, kissing her all the way up.

I reached her neck and nibbled on her ears. She moaned and her hands raked across my back.

"I want this to last as long as possible," I whispered and she shook her head.

"I can't. I'm already- "

I moved my hand to feel her arousal, she was right. She was already- ready. Her hand reached for me and I let her massage me. I let out a gasp. Her hand felt so much better than mine.

I stopped her and moved down to give her a turn. I spread her legs wider and teased her with my mouth. She squirmed and moaned underneath me, begging me to take her. She let out a sharp gasp and her entire body shuddered.

She ripped my head away and pulled me up. I laughed as she pulled me into her, demanding that I claim her. I obliged and we quickly rode the waves of pleasure together until we both hit our crescendos.

She fell asleep quickly, but I was wired. How could I sleep when I had this beautiful woman who truly loved me beside me? I could watch her forever. Eventually I got up and checked out the mini bar. I pulled out a bottle of water and gulped it down in one go. Jeez. I didn't realize how thirsty I was.

I sat on the edge of the bed and spotted my trunk against the wall. I went over and found that someone had washed my clothes. Hell yeah. Being on the road, I wore my clothes four or five times before I got the chance to get to the laundry mat. I'd have to thank whoever for doing me a solid.

I dug through the trunk until I found the small box I kept two different locks on. Grabbing my jeans from the bathroom I took the key out of my wallet and unlocked it. I plucked out the much smaller velvet box and opened it, examining the ring.

I had gotten it personally designed just for my goth queen.

It was some kind of Victorian style with garnets and black diamonds on the side, with the big white diamond in the middle. I knew when they showed me the picture that she'd love it. It would look beautiful on her finger, but then again, anything would.

I closed the box and locked it back up. Returning to our bed I wrapped my arms around her and fell asleep thinking about the end of the tour. I could not freaking wait.

Chapter Nine

NOT A STRANGER

DITA

I woke up a few hours later fully embraced in Derek's arms. I turned to face him and started to slowly kiss him awake. I wanted to make love to him until he had to leave. His reaction to my lips on his skin told me that he felt the same way.

His phone rang at around ten, telling us that our time was up. He had to check out and return to his bus. With slow, depressing movements we got out of bed, showered, and left the room.

I took our paintings and he took the obnoxiously large bag of stuffed animals. We hugged and I sent him on his way with his band mates. My heart ached already.

I called Grey as soon as their van was out of sight to meet up with him. I grabbed my own ride and met up with him at the hotel he had stayed in for the night. I felt a little guilty. The one Derek's band had booked was way nicer than the one I had rented for Grey and I.

When we first came up with the idea to follow the rest of the tour, our first thing we figured out was a rough budget. I pulled out everything from my checking and savings and Grey offered to drive, film, and edit for free.

"I've spent the last few years making money on the road. If I need to, I can pull a quick hundred or so when we need it," he assured me when I realized I wouldn't have enough money to get us through the entire tour. However, another demanding call from Emile Dahl prompted me to take him up on his offer of paying us to do the favors for him.

"Whatever you want. Just name the price," he said cheerfully when I accepted his offer. I was shocked, originally thinking he was just bluffing to not sound so rude.

"Uh, well I don't know," I stammered. He simply laughed.

"You must have something in mind since I've offered every time we've talked and you're only now accepting my offer. Come on, what do you need?"

I bit my lip and revealed our plan to him. He got quiet for a moment.

"Alright. I can help with that. Just let me know when you get to Chicago and talk to Leah. I'm sorry you wasted your time at the storage unit. I was sure the box was there. I swear this time that Leah can help. I'm going to wire you some money. Buy a vehicle, equipment, and save the rest for lodging and food."

I was shocked when I looked at my bank account two days later to find that Emile had wired me 25,000 dollars. Granted he was having us go to across the country to talk to a stranger about some key, I felt like it was a fair trade. I still didn't understand the man, but I'd take the money. His requests were strange, but it wasn't like I didn't have the time. Plus, it gave me the chance to see Derek.

When I told Grey what Emile had done, he only smirked. I wondered if he would ever get over his hang ups over the hot and cold rockstar. He was demanding sure, but also apparently very giving. With our new budget, we picked up a decently comfy van and started off on our tour of America. Despite Grey not liking how we got the money he didn't seem to mind the traveling itself.

We got back into the van the day after I spent the night with Derek and started off to our next destination. That was one of the things I loved about my youngest brother, he just went with the flow. It was like heading over to the lazy pool after riding the thrill rides all day; relaxing and no pressure because it was filled with others wanting peace as well.

"Did you get a video done?" I asked. He nodded, not taking his eyes off the busy road.

"Yep. I don't think he'll suspect a thing. We had enough footage of you and I before the show in costume."

I thanked him and relaxed in my seat. I was nervous about last night's show. We barely had time to change and return to the venue before the show started. I pulled out my tablet from my bag and found the video he had shared on our Fan Talk account. I watched it as he drove on to finish Emile's request. The video ended just as he was pulling into a parking lot behind a row of buildings. He was right, I don't think they'll put two and two together.

When we had started fleshing out the details of our plan, I realized that I wanted to completely surprise Derek and the rest of them. That, and if word got out that the person doing this fun project had direct ties to the band members, I was afraid fans would go nuts. I wanted this to be as authentic as possible.

Grey came up with our names and I figured out the costumes. I planned each episode and directed, while he edited and posted each episode. We both took turns filming to make sure we had equal screen time and further throw off the scent that it could be me under the mask.

Our accounts were already starting to grow with hundreds of new followers every day. I had to turn notifications off on my phone because it drove me crazy. I loved stepping into my costume and heading to the shows. The thrill of anonymity and the knowledge that Derek had no clue I was there was exhilarating. I could not wait until the end of the tour to surprise him.

"Is this it?" I asked my brother as he turned the van off. I looked at the buildings. Since we were behind them, nothing had a sign to indicate what was what.

"Yes. We'll have to walk around, but it's easy to find. Are you ready?"

I chewed on my lip some and then nodded.

"Yeah, let's get this over with." We got out and started towards the bookstore Emile had directed us to. Once we had gone through his entire storage unit and came up empty, he made some calls and asked if we were interested in picking up something near Chicago. It wasn't that much out of the way, since Derek had a show in the same city. Grey grumbled slightly about Emile always getting his way.

"How can you be so mad at him when they were separated when your friend passed?" I asked casually. He scoffed.

"Because if he wasn't cheating on her they wouldn't have been separated."

"What if that wasn't the full story? I mean, he's rude sure, but he doesn't really seem like the type to just purposely abandon or hurt someone. Derek and his friends have said that he's weird but nice overall. Maybe things weren't so one sided," I suggested. He scowled at me but said nothing.

We stopped in front of the building. It was just an ordinary bookstore. Nothing special about it. The storefront windows had featured books and posters advertising others. I searched for some sign that it was hiding something behind the rather uninteresting storefront, but I came up with nothing.

"I have a hard time seeing him as anything other than self-ish," Grey muttered. "Her funeral was small. He didn't even show up."

His words left me feeling uneasy. I forced a smile and reached for the door. The faster we did this the faster we could move on. We stepped in and started our search.

Just like the outside, the inside was just the same, exactly as you would expect a bookstore to look. Row after row of books, tables with magazines, knickknacks, games, and notebooks. It was crowded, but overall unremarkable. We walked through the store surveying the products. I stopped at a table that had a book on a pedestal and twenty copies surrounding it.

I picked it up and examined it. I had heard of this book, although I had never read it. It was on my to be read list. The front was simple, a red cover with the title and author listed.

'*Each Moment Counted by Gregory Dumas*'

"Can I help you with anything?"

We both turned to see an attractive red headed woman smiling politely at us. I gave her a polite smile and my eyes widened when I saw her name tag. *Leah*. I glanced at my brother whose expression matched my own. This was who Emile had told us to find.

"I see you have a copy of our bestseller. It's a very popular book here."

I glanced back at it and back to her in confusion.

"Isn't this book like ten years old?"

She nodded. "Yes, but the author came from this very town. In fact, his wife and son worked here. I knew him and his family very personally," she boasted.

"Really?" Grey asked. I don't think either of us were genuinely interested but we needed to keep her in a good mood. Emile warned us that if we weren't careful, she'd lock up and send us away.

"Yep. Not only did he become a millionaire with this book,

his kids went on to be very successful as well. Do you want me to ring you up, or are you still looking?"

I looked back at the book. It was thick. I knew I wouldn't read it any time soon, but she had me curious about its contents.

"I think this is it for me," I told her, and we followed her back to the front of the store.

"I was best friends with his daughter Libby for years. Now she goes by Olivia Dumas, you know, the famous designer," she bragged as she rang me up. The name rang a bell, but I couldn't quite place it. I repeated it over and over in my head until it clicked.

"The wedding dress designer?"

Leah smiled wide as she handed me the book in a brown paper bag.

"The very one. And her brother and I were close too. He goes by his stage name though. You heard of Emile Dahl?" She asked us coyly. Of course, we had. Everyone knew Emile Dahl. I pretended to act surprised. I mean, I was sort of surprised. I hadn't known about his family. Who knew he came from such an interesting background?

"That's actually why we are here. We're friends of Emile's and he sent us here to talk to you." My brother decided to just go for it. It was as if we had one mind. We didn't want to spend the afternoon listening to this woman name drop.

"Oh? How is he doing these days? I haven't seen him since he dumped me right after we slept together." Her smile was tight and her eyes holding back fury. Oh no, this was not good. Was this trip going to be for nothing?

"He's okay. He said you were a dear old friend," Grey lied. "He said you have something he needs."

"He wants the key? Sure, I can go get it. Stay here." Her mood shifted again back to the chipper woman from before. We watched as she went into a back room and returned with a key in hand. "Here you go. It's been hanging on the wall for years. It's about time it's returned back to his family."

"What's it to?" I asked as I examined it in my hand.

"I don't know. His mom left it here when she ran off. She abandoned them you know. Emile had to quit school and come work here full time just to keep their lights on. But then the book came out and suddenly they were rich."

I blinked. The more I heard about this man the more confused I became. After a long moment of awkward silence I smiled and thanked her.

"I'll be sure to give this to him." I waved the key. We turned to leave. I took a few steps but Grey turned back.

"Wait, why didn't you give the key to his dad or sister?"

She shrugged.

"Libby and I weren't as close after Emile left. She went to Europe for fashion school and then Mr. Dumas died shortly after. I guess I always hoped it would give Emile a reason to come back." Her face fell in disappointment. "He must be pretty busy these days."

I frowned. I understood why Emile hadn't wanted to come back now, but it sucked that I ended up being his lackey. It was cowardly of him. I had a feeling Grey would remember to tell him that when we saw him next.

"He is. He told me to tell you thank you, and that he appreciates you holding on to this for all these years," I told her. He hadn't, but that was besides the point. He should have said those things. Her eyes glistened and she simply nodded. Without another word Grey and I left.

We returned to the van and just as Grey was about to call the cowardly rockstar, my phone rang. I looked at it and saw that it was our oldest brother, Griffin.

"Griff?" I answered. Looking at Grey, I saw him roll his eyes and make a gagging motion. I ignored him and motioned for him to start driving. The further we got from this place the better.

"Hey sis, I have some great news. I'm officially engaged!"

"Congratulations! When was this?" I exclaimed.

"Just an hour ago. I just got home actually. Oh man, I was so nervous. I was shaking in my boots," he laughed and then began excitedly telling me all about it. I listened intently as Grey drove angrily through the city.

"That is amazing. I am so happy for you Griffin. When do you guys think you'll get married?"

"Ma thinks we should take a year or so to plan the ceremony. She's already talking colors and flowers. I haven't really talked to Cherry about it yet. I just wanted to call and tell you the good news."

Suddenly there was a distinctly female blood-curdling scream in the background. "Ma?"

"Griffin, what's wrong? Is everything alright?" I asked frantically. He hadn't hung up, but I heard the porch door open and slam shut, and then his heavy breathing as if he was running. Grey glanced over at me and began to slow down, seeing my terrified face. I repeated my brother's name over and over, but he didn't respond. I refused to hang up until I knew what was going on.

"Oh my God. Dad!" I heard him scream before the call dropped. I heard a dull beep and then the line went dead. Where was he? What was going on?

Tears streamed down my face as the echo of my mother's scream rang through my mind. Was my dad okay? Grey stopped the van and I started sobbing. He reached out and tried to calm me down.

"Dita, what is going on? What did Griffin say?"

I tried to calm myself but couldn't stop sniffling.

"Something's wrong with Dad. I heard them screaming. We need to go home."

Grey's face darkened. We were close enough that if we left now, we'd be back on the farm by nightfall. I didn't want to go back just as much as he didn't, but we didn't have a choice. We needed to go. With a loud swear he pulled away from me and put the car back in drive.

"Fox Farm, here we come," he muttered as we got onto the freeway.

No one was answering the phone back home, so we were left in fear and worry about our father until we drove onto the property. I was right, the sun had already set. There were no lights on in the house, which was surprising. My mother always kept the kitchen light on every night.

Grey put the van in park right behind an old tractor. There were two trucks in the dirt driveway, but plenty of space for more vehicles. Everything was just as I remembered it. It was obvious no one was home, so Grey and I sat in silence for a moment, taking in the sight of our childhood home.

It was a large, old farmhouse, like all of the others in the county. A faded white with sky blue shutters. The porch was newer than everything else. My dad had rebuilt it when I was a little girl.

A million memories of growing up here were flooding back to me and it was hard to process. I gulped and looked over at my younger brother. He was glaring daggers at the house.

"You never told me why you left," he said suddenly. I blinked.

"Yeah, and you were pretty vague on your details too," I shot back. Silence followed for a few beats before I felt bad. "Look, we've always been way closer to each other than to Graham and Griffin. It's always been me and you. I'll tell you my story if you tell me yours."

"This stays here. Especially with Griffin's... news..." he said bitterly.

"Jesus Grey, of course. What happened?"

"Cherry happened." He turned the car back on and put it in reverse.

"Where are we going?"

"The hospital. That's probably where everyone is."

While we drove, he told me the story of why he left home, barely a legal adult, but not before stealing our mother's most prized possession, her engagement ring from our father.

"You didn't sell it, did you?" I asked when he told me why he took it.

"No of course not. It didn't even make it out of the county. It's sitting in a locker at the bus station. I pay the fee every month to keep it in my name. No one's touched it in years. That ring was promised to me, no matter what anyone says," he defended.

"Yeah, but if you weren't going to use it anymore, then why not give it back?"

"Why? So my older brother can give it to her? Cherry McGowan was the first and only girl I ever loved and that was taken from me. That damn pastor's son. Him and his whole family always got what they wanted. I never stood a chance next to him. I'd been told that from the start and then when I saw... what I saw, I knew it was true. Gretch- I mean Dita, I don't think I can do this." His voice cracked as his midwest accent crept into his voice. He slowed down and then completely stopped. We were still on the road.

"What are you doing? What do you mean you can't do this? Do what?"

"See them. Ma, Dad. Griff and Graham. They hate me for what I did and now that he's marrying her, I can't tell them the truth. What's the point? Dad never loved me anyways," he muttered, rubbing the stubble on his jaw. I shook my head.

"That's not true. He loves you, just like his other children. Now come on. Let's get to the hospital, we still don't know what's going on."

With a long sigh and a few more long minutes of me coaxing him, he pushed on the gas and we started towards the next town over.

"Okay, so now that I've spilled my heart out it's time for you to pay up. What made you run away from home without even saying goodbye to me?"

"What do you already know?" I asked, not really committed to telling him everything. It was all way too horrible.

"Literally nothing. You left in the middle of the night and Mom and Dad told us that we weren't allowed to talk about it. You left and that was that. Mom had been crying but Dad looked pissed. We tried talking about it in private, but they knew just about as much as I did."

I gulped. I hated how I left. It was cowardly and done purely out of spite. It was wrong but I hadn't cared back then. I did what I had to do to get out of this tiny, crappy town. I couldn't say I wouldn't do it again.

"I slept with a married man. Mom and Dad found out and flipped out. Dad told me that I needed to get my act together or leave. So, I left. I didn't want to be just another farmer's wife." I left out the more embarrassing details of what I else had done to spare him. He wouldn't look at me the same if he knew everything. My story wasn't like his. He left because his heart had been broken. I had left because I didn't have a heart to begin with.

Pulling into the hospital's parking lot I saw a familiar truck and I felt a small sense of relief before panic returned. We at least knew they were here, but that also meant it was potentially something serious.

Grey parked beside the truck and we jumped out, hurrying

into the building. The receptionist looked up and her eyes went wide as if she had seen a ghost. I recognized her but couldn't place the name. That was everyone here in this area. We all knew each other.

"You're here for your father?" She said, her voice barely above a whisper. I nodded. She retained her shocked appearance as she shakily pointed us to his room. I thanked her and we hurried off down the hallway.

When we reached the room I stopped, my heart was pounding furiously. Was I really about to go in there? I hadn't seen any of them in years. Was this the appropriate time for a family reunion? I glanced at Grey who looked as nervous as I felt. Maybe this was a bad idea.

I gave him a weak smile and took a deep breath. It was now or never. I knocked on the wall and peaked my head in. All the heads in the room turned and instantly tears sprang from my eyes. They were all here.

My mom cried out when Grey and I took tentative steps inside the room. We stayed by the door, almost afraid to join them fully. I eyed them all one by one.

My mother looked just as I remembered her. Naturally pretty, with only a few laugh lines on her face. Her blonde hair was much shorter now, but nothing else had changed. My younger brothers on the other hand were all grown up.

Both boys were now full grown men. While the youngest Fox brother was slimmer, the other two had packed on the muscle. Probably just by working on the farm. Hay was heavy.

Last but not least, I looked down at my father. He had his eyes closed and appeared to be sleeping in the hospital bed. He didn't look like he was in pain. Actually, he looked very much like how I remembered him. Maybe with a little less hair on his head, but otherwise very much the same. Just like this town.

"Gretchen, how did you get here? How did you know we

were here?" My mother asked. I looked up at her and then Griffin. Griffin cleared his throat.

"I was on the phone with her when he fell. What'd you fly out here?"

I shook my head and motioned to Grey, who was still standing near the door.

"We were in Chicago. We drove here right away. What happened? Is he okay?"

"He's alright. His appendix burst right in the middle of helping a sow give birth. Ma saw all the blood and him on the ground and thought the worst. He had surgery and he woke up fine. They just gave him something for the pain and to sleep. We were about to leave," Graham said sharply. Instantly I felt unwelcome again.

I took a step away from my father and back towards Grey. He still hadn't moved.

"I didn't even know you were still alive," Graham said to him, his voice thick with hatred and sarcasm.

"Okay, well this was clearly not a good idea. We just wanted to make sure Dad was okay. We're gonna go. If you want us to stop by when he gets out, or if you are okay with us visiting, just call me." I held up my hands as I walked backwards, pulling Grey out the door with me.

We practically ran out of the hospital and to the van. Only when we closed the doors and he pulled out onto the road did our thoughts come out.

"Did you see how Graham looked at me like he wanted to toss me through a window?" Grey said. His hands were shaking as he clung tightly to the wheel. I couldn't tell if it was from anger or sadness. Probably a mix of both.

"We clearly aren't welcome back." I agreed with him. Just as I was going to suggest we drive through the night to catch up to Derek's tour bus, a text message alarm pinged on my phone. I pulled it out and saw that if was from Griffin.

Ignore Graham. He's just shaken up over Dad. Ma really wants to see you two. She said she's gonna brew some coffee when we get home and you guys can talk. Love you sis.

I stared at his words for a long moment before deciding to tell Grey to turn around and head back to the farm. He fought me on it, but eventually did as I requested.

By the time we made it back to our childhood home the trucks were there and lights were on in the house. We sat outside for a solid ten minutes, debating whether to go in or not.

"She's our mother. She wants to see us," I argued.

"Yeah but I don't think I can look at Griff. Knowing that he's going-. Gretch, I can't. And Graham wants to beat my ass. I can't even imagine what Dad's going to do when he gets out."

"If you don't go in what are you going to do?"

"I'll go down to the bar, it's still open."

"Grey Francis Fox. You will get out of this van and go up to that porch and talk to our mother. If I'm doing it then so are you."

"You screwed some dude; I robbed our parents. Big difference!"

"It was Peter Joyce!" I screamed back at him. He sat back in his seat, his eyes open wide from my revelation. He blinked a few times and then gulped.

"Pastor Peter Joyce?"

Yep, that's the one.

He stared at me, horrified. "How old were you?"

"I just turned eighteen when I was caught." I said, cringing at how old I was when we had actually started the affair. It was mortifying.

"He's like, mom and dad's age."

I laughed, but it came out hollow and dry. It seemed to

break the tension though because suddenly Grey joined me in my laughter.

"Gross," he said, ending the topic.

"Are we getting out?" I said finally and seemingly more relaxed, he nodded and opened his door.

Ma was sitting at the kitchen table alone when we knocked and came in slowly. She had been crying, cradling her coffee mug in her hands. She looked up when we came in and leapt up, wrapping her arms around Grey first.

She burst into a sob as she pulled away and reached for me. I hugged her and inhaled the familiar scent of her perfume. It smelled like my childhood. She let me go and reached for my brother again. His face was hard but quickly softened. I saw a few silent tears stream down his face as he hugged her.

I coughed awkwardly and they finally moved apart and we sat down. Ma poured us coffee and she sat down with us.

"You two have grown so much. You look so different now," she smiled through her tears. I could see her looking at our tattoos. She chuckled and reached for my hand over the table. "You don't have to tell me any of the bad stuff, but tell me the good things you've been up to."

I couldn't help but relax even further and smile wide. She really hadn't changed. She never wanted to think badly of any of us. Even when we royally screwed up, she was our first defender. She only wanted to hear good things, so that's what I'd tell her.

"I got my veterinarian's degree. I don't practice right now, but I can in the state of California."

"Oh, how wonderful! You always loved animals. Do we have to call you Dr. Gretchen now?" She laughed. I swallowed the lump in my throat. That was the perfect chance to move into my next important thing.

"They never called me that at the clinic I worked at. I actually changed my name a few years back."

Her mouth fell open. "Why? Did you get married?" She glanced down at my hand and I shook my head.

"No, I kept my last name. I don't go by Gretchen anymore. My name is legally Dita Fiona Fox."

She grimaced. "Dita? Where did you come up with that name?" I ignored her and shrugged.

"Okay. So Dita," she said my name slowly, as if dipping her toes in icy water. "You live in California?"

"I do. With my boyfriend. We have two cats."

Her eyes welled up with tears again, but this time they were happy ones.

"Oh, how wonderful. Perhaps you can come visit with him. And you, Grey? Are you still Grey Francis Fox?" She teased.

"Unfortunately," he muttered and then instantly apologized. "I travel a lot. I haven't settled down with anyone or anywhere yet. I just go wherever life takes me."

"So how did you two find each other?"

The next hour or so the three of us sat at the table and we told her the story of our reunion and other fun tales of things we'd been up to together. Like she had asked, only good things. I told her about Derek, and how he was a musician, currently on the road. She had never heard of the band, but it didn't surprise or hurt my feelings. Country was the popular genre around these parts.

"Well when he has time off, I would love for you all to visit. I think enough time has passed that your father has cooled off."

"Graham didn't seem too happy," Grey commented and she frowned.

"Graham is more like your father than any of my sons. Stubborn. But he has no real reason to be. You're his brother whether he likes it or not. If I say you are welcome, then that's that."

"Where are they now? Griff and Graham." He looked

around nervously, as if they were going to pop out of the shadows any minute.

"Griffin is at his new fiancé's house. She lives down the road, you remember little Cherry McGowan? I think she was in your grade, Grey."

I shot a look at him. He looked like he was fighting back something painful. He nodded silently.

"She's a nice girl. Has the sweetest little boy, Gavin Fletcher. He's going to fit right into the family." She got up from her chair and went into the living room, returning with a framed photo. She handed it to me first. It was a picture of Griffin with his arms wrapped around a beautiful brunette and her young son. She was right, he looked like he could be Griffin's biological son. I handed it to Grey who stared at it for way too long.

"He wants to adopt Gavin shortly after the wedding. The father isn't in the picture."

"How old is he?"

"He just turned four a few months ago. He's a doll. So polite."

With reluctance he handed her the frame back and asked for another cup of coffee. My phone started ringing suddenly. I reached for it and saw Derek's smile on my screen. I excused myself, taking the phone call outside.

"Hey! Where are you right now?" He said immediately after I answered.

"Right this moment?"

"Yes. Right now."

I paused. My knee jerk reaction told me to lie to him, but I knew I had to stop that. We would get nowhere if we kept lying to each other.

"Grey and I are actually back at the farm. My dad's appendix burst and he had to have emergency surgery. Since we were so close, we drove back."

"Is he okay?"

"Yeah, he's recovering already. Why, what's up?"

"There's a big hurricane coming, so they canceled a full week of shows. I'm at the airport booking my ticket now. I gotta see my girl," he said.

My heart stopped. He was going to meet my family. Oh no.

Chapter Ten

BACK TO THE MIDDLE

DEREK

We all hugged and said goodbyes as we took different flights. Adrian was headed to Louisiana, Mark and Cleo were flying home to L.A., and I was going to see my girl in Michigan.

I thought about calling my folks and driving to see them for a day or so, but I wanted to see what Dita wanted to do first. With her dad sick and all I figured she might want to spend as much time as she could back on her family's farm.

I was nervous and excited to see her again. Despite living in a small town similar to hers, I never actually spent time on a real farm. We lived in a plain lower middle-class neighborhood and was traveling with the band by the time we were 16, so we didn't spend any time doing the things other teens our age did. Well, some things. We partied a lot, but it didn't involve livestock or tractors.

The flight was a quick one. I barely had time for a comfortable nap before we were landing. Dita was there to pick me up. I couldn't even begin to describe how ecstatic I was to see her. It was like slipping into a super hot bath after a long show. She was my security blanket. All my worries and stress slipped away as soon as I saw her.

I grabbed her and hugged her tightly. It had barely been 24 hours, but I had missed her so much. It didn't matter. Hours or days, it all felt the same. Without her near me, life sucked. We got into a truck she told me was one of her brothers.

"Graham wasn't too happy about it, but our mom threw a fit until he gave me the keys," she laughed.

"It's late, are you sure it's okay to go back to their house? I can rent a hotel," I offered, suddenly my stomach fluttered. I had never met a girl's parents before. That was the best part of my career choice. Being on the road constantly gave me a great excuse not to do real relationships. This was a first, and I was suddenly terrified.

There was a reason she left, she told me that a million times. Was it because they were strictly religious? Would they immediately hate me because of my tattoos and profession? What if they didn't even give me a chance to win them over? I looked over at her, silently pleading for her to take me up on my offer.

"The hotel sounds great, but I have to return the truck. Let's do that first."

My stomach sank. I only had a few more minutes to prepare a great introduction. I was coming up blank. It was dark so I couldn't get a good view of anything, but I saw an old sign that said "FOX FARM" as we turned down a dirt road. So, this was where little Dita grew up. Well, little Gretchen, I guess.

We pulled up to an old farmhouse. It was huge. I guess it would have to be with four kids. The lights were on, despite the time. She took me inside and told me to be quiet. I tried but everything in this house seemed to protest against us. The door squeaked loudly as we opened and shut it. The porch creaked with every step. I could hear my heartbeat pounding in my ears. Was it hot in here? I was practically sweating.

A soft TV was playing in the next room. We stood in the kitchen for a moment. She offered me coffee and a muffin. I took the muffin but passed on the coffee. I wasn't really hungry either, but it gave me something to do with my hands. Something to focus on besides this new encounter.

It was crazy how quickly my life seemed to move. Just a few hours ago I was a rockstar, playing the cocky goofball on stage, nothing scared me. I was loud and proud, fearless and flightless. Nothing could stop me. Now I was just some nervous man-child about to meet my girlfriend's parents, praying they'd like me. I should have gotten flowers or something. Wait, is that too romantic for a mom? Maybe a potted plant.

We had played a small gig earlier today and then spent the rest of the day trying to reroute the tour to avoid the weather. We were able to get a few venues on board for last minute shows, but they were all afraid ticket sales would be low since they had little time to advertise.

Eventually Cleo suggested we take the week off and consider it a break for everyone. They fought it, of course, but finally realized that it was the only real answer to the issue. I had never jumped off the bus faster. Now, a tiny part of me wished I was back in my bunk.

No sooner had I sat down to eat the blueberry muffin did I have to stand up to shake the hand of a woman that had to be Dita's mom. She looked just like her. I tried to swallow my bite as fast as I could to say hello. She was blushing when she looked up at me. I couldn't help the grin that formed on my face. Sweet, this wasn't so bad. Her soft demeanor put me at ease.

"I uh, looked you up on the web when Gr-Dita went to

pick you up. You have taken some racy photos young man," she said, her eyes not meeting mine.

"Mother!" Dita squeaked. I laughed but she looked mortified. I was pretty sure I knew exactly what photoshoot she was referring to. They had lathered me in oil and gotten me down to my boxers. I had made a ton of money on it, and it was very popular. I couldn't help that people liked what they saw.

"What? They aren't bad. It's good to keep up with exercise considering your busy job."

"We're done with this conversation. Ma, he's had a long day. Me too, actually. Can we go up to my old room for the night?"

"Oh, your dad won't like that."

"Yeah but he's not here right now," she argued.

"I can sleep on the couch, Ma'am," I said politely. I really didn't mind. I looked at Dita and gave her a reassuring smile. I guess the hotel was off the table. "Really. I just want to rest."

With a sigh of defeat, Dita set me up on the slightly weathered, yet super comfy couch with a pillow and comforter. I closed my eyes and I was fast asleep before she could go up to her bedroom.

I woke up to the smell of eggs and ham. My stomach gurgled. I rolled off the couch and followed the smell. I froze and my body was jolted awake when I saw a table full of Fox's.

Dita was sitting beside her mother, while two big guys sat across from them. Both guys looked just like Grey and Dita. The only real difference was the hair styles and body shape. One was solid and had a beer gut and long beard, while the other one reminded me of Patrick Swayze in his prime. Jesus. The genes in this family were spectacular. They all could easily be models.

Mrs. Fox stood up and made me a plate of eggs, ham, and toast while Dita poured me a cup of coffee. I thanked them both as I sat down between my girl and the 80's teenage heartthrob.

"Derek, this is Graham and Griffin, guys, this is Derek Turtle, my boyfriend."

I gave them a polite hello. Larry the Cable Guy didn't seem too eager to acknowledge me, but Swayze seemed nice enough.

"What do you do?" The brother identified as Graham asked me.

"I'm a musician. I play bass in a rock band."

He grunted and went back to his food. Well, this was sufficiently uncomfortable. The siblings were more critical of me than her mom was. Joy.

"That's cool. Sounds like you guys are living it up out there in California," the other brother, Griffin said. His tone was much nicer.

"I like it out there. I'm originally from a small town about an hour or so away from here, so sometimes I miss having four distinct seasons, but my bandmates live out there, so I enjoy it."

"You're from Michigan? She didn't say that," Graham said, eyeing his sister warily. Everything in his body language told me that he was holding something back, just under the surface. It was like watching a pot boil, and one wrong move would make him spill over. I gave him a quick smile.

"Yeah. My folks and brothers still live up there. I don't visit enough though. I might make a trip up there this week."

"Well we're on the way to the hospital. Dad is probably awake and wondering where we're at," he said sharply, as if I hadn't spoken at all. I wasn't sure why he was so angry, and I didn't know how to respond. Instead I started shoving scrambled eggs into my mouth.

"Do you think it's a good idea for me and Grey to go?" Dita asked. The table fell silent. I suddenly felt like I shouldn't be here for this conversation. I felt like Dita and Graham were competing to see who could make the other flip the table first. They were both on the edge of screaming at each other. I just hoped I could finish my plate before they started throwing things.

"I think maybe I should go in first and tell him that you two are here. You can all stay outside until he is ready," their mom said calmly, but firmly. That seemed to dampen both of their anger a bit.

"Fine. Let's just hope Paster Joyce doesn't come to see how Dad's doing." Graham shot back with a glint of satisfaction in his eyes. Dita gasped loudly and her head swiveled to her mother. I couldn't keep up with this. My head was like a ping pong ball going back and forth across the table.

"You told them?" She accused her mother.

"Oh, don't act so shocked. Everyone knew. You were the talk of the town. You stole the churches money and ran. Probably where Grey got the idea to do what he did," he smirked.

Suddenly Mrs. Fox's hand reached out and slapped her grown son across the face. He fell back in his chair, landing on the linoleum with a thud. She stood over him angrily.

"How dare you talk to your sister like that. Before you judge another person's actions you better be sure your slate is clean. Now get up. We are going to visit your father as soon as everyone's finished eating."

The room fell deathly silent as Graham stumbled up and stormed out of the house. The four of us finished eating in silence and then they got ready to leave.

"Uh, I really think I should give you guys some time to do this alone. Is there something I can do maybe in town for the afternoon?" I asked. I prayed she didn't insist I go with her. I couldn't take any more of the tension. My family never fought like this. I wasn't used to it. She sighed deeply and scrunched up her face in thought.

"Well, I'm pretty sure Grey is uptown, waiting for the bar

to open. I can drop you off and you can hang out with him until I get back."

A stiff drink sounded heavenly. I glanced at the faded chicken shaped clock on the wall. It was barely nine in the morning. I mentioned it and she shrugged.

"I can guarantee he's probably already there. If they won't serve you any alcohol you can check out some of the stores up town while you wait. Maybe you'll find some charm in this little town," she sighed heavily at her last words. It was apparent that she never had.

Dita and I drove separate from her mom and brothers. Graham was still steaming from the slap earlier, so he just shot daggers at her as he hopped into Griffin's truck while she took his.

It didn't take long for her to reach town. There really wasn't much to it. Two long rows of shops. We passed a florist, post office, bakery, an accounting firm, and some other shops we drove by way too fast for me to catch their signs. She turned a corner and pulled into a parking lot, stopping the car.

"Bar's on the other side. Have fun. I'll call you when I'm done. If you get bored and need me to come get you, just call."

I gave her a quick kiss before I hopped out and thanked her for the ride. She gave me a tight smile and pursed her lips when I told her good luck at the hospital with her family. Her stiff body and the almost silent ride over told me she was stressing out about it. She nodded and after a long pause she pulled back out of the parking lot and headed down the road.

I walked towards the front of the building and saw the bar. The sign on the door said they were open, but I wanted to stretch my legs and check out the town before settling down for a drink. I didn't know how long Dita would be, and I was hesitant to sit around all day drinking. Being drunk around her family was not a good idea. Things were tense enough.

I started down the sidewalk, window shopping. There was

nothing of real interest on this strip. A laundry mat, diner, general store. I was growing bored when I stopped in front of an interesting window. There was an assortment of things that were seemingly random. I glanced up at the sign and saw that it was a second-hand store.

I stepped inside and chuckled. I swear, this entire town was just like every other Midwest town. You could get a checklist of things every tiny town has and this one would have a fully completed list. The list would include a second-hand store that was completely packed full of old clothes, cheap furniture, with an overhead radio that played an old country radio station that only played Dolly Parton and maybe one other artist. It felt like home.

Despite not needing any of this crap, I perused the clothing racks and shelves of knick knacks. The store consisted of two large rooms on the main floor and a basement level with a sign that said it had books down below.

I turned into the second room and stopped short. My eyes went wide as I stared at the tall wall directly in front of me. The entire surface from floor to ceiling, left to right, was covered in mounted singing fish. My fingers tingled with the strong urge to activate every single one.

I wanted to buy them all. I chewed on the inside of my cheek, debating it. I did have a brand new house to decorate. However, I think that might be the dealbreaker with Dita. But, on other hand, there was enough room for me to have a man cave. I had only taken a tour twice before I bought the place, so it was hard to remember where the rooms were and how big they were, but I was sure I had enough room for all of these fish. The place was huge.

I must have been staring at them for way too long because I was suddenly approached by a middle-aged woman with a kind smile and plump frame. She had a name tag pinned to her dark pink cardigan. Her name was Jan.

"Hello, I see you found our conversation items. Would you like one?"

"How did you guys get so many of them?"

She laughed lightly and nodded. I'm sure she was used to having this conversation, but that was also a Midwest thing. It was hard to describe how much I missed the familiarity of Michigan.

"We had a gentleman who collected them for years in his garage. His wife hated them, so when he passed away, she donated them. But don't worry, she got permission from him first," she smiled.

I looked back at them, my desire for them growing the more and more I stared at them. She repeated her first question. Did I want one? *No.*

"I want them all," I said, shoving my hands into my pockets and rocking on my sneakers. I could feel heat going to my face.

"What?" She laughed and I shrugged.

"I would like to purchase them all please," I said more firmly. Her eyes went wide and then she smirked, crossing her arms across her ample bosom.

"Son, there is over fifty fish on that wall and the cheapest one is fifteen dollars."

"That's fine. Do you have boxes I can put them in? Wait, can I pay to have them shipped to my home?"

She stared at me for a long time, trying to figure out if I was serious or not. Her eyes narrowed as she asked me one last time if I was joking.

"No, I really want them. I just bought a place and have a man cave I need to fill. I have the money. You can wait until the money clears before you let me have them if you want. I just know that I can't leave this town until I own all of them."

She shook her head, finally relaxing and letting out a loud laugh.

"Well alright then. You want them, they are all yours. Let's get you rung up."

While we sat at the cash register, we chatted a bit. She asked who I was and requested my ID.

"I don't want you to be some credit card thief." She glared at me as she read my California issued license. I sighed, understanding her hesitance, but slightly annoyed she didn't recognize me. Then I realized that I was being that guy who thought he was bigger than he was and felt like crap. Hollywood was a real shit place.

"Look," I pulled out my phone and clicked on one of my social media apps. I clicked on my profile and showed her the verified symbol next to my name and bio.

Derek Turtle, bassist and bestest member of rock band Maria Maria.

She read it and her mouth fell open.

"You're a rockstar?"

I nodded, a little sheepish.

"Wow, what brings you to this little town?" she asked as she eagerly took my debit card and swiped it.

"My girlfriend came to visit her family. I had some time off, so I wanted to see her."

"Oh, who is she? This town is so small everyone knows everyone." She smiled warmly. I frowned. Did I tell her the truth or lie?

"Uh, Gretchen Fox," I gulped. Her face dropped again, and she blinked rapidly for a moment.

"Well that's a name I haven't heard in a minute. How is she doing these days?"

I relaxed and smiled. "She's a veterinarian. She lives in California with me."

"How nice. It's good to hear she's doing okay. Not many

people leave this town. It was quite a shock when her and her younger brother both left. Broke their mother's heart. Her dad is in the hospital right now. Oh! Is that why she came back?" She asked, realizing that they were connected. I nodded as she handed me my card back. There was a brief moment where we waited for her bank to show that the card cleared and then she grinned and thanked me for my purchase.

"How are you taking these home?"

I pulled out my checkbook and filled out a blank check. I winked as I handed it to her. "Can I trust that you'll be honest with the shipping cost Jan?"

She blushed and then nodded very seriously.

"Of course. I am nothing if not a good, honest business woman. I'll get them packed up today and ship them tomorrow. I just need an address."

I wrote it down on a slip of paper and thanked her once more before leaving her store. Now that my impulse shopping was over, I was ready to get a drink. As I was walking back towards the bar, I passed the florist and realized that Dita would be home most likely when my boxes came in.

I made a sharp turn into the small shop and ordered two bouquets. A small, simple one with a mix of sunflowers and roses for Mrs. Fox, and the largest order of red roses I could get for my girl. They didn't have many options, but I knew she'd like them. Hopefully with the flowers on her mind, when my mass amount of motorized singing fish came to the door, she wouldn't be so mad.

I didn't have an address but when I mentioned Fox Farm he knew exactly where to deliver them. I thanked him and left, finally ready to sit down at the counter for a cold beer and maybe a burger.

It was noon by the time I stepped inside, making me feel better about ordering alcohol. But based on the other patrons I shouldn't have felt any embarrassment. A few of them were already looking pretty buzzed.

It was a nice sized bar with two rooms. I peered around the corner and saw what must be a dining area, with this room strictly for shooting darts, and serving drinks. The walls and floor were a dark wood and a modern country song was playing through the speakers hung in the corners of the room.

Even though she told me he'd be there, I was still surprised when I saw Grey sitting at the counter with a beer in his hand. I went and sat down next to him. When he looked up, I gave him a friendly smile but it stopped short when he looked up and I saw his face. His eyes were sunken in and his mouth drooped like it didn't know what happiness was. His hair was wild and his clothes were wrinkled like he had slept on the ground.

"What's up? Where's my sister?"

"She's at the hospital. You didn't want to go?"

A dry laugh came from him and I began to feel uneasy.

"They don't want me there. I'm only here until she's ready to leave."

The bartender came over to me and handed me a menu. I looked it over quickly and ordered an olive burger basket and a beer on tap. When he left, I turned back to Grey.

"So, you're drowning your sorrows for the next few days? Where are you staying?"

There was a pause before he replied.

"Last night I slept on a bench. Nothing I haven't done before. Enough about me," he gave me a halfhearted wave of his hand. "How's Derek?"

"Great. I met your mom and brothers."

He chuckled again. It was extremely unsettling.

"They are a treat, aren't they? Griffin and Graham."

"Who, Patrick Swayze and Larry the Cable Guy?" I joked and there was a pause before he let out his first genuine laugh.

"Yep. Those are the ones. Griff ain't so bad. Just likes to follow the rules a bit too much for my taste. Graham's just a dick. Always has been."

"I get it. Breakfast this morning was kind of crazy. Graham and Dita were throwing jabs at each other and eventually your mom slapped him clear to the floor."

"What?" He asked, his eyes wide with surprise. "What did he say? Ma's always been the passive one."

"Something about a guy. I'm bad with names, hold on." The bartender returned with my drink and I took a long gulp before I resumed my thoughts. "Oh, a pastor. I don't know. It set everyone off, I know that."

Grey blinked a few times while he stared at me hard. Like he was trying to read my face.

"What?"

He hesitated for a long moment, trying to decide whether or not to tell me something. I could see it in his face. My mind went back to breakfast this morning. What was Graham going on about? I snapped my head back up. He had said that she had stolen from the church. Was that true?

"Did she rob a church?" I asked, lowering my voice so that only he could hear me. He shook his head.

"I don't think so. Man, I don't know really. There were a lot of rumors about what happened. She hasn't told you about any of this?"

"No, she keeps her past pretty tight lipped. She didn't even tell me she was a stripper for like six years. My friend Adrian told me only a few months ago."

"She was a what?" He sat up like I had just shocked him. Crap. Apparently I wasn't the only one she was keeping secrets from. I cringed. Well then, what am I supposed to say now?

"Okay. So, we've established that she likes to keep her past private. Maybe we should just leave it," I said. He was staring at me in shock still, as if he was trying to piece things together.

"Six years, so like right when she left home?"

I sighed, seeing that he wasn't going to let me drop it.

"I think so. Until she met Adrian. She finished her schooling and then moved out to L.A. with us."

He swore and then slammed his beer, immediately asking for another. Was he an alcoholic? Dita never mentioned it before if he had a drinking problem. Maybe it was just a result of being so close to his childhood home. It was clear that whatever happened in this town traumatized these two.

"Let's talk about you, why are you so down about being here?" I changed subjects.

"The only girl I ever truly loved is engaged to my brother. Don't really feel like seeing either of them." His statement was blunt and I could see in his face that I was going to get no more information out of him.

Thankfully the cook was quick, and I escaped further awkward conversation by stuffing my face with fantastic beefy goodness. I smothered the fries with ketchup and enjoyed my meal while pretending that the guy sitting next to me wasn't on the verge of a mental breakdown. Despite hating his brother, he sure had the same temper as Graham. It was probably why they couldn't stand each other.

When I was done, I was almost tempted to go see if Jan at the second-hand shop wanted help packaging my fish. I turned around in my seat and scanned the room. I saw a pool table in the next room and perked up.

"You want to play some pool?" I asked Grey. He rolled his eyes but got up with a sigh, following me to the table.

I wasn't really any good, but it was something to do. Grey however was fantastic. He beat me every single game. Hell, it wasn't even close. He was starting to loosen up and relax, which made me do the same. Soon we were laughing and chatting about music and other stuff like we were old friends. All of his family drama was all but forgotten.

"How did you get so good at bar games?" I asked when we switched to darts and he once again was leagues ahead of me in skill. He chuckled.

"I'm a traveling musician. Sometimes a quick bet over a game of pool is how I eat for the next day or so."

The bar slowly started to fill up with people getting out of work and families sharing pizza and homemade breadsticks. The energy was pleasant. It wasn't wild like a concert, but it was comfy. The longer I stayed here the more I began to miss home. I would definitely have to call my parents and see what everyone was up to.

Eventually I went to the bathroom and realized I hadn't checked my phone in a while. I glanced at it and saw that we had spent almost five hours playing pool and darts. Jesus. I sent a text to Dita, asking if she was okay. She replied that she was fine and that they were going to eat dinner with their dad before leaving.

Since they were eating at the hospital Grey and I ordered more burgers, fries, and beer. I spent the meal trying to convince him to come back with us to the farm. He was adamant about staying away.

"Why? So I can hear Graham go on and on about everything I took and judge our sister about what she got caught doing? He acts like he's so high and mighty just because he goes to church every damn Sunday. Like a good ol' country boy," he smirked. I noticed the more he drank the thicker his country accent became. I had been monitoring my drinking, making sure not to get more than a buzz. Grey was completely drunk. He laughed dryly.

"If only he knew the truth about that guy. I remember his sermons. He always talked about being truthful and a God-fearing person. He has everyone in this stupid little town wrapped around his finger, and his son is the same way," he spat.

"Okay man, maybe we should stop drinking. I think you're blasted," I chuckled nervously, sliding his drink away from him. People were starting to glance our way. He laughed and put his hands up.

"I get it. I don't like hearing about guys my- she slept with. I know it was hard enough for my sister to come back, knowing that the bastard is still giving those sermons every week about how holy he is when he's probably the worst one in this fuckin' town."

"What did you just say?" I said sharply. He was speaking in half thoughts, but it sounded like he just said-

He turned back to me. His eyes were cold and full of hate and pain. It sent a shiver down my spine. He burped and looked me square in the eyes.

"I said, that she was having an affair with the town's married, middle-aged, preacher."

YOUR MUCH AWAITED ENTRANCE

DITA

Today had been nothing but one long migraine. Once I reached the hospital I had to sit in the lobby with my brothers until Mom came and got us. Griffin tried to play peacekeeper but was failing miserably.

Now that Derek was gone and we were alone, Graham and I didn't bother holding anything back. I wanted to shove him to the floor and fight like we were kids again. I think it would benefit us both if we could just get our frustration out. I would gladly take a few bruises just to shut him up.

Finally, Mom stepped out and said that our dad was ready to see us. I paused at the door, letting everyone else go in first. I was about to back out when I heard my daddy's voice.

"Come on in here Gretchen."

Tears immediately sprang to my eyes and slid down my cheeks. It was like hearing from a ghost. I hadn't really spoken to him since I left. Sure, I had heard him in the background of a few calls, but this was real. I was about to see him, awake and ready to talk.

I took a deep breath and came into the room. My eyes were focused on the man in the bed, but I noticed that everyone else had stepped towards the walls to give us space. My hands were shaking at my sides. My lips trembled and my heart raced. Awake, he looked just like I remembered.

"Daddy?" I said meekly. My voice was tiny and shaky. The slight accent I made a point to conceal quickly returned. I was terrified of how he was going to react to me. His eyes were cold and unfeeling as he eyed me. I reached out for his hand and he pulled away quickly. I straightened as if he had slapped me like my mom had slapped Graham this morning.

"What are you doing here? And where is your delinquent brother?" He snarled. I stammered and Graham answered for me.

"He's at the bar with her boyfriend. He looks just as trashy as her. Tattoos, piercings."

I heard a thump come from behind me. Most likely it was Griffin's arm shoving into Graham's chest.

"He too busy to come see his father? He all tattoo'd like you too? You look like you've been living the wild life like when you were a teenager. You are going to look stupid when you're older," Dad said in the same harsh tone. Suddenly my fear slid away and was replaced with the familiar anger I had felt towards him and the rest of my family.

"Wow, and here I thought this health scare would change you a little bit. Give you a little bit of a heart. Do you blame Grey? I came back to see if you were okay and you are already back to being an ass."

My mother gasped and my father's eyes grew wide with surprise.

"What did you just say to me?"

"I'm not repeating myself. I came back because despite

what you and everyone else thinks, I care about my family. It is clear that you are fine. You're not going to die. I thought we'd be able to bury the hatchet, but it's clear that you have no intention of being open to that."

"Gretchen Fiona Fox-" he started but I interrupted.

"I know Ma told you I had it changed. You and everyone else made me want to bury that name. You can keep calling me Gretchen all you want but it is not going to change the fact that you took his side instead of mine."

"Knock knock!" A familiar voice sang brightly at the door and I froze. My eyes went wide with surprise and it was my father's turn to get his pleasure from my pain. He smiled wide and I tightened my lips as I turned around to see Pastor Joyce standing at the door with a bible in his arms and the same look of surprise on his face as mine.

I had to leave. I didn't think seeing him in the flesh would bother me, but my entire body was shaking with the terrible memories of what he had done. I left the hospital without saying goodbye to anyone and went back to the farm. I drove all the way to the back of the property and got out of the truck, heading to my favorite tree on the property. The only place untouched by my wrong choices.

I looked up at the treehouse our father had built for us when we were children. It was well built and didn't look like there was much damage to it. I put my foot on the peg of wood he had hammered into the trunk as a step and took the rest of them up into the playhouse.

All of our old toys were still here, preserved in time. Griffin's monster trucks were now rusted over. Graham's plastic toy guns were faded from the sunlight and were cracked in various spots. I had left a small pile of baby dolls that were absolutely filthy in a corner, and Grey's comic books had been soaked from the weather over the years. They were thick, waterlogged, and the pages were wavy. The smell of wood and mold were heavy, but I chose to ignore it.

I sat down in the middle of the floor and looked around, letting the good memories waft over me. Memories that weren't tainted by all of my mistakes. I wished I could go back and undo things.

Peter Joyce wasn't my first lover, or even the best, but he was the one I regretted the most. I was always told that sex was bad. That there were consequences to my actions, and I didn't care. I didn't believe them. I wasn't stupid enough to get pregnant, so what was there to lose? It was just fun and games until we got caught. I had been too young and too naïve to see him for the predator he was.

I bunched up my legs and hugged them tightly to my body. What was I going to do? I refused to go back to that hospital. I was shocked to see that my father still talked to the adult man who slept with his teenage daughter but couldn't even look at his own flesh and blood eight years later.

This entire trip was a mistake, and now Derek was here with us. He was going to find out the truth and hate me. How could I possibly tell him? Just like everyone else, he wouldn't understand. I couldn't bear to see his face when he discovered what a monster I really was.

A message from Griffin shot me out of my dark thoughts. He told me that Pastor Joyce had left if I wanted to come back. I shoved my phone back in my pocket without responding. I laid down on the hard, cold wood and put my hands behind my head. Closing my eyes, I tried to pretend I wasn't a complete toxic mess. What was I thinking coming back?

I don't know why I did it. I knew it was a bad idea while it was happening. I wasn't in love and didn't want a future with him, I just wanted to feel... alive. Being bad was the greatest feeling as a young girl. Now it seemed like I was finally paying for all of the things I had done in my youth.

I had an amazing guy who loved me. He begged me to move into his enormous house and start a life with him. I had a degree in animal medicine, and I couldn't be in a healthier mental and physical state. Just like that though, it was now all in jeopardy. I wished I could find someone or something to blame, but it all fell back to me. I was the reason things were falling down around me.

I sat up, deciding that it was time to get out of here. I couldn't keep this pity party up. I would go get Grey and Derek, go to the hospital, apologize for my harsh words to my dad, but be firm that I am not sorry for my actions and that if he wants to hold a grudge, that was on him.

As I climbed down the tree, I went over what I wanted to say to my father. I couldn't let him think I was admitting anything. He obviously still believed anything Peter said to him. That was the reason I left. When I realized that my own blood had taken a perverted, middle aged man's side over mine, I knew I couldn't stay anymore.

I jumped back up into the truck and started back towards the house. No one was back yet, and I didn't know if I was relieved or not. Did I want an audience when I talked to my dad? I decided that it didn't really matter. They'd all know what I said to him when I left anyways. I drove right past the house and went back onto the dirt road, leaving the farm behind. *Again*.

I drove down the road slowly. I passed by other farmhouses, silently listing each family inside. I wondered whatever became of their children. The ones I went to school with. I didn't have any friends to keep up with, so I never really knew about anyone's future after school.

I drove around, reliving each and every painful memory I had of this small town. I wasn't looking for anything in particular, I just needed to be alone for awhile. Once I had gone through everything in town, I took the highway road to the high school. Our town was so small the kids had to be shipped to the next town over to go to school.

I sat in the school parking lot for awhile, trying to recall any good point in time. Was I ever truly happy here? I honestly couldn't find anything I missed here, at the farm, or anywhere else. I stayed at the school until it began to grow dark. I glanced at my phone and realized I needed to head back. I drove back, my mind completely in a daze.

Suddenly, without realizing it, I had turned down a road I had been purposely avoiding all day. I saw the sign for the Calvary Baptist Church. The center of all my problems. Where everything started. Without thinking, I turned into the gravel parking lot and drove around to the back. My heart raced as I stared at the back door.

My phone went off and I saw a text from Derek, checking up on me. This was my perfect excuse to leave this hellish place. However, instead, as if in a trance, I found myself telling him that I was having dinner with my family. I'd pick him up soon.

Unpleasant memories flashed over me. I couldn't count all the times I had taken the key under the special rock, unlocked the door and hurried inside, pulling my bike with me so that no one knew I was here.

I turned the truck off and stepped out. I didn't have to search hard for the rock. It was in the grass, right where it had been eight years ago. Lifting it, I saw that the key was still there.

I took it and stood back up. My hands shook as I stared at it. I gulped and as if I was someone else entirely, I put the key in the door and turned it. I heard the click as it unlocked. It was loud in my ears. I turned the knob and opened the door. It was dark inside, and the smell of dust and potpourri filled my nostrils.

I took a step inside and closed the door behind me. It was

deathly silent inside. I took tentative steps forward, finding the light switch quickly I lit the room. I was in the lobby on the main floor. It was as if I had taken a step through time. Everything was exactly the same.

The carpet was blood orange and the walls a faded yellow. A large wooden cross loomed over the room, decorated with swaths of fabric and fake flowers to make it look less menacing. Large paintings of Jesus, Noah and his ark, Moses and his staff, and other various people from the Bible were strung around the room, as if advertising the stories that were told here. It looked so clean, pristine, and untouched. Just like it always did.

I glanced at the glass doors that lead to the pews. That room always made me so uncomfortable. As a child I fought going inside and listening to Pastor Joyce talk about sin and damnation. It always felt like he was addressing me directly.

I walked past it and hurried onward to the hallway that lead to the classrooms. I ran my hand on the wall, smiling when I passed the nursery, Sunday school rooms, and the youth group room. I opened each door and took a few minutes to explore them, literally almost nothing had changed. It was eery but comforting to know that the evil things we had done down the hall hadn't tarnished the innocence and happiness that happened in these rooms.

I stopped a beat longer at the youth group class. That was where my good memories ceased. When our regular youth pastor and his wife moved away for his job, Pastor Joyce took over the Wednesday night program. What started with long glances as I walked past him and not so innocent smiles from me when no one was looking turned into something wicked when I had the courage and stupidity to ask if he could help me with a problem I was having. In private. After that night, nothing was ever the same in this building.

It wasn't all bad here. I remembered fondly my teachers, the lessons, and the songs. It didn't get bad until I did what I did. I stared at the room at the end of the hall and I suddenly realized that this was such a bad idea. Why did I think it was smart to revisit this place?

Maybe if I just peered inside, confront those demons, I could move on. I could get some kind of closure. I'm not the girl I used to be. I took a step forward and a moment later I was opening the door to Pastor Joyce's office.

His too musky cologne assaulted my senses when I closed the door. I quickly turned his desk lamp on. My heart was thumping out of my chest and my stomach turned sick. I needed to leave. *Now.* The door opening and slamming shut behind me startled me. I whipped around and froze.

"I knew you'd come here," Peter Joyce said. His voice low and husky. His eyes, the color of whiskey, were hooded with lust.

He wasn't an ugly man. Then or now. He was handsome, with dark hair and good bone structure. He kept himself fit. However, he was a sheep in wolf's clothing. I knew I did wrong, but he was worse.

"I don't know why I came here. I'll go. Please don't call the cops," I stammered and tried to take a step past him, but he grabbed me. I had forgotten how strong he was. Flashes of instances in which I had to nurture bruises from his spanking or gripping returned, and I let out a cry. I ripped my arm out of his grasp and he chuckled.

"I'm not calling the cops, and you're not going anywhere. Not yet. Tell me, Gretchen Fox, why did you come back to my office? Was seeing me in that hospital room spurring old memories of our time together in this room?"

I took steps back until I bumped against the wall. He quickly matched my steps, effectively pinning me against the wall. His breath was hot on my neck as he moved closer to me, smothering me in the heat of his body. I squirmed, trying to move. He put his arms out, keeping me in place.

"No. I want to go," I managed to get out. He was easily twice my size. I could not brush past him. He looked at me, fire in his eyes. He wanted something from me that I would never give him again.

"Fun memories in here. Do you remember that first time you came into my office? You were wearing that blue sundress and your hair framed your face in lazy curls. You were hard to resist," he said, his voice low and filled with desire.

"Must not have been that hard since you slept with me that very day," I said sharply. He chuckled softly.

"Oh yes. Do you remember what you told me when you came in here?"

I gulped. I did. It was embarrassing. I was a sexually charged teenager who thought it would be fun and dangerous to sleep with an older man. I had friends who had been with older boys, but I wanted to go for gold. I wanted to seduce the man who should never be looking at another woman let alone a young girl.

"I was young and very immature. We shouldn't have been doing what we did."

"You weren't that immature. In fact, that was what you told me, wasn't it? 'Pastor Joyce, I need help. You said that sex before marriage is a sin. I'm not a virgin anymore and I like sex too much to stop. What do I do?'" He mocked me with my own juvenile words. My face heated up hearing how stupid I sounded.

"Peter," I said as calmly as I could muster. "I don't want to walk down memory lane right now."

He lowered a hand to my shoulder and moved down my side, tracing my curves. A shudder went through my body and I flinched away.

"Really? Then why did I find you here? You know, I

wouldn't mind recreating some of those memories. I could bend you over and take you right across my desk. It's been years, I bet you've learned some new tricks since then. After you, I went and got a vasectomy. I won't have to use a condom this time," he whispered directly into my ear.

My body tensed completely like I had been struck by lightning. I ducked and tried to run from under his arm, but he stopped me. I yelped when his thick arm came into contact with my gut.

"No, you aren't going anywhere without showing me how you've improved."

"Let me go!" I squirmed in his arms as he whispered filthy, disgusting things to me.

"Tell me, do you still enjoy sex too much to stop yourself?" He groaned as he set me back up straight. Thankfully, he was no longer pressing his body to mine. I moved in slow steps around the room, watching him carefully. He eyed me with such heavy desire it made me sick. He was a lion and I was a gazelle. Whether I had wanted to believe it or not, this man was a predator. I had to be careful or he'd pounce.

My eyes shone with fear. I wasn't getting anywhere. I took a deep breath and spoke.

"I shouldn't have come here. You need to let me leave." My voice was calm and steady despite how I felt inside. He simply laughed and shook his head. His intense gaze kept me on high alert. I wasn't so certain that he'd let me go without a fight. With a sigh, he turned around and went to the door. Just as I thought he was opening it, all the air left the room as I watched him lock it with a key from his pocket. He winked at me and my stomach went sour. I was going to be sick.

"I picked that up after you left. I realized it was way too easy for people to burst in unannounced."

"Where's your wife?" I said loudly, trying to divert him as I moved behind the desk. He laughed.

"Gweneth? She's at home, with our grandchildren. I know you were disappointed when my congregation forgave me for my sins. They'd forgive you for stealing the money too, if you asked them."

"I didn't steal anything. You gave it to me," I said sharply. He shrugged as he slowly moved towards me. Every step he took towards me I took one back, away from him. He seemed to be enjoying this game. He wasn't moving any faster. If I could just get to the door, maybe I could bust it down.

"Yes. But they wouldn't understand why I did so. You needed that money more than anyone I knew. Much more than the women's committee. They had to cancel the quilting club until they could raise the funds you took."

What a bastard. He made me the villain in this story and him the hero. My phone went off and I reflexively reached for it. I was pulling it out when Peter stormed over and slapped it out of my hand. It fell to the floor and I quickly bent down to retrieve it but in one swift move he kicked it under his desk. It flew out to the other side, hitting the wall next to the door.

I swore and tried to move, but he was faster. He quickly snatched my phone up off the floor and smiled at me, triumphant, as he read the screen. He smirked and sat on the edge of his desk. I stared at him in shock. I jiggled the door handle, but it was solidly locked.

"Aw, your boyfriend is checking in, what should we tell him?"

"To call 911, you psycho," I spat. I could hear the distinct clicking of the keyboard on my screen did as he sent something to him. He slipped the phone in his pocket and gave me a tight smile, crossing his arms.

"There. Now we've got some time to play. You're going to take a nap. You'll see him later."

"I don't want to play. I want to leave. Let me out, Peter." I pleaded with him once more, but he continued to ignore me. I pressed myself against the door. He stood up and reached out. He tried to pull me back to him, but I moved away quickly. He was enjoying this game of cat and mouse far too much.

"I'm surprised you've settled down. I distinctly remember you telling me that you never want to be with one person. Isn't that what you said when you slipped your panties off and sat on my lap?" he said as he followed me around the room. I took slow, calculated steps, never taking my eyes off of him. He did the same.

I shuddered at his too sharp memory. I wasn't subtle. What was supposed to be a one-time thing with him had turned into an affair that lasted almost two years.

"I'm not that person anymore. I was a girl, not even of age."

"Yes, but you were all woman. You knew exactly what to do, what to say, where to put your mouth..."

"Please stop!" I shouted, covering my ears. I didn't want to hear anymore of his sick thoughts. He laughed and stormed over to me, covering the gap in three large steps. When he reached for me again, I let out a scream for help and dropped to the floor out of his arms.

"Stop it! If you stop fighting this, I'll unlock the door and we can talk. Afterwards."

"After what?" I screamed at him. "What are you not under-standing about this? I am not interested in sleeping with you."

He rolled his eyes and crossed his arms as I stood up and brushed off my knees.

"If you keep screaming someone will hear you and think the wrong things," he said sharply, reaching for me again. This time he caught my shirt. I pulled away so hard I heard the tear of the material. I cried out in anguish until the shirt gave way and stumbled forward. I turned back to see him holding half of my shirt in his hands, very much amused. I glared at him. I realized then that he wouldn't ever get the hint.

"That's the point. I need someone to find us here so I can get out. I don't want to be here anymore. Please let me go."

He shook his head. "Not until we talk about everything."

"There's nothing to talk about!" I shouted. He stormed around the desk, finally shifting his attention off of me. He looked down at his desk and I jumped when he slammed his hands on the surface.

"The procedure. How did it go?" He demanded. My blood ran cold and I opened and shut my mouth. I had forgotten about it. When he continued to glare his dark eyes at me, I relaxed and crossed my arms defiantly.

"I didn't do it."

His hardened face dropped into one of shock and then fear. "You... you didn't get the abortion?"

I shook my head and gulped, eyeing his pants pocket. The one with the key and my cell phone. I tried to figure out how I could move to grab them both and run. Was it possible?

His jaw tightened and his fists clenched. His face was turning beat red with fury as he processed my statement. That was what he had given me the money for, after all.

Suddenly we heard shouting and pounding as people hurried down the hallway. Someone was here. I turned to run to the door and pound on it to alert them we were in here. Suddenly his arms were around me, pulling me away from the door! Papers, books, and paperweights flew off his shelves as I kicked my legs in the air, not caring what I hit. He dropped me just as quickly as he had grabbed me. I screamed and he shoved his disgusting fingers in my mouth. I gagged as he tried to reach my throat and I bit down as hard as I could. He let out a cry and swore as he pulled them back.

"How could you not take care of it? Did you really think someone like you could make a suitable mother? You seduced a married man in the house of the lord. Look at you, covered in tattoos and holes in your face," he stumbled back, causing me to fall limp onto the desk.

There was a large thump against the door, and it shook. We stared at it. Me in joy, him in horror. Thump! Thump! Thump! With the fourth hit, the door cracked. Yes! I called out to whoever was on the other side.

"Help! He won't let me out!"

They hit the door again and again. Each time cracking it just a little more. I watched as Peter pulled out his own cell phone and dialed the police. I opened my mouth to start yelling again but he quickly clamped his hand over my mouth and pushed me against the wall. He held his hand tight as he made the call. My shouts were muffled as he told them that he had intruders in the church and they were breaking down his door. He said he was all alone with no protection. Only once he hung up did he release me. I wiped my mouth and gaped at him. Was I about to be arrested when he was the one who was trapping me here?

With one last thump a body crashed through the door and I screamed with surprise and glee when I recognized the curly, sandy blonde hair of my boyfriend.

"Derek!" I screamed as I ran to him. I tried to reach for him but the moment he was on his feet he was lunging at Peter. He shoved him to the ground and began punching him over and over. *Oh no*. I attempted to pull Derek off of him, but they began rolling. Peter was fighting back.

A second figure took a step through the hole in the door. I could tell by the look and smell of him that my brother was drunk.

"I didn't mean to tell him. It just came out. But you were a stripper so you can't get mad!" He smiled and gave me finger guns. I pulled him out of the room and let Derek and Peter fight. There was nothing I could do at this point.

I had the worst mistake and the best mistake of my life

throwing punches at each other. My brother was completely intoxicated as he told me about how they broke three different church windows until they found one that they could climb into. The police were on their way. My boyfriend knew my deepest darkest secret, and my brother was begging me not to go back to stripping.

I closed my eyes and put my fingers to my temples. What was going on? I felt like the world was crashing down on me. I couldn't handle things anymore. I felt like I couldn't breathe. I tried to take a deep breath but suddenly my head felt empty as everything went black and I crumpled to the floor.

I woke up on a stretcher, being wheeled into an ambulance. I lifted my head and saw flashing blue and red lights. We were still at the church. I scanned the parking lot for faces I recognized. Everything was fuzzy, and my vision blurry. I saw a mess of curls and I screamed out his name.

"Derek!"

"I love you Dita Fox!" A scream rang out from across the yard. I looked towards the sound and saw him with his hands behind his back, being led by a police officer to the flashing car. I screamed for him again as the doors to the ambulance were closing.

They pulled an oxygen mask over my face and I sat back and closed my eyes. Once at the hospital, Grey showed up. He had followed me in Graham's truck. I scolded him for drinking and driving and he shrugged.

"The sirens and fight sobered me up pretty quickly. I was okay to drive."

I stared at him for a long moment, debating how much and how long I wanted to argue with him. Instead, I closed my eyes and sighed deeply. I had enough problems to deal with at the moment.

"Okay, I'm lying. I called Griffin, who came and drove us."

My eyes sprung open.

"Griffin's here?"

Grey looked away quickly.

"He was. He had to go take Graham's truck back. He said he'll be back."

I swore silently and tried to relax again. What a mess.

We sat for hours just for them to make sure I didn't have a concussion and could walk on my own. I had apparently fainted.

"How did you know I was there?" I asked.

"We didn't. We were drinking and I accidentally told him about your affair with Pastor Joyce. He didn't know anything. Then we got a message from you that you were going to take a nap instead of picking him up. He took it as something was wrong and we got someone to drive us back to the farm. But then I saw Graham's truck in the back of the church. I made the guy stop and leave us. Seeing the pastor's car there too, we freaked out."

Oh no, I thought. Did Derek think I was cheating on him?

"Was Derek thinking that I went back for some kind of fling?" I cringed, saying the words out loud. He shook his head vehemently.

"Not at all. I told him to calm down and asked him the same thing. He rolled his eyes and told me very confidently that you were not cheating on him. Something was wrong and he was going to get you out of there."

My heart soared with his confidence and love for me. He really did know me better than anyone else in this world. I turned back to my brother and asked about his arrest.

"They arrested Derek for trespassing, vandalism, damage to

property, and assault, the list is probably more," Grey revealed. "I picked you up when you passed out. Derek told me to get out of there before the cops came. He took the blame for every-thing so that I could come to the hospital with you."

I had to wipe my eyes. What happened to my annoying goofball boyfriend? This man he was becoming was something to behold. I couldn't believe that Derek Turtle could be so strong, smart, and mature. I liked it.

"What about Peter?"

He rolled his eyes.

"We all know he's getting off. They didn't even question why you were locked in there with him. He didn't hurt you, did he?" He lurched forward, anger spreading though his face. I turned my head towards the wall.

"That man was a monster then, and he's a monster now. He may not have left any physical bruises, but he took everything good about this town and ruined it for me forever," I said flatly. My eyes grew heavy with tears again. My chin trembled as I wiped them away, turning back to my baby brother.

"I'll be fine. I always am." I gave him a forced smile, but he didn't reciprocate.

There was a knock on the door to my room before he could respond. We both looked up. The door opened and all blood drained from my face. Peter was standing there, bruised, and holding a bouquet of flowers.

"What the hell is your problem?" I shouted. He looked like he had showered and changed. His hair had been brushed but he had a very clear black eye. Good. He deserved it. I didn't want to imagine what could have happened if we hadn't heard Derek and Grey coming. He closed the door quickly when Grey jumped up and raised a fist.

"I told the police you had come for some private counsel-ing. You're not in trouble, at all."

"I don't care what you said. Get the hell out of my room. I never want to see you again."

"But we have a child together," he protested. I rolled my eyes and fell back in my bed.

"No, we don't. Peter, I conned you. I wasn't pregnant. There was no baby. You wanted me to stay, I wanted to leave, so I told you what I knew would make you panic and want me out of this town."

"But you told me exactly how much it cost."

"I guessed. I used that money to get a bus ticket out and put a deposit on an apartment near my college. Sorry for not using the church money you willingly gave me to abort your secret bastard baby like I told you I would."

The room fell silent before Peter threw the flowers down in a fit.

"You, Gretchen Fox, are the devil incarnate. You will rot in hell for your sins."

"That's the plan. Can you leave me alone now?" I said, my voice dripping with annoyance. I was over this man's bullshit. When before I had pain from betrayal and fear of judgement, now I had hatred for how insane he was and pity for his wife who had to live with that for the rest of her life.

He stormed out, leaving a mess of scattered leaves and petals all over the floor. Grey picked them up and tossed them in the trash. The nurses came in and took me to get my head scanned. We sat for another few hours until the doctor came in and told me that I was free to go. Other than some minor bruising and my ripped shirt, I was okay.

Griffin returned shortly before I was released. He asked if I was okay and when I told him I was leaving town he begged me to see our dad one last time. I shook my head.

"No, Griff. He said what he had to say, and so did I. I'm finally okay with that."

By the time they released us, Grey and I were able to pick

up Derek from the county jail. Peter had dropped all charges in exchange for paying to fix the broken door and windows. I think it was more likely he did it so I wouldn't tell anyone how he tried to keep me captive until I slept with him. He didn't have to worry though. I didn't want to spend another second longer in this town than I had to. *Lucky him.*

Grey drove us, giving me the freedom to relax into Derek. He reached for my hand and squeezed it tenderly.

"I would do it again. Don't ever think that I won't come for you when you need me."

"Whenever? No matter what?" I turned my head to look at him.

"Do you trust me?"

I paused and he gave me that award winning smile I loved so much. "Of course," I replied.

"Then yes. Whenever."

Chapter Twelve

ON AND ON

DEREK

INSTEAD OF FINISHING out my vacation at Fox Farm, Dita and Grey said their goodbyes to their mother and I invited them to visit my family. I asked her if she wanted to visit her dad one more time, but she shook her head.

"I have nothing more to say to him. His opinion won't change and I'm done trying. I think I'm finally okay leaving without guilt."

We invited Grey to come with us, but he opted out. He had apparently gotten a few gigs at some small bars around the area to keep him occupied. When I left back for tour, he'd go back to L.A. with Dita.

"I'm thinking about finding an apartment or something out there. I like it. Maybe I'll get a real job for once," he said when I asked about his plans.

I rented a car for the few days we'd be spending with my

folks. As we drove up to their place, Dita asked me questions about everyone.

"What are your parent's names again? Your brothers too. What are they like?"

I laughed, enjoying her nervousness. Not only did I experience my first meet the parents earlier this week, now I'd be bringing a girl to meet mine for the first time as well. Well, other than high school girls that barely made it past one date; and that was just because I lived at home still.

"Nancie and Larry are my parents. My two older brothers are Jack and Nick, they're cool."

"What do they do?"

"My parents? They owned their own architecture business for years, but my dad retired last year. Jack took over that and Nick is an electrical engineer, I think. I'm pretty sure that's what his degree is in."

"Wow, so everyone is pretty successful in your family."

I shrugged.

"I guess it depends on how you measure things like that. Everyone seems happy with their lives, so yeah, I'd say we all are successful. Money doesn't equal success with my family. You'll see. You're going to love them."

I was right. Our four days with my parents were so much better than the one night I spent with her family. That first night we were treated to my favorite home cooked meal, meatloaf. It wasn't anything fancy, but it was nostalgic and tasted heavenly. It was even better now that I was able to drink a beer with my meal. I don't think I'd ever had alcohol around my parents before. It had been so long since I was home for more than a day or two.

That second day my brothers and their families came over. Both of them were married and were making their own brood of children. Jack had three kids with his wife Nadia. Two girls, Melissa and Joan, and their son, Jack. Nick had one of each with his wife Candace, named Tarren and Kinsley. It was hard to remember the names, but they made sure to give me lots of photos to take home.

It made me feel slightly guilty watching my nieces and nephews play. The last time I had been home Melissa was the only one who had been born. Birth's and marriages were happening all around me but at the same time, not really. I was just missing them when they did happen. I made a promise to myself to at least come home for the holidays every year. Oh, and to send birthday presents to the kids.

My dad suggested a fishing trip, inviting Dita and all the other women. She surprised me however by offering to stay back with my mom and the girls while we had our guy time. Nadia assured me that they were going to have more fun with a girl's day than a fishing trip with us.

Right after breakfast we were off to the lake with my dad's pontoon boat in tow and coolers filled with beer, lunch curtesy of my mom, and extra empties for anything we caught. No sooner had we gotten into the water and were casting our poles did my brothers start teasing me. I was quickly reminded that I was the baby of the family.

"When was the last time you went fishing bro? It took you forever to get that worm on the hook," Nick smirked. I rolled my eyes. It didn't take that long.

"It's been a minute," I agreed. I didn't ocean fish, and most of the time I was so busy it was hard to get out to a lake to relax and catch something.

"Jack Junior can cast a better line," Jack teased. His son was barely a year old. I flipped him off. After my line was cast, I set it down and reached into the cooler for a beer. Popping the cap off I took a long sip and then relaxed into my chair.

"You guys got some good-looking families," I told them. They nodded.

"Yeah, Nadia's great with the kids. They're fun little guys. I love it."

"Candace is the best. I never really wanted kids until her, and now I can't imagine life without them," Nick added. All three men nodded in agreement.

"And look at you man," Jack grinned at me, tipping his beer towards me. "Never thought I'd see the day when the rockstar would bring someone home. Mom's over the moon."

"She called last night damn near screaming. 'Derek's home and he brought A GIRL!'" Nick laughed. I glanced at my dad, who was his typical self. Quiet and relaxed. He was enjoying the time with his sons and nothing more.

"Must be something serious." My dad winked at me and I agreed with him, nodding.

"I think so. Never really felt this way about someone before."

"How long have you two been dating?" He asked. I shrugged. It was a tricky question to answer.

"On and off for about two years now, but this year we decided to make it public."

"Aw, so no more groupie love?" Jack teased. I shook my head.

"I haven't slept with a groupie since I was in my early 20's. I ain't missing out on anything."

"Man, if I was in your shoes, I don't think I'd ever settle down. I could have a different girl every night. I'd live in my big ass mansion with peacocks wandering around. Ooh, and a Bentley," he mused.

"I'd have a bar inside of my pool and I'd own my own football team," Nick added. I rolled my eyes and then brightened.

"I don't think you realize that just because I'm in L.A. doesn't mean I've changed. Yeah, I have a big house, but I still live just like you guys."

They snorted and laughed.

"Mom showed us pictures of your place. It could easily fit all three of our houses in it," Jack said. I laughed.

"Alright, sure. But I'm not getting any peacocks. I did however just buy like sixty different singing fish to hang in my man cave." There was a pause before everyone burst into laughter.

"You can take the man out of the country, but not the country out of the man," my dad joked. They all agreed, and the conversation shifted to talk about their own designated rooms in their homes.

Throughout the day we caught some bluegill and walleye. We talked about football, some minor politics, and the family business. Mom had packed us enough food to feed a dozen people, which gave us the excuse to stay out longer. We knew they wouldn't care.

While I told them about my wild adventures with my other family out in Cali, they told me about their adventures with the kids. Jack took his brood camping every weekend in the summer. Carrying on the tradition, he was teaching his daughters how to start a fire and different plants and rocks while hiking.

Nick on the other hand, spent a lot of his time with his wife's family. She had six siblings and lots of rich traditions. Candace was black, so their daughter had her complexion and hair. He told us funny stories of him watching videos and then trying to do her hair just right.

"I picked her up and put her in front of the mirror so she could see for herself. Kinsley looked at her hair and then gave me the dirtiest look before she asked me when her momma was coming home," he chuckled. After the laughter settled, they asked me about kids.

"What about you? You gonna settle down and have a few?" Nick asked.

"I don't know. I like my nieces and nephews, and the band's

kids. I wouldn't be opposed to the idea, but I'm not actively trying either."

"Start with marriage first, Little Turtle," Jack teased. I scowled. They had been calling me that all day. I hated it when I was younger, and I hated it now.

"I'm working on it." There was a pause when they all turned away from their lines to look at me. I flushed. "I plan on asking Dita to marry me after this tour is over."

They all congratulated me and wished me good luck. My dad told me he was proud and happy for me. I was ecstatic. Even though my parents never once made me feel inadequate or less than either of my brothers, I always felt like I was stuck looking up to them. Like I was supposed to be doing what they were doing. It felt good to get my dad's verbal approval.

When we finally headed back to the house, we were greeted by the beautiful women in our lives looking refreshed, happy, and a little tipsy. They had taken the kids to a sitter and gone out for manicures and some light shopping.

Bringing in the cooler full of fish my mom revealed that they also had prepared a full meal for us.

"The fish can wait until tomorrow. Tonight, I made a roast for everyone."

We finished off the night with more food, beer, and great conversation. Dita held my hand most of the night and every time I made eye contact with either of my brothers or dad, they winked at me. I hoped she didn't notice.

The next day brought barbecues, bonfires, and lawn games all day. It felt like just another day at home. Like we were all kids again. I hadn't realized how much I missed stuff like this.

No one threw backhanded or obvious jabs at one another. Not a single mention of me never visiting came up. We all just celebrated the brief time I had with them. It was refreshing. It made me want to come home more, which I think was my parent's goal this week.

Dita fit right in with everyone. She helped my mom clean the fish and then cook every meal. She talked dogs with my dad, who was obsessed with golden retrievers. Over the course of his life he had had six of them. Dita taught him some basic remedies for their aging pup and he sat there for hours, fascinated by her knowledge.

My siblings gave their stamp of approval after she roasted her marshmallows to black. Not that I needed their positive words, but it was nice to hear that they liked her.

My parents were the best. We spent our vacation being filled with my mom's fantastic cooking and drinking beer with my dad and brothers. He showed me his newest addition to the house I grew up in. They added another room, giving him a brand new den. My mom wanted to use our childhood bedrooms for when grandchildren wanted to stay over.

On the last night of our stay, Dita fell asleep during a movie so I helped her to bed and went back down to the den to spend just a few more hours with my parents. I always hated to go, but they never once guilted me for leaving. Just like my brothers, they were proud of me too. My parents were relaxing with wine and popcorn, watching some crime show rerun. I plopped down on the couch and reached for my own bowl of snacks.

"We really like Dita, dear," my mother told me. I perked up.

"I knew you would. She's awesome. I love her more than anything."

My mom asked me about my plans for the future. Glancing at my dad, I knew that he had already told her and she just wanted to hear it herself. I pulled out the ring I had bought for Dita. I had taken to keeping the box in my pocket while I was with her. I was afraid she'd go through my things, find where I hid it and demand me to unlock it, revealing my plans.

"What kind of wedding are you thinking? Jack's was nice, I'm sure we could see about the hotel hall again if you'd like," My mom offered as she handed me the box back carefully. I tilted my head from side to side thinking it over. What did I want? Big, small, destination? Should we do it in California, or back here? What would Dita want?

"Let me get back to you on that one. I haven't really thought much past asking."

"Oh! How are you going to ask?" She asked eagerly. I frowned. I hadn't really thought about that either.

"I don't know. I don't think she'd like something huge. Maybe something in a more intimate setting."

I glanced over at my dad who was simply nodding and smiling his approval. After my mom's questions I couldn't really focus on much else, so I called it a night and went to bed.

Upstairs next to Dita's sleeping form, I stared at her mass of blonde hair, trying to think of how to properly propose. I fell asleep with not even a single good idea. However, I was thinking it should involve me riding in on an elephant. I decided to save that for plan B.

When we finally had to part ways it was hard to let go. I had loved the time we had together, just us. My friends weren't involved for once and that was kind of nice. I would have stayed longer if I could, but I had a show the next day and they'd kill me if I didn't show up on time.

I boarded the plane and just as I was about to shut my phone off, I received a notification from that pair of kids who were making those fan videos for us. I clicked on it and watched as it was a short montage of them putting their clothes and make up on and heading out to a concert with other waiting fans. It was a teaser to tell fans and us that they were on scene and ready for the next show. I commented under the video quickly and shut my phone off, knowing that by the time

I got off the plane there would be at least a thousand or so replies and likes to it.

I loved our fans. For the most part they were all pretty cool. We'd only had a few crazies actually reach us. Security was good about not letting us come into contact with those ones. But the genuinely good ones were the best. That was why I looked forward to these Fan Talk videos, it showed us the world that we didn't always see anymore.

I missed the days of being able to finish a show and then go out into the crowd and dance or hang out with fans. Now I'd get trampled. The fame was nice, the money even better, but sometimes it was the little things like that I craved.

The following shows were fun. All of us got the refresher we needed. We came back to the bus full of energy and ready to continue touring. Everyone had similar stories about their vacation. Cleo got to watch her twins perform in another play, Adrian and Chase were discussing another baby, and Mark got to watch Lola take her first steps. Babies were everywhere it felt like. I prayed that this wasn't some sign I was missing from the universe.

With each show came a new video from Fan Talk. They had thousands of followers and people were constantly talking about them, trying to figure out their identities and where they would pop up during the shows. Whenever I got bored, I'd pop into the comments and give them my thoughts on the newest video.

The rest of the band got really into it too. At one point we bunched together and made a thank you video in reply to them and the rest of the fans. We made some jokes about trying to figure out who they were and even offered a reward for their names.

"We'll give out some free signed merch for the unmasking of Trigger Finger and Death Wish. But seriously guys, please don't hurt these people. This is all in good fun. If you see them, give them a little courtesy check in. Make sure they have food, water, or are just okay in general. Being on tour can be rough, so be cool and make them and everyone else's experience at our shows awesome." Cleo ended the video and we all teased her for her little 'mom' speech at the end.

Tons of names came up after that, but Fan Talk shot down all of the theories. They replied with their own video, catching up with some of the bigger names on the list and proving that they weren't the culprits of these awesome videos. It was beginning to be the highlight of my days. That and talking with Dita.

I didn't get much time to call her, but we messaged each other as much as we could. She was busy with decorating the new house and taking pictures of cute babies. She claimed it was her passion but I really couldn't see Dita as the boring, cute babies surrounded by fruit person. She was more of a candid photos person. I saw her as more of a mountains and Chinese New Year party type girl. But, if this was what she wanted to do, who was I to stop her?

I asked her about my packages, without telling her what was inside. She told me she had received them and put them in my den. I asked her if she opened at least one and she said she was going to wait for me to get there before she opened them. Lame.

A full month had passed from the last time I saw her beautiful face in person and it was beginning to really wear on me. Before the night's show, I hid in a private room and called her. She didn't answer and it crushed me. I knew it wasn't her responsibility to answer every time I called, but I really needed to hear her voice.

I went on stage and played, but my heart wasn't in the performance. I did my job and went back to the hotel we were staying at for the night. I wanted to go back to my room and wallow in my misery, but Cleo insisted I join everyone in Mark's room for a little bit.

Nothing really exciting was going on. Everyone was just getting drunk, eating pizza, and playing video games. I grabbed a bottle of tequila and Cleo and I began slowly draining it.

The music was turned up and the party got wilder. I danced with Cleo as Adrian and Mark clapped their hands to the beat. Eventually though, my dark cloud of loneliness resurfaced and I was going on and on about how much I missed Dita.

"She didn't answer my call today, and I really could have used the reassurance today," I said miserably.

"What reassurance?" Adrian asked.

"I don't know, that she still loves me? That she hasn't run off with some hunk who doesn't leave her all the time," I moaned.

"I doubt she'll make that mistake again. She's crazy about you dude."

"Maybe she's mad at you," Cleo teased.

"You should do something to show her how much you love her," Adrian added. Drunk me nodded. That was a great idea. I stood up and wobbled on my feet.

"Yeah!" I paused. My mind was too fuzzy to think of something on my own. "Like what?" I asked the room.

"Buy her a car!"

"Send her a shit ton of flowers!"

"Get a tattoo!"

I thrust my hand up in the air at that last suggestion. Genius. I looked back at my bandmates who were eyeing each other nervously. I grabbed Cleo's hand and told everyone to follow me.

I don't know who called a driver, but sometime later a group of about eight of us were smushed inside a van and were heading to the closest, open tattoo shop. Everyone was chanting, "Do it! Do it! Do it!" The entire way there.

By the time we got inside the shop I already was sold on my decision. My artist was not too pleased about having a bunch of drunk idiots in his shop, but when he recognized us, he locked the doors and agreed to ink me.

"What do you want, and where?"

I thought about it for a moment. Where did I have room, was the better question. Before I could answer Adrian slapped my left pectoral.

"He's got space right there."

"Right near his heart," Cleo added and made annoying aw noises. I nodded when the guy raised an eyebrow at me.

"Okay, and what am I putting there?" Despite our celebrity status his patience was growing thin. What did I want?

"A fox!" I shouted unnecessarily.

"With a heart!" Cleo added.

"With a heart! Wait, what?" I said, turning to her. She shrugged. I considered her suggestion then agreed.

"I want a heart with a fox around it, right here." I pounded the middle of my chest. "And make it bad-ass," I told him. I saw him roll his eyes but told me to wait here. He returned with an anatomical heart and a fox wrapping its tail around it. I loved it. I ripped off my shirt and slapped my chest twice quickly.

"Lay her on me," I said.

It hurt like crazy, and I was pretty sure I fell unconscious more than once, but when I woke up, I had an amazing tattoo on my chest in dedication to the girl I adored. I popped my eyes open and groaned. The headache immediate. What exactly did I do last night? I had no recollection of returning to the hotel.

I grimaced as I rolled out of bed and went to the mirror in the bathroom. The skin was slick with fresh ink and still painfully sore. I couldn't decide which was worse, the hangover or the fresh tattoo. I looked around the sink and discovered a small tin of tattoo lotion I must have purchased afterwards. I had no memory of it but thank God I had some kind of sense to get some. I opened it quickly and rubbed it on my chest. It relieved some of the pain. Enough for me to calm down and think a little better.

Searching for my phone I found it on my bed, lighting up with notifications. I groaned and unlocked the screen, revealing a million different things. News articles from magazines, my socials, text messages from friends, and a few missed calls. Nothing from Dita though.

I ignored them all and tried her phone again. It rang and rang but again, no answer. Was she avoiding me? I started going through my messages and saw that Cleo had sent me a link to a video. I opened it and groaned.

There I was, completely wasted, in the tattoo chair. Everyone was around me laughing their asses off as I gave the camera a thumbs up and yelled. "I love you Dita Fox!"

The video cut to me paying the artist very well and then us walking around outside. I kept screaming my previous declaration over and over as we walked. Finally, Cleo stopped me under a light so I could show the camera my finished tattoo. I attempted a little explanation, but it came out super jumbled and then Cleo turned the camera on herself and smiled wide.

"This is what true love looks like guys." The video ended and another notification popped up. It said that someone had commented on my video. I groaned, putting two and two together. She must have posted it online.

I messaged Dita a few times, begging her to talk to me but

I received no reply. When it was time to leave the hotel, I got on the bus feeling more miserable than ever. Her complete silence over the video was maddening.

Eventually I began reading the comments under the articles and video. People loved it and wanted to know the artist. I was too upset to bother commenting.

Everyone on the bus tried to cheer me up. They made jokes all day. Whenever they saw me beginning to hide inside myself someone would scream, "I love you Dita Fox!" Which would prompt everyone else to repeat it.

Did I take things too far? Was she angry at how I was acting on the tour? This was the longest she had ever taken to respond to me. Even with her photography and other things, it was well over 24 hours from her last message.

Another day went by with no reply and I was beginning to tear my hair out. What was going on? Was she moving her things out as we speak? Was she ghosting me, and I just hadn't caught on yet? Every second that passed and no new ding from my phone alerting me that she still existed was agonizing. I was just about to take a sleeping pill and sleep until the next show just to pass time when suddenly I received a text.

It was an unknown number, but I clicked it anyways.

My phone was stolen. Just got a new one. Trying to catch up and get contacts saved. I lost a lot of stuff. X, Dita

My heart soared! She wasn't just avoiding a breakup. Simple misunderstanding. I quickly replied back.

Are you okay? I was starting to get worried.

There was a long pause before her reply came, as well as a notification that Dita Fox has posted a video on her socials.

Don't be. I'm fine. I love you Derek Turtle.

I replied back with the same and then went to check the video. Just as I was starting it, I heard Cleo squeal from the front of the bus and then come running to my bunk, holding her phone. She thrust it into my face and grinned.

"Did you see her video?"

I grimaced and pulled my head away. I waved my phone at her.

"No, I'm just about to watch it. Hold on."

I climbed out of my bunk and went to the front with her. Everyone in the room was staring at their phones and grinning. Had they already watched it? I plopped down and clicked play. It was blurry at first and then my eyes went wide when I saw my girlfriend, completely trashed, topless, and laying in a tattoo chair.

They had blurred out her nipples, but not much else. It didn't bother me though. I kind of liked how confident she was. It was hot. She smiled at the camera, and like me, gave a thumbs up and shouted. "I love you Derek Turtle!" As the chick artist drove that needle into her skin. Wait, I recognized that girl. That was Becca Boyce, from Wicked Little Tats. She did the portrait of me on Adrian's ass.

The rest of the video looked like a shot for shot remake of the drunken one Cleo had made of me, but with less people. She walked around with a tube top rather than topless like I had. All the while screaming out how much she loved me before turning to the camera and gave the world a good look at her own tattoo.

My breathing stopped when I saw it. It was just like mine, but the fox had been replaced with a turtle. The little guy was snuggling his little head against the realistic looking heart. He had his little red tongue peaking out in a playful way. I was in awe.

Right when the camera should flip and the director be shown the video cut for just a hair of a second. Dita's beautiful face appeared again. She wasn't outside anymore, but rather inside a small cramped room. There were dark red curtains all over the walls and boxes lined up in the corners.

"This is what true love looks like guys. I love you Derek Turtle." She blew me a kiss before ending the video.

I watched it over again and again, taking in her words and actions. She did love me. Every time she screamed out my name my chest beat a little harder. My heart soared a little higher. She was amazing.

Cleo came over and hugged me tightly.

"I'm so glad this worked out good. She's a keeper."

I agreed with her and pushed play on my phone again. Just as I was getting to the end of the video again something caught my eye in the background. I paused the video to stare at it.

It was barely visible. In fact, I had to squint my eyes to actually see what it was. My eyes lit up in shock when I realized that the little black thing in the background, almost hidden by the curtains, was a mask. A black, rather intricate spiderweb mask.

I could identify that mask anywhere. I had seen it a hundred times in videos. My mind suddenly swirled with memories of them. I stared hard at my girlfriend's face as I tried to picture the mask on it. I shook my head with disbelief, but I knew it was true.

This video was really put together. Even I was impressed with the quality and detail she put into this. How would she know how to make a video this good without having done it before? The answer was easy. It was because this wasn't her first time. She and her brother had been making videos for awhile now.

He was Death Wish and she was Trigger Finger.

Chapter Thirteen

EVERYTHING IS ALRIGHT

DITA

MY PHONE and tablet were going off non-stop for days after the video. Magazines, celebrities, and everyone else on the planet who knew Derek's name had contacted me in some way. I was overwhelmed.

I tried to remember conversations I'd had with Cleo or Renee about viral fame, or rather, fame by association. Not that I really considered myself famous now, but whether I liked it or not, my boyfriend was. Every time I reacted or responded to something of his online, it would be seen by thousands of people.

Derek loved it. The camera was his friend. He was born to shine, and I loved that about him. He wouldn't be Derek without his ridiculously outgoing personality. When I saw the video and the picture of his tattoo for me, I knew without a doubt that I had to do the same. I loved this man, and I wanted the world to know it too.

It was Grey's idea to recreate his video. He was actually way better at all of this directing and editing stuff than I was. I didn't know what I'd do when he decided to leave. He wasn't the same after we left the farm for the second and in my case, last time. I was okay with how I left things. I finally knew that my dad would never change, and I couldn't keep dwelling on it. I had my mother's love, albeit from afar. I could live with that. I didn't have to be daddy's little girl anymore.

Grey, on the other hand, wasn't as content with things. I knew that Griffin's upcoming marriage to Cherry, Grey's childhood sweetheart was still tearing him up. I tried to get him to talk about it, but he would clam up. All I knew, is that his love story wasn't over. I just prayed he didn't hurt Griff in the process.

My plan was only to stay at the house long enough to get the tattoo and post the video. The band was still on tour and we still wanted to continue with our Fan Talk videos. The longer we did this, the more difficult it became to do. The idea was definitely easier than the execution.

As we started repacking our freshly laundered clothes and filling the van with equipment and food for the road, I paused at the door to Derek's man cave. I opened it and peeked inside.

There was about a dozen boxes inside, organized neatly against the far wall of the otherwise empty room. Derek had asked if I had gotten the packages and I told him that I would wait for him to come home to open them. What did he buy? That was a crazy amount of boxes for something. Maybe it was some music equipment or something. I closed the door and returned to the task at hand.

We had one full day to get to their next show. We didn't have much time to waste here. Just as I was tossing a box of dry snacks into the van my phone rang. I sighed but answered it when I saw my boyfriend's face on the screen. Finally, a call I could answer.

"Hey Hottie," he greeted me when I picked up.

"Hey! What's new?" I asked coyly. He laughed.

"I don't know, just some dumb social media stuff. We're apparently going viral. Do you know anything about that?"

"Not a thing. I've been terribly, terribly busy."

"Apparently." His voice was cheerful and instantly relaxed me. There was a slight pause before he added, "You know you didn't have to do that. I wasn't expecting you to reciprocate."

"I know. I wanted to. But seriously, holy crap it hurt. I wish I had been as drunk as you were."

He laughed again. "No, you don't. Believe me."

We continued talking as I locked up the house and then the gates. I talked as Grey drove and only hung up when we pulled into Renee's driveway. I reminded him I loved him before finally ending the call. I told him I'd see him soon, knowing he didn't know truly how soon that would be.

We stopped in quickly to pay Renee for the constant favors I kept asking of her. She protested like she always did, but I reminded her that cat food and litter wasn't free, so at the very least my money was paying for that. We were on the road shortly after and onto the next show.

The band didn't disappoint. We jammed out with all the other fans in our plainclothes and interviewed them before the concert in our costumes. Grey suggested that I start wearing a wig to the concerts, considering people were starting to recognize my face. I told him that we'd cross that bridge when we came to it. Wigs were hot. Throw in the heat from the crowd and I'd surely pass out.

The concert ended and people were calling for a finale. They indulged the crowd with one last song and as the club's lights were being turned on Derek yelled into the mic for people to wait.

"Hold up!" He set down his guitar and ran backstage, returning quickly with the giant trash bag from our painting night date. I had totally forgotten about his prizes. I laughed as he went to the edge of the stage, opened the bag, and began throwing animals out into the sea of people.

He would pull one out and ask who wanted it. He'd look at some patch of people screaming and point at some random person before hurling it their way. By the time he emptied the bag, all of his bandmates had disappeared from the stage. He flipped the bag upside down, showing that it was empty, and gave one last wave to the room before bouncing off to his friends. I sighed, missing his face already.

The next few shows we were shocked and delighted to see that people were starting to dress up as us. At one show in Florida I counted six Trigger Fingers and three Death Wishes.

People were making videos about their own theories about who we were. Grey and I watched them all every night after each show. It was entertaining seeing people respond to us.

With our following building, so did the pressure the band was putting on us to be unmasked. However, despite their escalating prizes for our identities, people began urging others to protect our names.

We laughed, seeing the band's plans backfiring. It was a fun cat and mouse game before and after each and every show now. They even acknowledged us during the show. Every once in a while, in between songs one of them would point to a look alike and demand to know if they were the real face behind the videos. It was turning into something of its own.

After almost a solid month of back and forth action, we received a video from the band's account on an off day. Clicking on it, we saw the four of them sitting neatly in folded chairs. They had their hands in their laps and all had the same small smiles on their faces.

Cleo spoke first. "Hello again. We are Maria Maria and we're here today with another message for our fans and the pair of crazies we still can't seem to unmask, despite our efforts."

Adrian cleared his throat and put his hand on her shoulder.

"We're changing things up. You don't have to tell us their names. We don't want that. This is a challenge. Trigger Finger, Death Wish, if you can remain anonymous for the rest of the tour, we will all do something special for you two. Just name it."

Mark smirked.

"As long as it's doable, we'll do it. Souvenirs, hanging out with us, cameo in a video, hell, if you need a date to your sister's wedding, we got you. You just need to last until that final show."

Then, Derek spoke. He smiled wide. Too wide. I frowned. It was as if he was staring right at me. He stood up.

"Just know, that we are coming for you. We are going to do everything in our power to get you to tell us who you are."

"Fairly!" Cleo quickly said, pushing him to sit back down. "We won't get spies or security involved to do our bidding. But don't be surprised if you start seeing us popping up in odd places." She wiggled her fingers like a crazy scientist.

"We're coming for you," Adrian pointed to the camera and winked.

Derek stood up again and put his face right in front of the camera. He smiled evilly again. It sent a chill down my spine.

"I'm making it my mission to get you to tell us who you really are." With a click he turned the camera off.

I bit my lip and stared at the screen. *He knew*. Did he? Why did it feel like he was talking directly to me? Guilty conscience, perhaps.

"Well this can be fun," Grey said. I didn't agree with him, but before we could discuss it further my phone rang. My stomach flipped nervously when I saw it was Derek. I gulped and answered it. He answered it with his usual gusto. I tried to relax as he spoke quickly.

"I don't have too much time, I'm right about to go into a

meet and greet. I just wanted to see if you could do something for me."

"Sure. What is it?"

"Ethan's prom that he hosts for his charity house is in three weeks. We can't make it, so will you go in my honor?"

"I didn't know you had plans to go in the first place," I said.

"We didn't really, but I figured since you're still in L.A. there's no reason you couldn't go. I thought you would have fun. Go dress shopping with Renee, get your hair done, all that fancy stuff. What do ya say?"

I hesitated. How was I supposed to manage that?

"What's the date? I might have a photoshoot that day," I said lamely.

"All day? It's May 11th. Grey can go too if he wants. We have a show that night, so even if we took a plane, we couldn't make it."

I tried to think fast, but I knew the longer I paused the worse it seemed.

"Sure. Sounds fun. I'm actually leaving myself, I'll talk soon okay?"

"Yeah, okay. See you soon," he said, hanging up. My mouth fell open. He said, "*see you soon*". He knew; and he wanted me to know that he knew. This game we've been playing had just become interesting.

Grey and I spent the rest of the day trying to come up with a solution to our problem. He wasn't entirely convinced that Derek knew, but there was no doubt in my mind about it. Grey thought the best and easiest solution was to get a body double for the videos.

"All we'd have to do is avoid close-ups of her face. No one would be the wiser."

"Yeah, but that feels like it's cheating. If we get two of us, then it could easily be anyone. Or the actor can come forward later and try to say she was Trigger Finger this entire time."

"Okay, so plan B then?" He asked, frowning. I knew it wasn't ideal, but it was the best solution in my book. I nodded.

"I'll call Renee in the morning. I can almost guarantee you that she knows someone who will be willing to travel and film with you. I'll go back to L.A. for a few days prior to the dance and no one will be the wiser."

Grey sighed deeply and laid down on his bed and closed his eyes. We had rented a hotel for the night since we had some time in between shows.

"Whatever you say, Captain."

That next morning, I choked on my gas station coffee when I saw the band on the TV behind the counter. The headline near their feet said something about them staying at the small town's only motel. It had eight rooms and was in the middle of nowhere. I knew this, because Grey and I had also stayed there last night. They were messing with us.

I wondered if he had told his bandmates my secret. As we got back on the road, I tried my hardest to imagine myself in his shoes. Only when I had given myself a massive headache did I decide that he probably didn't. Derek loved this game within a game just as much as I did.

The next two weeks worth of shows they really did up their game. However, so did fans. The shows were starting to look like one of those 'find it' books you'd read at the dentist. Dozens of look alike's were at each show, and it rocked. We even did an episode with only look alike's to mess with them.

They showed up to restaurants and motels shortly after we had just left them, or in some instances when we were still there. We had to sneak out the back door of a Chinese restaurant not once, but twice! Grey scolded me for liking Chinese food so much.

"It's a dead giveaway! No more egg rolls for the rest of the tour!" He said as we sped away from the scene as quickly as we could.

Thankfully, Renee's theatre friend's, Erin and Justin, met up with us a few days early, giving me the opportunity to fly out early. I desperately needed a break. Derek was driving me insane.

He asked me how house decorating was going and asked for pictures. He'd ask about the cats, and again, asking for pictures. Thankfully, we had Renee on our side. She sent me pictures of Duchess and Hank. Big D was her normal grouchy self, but guilt hit my gut when I saw how big Hank had gotten.

Derek had gotten Hank for me so that I would have company when he was gone. I should have stayed home. I spent the majority of the last decade learning how to help animals, and I ditched my own as quickly as I could. What was I doing?

As soon as Renee picked me up from the airport I went to her place and picked them up to take home. For the first time, I slept in the large mansion alone. It wasn't as bad as I thought it'd be. I also made a point to take as many pictures of things as possible for later. I sent Derek pictures of me and Big D on the couch relaxing with wine and a movie. I realized that I needed to get used to this.

Being alone wasn't horrible. I wasn't unfamiliar with it. When I was dancing, I had a studio apartment by myself for years off campus. It was perfect for me to come and go as I pleased. I could stay up to study when I needed to, or sleep for days when I was exhausted. But that was different. I didn't have anyone to go home to back then. I was single and enjoyed it. I didn't keep boyfriends long and rarely let one sleep over.

I didn't have time or patience to maintain a relationship. I was completely happy with my life back then. Somewhere down the line, things changed though. I met Adrian, and then eventually Derek.

Adrian was the first guy who made me rethink relationships. He was cool with my career of choice and I thought I could handle him being busy as well. The moment I decided to make him a priority, he took me off his own list. But then Derek happened. He showed me that relationships were worth trying. I fought it for so long, but now that I was fully embracing it, it was hard being without him.

I thought about going back to practicing medicine. It was a shame to not use the degree I worked so hard for. I loved and missed working with all the little creatures. I decided that when the band finally returned home, I'd start looking for something.

Two days into my mini vacation at home, Chase called me. I hesitated to answer it. I had never really talked to him outside of group outings. It was kind of awkward. I was the ex right before him. With a lump in my throat, I answered the call.

"Dita?"

"Hi, how are you, Chase?" I greeted, cringing at how over the top I sounded. The cheeriness was obviously forced.

"Uh, good. Don't worry, this isn't a social call. I have a reason for calling, you don't have to make uncomfortable small talk for an hour today."

I giggled. "Thank God. What's up?" I relaxed.

"Prom. The band can't go. Ethan and Renee are going as each other's dates. You wanna be mine?"

I blinked rapidly. He wanted to go with me to the dance? Was that weird?

"Did Derek or Adrian put you up to this?" I asked. He chuckled.

"No, but I don't want to keep up this awkward shuffling we've been doing. You don't have to walk on eggshells around me. I don't care that you used to be with my husband. You guys didn't work out so that we could."

I thought about his words before answering. He was right. And they were so happy together. I wouldn't want to change that just to change things with Adrian and I. They were way better as a couple than him and I ever were.

"I'd love to be your date," I told him.

"Great. What color are you wearing?"

Renee and I went shopping for our dresses with our dates in mind. Ethan normally wore dark colors to events he attended with Cleo. Reds and blacks were their staple colors. Renee wanted to wear something lighter, to make people know that she wasn't trying to compete with his wife.

"It's insane that we even have to think about these things, but paparazzi are crazy. They will try to spin anything they can into something nasty. Cleo can keep the black, romantic dresses; I think yellow is a good color this year." She pulled a simple, soft yellow dress off the rack. It had a crew neckline and the skirt was multilayered, giving it just a touch of volume. Renee's curves would fill it out just right, and her pale skin with her bright tattoos would look perfect with the light color. As she tried it on, I continued looking through the racks for my own dress.

"Do you think people will think I'm trying to steal Chase?" I asked, only half serious. Even if I wanted to, I don't think it was possible. I don't think Chase was as fluid about his sexuality as Adrian was. The only way I was getting into that man's pants is if I had parts like him.

"I don't know. I mean, the easy answer is no because of the obvious. But considering how your boyfriend stole you from him some people might try to spin it that way. Why don't you call Chase and ask him what he thinks?"

I thought it was silly, but after going through racks and racks of dresses, I folded and pulled out my phone.

He laughed when I explained my problem.

"I don't care what you wear. Hell, wear a suit if you want."

I thanked him for his thoughts and hung up, feeling like I really got nowhere. I told Renee and she rolled her eyes as she continued to help me look through the racks. After hours of trying on dresses that were too sexy, too frilly, too short, too shiny, and just plain too ugly, I settled on a dusty rose dress that wasn't too revealing, but still feminine and framed my body well. It went down to the floor, but the neckline was low enough that you could see a hint of my newest tattoo.

I sent a picture to Chase and he sent me back a thumbs up. I had the feeling that he wasn't entirely invested in this event either. He was probably asked to go in his husband's honor, as I had been.

Renee and I got ready together, with Lola beside us. She was walking now and was curious about everything. She mimicked everything her mom did. Renee had bought the little girl her own play makeup and bows to put in her hair while we prepped for the dance.

This was my first real prom, as I had been too busy fooling around with Peter Joyce to bother going to mine in high school. Renee hadn't either, surprisingly.

"I got my GED on the road," she paused in applying her lipstick to think. "Actually, I think the only ones who went to their high school proms were Chase and Ethan. Crazy," she shrugged as she finished her makeup.

In the past, Cleo and Renee would go out to get their hair and makeup done for events, but today we opted to do the jobs ourselves.

"I hate it, honestly. I just feel like it's a waste of money and

I can do the job just fine," Renee revealed. I agreed about the makeup, but I absolutely hated curling my hair. It took forever, and I would much rather have someone do it for me.

"Cleo's used to it. She's been around stylists for years. I don't think I'll ever get used to this whole lifestyle."

I nodded. All four of the band members seemed to fully embrace the fame and the money it had gotten them. I was still getting used to it myself. Just as we were slipping our shoes on and Renee giving her last few kisses to Lola before the sitter took over, the doorbell rang.

I went to it and opened it, finding Chase and Ethan standing side by side with two small white cardboard boxes in their hands and matching grins. They opened them when Renee came to the door and revealed that along with matching suits, they had gotten us the corsages with the same colors as well.

While Ethan had chosen to go with a black suit with the soft yellow as an accent color with his tie and handkerchief, Chase had decided to go full pink. He reminded me of a singer from the 1950's. He had slicked his hair back just like the old style as well. I loved it.

Behind them, parked in the driveway was a black limousine. Renee and I turned to each other and giggled as they pinned our corsages to our dresses and offered us their arms. We confessed to them that we had already had a few drinks and they laughed.

"I had a scotch in the car," Chase said.

"I had this new tea Cleo is insisting I try. It's got apples in it," Ethan grimaced and any tension we had about tonight slipped away.

The men kept the conversation flowing on the ride over. Chase offered to pour me a drink and I took him up on it. I grimaced as the burning liquid hit my throat but relished in the familiar taste.

Once we got there, the door was opened for us and we were immediately greeted by dozens of flashing cameras and people yelling at us. Ethan got out first, pulling Renee out with him. Chase followed him, then offered his hand to me.

Despite my nerves I forced a smile as I put my arm through my date's, and we walked down the carpet slowly trailing the host of the event and my closest friend. It felt like an eternity until we were inside, but once we went through the doors and they closed behind us I let out the breath I hadn't noticed I'd been holding.

We were escorted to our table and only then did I relax enough to look around and appreciate the scene around me. The theme was 'One Night in Paris'. Everything was black and light pink. Soft twinkling lights were wrapped around a large, one dimensional Eiffel Tower on one side of the room. Large bushes of flowers were all around and on the tables were napkins that told us the theme just in case we hadn't caught on yet. It truly felt like a high school prom.

No sooner had we been seated did Ethan excuse himself. Renee shrugged. She knew that him inviting her was just to be polite. He was still on the clock, so to speak. Chase offered to get us drinks. While he was gone a song came on through hidden speakers that we both liked. I wiggled my eyebrows at my friend.

"Would you like to dance?" I asked. She stood up, and arm in arm we took to the dance floor. Around us a hundred other couples danced with us to Rick Astley's only hit. Chase found us shortly after. We slammed our drinks and as a group continued getting our groove on. When a slow song finally played Chase bowed out and Renee and I swayed awkwardly together.

We saw Ethan from time to time. He didn't come to dance with us, but he did stop and have dinner at the table. Our table had six other people at it. None of which I knew. Ethan introduced them as his bandmates and their respective dates. I couldn't remember any of their names, despite recalling some of the faces from other small gatherings the Andrews' have had.

Despite all of us trying hard to pretend we were having the best time, I caught on more than one occasion each of my friends looking disappointed that they weren't here with their loved ones.

Eventually, the more we drank the sillier we became. We danced with abandon, laughed about everything, and tried our hardest to forget our loneliness. Renee, Chase, and I, were making the best out of the situation. After a few hours however Renee began to yawn and told us she was going to head home.

"I miss Lola already. I'm gonna get Ethan to call the limo. I'll see you all later."

She exited before we could protest and convince her to stay. She had been our comfortable third wheel. Chase and I glanced at each other and he pursed his lips. He sighed deeply and then stood up.

"Hold on, I'll be right back." He left me at the table, returning about ten minutes later with a large bottle of scotch. He was grinning ear to ear as he waved it around.

"You wanna go sit outside and pretend we're sneaking this?" He winked. I took his extended hand and followed him out. We found a quiet spot behind the building and plopped down on the grass. I didn't care about my dress. I just wanted to relax. The cold air felt amazing on my sweaty skin. It was so stuffy in there with all the dancing bodies.

He joined me cross legged on the ground. Opening the bottle, he took a swig and then offered it to me. I took a drink and closed my eyes.

"So, you're Trigger Finger, huh?"

I choked and spit out the alcohol. It dripped down the front of my dress as I tried to swallow properly.

"How? Wait, who? Renee," I swore, coming to the answer on my own. He laughed.

"You're driving them crazy, you know."

"Am I?" I asked innocently. He nodded.

"Yeah, but in a good way. I think it's helped to get their minds off being away from home. Adrian misses Rocky so much. It used to be all he talked about. Now, he talks about you guys. They are having a lot of fun with it. But oh man, I can't wait for them to figure it out. I hope I'm there when it happens."

I laughed. "Maybe we'll do a video reveal or something."

"Derek is going to lose his shit."

I straightened. "In a bad way? Was this too much?"

He shook his head. "No, not at all. I think it was cool. The videos don't make you guys seem like crazy obsessed fans or anything. It's like you're reminding them of why they do what they do. The bigger they get the more detached they get from their fans. I think you brought that back. They like it.

But Derek, oh man. He's already crazy about you. I can't imagine what he's going to do when he sees you take off that mask."

I chewed on my lip. I couldn't imagine either. I knew he already knew, but what was he actually thinking? We fell silent, taking swigs of the bottle from time to time.

"Thank you, for offering to be my date tonight," I said after a while. He shrugged.

"Sure. I think it's about time we all embrace you into our little family. I know Adrian has been weird about it, which is understandable, but I think it's time he gets over it. You're here to stay, whether he likes it or not."

"He's still mad, then?"

"I don't really know. I honestly think it's an ego thing. He just can't get over the fact that a woman picked Derek over him. I mean, you've met Adrian. Sure, we're married but he still thinks he's God's gift to the world."

There was a moment of silence before we both erupted in laughter. He had a good point.

"I still feel bad. I shouldn't have slept with Derek before breaking it off with Adrian."

"Honestly, he only mentioned it once before the big fight. You weren't even a concern of his. He was over it. It's Derek who hurt him, not you. It's just hard for him to see you without thinking about his best friend's lies."

Suddenly he moved closer and put his arms around me. He leaned over and kissed my shoulder. "You shouldn't stress about Adrian. Everyone loves you. He'll come around. I am giving you my stamp of approval. You are by far the best partying buddy out of all of his friends. You're the perfect amount of crazy."

"Crazy?"

"Oh yeah, don't get it wrong. You're still insane; but I'm here for it. We all are. Anyway, we can help. Ethan, Renee, and I have your back."

Chapter Fourteen

I WANT TO BREAK FREE

DEREK

THAT SLY FOX. I watched the videos of prom night on loop. Dita looked radiant beside Chase and Renee. It sucked that I couldn't have been her date, but this worked too. She looked like she had fun.

It took everything in me not to call her out. I wanted so badly to ask her how she did it. When she was at the dance in California a Fan Talk video came out. She was a woman of many secrets, but even she couldn't be in two places at once.

I spent any and all free time trying to get her to slip up. I'd ask her if I got any mail that day, or I started buying stuff for the house just to see if she'd be there to get it delivered. I had a sneaking suspicion that she had gotten Renee roped into this as well. I was convinced that she was the one getting my packages.

I had one month left to catch her in an honest way. I still hadn't told my bandmates what I had discovered. I didn't feel right taking their fun away. Everyone was enjoying the chase so much, a few more weeks of keeping this secret wouldn't hurt anyone.

Every day we got closer to ending the tour, the more nervous I grew about my plans for the end. I still hadn't come up with the right way to propose. All the good ideas had been taken.

Chase and Ethan had both proposed on stage in front of huge crowds. Sure, I could do that too, but it felt like a cop out. I needed something original, something fun, and something perfect for her. Surprisingly, the answer to problems was handed to me one day when Fan Talk replied to an invitation Cleo had extended.

We were going to have a party right after the last show of the tour. We had rented a hotel suite and the bands, crew, and a few guests would be in attendance. Cleo told the secretive duo that if they lasted, they could come and party with us. I didn't think they'd go for it. I was almost sure Dita would keep this secret to the grave, and I was kind of okay with it. As long as I got to see her without the mask for the rest of my life.

To my shock, her and who I assumed was Grey agreed to come. Once I discovered the truth, I could easily see that they were in fact Dita and her brother. The bone structure, their posture, little ticks in their movements that I hadn't noticed before. It was laughable.

I started writing down all the things I wanted to say to her at the party. Or when we got home, rather. Writing them down helped keep me from word vomiting the truth. There were so many instances, especially when I had been drinking, when it almost came out.

I finally broke at a show 25 days before the deadline. Dita had messaged me right before I went on stage. I told her I wished she was here and she said the same. For some reason it irritated me, and I spent a lot of my performance stewing over it. Thankfully I didn't have to concentrate on anything other than playing my bass. Breaking both of your legs twice in one year made it hard to go crazy on stage like I used to. No one expected me to be jumping or running around anymore, which made it easier to focus on other things.

We were finishing up our set and Cleo was telling the crowd good night. I looked up and my eyes fell on a Trigger Finger look alike. I felt my jaw tense and I reached for my microphone.

"Trigger Finger, when I find out who you are, I'm going to marry you."

My heart was pumping out of my chest as my hands slipped off the handle. What did I just do? I felt Cleo's small hand on my shoulder as she pulled me away from the microphone. I couldn't hear the fans reaction to my words. Blood was pumping through my ears at a deafening level. I gulped, and after a few more moments of Cleo's pulling I turned and stormed off the stage. I tripped over my own feet trying to leave the thousands of eyes watching me. Cleo slapped my chest when I stopped moving to lean against a wall.

"What the hell was that?"

I gulped and wiped my face. It was dripping with sweat. I raised my shoulders.

"I honestly don't know." I looked away from her furious face. Mark and Adrian were standing a few feet away shaking their heads. Mark looked annoyed but Adrian's eyes showed his amusement. He was happy I screwed everything up. He didn't know that I knew the truth.

I fled the building, hurrying onto the bus. I tried calling Dita, but she didn't answer. I was sure her phone was going wild right now. Mine sure as hell was. When she didn't answer I tried Grey, Renee, and then out of desperation, Chase. The only one who answered was Chase, who had already flown back to his parents in Louisiana. I was getting nowhere.

Once everyone was back on the bus and moving on to the next show my bandmates came to talk to me. I tried pulling my curtain down to be left alone but they ignored it.

"Just explain it to her, if anything you'll just do a fake wedding thing with the chick for laughs. Worst case scenario, you get a restraining order on her after you give her a kiss and some cash or something." Mark laughed it away, but I wasn't so sure Dita would find it amusing. The rumor mill was working overtime right now.

Adrian smirked from the couch when I got out of my bunk to get a beer in an effort to relax.

"Looks like you screwed up your relationship on your own. No help needed. And you were so close." He pinched his fingers together. I sat down next to him and socked his shoulder hard. He clenched his teeth but said nothing.

I spent that night in agony. What was she thinking? Why wasn't she responding to my messages? However, I was finally given some kind of relief the next day when we got another video from Fan Talk. I was slightly disappointed when only Grey was on screen. He was in full Death Wish costume but sitting in what looked like an office. He addressed me directly.

"Derek Turtle, our little fandom's favorite bassist. Where to start. Unfortunately, my colleague and dearest friend Trigger Finger was unable to make it into the office today to make a statement about your offer last night. However, she gave me something that I will now read off.

'Derek, while you are by far the cutest member of the group, I will have to respectfully decline your proposal of marriage. I am currently in a very strong, happy relationship and have no intention of leaving that any time soon.

Marrying a celebrity crush is every girl's dream. However, I encourage everyone out there who offered themselves in my place to think of Derek and the rest of the band as real people. These people have real lives with real people. I happen to know that while Derek's offer was cute and touching, those behind the scenes probably didn't think it was amusing.

I can't wait to meet you all at the party in a few weeks, in which we will reveal ourselves and I can say with a certain level of confidence that it will be a night to remember. So, in conclusion, Derek, thanks but no thanks.'"

Grey shuffled the papers in his hand and smiled nervously at the screen.

"So that's it, folks. We'll see you guys at the next show."

The video ended and my entire body relaxed. She wasn't mad. Thank God.

Everyone spent the rest of the day teasing me about the viral rejection. Cleo even mentioned it in our next gig. The crowd laughed and I got to play it like I was offended when in reality I was so thankful that I was off the hook for my mistake. It really could have been a crazy fan behind that mask fully ready to put a ring on it.

After that show we were driven to a hotel for the night. We were staying in hotels at least once a week now. I thought back to our younger years, where staying in a hotel even once during an entire tour was a luxury.

Most of our nights were spent sleeping in the van or on occasion a stranger's couch. Sometimes when we were really desperate for a place to shower and sleep, we'd reach out to fans for a night. Those were some of the most fun and scariest nights of our careers.

I honestly forgot about those times until Fan Talk did an episode about it. They somehow found some of those people and talked to them. I seriously loved what they did. It was the best gift anyone could have ever given us. It was humbling. I couldn't wait to tell Dita in person how grateful I was for her being in my life. I spent my alone time in my hotel staring at the ring that was meant for her. It was going to look stunning on her hand.

Eventually she contacted me through her actual phone. She apologized for the ghosting and gave me some lame excuse about having to do something that kept her busy. I didn't really care about calling her out on the obvious lie. I was just happy to hear her voice.

I was awoken that next morning by someone knocking on my door. I groaned and sat up. Security wouldn't let anyone through, and important people would have keys. What the hell? When the knocking continued, I screamed for them to stop.

"I'm coming, hold up!"

I reached for my pants on the floor and slipped them on, foregoing a shirt. A headache was already forming from the rude wake up call. I looked through the peephole and saw a male figure, but his face was blurry. Who the hell was it?

Sighing, I rubbed the sleep from my eyes and cheeks and opened the door. I blinked when I recognized the familiar face. Jet black hair, striking green eyes, and a face that the rock gods themselves carved, Emile Dahl, in the flesh.

"Jesus, what the hell man?" I asked. He did not look even remotely amused. But that was just him. I don't think I've ever seen him genuinely smile in person. I let out a yawn and then moved to let him inside, closing the door behind him.

"What's up?"

"Nothing, is your girlfriend here?" He asked, looking around the room. I blinked, confused and already slightly on edge. Emile had an intensity around him that could be unsettling at times.

"No? Why would she be?"

He scoffed and turned back to me.

"When are you going to see her next? I need to talk to her."

"Uh, in about three weeks. When the tour ends. Can I ask what this is all about?"

"Her and Grey Fox have something of mine. I just need it back is all. For some reason I can't call them anymore."

"She lost her phone a few weeks ago. She got a new number. Hold up, I'll call her now and see if she can help." I reached for my phone on the nightstand and quickly clicked on her name. It rang and rang but no answer. I glanced at Emile who was pacing the room like a drug addict desperate for his fix. I eyed him warily.

Although I had seen him at events from afar and purchased his property, I had never formally met him. I used to make fun of Cleo and my other bandmates for being divas, but this guy took the cake. He wasn't used to being told no.

"She didn't answer. I don't know what to tell you man." I shrugged and he gritted his teeth.

"That's not going to work. Grey took the key. I need it back."

"What key?"

He ignored me. Plopping down on my bed he began pulling on his shaggy, unkempt hair. He looked stressed to the max. I sighed. I was developing a headache already.

"I'll send her a message and when she gets back to me, I'll call you. Give me your number."

He shook his head.

"He's dodging me on purpose. That bastard. I want to see them in person. You said you'll see them in three weeks?"

I nodded.

"It's a few days short of a month still, but yeah. We're having a wrap up party. You want to come?"

"And there's no chance they'll show up earlier?"

"I don't know. She might. What, are you just going to follow me around until she gets here?" I scoffed but his eyes lit up. Oh hell. What did I just do? He jumped up and grinned.

"Sure. Do you have room on the bus for me? I'll do anything. I just need that key."

Before I could protest, another knock on my door rang through the room. Emile and I looked at each other like deer caught in headlights for a moment. Another knock sent me to the door only to find my friends on the other side. I tried to keep the door open only a fraction, but Mark shoved it open playfully and Cleo gasped when Emile waved at them.

"I didn't know you had an evening guest," Adrian smirked. I ignored his joke.

"You guys know Emile," I said, my voice low. They all came inside and I shut the door quickly. "He wants to hang out for a few weeks. Until the wrap party."

"Hell yeah!" Cleo exclaimed.

"We'll make room," Adrian added.

I rolled my eyes at my friends. They were star struck. Honestly, I would be too if he hadn't bombarded me right when I woke up to demand my girlfriend's head.

"We should have a party tonight. We're actually about to hit the road in about an hour and a half. Hop on the bus and after the show tonight we'll do something fun at the hotel," Mark told him.

"Is that why you came to get me? I need to shower," I said from behind them. Cleo waved me off.

"Go then. We'll be here."

Despite my obvious displeasure, Mr. Rock Royalty followed us onto the bus and to our next concert. He chilled backstage with the other bands and crew. Our bus was already pretty full, but everyone made room for him. It irritated me to no end but if I protested, they would just say I was being whiny.

Dita messaged me in the afternoon. I explained the situation and she replied that Grey had sent the key to him through the mail. He should have gotten it by now. Great. It was probably sitting on his doorstep waiting for him to get home. He was probably being impatient.

The crazy, almost panicked man that had entered my room that morning had disappeared the moment he was in front of other people. He morphed into a charming, polite guest. He offered to pay for his stay, for everyone's dinner, and jammed with people on the bus.

Even though he was the singer in his band, Accepted Perversion, he also played bass, lead guitar, drums, trumpet, piano, and harmonica. He demonstrated his many talents time and time again over the next week. Everyone loved him.

I probably would have enjoyed his company too if every time he was able to get me alone, he was asking me about Dita and her brother. He was convinced that Grey was lying and still had the key on him.

I had become slightly anti-social with him around. Instead of hanging out and partying with my friends after the shows, I chose to go to my hotel room and enjoy the privacy. Cleo called me out one night, so instead of starting an argument I agreed to meet my bandmates downstairs for a few drinks at the hotel bar.

Everyone involved with the tour was here, but I had never felt lonelier. I didn't want these people. I wanted Dita. I missed her so much. I was so sick of this ruse. She knew that I knew the truth, so why were we still playing this game?

I had been drinking myself to sleep every night and I knew that she wouldn't be happy about it. Maybe some company would do me good.

We had all been taking shots at our table and I was beginning to feel their affects. My decent mood was beginning to tank again, so I decided it was time to switch to something lighter.

The room was so crowded I could barely move through the sea of people to get to the bar. I had only wanted a beer, but the waitress was busy and hadn't come to the table in a while. I was trying my hardest not to bump into anyone on the way back to my friends. Unfortunately, I was stopped by someone. A firm, yet dainty hand on the crook of my arm made me pause.

I turned and found myself eye to eye with a woman. One of the dancers. What was her name? You'd think after half a year with this crew I'd remember their names. The dancers were always difficult for me to remember. Especially since Dita left. She was the only dancer I ever noticed.

"Hello," I greeted with a forced smile. She smiled back at me. She was a pretty brunette with blue eyes and freckles all over her cheeks.

"Hello Derek." Her eyes were hooded, presumably from the alcohol I could smell on her breath. She moved so close to me that I couldn't help but get a whiff. "I've been waiting to get your attention." Her hands moved from my arm to my chest. She pushed me gently and I hit the wall.

Oh no. I looked around, but no one seemed to notice her cornering me. I gulped. "Yeah? Do you need help with something? I was kind of on my way to my table."

She pressed her warm, thin, dancer's body against me. I squirmed and tried to move away but she put her arms out on either side of me, effectively pinning me to the spot. I gulped.

"Do you know who I am?" She purred in my ear. I shook my head feverishly.

"No, sorry. I mean, you're one of the dancers, but I don't think we've formally met. I really should get going, my friends are waving me over," I tried once again to move but she held her arms tight to the wall.

"My name is Carly. You'll need to remember it when you take me to your room later," she winked at me.

"Oh, no. Look Carly, I'm not interested. I have a girlfriend and I don't sleep with fans." I lifted my hand and carefully removed one of her hands from the wall. I ducked under her arm, but she grabbed my shirt, revealing a shocking amount of strength for her small frame. I hit the wall again and my beer spilled over, drizzling down my hand.

"Oh, don't give me that crap. I know you've slept with girls on tour before," she smirked and pushed her body against mine again. My nervousness instantly shifted into anger. I was done playing this game. I tensed my jaw and looked down at her with cold eyes.

"Not anymore. You need to move before I move you myself," I warned her. She giggled.

"You can move me all you want, touch me anywhere," she purred again, and I was officially pissed. She pressed her small chest to me and put her wet, sloppy mouth on my exposed neck. Panic shot through me and I instinctively raised my hands and shoved her away.

"I said stop!" I growled. She stumbled back into a group of girls. They looked at me curiously and then her with disgust. I could feel heat rising to my face. I needed to get out of here. I set my nearly empty beer bottle on the nearest table and left the bar. Screw it. I was so sick of this damn tour. Everyone thought we were just pieces of meat that they could do whatever they wanted with. I was done.

I stormed outside looking for cold air and a smoke. I pulled out my cigarettes and began walking. After a few drags I was able to calm down. Between the vodka already in my system from the shots and the dancer's hands I was stressed to the max. I pulled out my phone and called the only person I wanted to talk to. She answered after the third ring. I didn't give her time to respond.

"Look, I know you're in town with me. I don't care. I don't need details. I just need you. Come meet me."

There was a long pause before she responded.

"Now? Derek, it's late."

"I don't care. I need you."

I heard a sigh on the phone then she agreed to meet me a

few blocks from the hotel. I reached the spot first and sat on a bench chain smoking until she got there.

She looked beautiful. She was wearing a simple black shirt and jean shorts. Her hair was down, flowing in soft blonde waves around her. I leapt off the bench and hurried to embrace her. She giggled when I lifted her up and spun her around. I inhaled the scent of her perfume and melted into her arms. I missed the familiar smell of jasmine. I told her so and she giggled again.

"You smell like sweat, beer, and cigarettes, but it's perfect. I wouldn't expect you any other way."

I took her hand and we began walking down the sidewalk. We didn't speak, but rather enjoyed the simplicity of just being together. Eventually though she did ask where we were going.

"I don't know. I just needed to get away from everyone. I am so sick of touring. I can't wait for it to be done. I need some real world life really bad right now."

"Real world life?" She asked, her eyebrow raised curiously. I grinned.

"You know, binging TV and making a meal at home. Shopping for laundry soap and cat food. Paying bills and complaining about the garbage man. Everyday life stuff."

"You really want that?"

"Sometimes. I mean, not all the time. I love my job. Playing live is the best. But I really want to sleep in my own bed. Just a small break, you know?"

She nodded and squeezed my hand tighter. She pointed to a sign a little bit down the road.

"I think that's a sign for a lake. You wanna go? We can dip our toes in."

The air was warm enough that the suggestion sounded perfect. We reached the sign and took the turn, following a long dirt road that eventually led to the water. There was a wooden gate that stopped cars from going in late at night, but there was nothing to stop us from hopping it and running towards the sand.

I lifted her first and then she helped me onto the other side with her. We slipped our shoes off when we reached the line separating the water from the sand. Her toes were painted black and looked adorable as she pointed her foot and dipped her toes in ever so carefully.

I stuck my foot in the cool water and splashed it playfully towards her. She squealed and demanded I stop.

"No! You stop that right now!" She laughed. I loved hearing that sound. It was heavenly. I splashed her again.

"The water is barely even cold," I smirked. She agreed with me.

'It's really not. It feels great actually."

"You wanna get in?" I wiggled my eyebrows as I lifted my shirt. She rolled her eyes.

"Are we fifteen again? I am not swimming in my clothes."

"Then don't." I tossed my shirt in the sand next to my socks and shoes. I slipped off my jeans and started walking into the water. I turned around and walked backwards, maintaining eye contact with her. She crossed her arms defiantly.

"I'm not doing it."

"Come on, the water feels great," I teased.

She shook her head again and I winked at her as I reached my arms into the water and removed my boxers. Her hands went to her mouth to contain her gasp.

"Derek Turtle! Put those back on right now!"

I bunched them up into a ball and tossed them onto the shore. They landed only a foot or two away from my dry clothes. I was a mildly impressed with myself. Dita smirked again as I urged her to join me. I bounced on the pads of my feet.

"Come on, stop being a puss and get in the water."

She scrunched up her face in the cutest way and then her

hands went to her shirt. She pulled it off quickly and shimmied out of her shorts. I whistled and catcalled her, prompting her to give me the finger. She stood there in her cotton panties and simple black bra, staring at the water.

"You're coming in like that?" I asked and she thought about it for a minute before reaching behind her back and unsnapping her bra. I pulsed in the water when I saw a tiny peak of a nipple. She quickly covered herself with one arm as she pulled the supporting undergarment off and tossed it on top of her shorts.

I shouted at her to get in and with one large gulp she closed her eyes and sprinted into the water. Water flew all around us with each large stomp towards me. I opened my arms as she flew into them, pushing my entire body under. I barely had time to shut my mouth before I was dunked!

We resurfaced with laughter, holding on to each other for dear life. I shook my head quickly, water flying everywhere. Dita squealed as some hit her face.

"Stop it! You're like a puppy!"

I playfully started planting wet soppy kisses all over her face. She tried to pull away, laughing all the while. I stopped and she relaxed in my embrace.

"So," I wiggled my eyebrows. "You gonna take off the rest of your clothes?"

"Why would I do that?"

I opened my mouth in mock offense.

"It's only fair. I did. If the cops come and I'm arrested for indecent exposure, then you better be right there beside me in the back seat in handcuffs. Panties off, Fox."

I crossed my arms and after a few moments of her glaring at me she sighed and removed them, tossing them onto the shore. "Happy?"

I pulled her in for a full skin on skin hug. "Very." Despite not wanting to feel like a perv, my body reacted to her nakedness. Her eyes went wide and I apologized, moving away.

"So, what now?" She asked, raising her legs up and relaxing her back to float on the surface of the water. "Marco Polo?"

I perked up. Naked, midnight Marco Polo? *Hell yes.*

"I'll go underwater and close my eyes. You've got until I can't breathe anymore to move." I told her. She must have been joking but I was on board. The thought of actually having sex in this murky water was... unsavory. Marco Polo sounded way better. I plugged my nose with my fingers and motioned for her to go. She ducked under the water and I followed suit.

I counted to 69 before I had to resurface for air. I gasped, letting the oxygen return to my lungs.

"Marco!" I shouted, keeping my eyes closed. There was a pause before I heard a distant but familiar voice.

"Polo!"

I followed the voice, holding out my hands and moving slowly through the unfamiliar water, calling out Marco. She replied but it felt like I was getting further from her. I knew she had to be moving every time I did. I heard a splash and I knew she had gone underwater. I whipped around towards the sound and dove under the water too.

I came back up and didn't hear her, so I called out again for her.

"Marco!"

Suddenly from directly behind me I heard a whisper.

"Polo."

I nearly jumped out of my skin. I whipped around and hugged her tightly.

"Gotcha!" I shouted. She giggled as I lifted her up.

"I think I got you."

I kissed the tip of her nose.

"Forever baby. You wanna get out of here?" I asked when I

felt her shiver in my arms. She nodded eagerly and we started towards the shore.

Shoving my wet boxers in my pocket I pulled my clothes on and shook my head a few times to try to get some of the water out of my curls. Dita dressed quickly beside me and rung her long hair out as best as she could. Just as we reached for each other's hands we saw headlights near the gates and we both froze.

We turned towards each other and I put my finger to my lips. I pulled her forward slowly, trying to see what kind of vehicle it was. I didn't know what would be worse. Cops or pedestrians who'd recognize me.

Thankfully whoever it was eventually reversed and after a minute or so their lights had disappeared. We let out sighs of relief and then looked back at each other and laughed.

"Let's go," I chuckled.

"Where?" She asked as we climbed the gates again.

"You wanna stay with me tonight? You can go back to your thing tomorrow?" I offered. She bit her lip but then snuggled up to my side.

"That sounds lovely."

By the time we reached my hotel we were only just a little damp. I glanced over at the bar on the ground floor and saw that the party was still pretty solid. I couldn't see any of my bandmates, but that didn't mean they weren't in there. I'm sure when I checked my phone, I'd have a few messages from them. I squeezed Dita's hand and urged her to the elevator. My phone could wait until the morning.

Not wanting to draw attention to ourselves we were quiet on the way up and didn't speak until we were safely alone inside my room.

As if there was a fire in us that was waiting for the perfect moment to erupt into a blaze, the moment the door closed our mouths were on each other's and our hands were pulling on our clothing.

I moved us to the bed and as her head hit the pillow, I kissed her exposed neck.

"Are you sure you want to stay? I don't want to blow your cover," I teased, nipping and sucking at the places I knew she loved. She groaned and twisted to give me more access to her neck.

"I'll just sneak out in the morning," she moaned as my hands explored her lower body. I lifted my head and chuckled before I kissed her more softly.

"Well, I guess it's not like we're not used to it. One more time?"

"What they don't know," she whispered, and I finished the sentence as I parted her legs.

"Won't hurt them."

Chapter Fifteen

HURRICANE

DITA

THE NEXT TWO weeks flew by in the blink of an eye. Getting to see Derek for a night made it so much easier to see the finish line.

We didn't talk about my secret identity that night. I offered to explain but he told me that we had all the time to discuss it once the tour was over. The less he knew the better.

When I got back to mine and Grey's much simpler and significantly cheaper room I fell onto my bed and closed my eyes, still mentally with Derek.

"Fun night?" He yawned.

"Amazing." I didn't go into details for obvious reasons, but the good feeling didn't really leave me for weeks. Every time I thought about Derek my heart sped up and my stomach fluttered. However, the feeling disappeared the morning of the last show. I woke up to about a dozen missed calls and a text message from Derek. I opened the message first and my stomach dropped.

STAY OFF ALL SOCIAL MEDIA.

What? The warning made me realize that I had a million notifications as well. That was nothing really unusual, but the sudden urge to check them struck me. What happened?

I looked up from my phone when Grey came out of the bathroom. Our eyes met and he looked away guiltily. I frowned. What did he know?

"What's going on?" I asked him. Before he could answer me, my phone rang again. Derek's face popped up on my screen and I slid my fingers over the screen to answer it.

"Hello? Derek, what's going on?"

"Dita? Thank God. Okay, I need you to do me a big favor. You need to delete all the social media apps on your phone and just stay inside today. Don't go to the concert. Don't do the Fan Talk."

"It's the last concert. I can't miss it."

"Yes you can. Promise me you won't go."

"Derek, what is happening? Are you okay? Is it a safety thing? Maybe they should cancel the show." My mind raced with all the scary possibilities.

"No, no it's nothing like that. They won't cancel. I just-. There's a problem that I'm trying to fix right now and until I get it figured out can you please just avoid everything for a little bit?"

"Tell me what's going on and I'll do what you want. Maybe I can help you."

"You can't help. Fuck! Dita, just turn your phone off!" he shouted.

My stomach turned sour. I gritted my teeth.

"Fine." I said and hung up before he could add any more

demands to the list. I tossed my phone on the bed and looked towards my brother who was trying his hardest not to meet my eyes.

"What is on the internet that he doesn't want me to see?" I asked. Grey ignored me. "I know you know."

"I don't think I should be the one to tell you. Maybe you should just listen to him. I'm sure he'll explain things when he can."

I swore at Grey and started pulling out my costume for the concert.

"You're really going to the show? I heard him ask you not to."

"Yeah but he didn't tell me why he doesn't want me there. How can I miss the last show? Am I supposed to miss the after party too?"

"I can go and we can edit the video so it appears as if you were there. We've done it before, and it worked just fine. Dita, I'm telling you. It's a bad idea."

I scoffed. "It's funny for you to be giving me advice on good and bad ideas. You may run from the truth, but that's not me."

Grey's face turned from worry to anger.

"That's low. Fine. Go to the show and screw up your relationship. I'm not stopping you. You want to spend the night crying? By all means, get dressed." He stormed out of the room, slamming the door behind him.

My phone lit up and I stared at it. Did I dare look at what just popped up? Was Grey right, would my relationship be ruined? Did I trust Derek enough to not pick up my phone? I paced my room, trying to figure out a plan. No matter what I did I would end up disappointing someone.

My phone rang again and I launched myself on the bed to answer it. It was an unknown number. Should I answer it? He didn't say not to answer calls. With the newfound loophole in existence, I answered the call.

"Hello?"

"Dita? This is Emile. I've been trying to contact you."

I sighed. "Yes, and I already told my boyfriend that Grey sent the key through the mail. We don't have it."

"I know, he told me. I was hoping to talk to Grey in person. Is he available today?"

"Uh, yeah for a bit. How do you know where we are?"

"I've been hanging out with the band the last few weeks. Derek told me that you guys are going to the tour wrap up party. You gotta be close, right?"

"Oh. Yeah, of course." I felt stupid for not realizing that.

"Where are you guys? I'll come to you."

I was hesitant to tell him the hotel name, but I hoped that maybe if I helped him one last time he'd be able to tell me what was going on with Derek. I gave him the address and he told me he was on his way. Grey popped back in shortly after with donuts and coffee. I told him who was coming and he swore.

"Are you serious? I thought you told him I mailed the key."

"I did." I looked at my brother who was sweating furiously and looking around the room nervously. "Did you?"

He froze and that told me everything I needed to know.

"Grey, what did you do?"

His eyes shone with tears and his face morphed into fury.

"You don't know him. He's a bastard. He plays with people. He uses them for his own gain and then tosses them away the moment they are no use to him. He wants this key so bad?" He pulled the familiar key out of his wallet. My breath stopped. "Well too bad."

Before I could argue with him someone knocked on the door. I closed my eyes and took a deep breath. I knew it was our guest. Grey crossed his arms, sticking to his guns. The knock came again so I hurried to answer it.

Sure enough, Emile, in all his glory came storming in. Dressed in casual clothes, he looked approachable, but his gorgeous face was riddled with anger that would make anyone stop short. How in the hell did he get here so fast? Before I could ask, he launched himself at my brother.

"You! Give it to me." He reached out his arm and in less than thirty seconds he had Grey pinned to the wall by his neck a foot off the ground. Grey squirmed and tried to kick him but Emile held firm.

"What are you talking about?" Grey got out finally and I sighed, lifting my head to the ceiling. What was he doing? Still playing innocent. Emile dropped Grey's neck and let him fall to the floor. My brother spit at his feet.

"My key. I know you have it."

"Why would I have it? Just because Dara was my friend? You think I'm holding a grudge?" Grey stood up and stood toe to toe with him. I watched Emile's jaw and fists tighten. I was frozen to the spot. Was I about to witness my brother get beaten to a pulp, and kind of deserve it?

"It wasn't my fault. I wasn't there." Emile argued through gritted teeth.

"Exactly. You. Weren't. There. Tell me, were you screwing that chick before you married my friend? The whole time you were making her all these promises of a magical life together and not even a month later you are asking for a divorce. What kind of man are you?" Grey scoffed at him. Emile was seething. The look on his face was deadly, but I could tell that my brother's words must have held some truth.

For a long moment no one in the room spoke. All that was audible was the two mens heavy breathing. Minutes passed before Emile relaxed his stance and ran his hand through his hair.

"Look, I admit that I wasn't a great person to her. I'll never forgive myself for breaking her heart. She got caught in the middle of something more powerful than what was between her and I. If I could go back, I wouldn't have tried to pursue her, knowing that my heart belonged to someone else."

Grey clenched his jaw. "She loved you. When you left, something in her broke." His voice cracked and a small tear escaped his eye.

"I'm sorry. I never wanted to hurt her. She deserved a better partner."

Grey pulled the key Emile was so desperate for out of his pocket. His green eyes widened with desire. My brother raised an eyebrow.

"You need this to get the girl? The one who you left Dara for?"

Emile shook his head but didn't take his eyes off the key in Grey's hand.

"No. You're not understanding. Cotton and I go back way farther than Dara and I. I gave my heart to her when we were young and never really got it back. I need that key to finally show her that. Dara just- Dara was an unfortunate mistake."

"Mistake?"

Emile shook his head and sighed. He was getting frustrated again.

"Not like that. I thought I loved Dara, Grey. I wanted to love her. I told myself if I married her that I could forget the girl I thought I lost. Well, I was wrong. I need that key. Please."

Grey stared at him for a long time before taking a breath so deep it looked like his entire body was going to collapse into itself. It was heartbreaking. Finally, he relaxed his hand and held out the key. Emile took it like it was the one ring to rule them all.

"Thank you. Grey, thank you so much."

"I hope she's worth it."

"She is." Emile shoved the key in his pocket as if Grey was going to take it back at any moment. He then looked around the room as if this was the first time he was seeing it. We made eye contact and he blushed a little.

"I'm sorry for my actions. I wish I could explain how much she means to me."

I nodded. "It's all good. I would do anything for Derek. If I lost him, I don't know what I'd do."

He stretched his mouth out in an awkward grimace.

"Yeah, I heard about the whole situation going on right now. I'm sure he'll figure everything out. I really don't think he did it. Derek's a good guy."

My heart stopped and my mouth fell open.

"Wait, what? What did he do?"

Emile blinked and then grimaced again.

"You know, the sexual assault thing. With the dancer? Shit, you didn't know. Okay, I should go. Call him. Sorry. I'm not good with this stuff. I've got to go." Before I could comprehend what he was saying he was running out the door.

Sexual assault. He said the words sexual assault. What did that mean exactly? My eyes flew over to Grey who was staring at me, gauging my reaction.

"What is going on?" I asked slowly. I was afraid of the answer, but also afraid of the unknown. Grey sighed and motioned for me to sit down. I did so and he joined me on his own bed. Biting his lip for a moment he finally told me what was happening.

"Obviously this is all new and developing. Only the girl has spoken out, so the story is only one-sided right now. Derek hasn't given his version of events to tell us if any of it's true." Grey was rambling. I was getting frustrated. I snarled and he held up his hands in innocence.

"Okay, okay. One of the dancers came forward and said

that two weeks ago Derek touched her without her consent. That's all I know. Obviously, it's not looking good for him right now. That's why he wants you to stay off the web. People are not being kind to him."

"Touched her? How? Where?"

"I read the statement she wrote. I guess he grabbed her chest at a party."

I pressed my lips together. Two weeks ago. That would be around the time we had our lake date. I remembered when we got back to his hotel, we passed by a party going on in the bar. Did he assault her and then call me as an alibi? Oh my God.

I jumped when my phone rang. I knew it had to be Derek, but did I really want to talk to him right now? After the ringing stopped it was only half a minute before he called again.

"You should answer it. Emile probably told him."

I thought about it and reached for my phone. Shakily I pushed answer.

"Hello? Dita? Emile called me. I need to explain."

"Explain what, Derek? You sexually assaulted someone? What were you thinking? Did you use me as an excuse to play it off like it didn't happen?"

"It didn't happen! That's the thing. The chick is nuts. She came on to me, I turned her down, and now she's trying to get me for something insane. I would never do something like that."

"Why would she lie? That's not something people kid about. People are pissed, Derek. Are you going to be arrested?"

"How do you know people are mad? Did you look on the internet? You saw what they are saying about me. Why couldn't you trust me?" His voice cracked and before I could reply I heard the click of him hanging up.

I tried to call him back, but it went straight to his voice-mail. I tried a few more times and I knew that he had shut his phone off. I swore and fell onto the bed.

Grey was on his phone, shaking his head.

"The show got cancelled. Everyone is demanding Derek be kicked out of the band."

I turned my head towards him.

"Are they going to?"

He shrugged.

"Who knows. No one even knows if it's true or not."

"Yeah but girls don't lie about stuff like that. It's just wrong."

Grey didn't say anything.

I sat up. I couldn't stay here. This room was suddenly extremely suffocating. But where did we go now? The tour was over. I was supposed to go back to Los Angeles with Derek. I couldn't very well do that now. I didn't know what to believe. He was right, I shouldn't have pushed it. I would much rather still be completely blind to whatever was going on.

"Come on, we're going." I gulped and started gathering my things.

"Going where? You don't want to wait for Derek?"

I shook my head. "No. I need to leave. Get some distance. Some air." I couldn't think in this stuffy room. We packed up our things and checked out of the motel. Once we were in the van, I reached for my phone again.

My finger hovered over the internet app. Did I dare look at what was going on? Derek's last words to me cut into my heart again. I hadn't trusted him, he was right. But I hadn't looked online. He had just assumed. I swallowed and quickly moved my finger to the little telephone symbol instead. Renee answered quickly, her tone in her greeting told me she knew what was going on.

"Dita," she said sadly.

"Renee," my voice cracked, and my chin started to quiver. "I need someplace to go. I can't go back home. Derek and I…"

I choked on the last words as slow tears started falling down my cheeks.

"It's okay, stay calm. I'm not in LA. I went to visit Chase and Rocky. Come down here to Tickfaw and we'll find you a place to stay. Chase has a friend who he thinks can house you two. She's really nice."

"Tickfaw?" I sniffled, wiping my face with my hoodie sleeve.

"It's like an hour or so from New Orleans. Don't let the keyboard warriors get to you. The band is already trying to figure out what really happened and what to do."

I nodded even though I knew she couldn't see me. Her solid, strong voice helped me relax and even my breathing. She repeated her simple directions and hung up. Louisiana was a few hours away, so I had nothing else to do but stew on my last conversation with Derek.

I wanted to do as he had asked. If Emile hadn't told me anything, I'd be perfectly fine staying off the web. However, the longer we were on the road the more carsick I began to feel. I felt like Pandora, and my cell phone was the forbidden box. I'd already had a peek; did I go for it and unleash the monsters into my world?

It was eating me inside, until eventually I caved and brought out my tablet. The small phone screen wouldn't cut it. I closed my eyes and sent a quick prayer to the powers that be that going through with this didn't destroy my relationship. However, if what he was accused of was true, it already was. I tapped my pointer finger to my go-to app for the socials.

Immediately I was bombarded with articles featuring Derek's face. They all used the same photo of him unshaven, tired, and glaring at the photographer. That alone could make him guilty in the public's eyes. My heart sank and stomach rolled when I saw the titles of the articles.

Bassist Derek Turtle Accused of Sexual Assault

Dancer on Tour Tells All: Derek Turtle Assaulted Me

Musician Derek Turtle is Revealed as Sexual Abuser

I was too scared to click on the articles, so I clicked on the trending topics and was flooded with more horrifying news.

#DerekTurtleisover

#DirtyDerek

#KickTurtleout

#MariaMariacanceled

Tears stinging my eyes I clicked on the hashtags. The statements were angry, demanding, and absolutely horrific. They wanted his head on a stick. I understood why he didn't want me to look. These people had already found him guilty. Day one and he was already deemed an abuser. But it couldn't be true. Not my Derek. That wasn't him.

With a large gulp, I braced myself for the articles. I chose to start with the one that people kept mentioning and sharing. I figured it was the best place to begin, since that was probably where the story broke. The article was from someone's personal blog. I recognized the name and face in the profile pic. My blood ran cold. *Carly.*

> *I planned on keeping quiet about this situation, but I've decided that my mental health means more to me than my career. While I was on tour with Maria Maria, Derek Turtle sexually assaulted me.*

From the beginning of the tour we were told that the dancers and the band were not to have any interactions with each other for our own safety. I figured it was because they didn't want us getting involved with any of them and causing drama during the six-month travel around the country. However, I sadly discovered two weeks ago that the rule was put in place for our protection.

With the tour coming to a close, the rules were starting to relax a little and the entire crew rented out the bar of the hotel we were staying at for a party. The bar was packed and I had just left my group of friends to go to the bathroom. On my return I happened to see Derek Turtle, bassist of Maria Maria, leaning against a wall holding a beer. He looked miserable, so I thought I'd go over and see if he wanted to join my group. We were having a good time and everyone was more than friendly, so I knew they'd have no problem making room in our booth for another person.

I introduced myself and he gave me that crooked smile that makes the girls go crazy over him. He told me that he's always wanted to talk to me, and when I pointed out that I knew he had a girlfriend he rolled his eyes and whispered in my ear that he loved sleeping with fans.

Pinning me to the wall, I couldn't move as he continued to tell me how much he wanted me and that his relationship with his girlfriend wasn't serious. His hands were all over me. I told him repeatedly that he needed to stop and when I tried to move away, he reached out and grabbed my breasts. I jumped back, falling into a group of girls. I was speechless and when they asked me if I was alright, he stormed out of the bar.

I spent the rest of the evening in my room sobbing and trying to process what happened. There were moments when I thought it was my fault for approaching him even though I had been warned not to. When I saw him the next few days happy as a clam, as if nothing had happened, the more stressed I became. I was so sick to my stomach I was throwing up before every show.

Finally, I decided to tell someone, and they told me I needed to tell my story. Derek Turtle and other men like him should not be allowed to get away with gross, disgusting acts like this.

I read the blog post over and over, trying to process what I was reading. I remembered seeing the party when we were going up to his room. He was avoiding it. Again though, nothing about her story sounded like the Derek I knew. He was never pushy like that. Even when I asked him to be, that wasn't the kind of guy he was.

I wanted to vomit. I felt like the most garbage person in the world for not wanting to believe this woman's story. I was part of the problem. Too many victims were not heard, and Derek's celebrity status just made it that easier for people to sweep it under the rug. I didn't know where my loyalty belonged.

Scrolling down the page I found thousands of comments from people, and surprisingly, she was responding to them. People were asking her if she had witnesses and she told them that the only people who saw where the unknown girls she fell into. Then someone asked if she was going to press charges. She responded with no, that telling her story was enough. Plus, she didn't have any evidence. She was sure that he would use his money to ruin her in court.

I went through hundreds of comments telling her to go for the jugular and ruin his life like he did hers. She made a point to comment to a lot of those responses. However, every time someone asked for some shred of proof or mentioned that her story didn't sound right, she ignored it. That led to people accusing those people of victim blaming. It was a mess.

I spent the rest of the ride reading articles and comments, watching video's, and trying my best to piece this mess together. It couldn't be true. The man she was describing was not the Derek I knew.

I wanted to believe Derek. He was a gentle man with a big

heart. I had never once felt forced into anything with him, so it was hard to imagine him doing something like that to someone else. He may be an annoying clown to the outside world, but he was a giant teddy bear in real life, and he was definitely not a monster.

Grey and I didn't talk much on the drive to Tickfaw. There wasn't much to say. My mind was too full of questions and possibly unfair accusations. I had hopes that the woman wasn't telling the truth, but it felt wrong to want that. Too many people are abused every day and you hear way too often about them speaking out, not being believed, and thus repeating the cycle. I didn't want to be one of those people.

Derek's last words to me rang in my ears like a haunting echo in a dark cave of heartbreak. It was as if I could hear his heart splintering right down the middle when he said it.

"Why couldn't you trust me?"

When we were finally within a half hour of Tickfaw, Louisiana, Chase's hometown, Grey cleared his throat and made an announcement.

"I've been thinking about what you said earlier. About me running from the truth. You're right. I still have a lot of unfinished business back home. I'm going to drop you off and then I'm heading back to the farm."

"Are you sure?" I was genuinely surprised by his decision. I looked at him, and my baby brother seemed to transform from a silly boy to a grown man right before my eyes. I smiled, proud of his decision. He nodded, keeping his eyes trained on the road.

"Yeah. It's about time. I put it off when we were there, but now that Dad's healthy and the dust has settled, I need to go back and attempt to fix things. I need to talk to Cherry."

He didn't need to explain, I knew what he needed to do. I gave him a playful punch on the shoulder and smiled.

"Aw, my baby brother is growing up."

He rolled his eyes. "Shut up before I change my mind."

I called Renee right before we reached town to get the address. By the time we reached the Wilson's house it was early evening. Renee and Chase were standing outside with their children on their hips. It made me smile instantly and my tense stomach relaxed for the first time all day.

Grey only got out of our van to unload my things and give me one last hug goodbye.

"It's been a wild ride, sis. I never imagined this was how I'd spend the better part of this year, but I wouldn't change it for the world."

"I know. Me too. I'll miss you."

He pulled away and hopped back in the van. He gave me one last salute.

"Let me know how that talk with Cherry goes," I winked. He rolled his eyes.

"Sure thing boss. And Gretch, hear the guy out. He's a good guy, give him a chance."

I nodded and just like that the van was down the road, turning, and then disappearing. I turned back to my friends. Chase was grinning and Renee was wiping a tear from the corner of her eye.

"Come on, let's put your stuff inside. Have you had dinner? We were going to meet up with Cotton at the bar." Chase greeted me with a quick half hug and Rocky tugged on my hair as his only little hello, gently taking my hair out of his hands I forced a smile and followed them inside.

"Food sounds great."

Chase's parents were warm and inviting. They were more than happy to take the babbling toddlers and let their parents have some time off.

The town was so small that it only took a five-minute ride in his dad's truck to get us to the bar and grill. When we stepped inside the small, simple restaurant I saw a girl with deadly dark hair wave to us. Chase perked up and motioned for us to follow him. He quickly introduced us. I was immediately intimidated. She was gorgeous. The red ribbon in her hair stuck out against the sea of black. The innocence of the bow contrasted with the tattoo's all over her exposed skin. It made her slightly more approachable. I shook the beautiful woman's hand. Her smile was huge and friendly. I relaxed. For some reason I thought she'd be rude.

"Cotton, this is Dita, Derek's girlfriend. Dita, Cotton. She's..."

"Single!" She declared, giving him a look. He gave a light laugh but took his seat beside the model worthy woman. Her dark hair contrasted with her pale skin and naturally full red lips, making her look almost like otherworldly. Her brown eyes were big and doll like, which paired well with her small frame. Despite her striking features she seemed to not really care about how she looked. Her clothes were slightly baggy and simple, and she had barely any makeup on if any. I wished I could look that effortlessly flawless.

"Sure. She's just got two men desperate for any shred of attention she'll give them," Chase added with an eye roll.

"I do not. Max is just a friend."

"Sure, and Adrian is just my roommate."

"Enough about me. I'm boring. Dita, you're my guest for the next few days? Weeks?" She dismissed Chase's comment with a wave and turned her attention to me. I shrugged my shoulders.

"I guess? I would appreciate a place to stay until I figure out what's going on." My stomach rolled again thinking about Derek. She smiled again and I forced myself not to dwell on what was going on.

"Well any friend of Chase and Adrian's is a friend of mine. Come on, let's get drinks and some food. I'm starving."

A waitress came and took our orders and only when she returned with the first round of beer did someone mention the reason I was here.

"So, Derek's in some trouble. Do you know what is going on?" Renee asked bluntly. I nodded.

"I saw the woman's statement. Derek told me it's not true. Do you know anything I don't?" I asked, silently pleading for her to tell me he's innocent. She shook her head sadly.

"Not really. Derek is swearing up and down that she's lying. They plan on making a statement about it. Last thing I heard was that they were trying to find proof that he's innocent. I don't know how, but they are trying."

I let out a deep breath. Well, that's something. If he was adamant about proving his innocence, then maybe her story wasn't true. I had to stay positive. Nothing was proven yet.

"Well, Adrian said it's a red flag that she refuses to go to the police. But there are a million reasons why a victim wouldn't want to do so. Too much victim blaming. I think all we can do is let this play out. Wait by the sidelines," Chase added. I bit my lip. I didn't want to wait for answers. I wanted the truth now.

"Social media is a powerful but horrible thing. I wouldn't worry about it," Cotton added. I turned to her, eyebrow raised. She shrugged. "People like to raise their pitchforks at anything these days. People also like to use other people's celebrity status for personal gain."

"What would anyone gain from this?"

"Exposure, followers, revenge. Just watch in the next few days what this woman does with her new platform. That will tell you the truth."

She tipped her beer to us and shrugged again.

"Been there, done that. Being famous is completely overrated."

There was a pause before Chase brightened.

"Speaking of celebrity boyfriends, let's talk about yours."

"Oh my God, he's not my boyfriend!" Cotton squealed. Her mouth was turned down in a scowl but her eyes shone with laughter.

"Who?" I asked. Renee and Chase turned to me.

"Emile Dahl," they said in unison. Cotton crossed her arms over her breasts and sat back with a sigh. I laughed.

"I just saw him. You're the girl he's obsessed with?"

Cotton was not amused. She glared at us.

"Unfortunately," she sighed and lifted her beer to her lips, downing the rest of it and slamming the bottle on the table. "Emile and I... have a long history."

Renee and Chase laughed like they'd heard this a million times. I eyed her curiously. So, this was the woman who had captured Emile's heart. I could see why.

A waitress came and took our orders. I didn't have much of an appetite but ordered some chicken fingers and fries anyways. The three of them kept the conversation alive with funny stories and things they'd read and watched. I chimed in when prompted but my mind was still on Derek. He still wasn't answering my phone calls.

At the end of the meal Cotton invited us back to her place for more drinks and dessert. The three of them had already had at least three or four beers, so I volunteered to take us there despite never having been to her home. We stopped back at the Wilson's to grab my bags, and moments later we were headed to Cotton's place.

Thankfully it wasn't a difficult trip. She only lived a few miles away from everyone else. It was dark so I couldn't see much of the outside, but I noticed that she had a humongous flower garden in the front yard. I was sure in the daylight it was gorgeous.

When we got there, Chase and Cotton went right to her kitchen and began pulling out large glasses and spoons. Renee and I sat in the living room politely waiting. I glanced at my phone and put it away with disappointment. No missed calls.

The pair returned with glasses full of ice cream and a root beer flavored beer. They plopped down on the recliners around us and relaxed. We poured the beer into the ice cream and made tipsy root beer floats.

"Okay, real talk. Derek. Dita, do you think he did it?" Chase asked bluntly. I almost choked on my ice cream. Taking time to swallow, I then answered him.

"I don't know. I don't want to think he'd do something like that. That's not the man I know. But on the other hand, that's a serious accusation for someone to make. He could lose his job."

"Do you think he cheated on you, told her it was a one-time thing, and then she said this to get back at him?" Renee said quickly. I whipped my head towards her with surprise.

"I didn't before. Now I do, thanks for that," I said sharply. She wasn't helping my crazy mind right now. She apologized and started in on her ice cream.

"Adrian said he thinks she's lying. He never saw him with the girl in question," Chase said reassuringly.

"If it's true, what are you going to do?" Cotton said in a much softer tone than my friends. I blinked. That was a good question.

"I don't know. If it's true, then he's been lying to me for weeks. That with the assault, I don't think it would be wise to stay together. I'll probably move out of the house. Find an apartment or something. It's hard to think about right now. I feel like I'm giving in to all the rumors and not giving him a chance to explain, but shouldn't he have said something by now?"

The room fell silent. They all agreed with me but didn't want to say so. Great.

"Okay, we gotta change topics. Until we find out the truth or something new, we won't bring him back up." Renee gave us a scout's honor salute. "Cotton, I demand you tell us about Emile. The first time you met, the last time you talked, I don't care. Give us something!" She giggled.

Cotton rolled her eyes, but she was smiling.

"Fine, okay. What do you want to know?"

"Tell us how you met," Chase suggested. She pursed her lips.

"The very, very first time? Or like when we realized that what we had was more than just friendship?"

"Both?" Renee asked.

"I met Emile when I was eight. He walked into my flower garden."

"That's boring. Let's hear the juicy stuff. Fast forward!" Chase laughed.

"Okay, well we found each other the second time at a bookstore. My brother Tod and I were traveling artists. He had found a tattoo artist who agreed to let him be his apprentice in the town, so we rented a place while he earned his license. I was bored one day and decided to walk into the local used bookstore down the street. He was working there. I was looking for a particular book and he found it right away. We clicked immediately, just like we had when we were little. Emile and I have always had a mutual love of literature."

"Emile likes to read?" I asked. Granted I had only met him in person once, but he never struck me as someone who read for enjoyment.

"Oh, very much so. He's a collector. He had thousands of books at one time. We used to spend our time with my head in his lap while he read to me. Or vice versa. We went through so many books." She sighed and a gentle smile rested on her face with the memory. A small smile of my own creeped onto my face. It was obvious, despite her vehement denial, that she was still very much in love with him.

"Did you ever think he was going to be famous one day?" Chase asked. She nodded.

"I never doubted it. He could pick up and learn any instrument with ease. He taught me how to read sheet music. We used to play guitar together. Reading is his hobby, but music is his passion. I expected nothing less of him."

"So why did you guys break up then?" I asked. Emile's brief and vague explanation this morning came to mind. I tried to remember his exact words but with the alcohol mixed with everything else going wrong in my life his words were lost to me.

"Tod got his license. He wanted to travel for his work and I had no choice but to follow him. I wanted to learn the craft too."

"So, it was purely coincidental that you set up a permanent shop in L.A.?" Renee asked. Cotton nodded.

"Wicked Little Tats? Man, I haven't been there in years. I hear it's doing well."

"I was just there for this!" I pulled down my shirt to show her my chest tattoo. "Becca Boyce did it," I told her. She grinned ear to ear.

"Becca was my apprentice! She's such a sweetheart. I remember her and Boogie were always flirting with each other but never did anything about it. They were so cute."

"You're avoiding the question," Renee accused. Cotton rolled her eyes and sighed.

"I hadn't talked to Emile in almost five years when I opened the shop. I mean, I knew he was becoming hugely successful in the music industry, but I had absolutely no intention of reconnecting. I had already broken his heart once. It wasn't fair to do it twice."

"What made you so sure you would do it again?" I asked, curious. She shrugged.

"Emile wants more than I can give. We've always been in different places in our lives, if that makes sense. He wants one thing. I want something else. By the time I change my mind to want his thing he has flipped and only wants my thing. I don't know if we'll ever match up."

Suddenly there was a sharp knock on the front door. Everyone froze and Cotton got up to open it. We all sat silently as we tried to listen in. I smirked when I heard Emile's distinct voice. Man, he moved just as fast as we did.

"Emile," Cotton sighed deeply. "What are you doing here?"

"I need to give you something."

There was a significant amount of silence before Cotton stepped back into the house.

"Thank you," she said before closing the door in his face.

We sat in the living room staring at the entryway as she came back to us. Tears were streaming silently down her face as she cupped something in her hands.

"What did he bring you?" I asked. I wondered if this was what he needed the key for. He sure got here quickly. Why didn't she invite him in? She plopped down on the couch. Her face was blank. She had been rendered speechless.

Renee reached out and gently pried her hands open. The three of us leaned forward to examine her palms. Inside her cupped hands was an interesting looking crystal flower. It reminded me of a morning glory, only it was deep red, almost like blood, and the petals were wavy. Nevertheless, it was beautiful.

"What kind of flower is that?" Chase asked. Cotton's lower lip trembled. She set her open hands down in her lap.

"It's a gloxinia. I was tending to them when we first met. He wanted to give me one then, but I told him if he plucked that flower from it's home and killed it, I'd never forgive him." Her mouth lifted into a smile as more silent tears began sliding down her face.

"He brought you one that'll never die," I sighed.

"It's a pretty flower," Chase offered. More silent tears slid down her face. I couldn't tell if she was upset or happy. I think it was a mix of both. She nodded.

"They stand for love at first sight."

Silence fell over the room as we let Cotton cry. No one really knew how to react. Suddenly, she stood. We all looked up at her as she started towards the front door. She turned and wiped the tears off her perfect face. "Dita, go ahead and stay. You all are more than welcome to stay the night. I've gotta go."

"Where are you going?" Chase asked, standing up. Cotton held up her hand to stop him as she opened the door and took a step out.

"I'm going to go tell Emile I still love him."

Chapter Sixteen

ALL I WANTED

DEREK

I STARED at the screen and reread the statement I was just about to release. What a fucking shitshow.

To my fans,

Yesterday a young woman who was on tour with my band this summer accused me of sexually assaulting her. These are words that I nor anyone should take lightly.

The night in question, I was at the bar. She did introduce herself. However, that is where the truth to her story ends. Several times I tried to excuse myself from her advances and when she attempted to kiss me, I pushed her away.

I have struggled with how to express how I am feeling at this time, but for now I just want to apologize to anyone who was hurt by these accusations, and just know that I will not stop until I can prove my innocence.

Thank you,
D. T.

The whole letter felt forced and gross. Honestly, I didn't really write it. Sam got our PR person to. All I had to do was push send. I tapped the button, watched for the notification to pop up that informed me that it was uploaded, and then shut the app down. Dita's face popped up as my wallpaper and I sighed. She deserved so much better.

Since the blog post came out, Sam insisted I change hotels, but not go home. I was registered under a fake name and my bandmates were recommended to stay away for the time being.

They were going home today. Well, back to their families. Cleo was heading back to L.A., but Mark and Adrian were headed to Louisiana. I was staying in Tennessee.

Sam sat with me around the clock while on his phone attempting damage control. There was a petition going around to get me kicked out of the band. Everyone assured me that it wasn't going to happen, but social pressure had a way of ending innocent people's careers.

It didn't matter if either side had proof or not at this point. I was guilty by her word alone. I honestly didn't know if my career or relationship with Dita would ever recover from this.

I held my phone in my hands and fought back the urge to call her. I almost called her about 30 times yesterday, but I couldn't talk to her right now. Not in a rational way. I was upset, confused, and scared. Anything I said to her or anybody right now would do more damage than help the situation. I needed to wait to clear my innocence before reaching out.

I spent the rest of the day pacing the suite in one room, while Sam did the same thing in the other one. I ordered room service even though I had no appetite. I had them bring up enough alcohol to intoxicate a horse.

Eventually Sam came in and told me that he was leaving for a bit, but security was sitting outside my door to assure that no one came in or came out. He emphasized the out. I wasn't to leave this suite until he gave me permission.

"Is there anything I can get for you while you wait this out? A guitar, a book, some video games?"

"How long do you expect me to be here?" I asked. There was no way I could stay trapped here for much longer. I did nothing wrong. This wasn't fair.

"Just a few more days. I'm working on some stuff. Anything?"

I sighed and thought about it. If I had to hide, I might as well make the best out of it.

"My acoustic guitar and a notebook please."

Sam smiled.

"Ah, gonna try your hand at writing some music huh?"

I shook my head.

"Nah, just want to write down my thoughts. Maybe it'll help clear some things up."

He gave me a thumbs up and left quickly. My phone rang and I dove for it. Dita's beautiful smile popped up. I stared at it. Did I dare answer it? Was I in a good frame of mind right now to talk to her? Her cries of accusations yesterday completely shattered me. They repeated in my head on a loop. I watched the phone ring and let it go to voicemail.

When my phone pinged with a text message however, I did check it. It was from Cleo. It was a link to a website and lots of exclamation marks. I clicked on it quickly and saw why she was sent it to me.

I read it slowly, trying to process what I was seeing. This had to be a joke.

Hello new and old followers,
    As many of you know, I recently came out as a sexual assault

victim of Derek Turtle, bassist of rock band Maria Maria. I knew when I exposed the truth of what happened that night that my career as a backup dancer in hollywood was gone.

After the post went up, a few hours later I was promptly fired from my job. I attempted to call some of my friends in the biz, in hopes of getting a new job when I got back to L.A. Most would not take my call and the ones that did told me they could not help me. I am essentially blacklisted from ever working in my chosen profession.

I do not make this request lightly. I have spent as much time agonizing over my next steps as an artist as I had about revealing the truth about what happened that night, and I have come to the conclusion that it's necessary for me to make a career shift.

As some of my personal friends know, I have always been passionate about film and being in front of the screen as much as behind the screen. For some time now I have been working with screenwriters and other professionals to make my dream come to life. Now that I have nothing but time on my hands, I am going to devote my career to directing and starring in my first film, titled 'Precious June'.

I am asking anyone who is interested in supporting me and my dreams to click the link below and donate what you can to help get this movie off the ground.

I want to take a moment to thank each and every one of you who has reached out to show their support for me and my situation. I know it's unfortunate and triggering to some, but just know that just like I have your support, you have mine. In time, hopefully we can all heal from this mess, and people like Derek can be forever stopped.

All my Love,
Carly.

What the fuck did I just read? I sat down on the couch and

read it once more. She was using this as a crowd fund? And I was the monster. What a joke. I rubbed my face, noting the significant amount of stubble I was growing. I needed another drink.

I stopped using a glass a few hours ago, so I took a swig straight from the bottle of whiskey they had brought up. No sooner had I relaxed into the couch did the alerts start coming. Another long drink was needed.

I wasn't in the mood to answer any of them. Once they realized the messages were being ignored, they began calling. Groaning I picked up my phone and shot a quick message to the band's group chat. Yes, I knew about Carly's newest stunt. No, I didn't know what I was going to do yet. Yes, Dita has tried calling. No, I haven't answered. Yes, I am getting drunk. No, I'm not going to jump out the window. I was going to be a good boy and sit and wait for Sam.

I shut my phone off and flung it across the room like a deflated football. It hit the wall and I heard a crack that I assumed was the screen. Screw it, I was so sick of it going off. I hoped it was completely broken. I reached for the bottle again but was surprised to find it almost empty. I swashed it around for a moment before bringing the bottle to my lips. I hiccuped as I took gulp after gulp of the burning liquid. I didn't stop drinking until the bottle was empty.

The room was silent for the first time in hours, and I closed my eyes, enjoying the silence. However, after only a minute pause my phone began ringing again and I let out a cry of anguish. Would this ever stop? Bottle still in my hand I threw it as hard as I could towards the offensive ringing. It hit the wall almost exactly where the phone had. The sound of the glass bottle breaking however, was much louder.

I couldn't get away from the noise. Rolling off the couch, I stood up and stumbled to the bathroom, slamming the door. I turned the shower on and stepped inside, clothes still on. I closed my eyes and let the freezing water soak me down to the bone. I just needed to get away from the constant beeping. The ever reminder that I royally screwed up my entire life.

Eventually my knees buckled and I sank to the floor. I curled up in a ball and tried to drone out everything I possibly could. Sam found me sometime later. He ran into the bathroom and I heard his muffled screaming as he opened the glass door and shut the water off. I didn't move. The alcohol had completely saturated my brain. I couldn't respond to him if I wanted to.

"Jesus, Derek! Are you okay? Can I get some help in here? I don't know if he's breathing!"

I felt a pair of hands on me, rolling me over. I groaned but refused to open my eyes. Suddenly a second set of hands were moving under me and I felt myself being lifted off the tile floor with ease. I heard someone call for a paramedic. I was still too gone to respond with anything other than grunts.

All around me people were shouting and talking frantically. I heard phones ringing, one right after another but was unable to respond. I was placed on something soft. It had to have been a bed. The feel of my soaking wet body against the dry comforter made me moan.

"He's alive. Thank God. How long until someone gets here? Should we get him to throw up?" I heard Sam speaking quickly.

"No. We need to sit him up and get him warm. He's freezing." A strong voice I tried to place but couldn't told him. Like a rag doll, I was lifted up and my clothes were being ripped off me. Whoever was moving me was swearing as he struggled with my heavy body. I was completely dead weight. Add the weight from the water, I knew it was a bitch.

"Has he ever done this before?" The voice asked.

"No. I mean, they all drink, but nothing like this. Shit, we should have had someone sitting with him. I never thought he'd…" Sam was cut off by voices coming into the room.

A blanket was wrapped around me and I was being lifted again. I was trying my hardest to stay conscious, but I couldn't anymore. I felt arms place me on a stretcher and Sam's voice close to my face.

"It's gonna be alright buddy, we're not losing you tonight."

I tried to open my eyes, but the effort was too much. Everything went black.

I woke up in a hospital bed surrounded by half a dozen people. The only light in the room was the dim one above my head. I blinked, trying to get a grip on my bearings. What happened?

I raised my hands to my face and cringed when I accidentally tugged on the IV in my hand. I hadn't realized it was there. I heard a familiar sniffle and I sat up sharply. Cleo was here.

I shook my head, trying to adjust my eyes to the darkness of the room.

"He's awake," she sniffled.

I looked around and saw all of my friends. I counted. Adrian, Chase, Ethan, Cleo, Mark, Renee. My heart completely shattered in that moment. She wasn't here.

"I'm gonna go get Sam," I heard Mark mumble as he shuffled out of the room. I knew my face was showing how destroyed I was. The tears were coming without my consent. My lip was trembling, and I turned my head away from my friends.

"Derek, what happened?" I felt a soft, manicured hand on my arm. I turned my angry eyes on Cleo. They weren't intended for her, but she was the one asking.

"What the fuck do you think happened?" I snapped. My

throat was on fire. I desperately needed water. I cringed. She pulled away quickly as if I had slapped her.

"We're looking for her," she said. She wiped her wet cheeks and nodded, as if reassuring herself more than me. "She'll be here."

"What do you mean, looking for her?" I said through gritted teeth. Cleo reached out again and pushed back my hair. Her eyes were full of pain. Pain I had caused. My anger started to deflate. Once again, my selfish actions hurt the people around me.

"She was staying at my friends. You knew that. When we went to get her Cotton had said she had left sometime in the night. She's not answering her phone. We think it's dead."

I closed my eyes and shook my head. The phone wasn't dead. Just her love for me. I knew Dita better than anyone. Running was her MO. She panicked, couldn't take it, and ran. Guess I should have known better than to trust her with my heart. Mark came back in with Sam and a nurse. I glanced at my friends but focused on the nurse coming to check my chart and vitals.

"Well hello Mr. Turtle. We're glad to see you awake. You scared a lot of people last night."

I only stared at her. She smiled and I hated her for it. How could anyone be happy right now. In less than 48 hours my life had been completely destroyed.

"Do you want some water? Your throat probably hurts."

I nodded.

"Did they pump my stomach?" I asked, my voice barely above a whisper. It hurt so much to speak.

"Nope. We actually don't do that anymore. We intubated you and then put a tube down your throat all the way down to decompress your stomach. Then you were on oxygen until you started to come to. How do you feel besides your throat?"

I shrugged. How was I supposed to feel? I felt like shit. Inside and out.

"I'll bring you some water," she said, ignoring my shitty attitude.

"You didn't do this on purpose, did you?" Adrian asked. I looked up at him. Was he serious right now? He was the last one I wanted to talk to at this very moment. I didn't even bother responding to his stupid question.

"Shut up, Adrian." Cleo came to my rescue, her hand returning to my hair. I knew she meant well but I jerked my head away. She frowned and dropped her hand.

"We know it was an accident. It's the stupid media going wild with rumors." She rolled her eyes. I groaned. I could only imagine. They probably said this was just an attention thing. Was it? I don't even know. I could barely remember anything from the last few days.

"We're going to make another statement. You'll be fine. They said once you're stable, they'll let you go," Sam told me. I glared at him. What was the point? So I could hole up in some hotel room while some stranger continued to ruin my life?

"We know you didn't do what she's saying," Cleo said softly, reading my thoughts. I turned to her. If only the world could see that. I felt my eyes growing heavy with tears again. I hated this. I was a mess.

"Do you want us to leave for a little bit? I can try Dita's phone again."

I nodded to Cleo and everyone quickly shuffled out. Sam was the last one out. He gave me a tight, awkward smile and left with the others. Only when I heard the door close softly behind them did I break down.

I let myself cry for her. I didn't blame her for running away, but the truth still stung. I thought our love was more than just a passing fancy. I felt that way, how could she not?

I sobbed until I could barely breathe. I couldn't figure out what was worse, the pain in my chest or my throat. I don't think I could talk if I wanted to anymore. I was just as broken as I felt.

Eventually there was a knock on my door and I wiped my eyes and cheeks. I was such a crybaby. Why was I acting like this? I had never cried like this over a girl. It was embarrassing.

The nurse came in with a styrofoam cup complete with bendy straw. She gave me an awkward smile that told me she had heard me sobbing like a teenage girl whose prom date just dumped her right in front of everyone. I was suddenly exhausted. I didn't have the energy or voice to make a smart comment. She left me to wallow in my misery.

I had hoped everyone else would leave but I knew they were all most likely sitting right outside of the door, waiting for me to stop bawling. When I had finally been reduced to only a few sniffles here and there, Cleo came in and wrapped her small arms around me.

Her intentions were pure, but they only caused me to start crying again. This time my tears came silently. It was easy to comfort someone when they had their happily ever after. Ethan wasn't going anywhere. Lucky girl.

I don't know how much time had passed, but eventually I was calm and no longer hiccuping. Despite downing four large cups of water I still couldn't speak, which was well enough. I didn't have anything to say.

Cleo asked me if I wanted guests and I shook my head no. She didn't ask if she could stay, she just did. I was grateful she didn't ask, because I would have told her to go. I wanted her here, but I also wanted to be alone. Misery loves company, I guess.

She was my voice while I rested. People knocked every so often and she would go to the door and answer any questions anyone had. The only people she let in were doctors and nurses.

The doctor informed me that I was going to stay another night for monitoring and to pump me full of fluids and vitamins. Apparently eating junk food and drinking for months on end had my body lacking more than a few necessary nutrients.

I didn't argue his decision. Despite having my saline bag changed twice since I've been conscious, I still felt like complete garbage. I was offered jello and popsicles, which I ate three of each. They then brought me chicken broth for dinner, and I managed to get a few spoonfuls in before I lost my appetite again.

Despite not having a cell phone any longer and the TV being kept off, I couldn't stop feeling the pressure of what was going on outside of this room. What were people saying about me? Was I still a monster? I didn't want people to start pitying me or turning to my side just because of this. This wasn't a cry for attention. Honestly, I just wasn't thinking. If I hadn't been so stressed out, I would have known better than to drink as much as I did.

When the sun finally dropped below the skyline, I croaked out that I was going to sleep. Cleo frowned when the nurse came in and gave me something to help me get there faster. I knew she didn't want to go but staying here while I slept was pointless. She needed to get some rest too.

I squeezed her hand and gave her my best half-hearted smile. It was weak but she returned the smile as she leaned forward to brush my curls off my forehead one last time. She kissed my forehead quickly.

"I'm glad you're still here." I watched her brush a tear off of her cheek as she turned and left the room. I relaxed into my pillow and closed my eyes. I heard a nurse come in right before I fell into a deep slumber and pull the string to my light, enclosing me in darkness.

I was awoken by the door to my room being thrust open and hitting the wall with a hard thump! I jerked my head up and blinked rapidly. What was going on? My head was fuzzy from the drugs. Mark came and shoved his phone under my nose. I moved back, pushing it away but he insisted.

"You're saved. Watch."

Confused, I took the phone he was shaking at me and looked down. He had a video pulled up. I hesitated before I pushed play. I gulped hard when it started.

The video was dark at first and started with loud music and people chattering. Whoever was filming moved the camera around the room and that's when I recognized the location. That was the bar from that night. The one in the hotel. Holy shit.

The cameraman was talking to the people he was filming. Telling them to wave to the camera or tell him what they're drinking, nothing of real importance. He was traveling around the room, filming the party. I watched the screen unblinking. My entire life hinged on what this guy caught on video.

"Ooh, and what is this? Is hot shot rock star getting a little on the side?" He said and that's when he turned and zoomed right into me being shoved into the wall. I watched in shock as Carly pressed herself into me as I continued to shake my head and try to gently remove her from me. The video was crystal clear. That was my face. This was it. *Proof.*

The guy stopped moving the camera and kept filming the two of us.

"Ooh, shot down Carly! I'm not going to let you live this down."

I watched in silent horror as she leaned up and attempted to kiss me. I reached up and shoved her chest. Her breasts. Fuck.

The camera man was laughing as he watched me storm off and then return back to Carly, who was screaming at everyone to stop staring at her. She was mortified. He continued filming her meltdown up until she saw him holding what was presumably his phone. He swore and then the video stopped.

I stared at the dark screen, mood deflated. I did touch her. It wasn't intentional, but I still touched her. The media was going to slaughter me. I was done for. I handed Mark his phone back and looked around for my cup. The nurse thankfully had brought me a fresh cup some time ago. I gulped it down before I attempted to speak. My throat was still raw.

"I guess that's it," I said with the finality of a closing coffin. He gave me a confused look.

"What? No, dude, she approached you. She was grabbing you, despite you continually trying to leave. Everything she said was a lie. This video is everywhere. She already recanted. People are already apologizing to you and the band. They are demanding justice for you and praying for your recovery."

"Recovery?" I croaked, confused. Mark gave me an apologetic smile.

"We told Sam not to, but PR insisted we say something. Everyone knows what happened. But that only solidifies your case. You knew you were innocent and the fact that people were wanting to murder you caused you to.... do what you did."

I shook my head. It didn't feel right. None of this felt like I was free. I made the motion I had made in the video when I pushed her away. Mark frowned, understanding where I was getting at.

"It's kind of a gray area. You weren't grabbing for her chest. It was clear that you were trying to get away and her actions were the unsolicited ones. I can ask Sam to get our lawyer's opinion if you want."

I nodded and he patted my shoulder.

"Don't worry bud. I really think you're going to end up on top with this one." He straightened to start out the door. I gulped again, welcoming the pain as I called out to him.

"Dita?" My voice came out hoarse and barely above a whisper.

Mark stopped and didn't turn back around to face me for a long moment. When he did, the look on his face deflated any good mood I was developing. He shook his head.

"Nothing. We still can't find her. I'll call Cleo again."

I sunk back into my pillow and let him leave. Soon after he left the rest of the band, Sam, and the nurse returned. Everyone was all smiles and full of cheery conversation. I felt the exact opposite. I couldn't just get on board with their assumptions that this was all over. How could it be that easy?

"People are talking about us playing that last show. I wouldn't mind finishing out the tour as intended," Cleo shrugged, not looking up from her phone.

"I'd be up for that. Show everyone that we aren't phased by this. The only problem is, everyone has already gone back home. Are they really gonna come back for one last concert?"

"Or even if they'll let us have the dancers. They probably won't want to deal with it. I can't imagine they'd want them back," Adrian smirked. I glared at him and he looked away quickly. Did he honestly think this whole thing was my fault? If I had the energy I would have reached out and socked him.

"You're right. If anything, they'll let us play the venue bare bones. Just us, maybe some local bands. That could be fun still," Cleo perked up. My bandmates looked up at me expectantly. I really didn't feel like getting up on a stage in front of people who less than 24 hours ago wanted me dead. They could all kiss my ass. I wanted to say that, but instead shrugged noncommittally.

"We can figure it out later, once you're out of here and back home." Mark gave me a pat on the leg and I grimaced. I didn't want to go home. Well, not home home. I was ready to leave this bed as soon as possible.

Eventually the doctor released me after I assured him that I wasn't suicidal or going to drink anytime soon. The thought of alcohol made me sick. A cigarette on the other hand, sounded fantastic. As soon as I stepped outside, I bummed one off of Adrian. I popped it in my mouth and took a long drag. Everyone stood around me expectantly. I raised an eyebrow. "What?"

"What do you want to do now?" Cleo asked. The cab came right as I was putting my smoke out and we climbed in quickly. Sam told the driver to take us to the airport.

Although everyone made a point to keep the conversation moving as to not allow any uncomfortable silences, I chose to keep quiet. Sure, everything was alright in their worlds now, but mine was still collapsing around me.

"Does anyone have my cell phone?" I asked. Sam snickered.

"We found it on the floor, with a small dent in the wall where you must have thrown it. Screen is shattered and it isn't turning on."

I sighed. Go figure. Even if she was trying to contact me, she couldn't. I sat back in my seat and sulked the rest of the way there. Once we got to the airport and checked in, they announced that due to a storm somewhere we were being delayed. My day was getting better and better. It was only a few hours, so there was nothing to do but sit around and wait.

While everyone else sat in the first class lounge and hung out, I decided to take a few laps around the large building. I couldn't just sit there. I needed to be doing something. My mind was going crazy.

The walk that was supposed to clear my head only seemed to make my anxiety and depression worse. Everywhere I looked I saw her. Well, not her but memories of her and I. A little girl carrying a pink bear, two girls taking pictures with an old Polaroid camera, a man with two crates at his feet, cats inside of them. I was going to drive myself insane if I kept doing this to myself. I was turning every small, obscure thing into something Dita related. I saw a guy scratch his chest and my heart cried, thinking about the tattoo Dita and I shared in that same location.

On my second loop around I stopped by the small, over-priced arcade and found the claw machine. It only took cards, go figure. Airports were a joke. Despite the price per game, I pulled out my wallet and slid my card into the machine. I was surprised when I was able to successfully capture and claim a yellow seahorse.

The big red button next to my joystick flashed, asking me if I wanted to play another game. I tapped it quickly and moments later claimed a giant green worm. The bin was full, so I pulled them out, setting them on the ground by my feet, and pressed the button again.

I made myself focus on the claw machine instead of my actual problems. Soon I was lost in concentration and wasn't dwelling on how every animal I snagged was like my girl. *My Girl.* I guess she wasn't mine anymore. Just as I was leaning down to the bin to retrieve three bears, I heard familiar voices behind me.

"He's here! Hey, over here!" Adrian shouted. I turned around, animals in my arms. My bandmates were sprinting over to me from all directions. My eyes went wide with confusion as Cleo waved her cell phone up in the air wildly. I stood still as they reached me. Cleo saw my prizes and rolled her eyes. With one quick swipe of her hand she slapped my arms down, bears flying everywhere. She shoved the phone at me.

"It's Dita," she said, out of breath. My heart jumped into my throat. What? I snatched the phone out of her hands and put it to my ear.

"Hello?"

"Derek, my phone died while I was on the road. Where are you?"

"I'm in Tennessee, I'm stuck at the airport. Where are you?"

"I'm back in L.A. When will you get here?"

"Around ten, are you mad at me?"

"No. I saw the video. You were telling the truth. I shouldn't have doubted you. I'm sorry."

"It's fine. Seriously. I don't care. I just want to come home and have you waiting for me there. That's all that matters." There was a long pause. My heart stopped beating the entire length of her silence. "Will you be there?" I gulped.

"Yes and no. I am not at the house right now. I'm going to need you to come get me."

"Okay," I said, confused. "Where are you?"

"County Jail. Bring bail money."

Chapter Seventeen

MOAN

DITA

"Dita Fox, you're free to go."

I stood when the officer came to unlock the cell and escort me me out of the jail. She went through a door and popped back into view through the window on the other side. She handed me my cell phone and car keys with a smirk.

"Matching mug shots. Couple goals." The sarcasm was thick, but I smiled right back. I leaned over to see the photo on her computer screen she was referring to. Hm, not that bad. Despite Carly's blood splattered across my face it was a pretty good picture. Actually, the blood made it better. I looked like a proud badass. I mean, I guess I was.

"Matching?"

She rolled her eyes as she left the room and returned back to my side. She stood back and motioned for me to follow her out to the lobby.

"I checked in your boyfriend a few months ago. Same stupid grin on your faces."

I laughed and shrugged. I didn't really care about her judgmental opinion. I would one hundred percent do it again.

"Wait, how do you know who my boyfriend is?"

"Honey, you are all over the internet right now. They've got you on camera, from start to finish. Broke the girl's nose."

I didn't say anything. I didn't want to incriminate myself further. I knew I had to be facing some time. Or a hefty fine at least. She raised an eyebrow at me, but I simply blinked. Did she expect me to feel guilty? I didn't. Not one bit.

We went through those doors and my stomach filled with butterflies as my eyes settled on the man who had my heart forever. He gave me that amazingly crooked grin of his and opened his arms for me to gladly run into. I threw myself into them. He lifted me up and spun me around. I heard the officer snicker, but we ignored her.

I inhaled his perfect Derek smell and pulled on a curl, letting it bounce back to the comfort of his head. He was here. In the flesh, here. I stared up into those eyes that could start wars. He set me down and my arms went from his waist to his neck. I looked up at him and leaned up to kiss him with everything I had. His movements echoed mine in intensity. We both felt the distance we'd had for so long dissipate. We were finally together, for good.

"Can I still be all yours?" He asked me. I laughed.

"Will you please be all mine?"

"Alright, it's time to get a move on. It's almost midnight."

I turned back to her, releasing Derek only slightly. I had been so entranced by him that I had completely forgotten where we were and who was watching.

"Do I have to go to court or anything?" I asked, realizing she hadn't explained how my charges really worked. This was my first time in the clink. She smirked.

"Girl changed her mind about pressing charges. Looks like you're off the hook."

"What? So why did I have to stay so long?"

"We just got the call. The prosecutor could care either way. It's your lucky day."

I looked back at Derek and nodded.

"It really is."

I thanked the police officer before taking my boyfriend's hand and rushing out the door to freedom. It felt like we were free in more than one way. For the first time ever, we were truly free.

I was greeted by the fresh air and cold wind. I shivered. I had been wearing jean shorts and one of Derek's band tee's when I left the house. Derek saw me and frowned. He didn't have a jacket to give me, so he hurried me along. I giggled as we started moving faster. I couldn't help it. Having him here, holding my hand- it felt surreal. Every moment with him was like this. It's what made him so amazing. We walked across the parking lot to my car where I slid into the passenger seat.

I couldn't keep the perma-grin off my face. I didn't want to let go of his hand to get in the car, but he traded his hand for a kiss on my cheek. I laughed when he closed the door and practically sprinted to the other side to hop into the driver's seat. He turned the car on and quickly took my hand again.

"You grabbed my car. So, you went to the plaza," I said, wondering if he saw the ice cream shop. I had been told that there had been no actual damage to the business, thank goodness. I didn't need more charges added to my rap sheet. Although I was told that they respectfully asked me not to return to their establishment. I felt that was pretty fair. I had run in, grabbed a chick by her hair, and beat the living shit out of her in front of all of their paying patrons.

"You're amazing," he chuckled.

"I know," I said proudly. He laughed again.

"Her nose is broken."

"I know." She deserved it. "Maybe a nose job will be the next thing she crowd funds."

He smiled but said nothing, squeezing my hand tighter instead. I closed my eyes and relaxed into my seat. I hadn't really slept in three days. The bus ride back to L.A. was long and uncomfortable. It drained the rest of my bank account. Perfect timing, I guess.

Once I was back in town I went straight to the house I had been planning to share with Derek and looked around. Was this where I was supposed to be? Was this right? Was me being here the right thing to do? I wandered around the house, picking up random items trying to force myself to feel something. Something that told me to stay. It wasn't until I stepped into what would be his den when he got home that I found what I was looking for.

I looked around the full but bare room. I had forgotten that he had told me about a huge order of things he had bought for the house. I hadn't even bothered to see what they were. They weren't labeled with anything special. Suddenly suspicious I tore into the first one. Shoving my hands through all the bubble wrap I pulled out a plaque with a rubber fish nailed to it.

A smile somehow got through my stone cold mood. I pushed the little red button under the fish and it came to life, singing a song about beer. Something shifted in the box, so I set the fish down and reached my hands back in, pulling out another one.

I went through every single box and by the time I had pulled out every one I was sitting on the floor surrounded by singing big mouth bass' laughing and sobbing simultaneously. This was the sign I was looking for.

Eventually I stood up, put on his favorite playlist, and went to find a hammer and nails. Only once every single fish had a home on the wall was I able to sleep comfortably.

The next day I decided that I had to fight alongside him. Things weren't adding up in Carly's description of that night. I got online and searched for an update on the situation. I found tons and tons of people on both sides of the story. A significant amount of people started questioning her case once she posted her crowd fund for the movie.

That pushed people to dive deeper into the incident in question. The more they asked the more defensive she got. She was insisting that everyone was victim blaming and that she didn't need to provide proof. That was her right, after all. I was beginning to feel slightly at a loss. That was until I got a surprise text from my old dance partner, Grant. I hadn't heard from him since I had left the tour.

I opened his message and saw that he had sent a video. I sat for five minutes and watched in horror as my heart was saved. Derek was innocent. He could come home. We could have a life together. We could be happy. *Finally.*

I sat by the pool for hours just wondering what to do next. I couldn't just sit back and let this woman ruin his life. Not when I had the proof sitting in my phone. I had to do something. I had screwed this up enough already. I couldn't just let her win. I ended up passing out on the couch from exhaustion, laptop still on my lap, opened up to her profiles. I was going to find her. She was going to pay for what she was doing to him.

I got dressed that morning, knowing that when I found her it wasn't going to be pleasant. She had posted that she was spending the day with her girlfriends, shopping for a new life, as she put it. That was my boiling point. I snapped. I left that house determined to confront her. She was going to admit what she did for the cameras. I was going to ruin her life just as fast and hard as she had Derek's.

I felt like a creep watching her go from store to store with her friends. I sat at the coffee shop Derek and I favored and watched from the window as she laughed and danced across the strip, collecting bag after bag of goodies to take home and bask in her successful scam. Every bag she added to her arm the more furious I became. I was shaking in my seat.

"Why were you ignoring my calls?" He said suddenly, pulling me from my dark thoughts. I pulled my head back up and looked over at him. I blinked away the sleep my body craved. It could wait.

"My phone really was dead most of the bus trip. But once I got back to our place, I wasn't in the right frame of mind to talk. I knew about the video, but it hadn't leaked yet, so I didn't know how to talk to you about it. Why? You didn't do anything to make things worse did you?" I teased but seeing his reaction to my comment made me stop smiling.

Derek clenched his jaw and his eyes furrowed. Unlacing his hand from mine he put both hands on the wheel and pulled us into an empty parking lot. I hadn't even noticed it. There were no streetlights anywhere. Nor were there any buildings. How did he catch it fast enough to stop?

He parked the car and turned it off. Silence echoed throughout the car for a long moment. My good mood slowly began to fall. What had he done during those three days? I had spent those days trying to repair our relationship, had he been doing the opposite? Finally, he unbuckled himself and turned his entire body to face me. I matched his movements in order to give him my full attention. Everything moving forward depended on his next words.

"No one told you?" He fidgeted with his hands. His head dipped, but then he lifted his eyes to me. It reminded me of a little boy confessing he did something naughty to his teacher. My heart started racing. There's no way he could have made this worse, was there? I had already broken the girl's nose, what more damage could have been done?

"Dita, the day after we talked, I was having a really hard time dealing with everything. I was stuck up in a stupid hotel room with Sam while everyone else went back to their families. I couldn't leave, I wasn't allowed to say anything, and my phone was going off nonstop. Things were getting worse hour by hour and I felt like my entire life was just crumbling around me."

I reached for his hands to stop them. They were stressing me out more than his words were. I nodded, encouragingly.

"I know, it was horrible. What she did to you is unforgivable."

There was a pause as a single tear slid down his cheek. "You really didn't see anything about it?" He seemed confused and hurt by my apparent ignorance.

"About what?"

"I was hospitalized for alcohol poisoning. I almost killed myself by accident."

I pulled back, sitting up straight as if he had just slapped me.

"What? How? Are you okay?" I stared at him, confused. What did he mean 'by accident'? It didn't make sense. He didn't look any different than when I had seen him last. I cringed remembering how I threw my entire weight at him after I was released. That probably didn't help his healing body.

"I just wasn't in a good place and didn't have anyone telling me no. Not that it's any excuse, but I was trying to hide from my problems. I didn't want to deal with it anymore. I was guilty before I could even speak. My career was ruined for no real reason. Because I rejected a girl?" His voice started to rise with frustration. I tried to keep my face relaxed and let him vent.

"So, they took you in to the hospital, was there any lasting damage? Are you going to be alright?" I asked. He shrugged.

"Yeah, I mean my throat was sore and they made me stay a

couple days because I was severely dehydrated and stuff but I'm fine now. It was just kind of like, my rock bottom. I was semi-conscious when Sam found me at the hotel and all I kept thinking was that it didn't really matter if I was dead or not. I had lost everything already, what was the point?"

I reached over and ran my hand across his stubbled cheek. The bone structure so familiar I knew I could identify it if I ever went blind. I would have missed it so much if they hadn't found him in time. My heart would never have healed. Tears stung my eyes as they began to fall quickly and unashamedly.

"I'm sorry I wasn't there. I'm sorry I abandoned you," I said mournfully. This was my fault. If I had just trusted him, he wouldn't have been trying to hurt himself.

He shook his head.

"No, you didn't. I was in trouble for something serious. I don't know how I would react in that situation if I were the other person either. It was an honest accident. I wasn't watching how much I drank. I was using it to mask my pain but wasn't thinking about the consequences. I just wanted to stop thinking. Things couldn't get worse if I was black out drunk."

"Oh Derek," I sighed. My heart ached for this broken man. I had never seen him so vulnerable before. I had thought hearing him crack on the phone was hard, seeing it in person was like a punch to the gut. He chewed on his lip and I pulled him towards me. He let his head dip, but the armrest stopped him from moving closer. Without hesitation I tossed my hair back and swung my leg over the armrest, climbing onto his lap.

He let out a sharp breath as we were suddenly squeezed together. There was hardly any room for us in this position. With a chuckle he reached his hand down and adjusted the seat to allow for us to relax into each other's bodies.

"What are you doing Ms. Fox?"

I wrapped my arms around his neck and he moved his hands to my hips. My fingers moved to play with his curls gently, teasing him with soft pulls.

"I have been waiting patiently Mr. Turtle, and I can't wait any longer," I said, my voice filled with lust. He chuckled.

"Waiting for what?"

My head dipped to kiss his neck. His breath hitched as my lips danced across his sensitive spot. I pulled up for just a second.

"For you to come home. And be mine forever."

With a huge grin he closed his eyes and let me continue my exploration of his body.

"You know you still have blood on your face, right?" He muttered. I shrugged, brushing my hair back.

"I don't care. Do you?"

"No, it's kind of hot."

"Well then, shut up and let me kiss you," I demanded as I began moving my body lower and we both jolted when my ass tapped the horn. It was a short, yet sharp noise that completely took us out of the moment and brought us back to the world around us. We stared at each other for a moment, trying to gauge each other's intentions. Did we dare continue, or did we take the beep as a warning for me to climb back to my side and head home?

Derek's Adam's apple bobbed nervously. I could see in his eyes that he was going to let me take the reins on this one. His body was eager underneath me, but his soft eyes told me that he could wait just a little bit longer. He raised his eyebrows expectantly. Well, what did I want to do?

I grinned and kissed him feverishly.

"You wanna move to the back?" I asked. His eyes grew wide with intrigue and excitement. I waited for a verbal response but instead he adjusted us and pushed me back slightly. I fell back onto the horn again as he quickly ripped off his shirt. I giggled as he shoved the door open with a kick of his foot.

I traced the lines of his flawless chest and abdomen. Marred only by time and ink. He bit his bottom lip when my hands began teasing the edges of his jeans. I looked up at him and he tilted his head, motioning to the back seat.

With quick glances around, we watched a few cars drive by, not slowing down even a fraction. With this place so badly lit I doubted we'd be caught. This parking lot was abandoned, so why not take advantage of it?

Opening the back door, I let him climb in first. I almost clapped for his near perfect execution of a swan dive as he eagerly got inside. He leaned his upper half against the other door and gave me that devilish smile I knew all too well. Kicking off his shoes, he lifted his hand and motioned for me to join him with one crooked finger. Paired with his lifted eyebrow and those downright sinful lips I was putty in his hands. I quickly joined him, shutting the door behind me.

Climbing back onto his lap, our lips returned to our heavy make out session. While I explored his muscles, his hands dove under my shirt and cupped my breasts. Needing to feel his warm hands on my bare skin I put my hands behind my back and unclasped my bra quickly. With his lips on my neck he paused to thank me as I pulled the undergarment out through my arm hole and tossed it in the front seat. His hands quickly replaced the lace material I had been wearing. He let out a satisfying sigh.

"God, I missed these."

"These? What about the rest of me?" I laughed.

"Oh, I missed every little bit of you, don't worry."

I felt a throb underneath me that told me he meant it. My hands quickly shifted from his chest to the button on his jeans. I undid his pants and started pulling them down. He lifted his lower half to assist me in removing his pants and boxers, leaving him in just his socks.

I tossed both items in the front and pounced on him. He let out a small oof as the breath rushed out of him. He chuckled and lifted me up slightly.

"Hey now, this doesn't seem very fair."

"What do you mean?" I asked innocently. He blinked at me.

"Well, my bare ass is pressed against your seat and all you have taken off is your bra."

"Yeah, but I'm on top. If someone were to stop, they'd see me first," I defended as I placed kisses starting from his neck down to his belly button. He groaned with anticipation as I went lower, ultimately silencing his complaints.

"Just shut your eyes and relax," I told him as he arched his body closer to me and I eagerly took him into my mouth.

He gasped with delight as I moved my tongue around his most sensitive parts. His hands dug into my shoulders as he writhed with pleasure. It turned me on seeing how much he liked what I was doing. Suddenly every muscle in his body tensed and he swore. Quickly he pushed me away from him and sat up.

Leaning towards me he reached for the bottom of my shirt and I no longer cared about possible onlookers. Our hands fumbled over each other's as we both tried to pull it off. I started to giggle at how eager and awkward we both were. This was why I loved this man so much. Every day was a new adventure with him.

Once he realized I could get my shirt off on my own his fingers went to my shorts, unbuttoning them with ease and practically ripping them off me. My legs flew up in the air almost comically. I grinned at him, but his face was serious, controlled, and full of concentration. He was a man on a mission. It was extremely sexy.

Picking me up with ease he helped position me just right on his lap. We sank into each other's all too ready bodies. My core was aching to feel him inside of me. My body let out a small cry as I felt all of him.

A quick flash of lights from passing cars made us freeze and then quickly get into a familiar rhythm. This was not the place for slow, sweet lovemaking. We had a goal in mind and not much time to make that happen.

As if reading my mind, Derek came alive. He reached for my hips and we started moving in furious, glorious sync. Taking a nipple in his mouth I could feel myself spinning out of control.

"Oh God," I gasped as I was quickly moving to the point of no return. He gently nipped at my breast and with one last thrust from him, my body exploded in a giant crescendo. I let out a cry and I felt his body tense under mine. With a large groan, Derek felt his own release moments later.

Collapsing into each other's arms I tried to steady my racing heart. Derek wrapped his large arms around my bare body, enclosing me in a whole different type of pleasure. I had spent the last few months traveling all over the country, and still, this was my favorite place to be. I snuggled my head closer to him and he let out a light chuckle, kissing the top of my head.

Eventually more lights from passing cars roused us from our comfortable bliss. I pouted when he sat up more and gently removed me from his chest. He reminded me that the longer we stayed the more likely someone would see the car and question our presence here.

"The last thing we need is a cop passing by and deciding to check on the suspicious vehicle. I'd really rather not make a second trip to the county jail tonight," he laughed. He had a point.

I slipped on my shirt and shorts and we started looking

around for his clothes. "Aw man, you threw them all the way in the front. I can't reach them from here. They are down by the pedals."

"Just come out and we'll move fast. No one will see you," I assured him.

We moved quickly. I got out and he followed, cupping his hands around his groin. I turned back to the car and realized I dropped my phone during our escapade. I climbed back in to retrieve it. Snatching it up from the floor I backed out again and shut the door. The air around us stopped as we both heard the loud and distinct sound of the car locking. *Oh no.*

My eyes shot to Derek, still holding both hands to his naked body. His face went completely white, realizing what that noise was. I gulped. He gave me the death glare as he removed one hand from his body and went to open the driver's side. Nothing. Shit.

"Where's the key?" I asked, although I knew I sounded ridiculous.

"Where do you think?" He snapped at me. I scrambled to try the other doors and the trunk, but nothing was opening. I went back to him, cringing.

"This did not just happen." He leaned his back against the car and threw his head back in frustration. He closed his eyes and I watched his chest rise and fall deeply as he was trying to keep calm.

"I don't know- I didn't realize- that shouldn't have happened," I stammered. He sighed and turned his head to me. He popped one eye open and smiled. I bit my lip to hide my laughter. He looked absolutely ridiculous. A well-built tattooed man wearing nothing but those playful curls on his head and white socks on his feet.

Once he heard a little giggle slip, he began chuckling, which turned into a full on belly laugh. I couldn't help it either, joining him in gasping for air. He bent over and grimaced.

"Stop! I can't hold my breath and my dick at the same time!" He cried, which only made me laugh harder.

I wiped the tears from my face and tackled him in a hug, wrapping my arms around him. He pretended to fight me but eventually we stilled, and he accepted my embrace.

"So, what now?" He asked.

"Well, I have my phone. Thank God I went back for it. I can call someone," I offered. He swore.

"Who do you call for that?"

"Well I think my insurance will cover it," I said as I began scrolling through my contacts. I frowned, not finding the number. I remembered they had an office number and the emergency number, neither of which I had bothered to save into my phone.

"We could always call for someone to just come get us while we figure this out?"

"No, hell no. The guys are not seeing me like this. Where's your brother?"

"He went back to Michigan. Derek, I don't think we have too many options right now."

We stared at each other for a long moment before he finally conceded.

"Fine," he sighed deeply and rolled his eyes. "But don't call Adrian. Try Cleo first." I clicked on her name and pushed call.

"Do you want to talk to her?" I asked. He shot me another look and tilted his head for me to place the phone to his ear.

"We are going to need to figure something out. My hands are getting tired," he muttered.

"Hello?" I heard Cleo's distinct, raspy yet feminine voice say from the other side of the phone.

"Cleo? Hey, we uh, we need some help." Derek said into the phone.

"Oh no, are you stuck in jail too?"

"No, we actually sprung her an hour ago. We uh, got locked out of her car and now we're stranded."

"Do you want someone to come get you?" She asked.

"Yeah, could you?"

"Hey, Chase and Adrian are here. Chase says he has a hook in his car. He can unlock it for you."

"No! I mean," he paused, gritting his teeth. He glanced at me and realized that he had no choice but to agree. "Sure, that'd be great. Thanks."

"Where are you?"

Derek listed off oddly specific instructions to her. I tilted my head in confusion.

"Why are you out there? There's nothing out there."

Suddenly we heard another voice yelling from the phone.

"They were having sex!" Adrian. I rolled my eyes and shook my head at my boyfriend. He shrugged innocently at me.

"Oh! Well... alright. Ethan and Chase are leaving now. Hang tight."

Derek thanked her and I took my phone back. Hanging up the call I turned to him.

"How did Adrian know what we were doing up here? Have you taken girls up here before?"

He shook his head furiously and removed one hand to raise three fingers.

"Scout's honor. Adrian has though. He used to tell me about it."

I crossed my arms. "You took this road and then pulled in here planning to do it?" I accused. He shook his head again.

"No, honest to God, it was an extremely happy accident." He grinned and my anger melted away. Damn it. I wished he could turn that charm off. We leaned back against the car again and made small talk about my stint in the clink while we waited for his friends.

Thankfully the few cars that passed during our wait didn't

slow down or even worse stop. Sometime later a familiar slick, black Cadillac Escalade pulled into the parking lot and flashed it's brights in our direction. We flinched from the harsh light.

Both doors opened and laughter erupted from the vehicle. I saw a phone's camera flash as Ethan came around with Chase and snapped a few pictures of Derek clutching his privates. He attempted to move his body to shield himself from the impromptu photoshoot but there was no saving himself. He was either showing off his front or his back.

"How in the hell did this happen?" Chase asked as he wiggled the hook he had brought against my window. I watched, surprised by how easily and calculated he moved the wire. This was obviously not his first time. Derek muttered something about not wanting to talk about it, but of course Ethan and Chase reassured him that the pictures would be shared amongst the group.

I could see Derek was growing more and more irritated by the moment with Ethan's incessant teasing. I just shook my head and focused on Chase. A few more moments of wiggling the wire and we heard the beautiful click of my car unlocking. I quickly ripped the door open, afraid it would somehow lock again.

I pulled Derek's pants out. Just as I was turning around to hand them to him, I watched as Derek straightened, thanked Chase, and then smiled widely at Ethan. My stomach flipped, knowing that devilish smile. Suddenly Derek's hands flew up, revealing himself to the parking lot. Ethan put his hands up and told him he was done with the jokes, but my boyfriend just laughed; and then without warning he threw his entire weight at him, tackling him to the ground.

Chapter Eighteen

PAINTING FLOWERS

DEREK

I SAID a silent prayer to the powers that be, thanking them for not letting Dita go searching in my pockets. If she had, she would have found the small box containing the engagement ring.

Thankfully, wrestling Ethan to the ground caused her to drop my pants, leaving me to collect them once I released the blue-eyed bastard.

Getting back on the road, I drove us to the house I had bought for her and I to share. I was nervous. I hadn't actually been there since I had bought the place. Would it really feel like a home? Our home?

I was shocked to see what Dita had done with the place. When I had originally seen it, the place was cold and almost felt like it had been a staged house. The realtor told me that these were in fact all Emile's belongings, but they would be moved out shortly after the sale went through. It didn't leave me any less confused, but that was kind of Emile Dahl's thing. That guy was just an odd one.

The house had barely any sign of use. It looked like someone had taken some basic decor out of a magazine, placed it inside the mansion, and called it a day. It was devoid of any personality. Besides the bedroom and library. Emile had a ridiculous amount of books. Once all of the shelves had been filled, he had started stacking them on the floor in tall piles all throughout the room. With all of his success in the music industry, how he had time to read so much was beyond me.

But Dita, Dita had moved into this cold, empty mausoleum and turned it into a real home. A place that as I was moving from room to room, I knew I wanted to spend the rest of my life making memories here. With her.

Once we were showered and settled in for that first night together Dita took my hand and gave me the full tour of the house I had bought with our future in mind. It was odd. Even though I already knew the place, it felt like she was taking me through an entirely different home.

Everything looked and felt perfect. Dita had put her style all over the place. Lots of black, spiderwebs, and other spooky stuff. It was amazing. Everywhere I looked, hints of her were there. Except for my den. That was all me. I had all but forgotten about the fish until we walked inside and saw them all hanging on the walls in their deliciously tacky glory. I burst into laughter and hugged her tight.

"I totally forgot about these guys!"

She rolled her eyes, but her beautiful smile peeked out from the pretend scowl.

"Were all of these necessary?"

I pulled back, feigning offense.

"Absolutely. I couldn't separate the collection. That would have been cruel."

With another large eye roll she walked over to a card table I hadn't even noticed and picked up a piece of paper. She held it up and waved it in my direction.

"I made a list of all the batteries we'll need to get them all running."

We'll.

That one word completely ruined me. We, as in me and her. We live here, together. I still couldn't fathom it. I would have never believed this would happen. After all we'd been through, it was insane to think that she was here, talking about things that we'd be doing. I gave her a tight smile. I didn't need to get mushy on her. She'd run away.

I went to her and pretended to read the list. Honestly, I didn't really care. I couldn't think about anything other than where we were. The tiny box in my jeans suddenly felt like a brick. This was as good a time as any. My hand went to my pocket and I played with the gift that only promised good things. Could I?

I gulped as my stomach fluttered nervously. My breaths quickened. I was ready. This was it. This was my moment to show her how truly amazing she made me feel. How I would do everything in my power to show her each and every day what a blessing she was to me, and I would never stop trying to prove myself worthy of a woman like her. If she agreed to be my wife. Finally, I took a deep breath and turned all the way to her, fingers wrapping around the box.

"Hey, you want to get some dinner? I am dying for some chow mien."

I blinked. My hand dropped the ring and I gave her my best smile.

"Hell yeah. Please tell me we have menu's here. I need my egg roll fix."

She led us out and just like that, the moment was gone. But I wasn't disappointed. I knew there would be better moments. As we walked to the kitchen for menu's, images of flowers, candles, and heart shaped chocolates came to mind. I would pull out all the stops if I had to. She deserved nothing less.

As she called our favorite place and placed our order I glanced around. Spotting the litter box in a corner I frowned. I missed Big D. Once Dita hung up the call I asked her about the cats.

"We can grab them from Mark and Renee's tomorrow." She came around the island and wrapped her arms around my neck. Reaching up on her tiptoes she planted a quick kiss on my lips. "Tonight, I need you all to myself."

"Need?" I grinned. She nodded.

"Need."

"How long do we have 'til the food gets here?"

"Forty minutes."

"Plenty of time," I said and with one swift movement I bent my knees and picked her up quickly. She squealed with surprise and delight as I carried her out of the kitchen and to the living room to pass the time.

That entire week, if we weren't in the throes of passion, we were doing everyday couple stuff. I couldn't decide which I liked more. Well, I did, but activities that forced us to wear clothing weren't so bad either.

That week was pure heaven. If I could choose how I wanted to spend eternity, I would tell whoever was asking to let Dita and I stay together, wrapped in each other's arms. I think we spent more time in our bedroom than any other room in the house. I swear dehydration was imminent.

We left the house only to retrieve our cats and grab groceries. Of course, when we stopped at Mark's place everyone was there and ready to roast us. At first, I thought it was just a happy accident that everyone was there, but when Mark came from the kitchen holding a bakery cake with mine and Dita's mugshots on the top I realized they had been anticipating us.

"We knew you'd have to come up for air eventually," he joked as I read the inscription under our matching photos.

#Couplegoals

I laughed, until Renee hurried into the kitchen and returned with a smaller, round cake. My face fell. I didn't want to see the photo. I was pretty sure I knew what it was. Sure enough, on the smaller cake was my buck ass naked self, holding my junk with my eyes bulging out of my skull. Everyone got a great laugh out of it. Cleo came up and playfully ruffled my hair.

"Only you."

I nodded, she was right. Shit like that only happened to me it felt like. I gave the room a smile and dug into my slice. Photos or not, the cake was good. We ended up bringing most of it home.

Returning home, our friend's jokes and outside world problems simply disappeared once we went through the front door. I didn't want it any other way. With Dita it felt like I was finally starting my next chapter. I was getting my happily ever after.

Eventually though, we had to start interacting with beings outside of our home. We had turned our cell phones off and had a home phone installed. Only our closest friends and Sam were given the number. For that first week, we both wanted a break from the world. We had plenty of time to read posts, watch videos, and make statements. On day eight or nine of pure domesticated bliss we finally grabbed our cell phones and put some underwear on. We couldn't hide forever.

Once our screens turned on there was a solid five minutes of them vibrating and chirping. We had missed a lot, apparently. Thankfully, it was mostly about three topics. Just lots of comments and opinions. It was quick to get the jist though.

Carly made a public apology to me, but I couldn't give a rat's ass. She was lucky I didn't sue her ass for defamation. She posted a video of her in the hospital right after Dita beat the shit out of her. She was attempting to garner sympathy by telling the world what happened through her perspective.

"I was just about to go back and make a public apology for hurting Derek and his loved ones. I had seen the video and realized I had been more drunk than I thought. I was talking to my friend about how I didn't know what to say when this insane woman just came out of nowhere and picked me up. I didn't even have time to react before her fist went right through my nose. Guys, I was on the ground, bleeding from a shattered nose and she continued hitting me. I was completely defenseless. It wasn't until later that I realized who it was. Dita Fox. His freaking girlfriend!

Thankfully someone called the cops and she was pulled off of me. I was going to press charges, but I knew that if I did, I would only continue to look like the villain in this story even though that could not be further from the truth. Derek and Dita are the definition of a toxic couple and the sooner I can move away from this whole situation the better. So, I'm not pressing charges and I am publicly apologizing to Derek Turtle for what I did. I hope this is enough."

Her video of course prompted hundreds of response videos and thousands of comments. I didn't even bother to sift through them all. They all seemed to see through her crap just like I did. She wasn't even worth responding to.

After her sad excuse for an apology, fans began asking about one last concert to end the tour. Petitions had been put up and sometime last week we had apparently been trending. People wanted us to play. I wasn't so sure if I wanted to give the fans who had so quickly turned on me before a memorable show. They didn't deserve it.

Lastly, people were asking about Fan Talk. I turned to Dita for that one. They had promised to reveal their identities at the end of the tour. With the chaos of everything they must have scrapped the idea. I asked her about it, and she blinked, as if she had all but forgotten about how she had spent her last few months.

"Oh, I don't know. Grey went back home. I'll call him and see what he wants to do." She reached for her phone on the counter and dialed him. When he answered she gave me a tight smile and walked out of the room. I took that opportunity to call Adrian. Someone had to know what the plan was for that last show.

"Yeah, I know you weren't wanting to do it. Sorry, but since you've been in solitude all week Sam went and started planning it. I think it's gonna be in Vegas next week."

I swore. I chewed my lower lip, trying to figure out how much I could argue this.

"If you don't show they'll flip. It's one last show for a while, suck it up. We can be there and back in less than a day."

"Really? Would you want to go in front of thousands of people who wanted your head on a platter just a week ago?" I shot back.

"Dude, it doesn't matter. It's our job. They all came back. Don't you remember how much Cleo went through when Chris was around? She put up with it for years, while they were married and long after their divorce. If she can do it for that long, you can do it for one last concert this tour."

I sighed. He was right. I didn't have a leg to stand on.

"Fine. I've had some contact with those kids from the Fan Talk thing," I said, moving on. His energy perked up.

"Really? How?"

"I think they might be willing to come to that last show.

We could still do a party and reveal like we had planned on doing," I told him, avoiding his original question.

"Awesome. I'll call Sam now and see if the details are hammered out yet. I'll call you later." We hung up just as Dita returned with a half-smile on her face.

"He's going to figure stuff out and call me later. Hey, is it alright if I go to lunch with the Cleo today?"

"Go for it. Have fun," I said absentmindedly as I was about to message her myself about the show.

That next day Dita got up bright and early and told me she was going to start looking for work. I told her she didn't have to get a job but she insisted.

"I have a few places I want to check out. Hand out my resume. I'll be back in a few hours."

No sooner had Dita left did Cleo call me, demanding that I open the gate to the house. I shoved some pants on and went to the door. I had barely cracked it open when she bellowed in like a hurricane.

"You haven't proposed yet?" She demanded. I blinked rapidly and held my hands up.

"Whoa, hold on. What?"

"You." She poked my chest with her small, yet surprisingly sharp finger. "Were supposed to propose after the tour."

"The tour's not over," I said sarcastically. She was not amused.

"Are you going to back out then? Did you change your mind?" Her voice was significantly calmer as she began moving through the house. I realized then that she was my first guest. We'd have to plan a party or something soon so everyone could see the place. I followed her as she examined the rooms.

"No, I still want to. There just hasn't been a good time. Nothing feels right."

"Well what do you want to do? Maybe I can help."

I shook my head.

"I honestly don't know what I want to do anymore. She deserves everything, yet I get the feeling that a simple proposal is what she'd want. I think I'll just wait until the show is over. I'll ask at the after party," I assured her. She stared hard at me for a long moment before shrugging.

"Alright. Fair enough. Well, I'm here for you."

I raised an eyebrow.

"What's that supposed to mean?"

She blinked. After a long pause she answered.

"I'll stand right up at that altar right next to you if you want me to," she teased. I playfully punched her shoulder.

"Duh. You'll have to wear a suit though. Gotta match the guys."

"Will do, now, show me this mega mansion."

I took her on a tour through the place. She kept whistling and complimenting Dita's decorating style.

"I love it. She needs to come over and do my place next."

When we did a complete wrap around, returning to the living room, we stood there awkwardly for a moment.

"So, did you come over here just to berate me for my nervousness?" I joked. She looked down at the watch on her wrist and grimaced.

"I've got a few hours to burn, want to chill?"

"Here? Sure. What are you waiting for?"

She blinked, like she was confused with the question.

"Uh, the kids," she said vaguely. "Let's go back to your jam room and have a sesh. We'll make a video for the guys and show them how much fun we're having here at your new place. Make 'em jealous."

I laughed and followed her into a room towards the back of the house. There wasn't much in it right now besides a large rug, my guitars, a drum kit and a mic. It was all that was needed I supposed. I picked up my favorite bass and motioned for her to take her pick of what was left. She picked up the one

Adrian bought for me last year from my small collection and put it around her. I offered her a pic from the bowl on a shelf and she started playing as I plugged her in.

I cringed, listening to her butcher whatever song she was trying to play. She was not very good at the electric guitar. She could play our songs, kind of, but not well enough to perform live. She was much better with an acoustic. She saw me grimacing and stopped.

"What? I'm not that bad," she pouted. I didn't say anything for a moment, so she flipped me off. "Come on, why don't you sing while I play?"

I kicked off the wall I was leaning against and snatched up my acoustic.

"Take this, have a seat, and I'll sing. You play this instead."

She rolled her eyes but slipped the electric guitar off and placed it back on its stand. She grabbed one of my stools and I brought a second one to sit beside her.

"What do you want to play?" She asked me.

"Let's just have some fun. Nothing of ours. Want to bust out some old school country?" I smiled, memories of teenage us trying to learn how to play music bouncing through my head.

"Okay, I think I can handle that. Let's see," she said as she began plucking the strings aimlessly. A few moments later a rough but simple version of a familiar Randy Travis song, "Forever and Ever, Amen" . I sang the words as best as I could, but the lyrics were lost to me from time. It was bad. Cleo picked up the lyrics as I stumbled. Oddly enough Cleo's guitar playing was better than my singing.

We ran through a few other songs together. Some I remembered better than others. Eventually I pulled out my phone to help me sing the proper lyrics. She had laughter in her eyes but said nothing.

Eventually I got tired of her laughing at me and I forced

her to trade me spots. I took the guitar and with ease started playing a Clay Walker song I remembered better. We recorded a few videos of us playing and sent them to Mark and Adrian. They replied with messages of jealousy and irritation that they were missing out. *Oh well.*

Eventually we took a small break and I glanced at the time. Dita was still gone and it was heading towards lunch. I sent a text to check in and then asked Cleo if she wanted me to order food.

"A sub sounds glorious. Make it a club with extra veggies and mayo!" She shouted from the other room. I called and put in our order and no sooner did I hang up did Mark call and demand an invite.

"We just ordered lunch. It's nothing serious, we're just hanging out," I said, rejecting their demands.

"Where did you order?" He asked and hung up the phone as soon as I told him. Half an hour later my gates were being buzzed and when I looked at the camera, I saw my friends hanging out the driver's side window with bags of food in their hand.

Mark and Adrian came in like a hurricane. Their energy was electric and contagious. Despite me wanting to be irritated by their need to be included, I suddenly didn't care. I was glad they came. We ate our food and picked up our instruments to jam together. This was the stuff I liked, no pressure fun. We could screw up, take breaks, learn new songs and instruments without anyone scolding us for not being on schedule.

We kept with our previous, smaller session of classic country. I think everyone was happy to not play the same old songs we'd been doing for the last year or so.

"Ooh, I know!" Cleo said and stepped away from her stand and went to Adrian, who leaned down for her to whisper in his ear. He glanced at me and shrugged. I scrunched my nose as she did the same to Mark sitting behind the drums. He removed his headphones to hear her and then moved them back quickly with a grin. He perked up and picked up his phone. She winked at me as she went back to her stand. I glared. I didn't like this game. She knew that.

"You got it?" She asked Adrian. Adrian frowned and then shrugged.

"I think so," he mumbled as his head dipped to watch his fingers as he began strumming the guitar in his hands. The chords came slow, but familiar. I tilted my head as I tried to remember the song. When Mark came in it hit me. My head ripped back to Cleo who was grinning ear to ear as she stared at me. She raised her hand and pointed it at me.

"This song is dedicated to you, my dearest friend. From us, to you. You've grown up so much this last year and we are so proud and happy for you and can't wait to see the man you're gonna be."

My eyes involuntary started to well up as she began singing "God Only Knows". I shook my head and pressed my lips together. This was dirty. She knew I'd get emotional. She was the worst, no, she was the best. They all were. I couldn't ask for better friends. I rolled my eyes and glanced at my other friends who were grinning. Mark pointed his stick at me and Adrian gave me a head nod.

"This isn't country!" I shouted over the music. Cleo shrugged but continued singing about how they didn't know where they'd be without me. Dammit. I stood there, trying to pretend I was annoyed, but I couldn't. The longer I fought it the mushier they'd get. I wiped my wet eyes and when they finished, I addressed them all.

"What was that? Are you giving me some sort of approval or something?"

Cleo nodded.

"Even though you don't need it, we wanted to give you our

blessing. Dita is good for you. You guys are gonna be so happy."

I glanced at everyone individually. Mark and Cleo beamed while Adrian's smile was tight and didn't meet his eyes.

"Really?" I was skeptical that she spoke for everyone. I crossed my arms and leaned against a stand. Her head whipped to Adrian and she glared.

"Yes. *All* of us."

I smirked when Adrian looked away guiltily.

"You think she's gonna say yes?" He said, immediately causing the smile to fall off of my face.

"Are you for real right now?" I said, uncrossing my arms and standing up straight. My hands instantly turned into fists. I thought this was squashed. Why are we still arguing over this? Adrian smirked.

"We all know she's a runner. You put her in a corner and she's going to panic. How long did it take you to convince her to move in with you? You didn't even tell us you were sleeping together for like two years. You think she's gonna jump to marry you?"

Suddenly all I could see was Adrian and the few feet between us. I heard a clamor as Mark stood up, but I didn't care. I blinked and all the tension left my body as I spoke to Adrian.

"Get the fuck out."

"What? Really? Dude, I was just messing with you."

"No, I'm really sick of this. I get it. No matter what I do, what we go through, you still want to hold on to this stupid grudge. So, until you are ready to truly give me your blessing with absolutely no hate behind it, don't come back. I don't need your damn blessing, but I think the band does."

I looked at Cleo and Mark who had moved to stand next to each other. Their eyes were wide as if they had just witnessed a car crash.

"I'm not playing at the show. Go ahead and let them fine me or whatever. I don't care. I'm done."

I left the room. It took every fiber of my being to remain somewhat calm as I went up to the second floor and to my room. Silence flowed behind me as my bandmates processed what I had just said. Closing my bedroom door, I fell against it and exhaled deeply. What a mess.

Moments later I heard shouting. I couldn't hear distinct words, but I could identify the voices. All three of them were yelling at each other. I moved to my bed and laid down on top of the blankets. I put my hands under my head and listened to them argue. Somehow, I wasn't furious or saddened by what had happened. I was oddly calm. I simply didn't care anymore. Either he accepted my relationship with Dita fully or I didn't want him in my life anymore. I didn't need the stress or hate.

Doors were being slammed and I groaned when I heard small, quick steps on the stairs. Moments later there was three quick, sharp knocks on the door of my room. When I didn't reply to them, they came again with Cleo's voice that had clearly been crying. Her voice was high as she sniffled.

"Derek, I know you're in there. I'm coming in."

I sat up just as the door creaked open and she peaked her head in. Her eyes were red and swollen. Guilt hit my gut like a hard punch. I had to look away from her.

"What do you want?" I asked, my voice more exasperated than angry. She opened the door wider and stepped in despite the lack of real invitation. She stepped inside and shut the door behind her. I moved to set my feet on the floor as she came to sit cross-legged on my bed.

Silence followed for a long moment. I didn't have anything to say, so this was all her. She stared down at her hands in her lap. Finally, she sighed.

"Do you remember what I told you when I found out about you two? That Adrian wasn't going to take it well?"

I chewed on my lip and nodded. "Yeah. And he didn't."

"We all would have reacted that way if you had been hiding something like that from us. In the fifteen plus years we've known each other, no one has done anything like that. It was just as confusing and hurtful to Mark and I as it was to Adrian. When you and Dita were having- whatever, it affected everyone."

"Okay? And? Honestly Cleo, I am so sick of having to deal with this guilt. I'm over it. If you guys want to keep bringing it up, fine. I'm just no longer going to be a part of the conversation."

"I get that. One hundred percent. I got tired of people telling me what to do regarding my relationships too. It gets old. You and Dita deserve to move on. You've grown up so much since she came into your life and I am so proud of you. But leaving the band is just throwing yourself right back to where you were. It's going to make things so much worse. Just like before, your feelings are focused on Adrian, but you're hurting all of us."

I took in her words. I hadn't thought of it like that.

"Look, Adrian is a jerk. We all readily agree with that. It's stupid that he's still bitter about it. He's happy with Chase and Rocky, so there's no reason for him to be like this, but stop hurting everyone just because of him."

"What am I supposed to do then? Just let him continue to throw shots at me and Dita for the rest of my life? That's not an option."

She nodded. "I agree. It's not an option. He needs to grow up. If he can't then maybe he doesn't need to be around."

"I don't know what you're getting at."

"Mark and I gave him the choice. He can either come and genuinely let this go and give you his blessing, or he can part ways with Maria Maria after the Vegas show."

"Bullshit." I didn't believe her. She shook her head.

"Swear to God. He's down there right now pacing and yelling. He doesn't want to come up here. He's got until the show to decide. If we can't get up on stage as friends, then that will be our last show as *us*."

For the first time in my life, I didn't know what to say. They chose me over Adrian. I would have never, ever, thought this would happen. I didn't want it to happen. I hated that Adrian and I had torn our friends apart. Cleo reached forward and wrapped me in a hug. I didn't hug her back, but she held tightly to me.

"You will always have my blessing," she told me as she pulled away and gave me a sad smile as she hopped off the bed and left my bedroom with one last look back. She shut my door and barely a minute later I was startled by Mark bursting into the room. He came in with a flourish, slamming the door behind him and belly flopping onto my bed.

"Man this is so soft. What is this? It's like a giant marshmallow."

I rolled my eyes. "And what are you here for?" I asked sarcastically. He rolled and propped his head up with his arm.

"Cleo told you what we decided. Adrian's down there throwing a tantrum about how you always get your way and you're up here gloating. It's a mess. I don't think I've ever had the chance to say that you're the mature one. That's weird. It sounds even weirder out loud."

I laughed. It felt good to relax a little. Mark was always good about that.

"What do you want?" I asked. He shrugged his shoulders.

"It's a bummer. Out of all the women in this world, you fell for the one that you shouldn't have."

"Believe me, I wasn't trying."

"I know. Cleo knows, but Adrian. I think a small part of him still thinks you did it on purpose. He doesn't trust you."

"Why not? It's not like I'm going to steal Chase from him.

The only time I truly screwed him over was the first time. After they broke up, Dita was fair game."

Mark shook his head. "The sex is literally the last thing he cares about. Truly. He can't get over the fact that you slept on his couch for two years, ate every meal together, and had every opportunity to tell him the truth and you didn't. There was nothing stopping you, and yet you continued to lie to him about where you were going, what you were doing, and all sorts of stupid stuff. It was stupid man. If you had just told him, I think he could have gotten over it."

"Dita didn't want me to tell him."

"Yeah, but you should have fought it a little more. Things would have been so much better if you hadn't waited."

"Well I can't fix that now. This is conversation is pointless."

"You're right." There was a pause before he asked me if I trusted Adrian. I thought about it for a long moment.

"No. I don't."

"Why? If you and her are happy and Adrian and Chase are happy, then why can't you trust him?"

"Because of how pissed off he is!" I yelled back.

"So, you can't trust him because he can't trust you. Makes sense." His voice remained calm and it irritated me. How dare he be the voice of reason. "I think you both need to let go of your anger towards each other. He's in the wrong in this situation, there's no denying it. But if you can't stop the glares, comments, questions, and getting so defensive when him and Dita interact with each other, he will never let it go."

I stared at him. He was right. I hated whenever he spoke to Dita. Even casual conversation, I was on edge. He wasn't the one who cheated. We were.

Making me jump again Mark popped up and slapped his hand down on my shoulder.

"I'm giving you my blessing. You and Dita really are meant for each other. Way better than her and Adrian. I'm happy for you, regardless of how it started. But my blessing isn't the one you want, and that's okay. Adrian will make the right decision."

"Will he?"

He didn't look at me but stared straight ahead towards the door.

"He better," he muttered. He opened the door and we both froze when we heard Adrian shout.

"Well look who's here! Dita freakin' Fox!"

I jumped up and shoved past Mark out the door. I couldn't get down fast enough. I tripped over him and fell flat on my face. The carpet burned as it scraped against my cheek. I could hear them all downstairs clearly.

"What are you guys doing here?" Dita's soft, beautiful voice floated upstairs. I could tell she was slightly startled. Probably by seeing Adrian flipping his shit.

"Oh? He didn't tell you? How surprising is that, Derek not telling someone he cared about something."

"Adrian! Stop!" Cleo ordered, but he ignored her. I stumbled up and started towards the stairs. I was going to beat his ass.

"I'm so confused. Did I miss a party or something?"

"Oh no, we're just here to give your dear boyfriend our blessing so he can ask you to marry him."

Silence. Everything around us stopped. I reached the bottom of the stairs and she turned to stare at me. Her eyes bulged and her mouth fell open. The moment lasted an eternity. We stared at each other, neither of us speaking, moving, or even breathing. Then, as if the time spell had been broken, she blinked, closed her mouth, and gulped.

"I need to go." She turned and ran out the door, ignoring my screams for her to come back.

Chapter Nineteen

RUNNING

DITA

I sᴀᴛ in the parking lot of my old apartment, staring at the ring I had just bought for him. A thick black band with a thin line of blood red in the middle that matched the interior color. I couldn't wait to see him put it on. If he would. After what just happened, I didn't know if he'd want me anymore. I wouldn't blame him.

I didn't know where to go that he wouldn't find me. Every time I remembered how he looked when I left tears returned to my eyes. I never wanted to see that look again. It was pure torture.

He called me over and over, but I forced myself to ignore it. I had to. If I was going to pull off this one last thing, I had to fully commit. Eventually the calls stopped and my phone chirped with a text message. I closed my eyes and took a deep breath as I checked it. It was from Adrian.

He bought it. We're heading to Vegas tonight. You want to ride together?

I replied quickly. My heart was still beating furiously. I wanted to throw up. What was I doing?

Sure. Thank you. How is he?

There was a long pause before his name popped back up on my screen.

Cleo and Mark are dealing with it. Don't worry. Everything is going to work out.

My nerves were on edge the rest of the day. The three Wilson men and I took my car and drove to Vegas. The four hours it took to get there gave me tons of time to think. I almost turned around countless times. I spent the entire time either crying or blubbering about how much I loved Derek. Chase sat in the front with me and held my hand, letting me vent.

"I promise you, when this is all over, it's going to be worth it." His words were meant to be reassuring but I was still unsure. It was Adrian's idea, but with everyone else's approval, I knew he wasn't just trying to ruin things.

Everything in the last 36 hours or so had happened so fast. My life was perfect. I had gone to Cleo's to pick her up for lunch. I went inside and found her other two bandmates sitting around in the living room. I waved and they all stopped talking at the same time. They stared at me like I had a wart on the tip of my nose.

"What?" I asked. Cleo stood up and gave me a tight smile.

"How are things? How was your week back home with Derek?"

"Great. Well, more than great. Why are you guys looking at me like that?"

"Did he propose or what?" Mark blurted out. I blinked a few times, processing what he just said. Propose?

"No. Was he supposed to?" I asked, my voice tight. Cleo reached for my hand and then held it up. It was bare. No ring. Sorry. She stuck out her tongue and frowned.

"Yes. Right after the tour."

"The tour's not over," I said reflexively, and she rolled her eyes. There was an awkward silence that lasted way longer than normal. I didn't know what to say. They were all giving each other looks, as if having a silent conversation without me.

"Why don't we all go for lunch?" Adrian said suddenly. They all agreed and before I could argue Cleo grabbed my arm and pulled me forward. We piled into my car and they made forced conversation about nothing of importance. I remained silent. One word kept bouncing around in my head. Propose. Only once we sat down at this bizarre burger place Mark insisted we go to did they decide to discuss the elephant in the room.

"Did you know this place used to be this upscale Italian place until the owners had to sell it. The new owners kept the decor but changed the food," Mark told us. Cleo kicked him under the table and he yelped.

"No one cares. So, we should talk about our screw up. Obviously, we weren't supposed to tell you. Thank you, Mark, for that." She shot him another dirty look. He raised his hands up.

"Well he's been holding on to the ring for long enough. What the hell is he waiting for?" Silence returned before Adrian cleared his throat and turned to me.

"Now that you know, what would you say?"

I grimaced and he turned red.

"Are you all asking for him?" I shot back and they all

looked guilty. I thought about it for a moment and then answered very quietly, but honestly. "I'd say yes."

The group let out small cheers. Adrian patted me on the back and Cleo gave me a side hug.

"I knew you would. You two are crazy about each other."

"I'm happy for you," Adrian told me, looking me square in the eye as he took a drink of his beer. Adrian and I have had a strained relationship since the day he saw me after finding out the truth. Everything he said to me had an edge to it and made me uneasy. But his last few words, they were genuine. I just knew it. For the first time, there wasn't any tension between us. The weird triangle we had been in for so long was completely gone. He had given me his approval. I thanked him.

"I don't know what I'm supposed to do with this information. I can't just ask him about it. He'll ask when he's ready. It won't feel right if I bring it up."

"Well just pretend we didn't say anything," Cleo suggested, and I shook my head. It didn't work like that. Mark apologized again and I gave him a tight smile. For once, I didn't find him amusing.

"Why don't you ask him instead?" Adrian suggested. I choked on my drink and Cleo patted my back. I stared at him, taking in his idea. Could I? How?

"I don't have the money right now to afford a ring," I said simply. Adrian scoffed.

"I'll pay for it. Consider it my wedding gift."

"You would do that?"

"Sure. I've given you enough crap, it's the least I can do. You two are good for each other."

My lip trembled and before I could stop it my eyes welled up. I mouthed a thank you to him and he simply nodded again. Cleo put her arms up on the table and rested her chin on her hands. I turned and she grinned at me.

"So, now that you've got the ring covered, how are you gonna do it?"

I tilted my head back and forth, trying to think of something good but came up blank.

"I have no clue. What do you think?"

"Something big. Huge. Derek would love that. Make it a whole spectacle. A declaration. He's a ham," Mark said.

"We can bring you on stage for our last show and you can ask then if you want," Cleo offered. I shook my head.

"That's been overdone. I agree that it should be something grand. That screams Derek. Maybe we could throw a huge party at our place and I could ask there?" They all grimaced at my idea and I frowned. The idea wasn't terrible, but their faces all expressed to me that they thought it was.

"What if you tricked him. Throw him off your scent. Let's face it, one of us is going to spill the fact that you know. My money's on Mark." Adrian shot him a dirty look and the drummer cowered. "If we cause a distraction, we could surprise him with it."

"We?"

Adrian smiled and waved his hand around the table.

"Welcome to the family. We do everything together. So, let's break you two up."

The rest of the afternoon they helped me create this elaborate plan in which Adrian and Derek would have this massive fight. While that was happening, I would take Renee and Chase and we would go pick out a ring for him. Then, I would come home and Adrian would reveal Derek's plans. I would freak out and run. After that I would get picked up and I would tell Derek I was going to Vegas early to think about things.

Then, Adrian still being in a fight with Derek, would decide to join me in Vegas just to make him jealous. To Derek's knowledge no one will have made any contact with either of us. All the while, Adrian, Chase, and I will be in Vegas together making wedding plans. The show was on a Friday night. On the day of the show I would ask him to marry me and we'd get married on Monday. It was horrible, too much, and yet, perfect.

As soon as we got to the hotel and I stepped into my room I called Cleo to see how he was.

"Not great. I mean, good for our plans, but still rough. Mark is still over there. Probably going to stay the night with him. How are you?"

I sniffled. I didn't want to break down again.

"I'm okay I guess. I know the payoff will be worth it, but man, this is hard. He's my everything."

"Don't worry. We'll make sure he's okay. Just get that wedding planning done. As fast as you can if possible."

I thanked her for the update and when I hung up, I felt all of my energy drain from my body. I had planned to shower, but instead I went to the bed and promptly began crying again. I fell asleep from pure exhaustion and tears staining my face and pillows.

The next day I was woken up by Chase pulling the blankets off of me and scolding me for wearing my jeans to bed.

"Come on, everything is going to be fine. We can't have you breaking down the entire time. We have a busy schedule today, so get showered and come knock on our door. Adrian's grabbing breakfast now."

I groaned and attempted to reclaim my blankets, but Chase was strong. Eventually I got my miserable butt up and did as ordered. I showered and put on new clothes but I didn't even bother with makeup. I didn't care how tired I looked. I deserved to look as miserable as Derek was.

After we ate, the three of us went to a bridal store. I tried on a few dresses but everything felt way too upscale and fancy. Everything had been chosen for me by Chase and Adrian. After rejecting my third mermaid style gown Adrian crossed his arms and huffed.

"What do you want to wear?"

I did an awkward waddle to turn to face them.

"Everything you've had me try on was either too tight or too revealing."

"You are stunning in all of them," Chase argued. Rocky, strapped to his dad's chest, babbled his agreement.

"They are beautiful dresses," I conceded. "But they aren't the dress I was meant to marry Derek in. I need something as..." I trailed off, trying to think of the right word.

"Obnoxious?" Adrian suggested and I lit up.

"Yes! I need a dress that fits the man. We need to go to a secondhand dress shop." With that we began to search for the most ridiculous bridal gear we could. We went to three different thrift stores before I found it. The perfect dress.

The large ball gown was the perfect mix of over the top, yet gorgeous. I spun around in the ball gown, showing it off to my shopping partners. They smiled and agreed with me, it was the right dress.

The top was all embroidered with a ton of shiny beads and small roses. The sleeves were off the shoulder rosettes, matching the bust. It wasn't as big as I had imagined, but it was just enough over the top without turning into a monster from the 80's. The sales clerk smiled when she saw me spinning.

"Would you like the veil that accompanies that dress? I think you'll like it."

"Yes please."

She returned a few moments later and I gasped when she set it the crowned veil on my head. It was perfect. She fluffed out the tulle, making the entire ensemble just absolutely wonderful.

"You look like you're marrying a rockstar," she commented,

eyeing my tattoo's appreciatively. A giggle slipped from my mouth as I looked back at my friends, grinning ear to ear.

"That's the plan."

"What do you think? Is this your dress?"

I nodded. "I'll take it," I told her breathlessly. With my dress and veil safely in a bag we left the shop and went to work doing everything else. It was noon by the time we left the shop, so we got a quick lunch and Rocky started rubbing his eyes. Adrian reached for him and offered to take him and the dress back to the hotel.

"You guys go on without me and get more stuff done. We'll catch back up in a few hours."

Once he left, Chase pulled out the list he had made of things to do and I gaped at it.

"Are you serious?" I asked. He blinked at me.

"Well yeah, planning a wedding is no joke. There's a lot to do."

"I've got what? Eight days? To figure this out. Less, really. Seven. I've got Seven days to figure out all of this. No, we have to cut some of this. A lot of this. Let me see this." I snatched the list from his hands, and he handed me the pen.

"Venue? Easy. Elvis. We need to find an Elvis chapel. There's got to be a ton around here. Colors?" I looked up at him and he rolled his eyes.

"Yes. For flowers, dresses, tuxes, decorations for the reception. Usually people pick one or two."

I chewed my cheek a little, trying to imagine my perfect wedding. What did I want?

"What about maroon and black?"

Chase grinned and pulled out a second pen and reached for the list.

"That is totally perfect for you two. A gothic Elvis wedding it is. What do you think of maroon, pink, and black? I bet the contrasting colors would be gorgeous."

I gave him an odd look and his face went red.

"Sorry, I enjoy planning events. Renee kind of got me hooked."

I sighed. "I wish she was here." I didn't tell him I wanted her here not only for moral support but to also get me out of planning all of this. This wasn't my thing. It all felt too forced. I just wanted to go and be with Derek. Chase raised an eyebrow.

"I think we can make that work."

The next day I was greeted by Renee and Lola at my door.

"We told Derek that I was coming out to talk some sense into you. Come on, the guys said we are food testing today."

I pushed the thoughts of how Derek must be feeling aside and focused on the tasks at hand. By the end of the day I had picked a red velvet cake that was going to be covered in black fondant and red and pink roses. We were going to have the reception at the Circus Circus hotel. We could watch various circus acts and play arcade games while we celebrate our special day.

While Renee and I picked out the rest of the food and dessert, the guys went and picked out a suit for Derek. They had to call Mark to get his measurements, but they assured me he'd look good. On Saturday I finally answered Derek's phone call. When I said hello my heart broke instantly with his cracked reply.

"Dita? Why have you been ignoring me? Are you still in love with me?"

I gulped. How could he even think that? I was horrible. What was I doing to him?

"Yes, I still love you," I said, forcing myself to stay strong.

"Is Adrian with you? How about Renee? She said she was going to bring you back. Come back, please. We can talk about it." The urgency in his voice absolutely destroyed me.

"I'm not ready to talk about it. Can you please just give me some more time?"

"How much more time? Dita, this is killing me. Is the thought of marrying me that horrible?"

Tears were freely falling down my face. I pressed my lips together to stifle a sob. I didn't know how much longer I could do this.

"When are you coming for the show?" I asked. He sighed deeply.

"The rest of us are scheduled to fly out Thursday morning. Sound check in the evening." His voice was filled with absolute misery. "I think we've got an interview during the day and an appearance before the show. Can I see you before then?"

"How about we play it by ear? Please, I need you to stop calling me. I can't handle this. Not right now. I promise it's what's best right now." My mouth trembled as I forced myself to keep my plan a secret. He didn't say anything for an agonizingly long time. When he did speak, I barely kept it together.

"That last week we had together was amazing. Just you and me in our own little paradise. I want that back. If that means never marrying you, so be it. I'll take whatever piece of you I can get."

"Okay," I whispered.

"Goodbye Dita Fox."

"Goodbye," I said, hanging up the phone quickly so I could bury my head in my pillow and wail. Was all of this worth it? Did we take this too far? Only time would tell. I'd have my answer on Thursday. When I asked our little group the next day that question no one answered immediately. They answered with their silence.

"Possibly. From what Mark says, he's a wreck. He's never seen him like this before. He's crazy about you," Adrian shook his head incredulously. I shot him a look.

"Is it really that unbelievable?"

"Whoa, that's not what I was saying. I meant that Derek has never been like this for any girl before. It's just different. In a good way. Would I be here planning your guy's wedding if I didn't like you?"

I scrunched up my nose but said nothing. It was Sunday now, giving us four more days to finish Chase's list.

"What's next?" I asked, already exhausted.

"Music. What songs do you want to dance to?" Chase explained.

"Oh, do you want a DJ or live music?" Renee asked.

"What's easier?" I sighed. They frowned.

"Do you need a break?" Renee asked.

"Is that an option?" I said sarcastically and then sat up straighter in my seat. "No, I'm good. You're right. It would make me feel better if Derek was feeling better. If that was possible."

The faces around the table fell around me as the guilt I was feeling seeped into them as well. I sighed and shook my head.

"Look, I don't think any of this is right. I don't know if it ever was. I know you guys just want to help, but I don't want to do this anymore."

"You don't want to marry him?" Adrian asked me, his eyes almost bulging out of his head.

"No, no I do. I don't want to plan this whole, grand affair. I don't care if we have salmon or ribs. I doubt Derek would even notice who's wearing what or what our accent colors are. I'm over this entire wedding planning thing."

Chase eyed me for a moment, before crossing his arms and sitting back in his seat.

"You know what, how about we take care of everything?"

"Fine! Great. I don't care. Change and do whatever you want. All I care about is Derek and I at that altar." I stood up and let out a deep sigh of relief.

"Where are you going?" Renee asked me. I grinned.

"I'm going to go propose to my boyfriend."

I drove back to L.A. and barely had my car fully parked before I jumped out of it and ran to door. I tossed it open like I was storming a castle.

"Derek!" I shouted. The house was silent for a long moment before I heard a door from upstairs open. I looked up just as my gorgeous guy's silly curls popped over the edge. Our eyes met and his jaw dropped.

"Dita?"

Before I could stop them, tears started falling down my face. This was the moment both of us had been waiting for. I just knew it in my heart. Derek's head disappeared and a moment later he was stomping down the stairs. I hurried over and greeted him at the bottom.

He wrapped his arms around me, and I greedily inhaled his familiar scent as I buried my head in his shoulder. Why did I think his friends plan was a good idea again?

"What are you doing here? I thought you needed time?" His cracked and sore voice killed me. I pulled my head away from his shoulder and kissed him hard. He had apparently stopped shaving. The scruff irritated my cheeks, but it had never felt more perfect.

"No. Not at all. It's a whole big thing, but we can talk about all of that later. I need to do something." I removed myself from his arms. His smile remained as he watched me. I didn't take my eyes away from his as I pulled out the velvet box I had stuffed in my pocket before I ran away from our friends. Cupping the box with both hands I knelt down on one knee. He started laughing as a few tears started sliding down his rugged, unshaven cheeks.

"Derek, our relationship has always been a mess. I'm bad news and you don't care. You never cared what anyone else thought about me." I laughed as my own tears returned. "I told you I was a stripper, that I had sex with the town's pastor, and that I had been secretly following you around the country dressed in a costume just so I could be with you in my own way. Each time, you smiled and told me that you loved me more for it. I know I'll never find anyone more caring, more accepting, and more adorable. You make me laugh and to be honest, I never thought I'd feel like this about anyone. I don't want to spend another minute without you. Will you marry me?"

He didn't say anything for a long moment. Each beat that passed I was afraid my heart was going to stop. He reached for my hands and lifted me to a standing position. He took the box from me and closed it softly. The click of it shutting echoed in my ears.

My eyes were hopeful as we stood in front of each other. I pressed my lips together, afraid I'd start wailing. His kept his smile on his face as he let go of one of my hands and brought it to his pocket. Quickly he dug inside and pulled out a box similar to mine. He pried it open with one hand and revealed the most beautiful ring I had ever seen.

"Only if you'll marry me."

I laughed as I took the box and we put our rings on. We held our hands up together to view them. They looked good together, just like their owners. I turned to let my back relax into his body so he could wrap his warm, familiar arms around me.

"So, do I get to know what this whole big thing was now?"

I laughed and wiped the tears away from my face.

"Sure. But let's talk while we get you packed."

"What do you think I was doing before you got here?"

I laughed and rolled my eyes.

"You were coming to find me?"

"Like I could really just let my best girl slip away? Of course I was. I had this whole big speech planned. But I liked yours better. I'll go grab my suitcase. The cats are already at Sam's. His wife is gonna watch them."

"Sam's?"

"Yeah, everyone else is headed to Vegas tonight. I wanted to get there early, just in case I made a fool of myself I wouldn't have an audience." His eyes saddened again, and I playfully pushed his shoulder.

"Stop it! We are officially engaged now. No more sad eyes. How else can I show you how much I love you?"

He wiggled his eyebrows at me and grinned. "Well I know a way or two you could…"

I cut him off with a tender kiss that ended with me gently biting his lower lip.

"I think that can be arranged. Only if you show me how much you love me too."

"Gladly."

By the time we made it to Vegas everyone was sitting down to dinner together. We had called ahead to see where they were, and they told us that they had reserved a private room at the restaurant they had picked. The doors were closed, and we were escorted to the room by the maitre'd.

When he opened the door Derek and I entered the room with our arms extended and hands dropped loosely to proudly show off our rings.

"We said yes!" We said in unison.

They greeted us with loud cheers and asked the waitress to bring another bottle of champagne and two more glasses. I was surprised when Derek held up one hand and politely requested a glass of cola instead. I shot him a surprised look, but he simply shrugged.

"I think it may be time to start slowing down a little. My

last hospital trip was a little wake up call."

Ethan held up his own glass of pop and gave him a half smile.

"Been there, done that. It's not fun. Rehab sucks, good idea to stick to something else for awhile."

The rest of the evening was filled with tons of laughs, stories from their tour, and the semi-failed plan of my proposal. Derek didn't seem too amused when they glossed over the fight that led to me storming out but overall, he seemed okay. I think me telling him privately on the ride over may have helped him ease into the situation a little.

"Are we cool?" Adrian asked him at one point while everyone was busy chattering away about something else.

"Yeah. I mean, you guys really sold me on everything which is kind of scary, but it worked out in the end. I can't really be mad when I've got my girl forever now. Are we cool?"

His simple question was loaded with so much more than could be discussed tonight. Derek was asking not about their most recent fight, but about these last few years. Were they finally going to bury the hatchet? Adrian stared at him, face stone cold for a brief moment before grinning ear to ear and raising his hand to him. They clutched each other's hands for a quick moment.

"Yeah. We're cool."

"Finally!" The rest of table shouted together. The three of us turned and started laughing with everyone else. Cleo got my attention when the laughter died down. She stared at me with a grin so terrifying I looked around nervously.

"What?" I asked.

"Chase told me that you gave us permission to plan the rest of your guys' wedding. He said he could use some help from the people who know Derek the best."

I laughed. "Oh gosh. I can only imagine what you guys are gonna do."

"Let's just put it this way, we scrapped everything but the location and your dress. All you have to do is show up to the Graceland Wedding Chapel," Renee said.

"I don't know if I'm supposed to feel offended or not," I laughed.

"It wasn't that your ideas were terrible. We just all agreed that your heart wasn't in the planning." Chase added. He wasn't wrong. None of it was anything I'd really miss. As long as I'd get to spend the rest of my life with the best man I had ever met, I didn't care about the rest.

"Sounds perfect to me, what do you think babe?" Derek asked me, reaching for my hand under the table. I leaned into him and put my head on his shoulder.

"Absolutely perfect," I sighed. Under the table our hands sat on his lap, intertwined. My new ring felt oddly smushed against our fingers. It was a beautiful ring. When I took my first good look at it, I started laughing. He took offense until he looked at his own. They matched. Black and red. Perfect for a rockstar and his goth bride to be.

I was glad his friend's proposal plan hadn't worked out. I wouldn't have been able to say everything I needed to say to him in front of everyone. They had meant well, but their idea was right for them, not Derek and I. Derek agreed with me, what ended up happening was a much better proposal than anything they could have arranged.

Quiet suddenly fell over the table for the first time since we arrived. It was a nice calm before the storm. Someone cleared their throat, breaking the silence. Cleo stood up and popped her hip in a dramatic pose that I instantly recognized when she picked up her spoon and raised it to her mouth like a microphone. She looked at us and with a wink she spoke directly to Derek and I.

"I was told to keep everything a secret until you got there, but I just wanted to say, thank you. Thank you very much."

Chapter Twenty

BABY IT'S FACT

DEREK

"Are you going to announce it live?" Cleo asked me while we sat in four identical chairs in front of makeup stations preparing for our TV interview in an hour. I tried to turn my head, but the stylist grabbed my chin and moved me back to continue messing with my hair.

"Should I? Am I allowed to? Sam!" I called out, hoping our manager was nearby. I looked into the mirror and tried to see behind me, but those damn bulb lights were too bright to see much.

"Yeah? What's up?" Sam came up and tapped my shoulder.

"Can I talk about my engagement during the interview? Or is this one of those 'we talk to Cleo the entire time and everyone just nods along' things?"

"No, go ahead. Actually, I think they want to talk to everyone individually at some point. But I would definitely keep a level head when they ask about the dancer thing. They asked if it was okay to ask you about it. Bringing up your good news instead of feeding into their gossip is probably better."

"Do you want me to avoid the whole thing when they ask then?"

"No, don't do that. That will be just as bad as admitting guilt to them. Just say something about how you're glad your name was cleared and then bring up your engagement. Distract them."

"What are they gonna ask me?" Adrian said from my other side. Sam moved over to talk to him.

"Your curls are so cute," the stylist complimented. I thanked her awkwardly. Maybe I'd shave it all off soon. I scratched at my chin. I still hadn't shaved yet. I wasn't used to the scruff. Even on the road I always managed to find a truck stop bathroom to shave in. I was going to shave this morning but Dita asked that I keep it.

"I kind of like it. Beards are sexy," she crooned into my ear as we stepped into the shower together. God, I'd do anything for her if she'd keep that up. Her appetite was insatiable.

I pulled out my phone and checked in with her. She was picking up her brother from the airport. He was flying in just in time for the show tonight. Fan Talk was finally going to reveal themselves. We were going to officially see them at the meet and greet before the show, I already given Dita their backstage passes. The other band members still had no idea it was her and Grey beneath the masks. It was going to difficult to act surprised. I don't think I'd be able to keep my knowledge of their identities a secret long. My face was always too telling.

A woman with a clipboard and headset came over and told us it was time to go. I stood up and stretched. I held my microphone in my hand before I shoved it in my pocket. I hated these things. They were irritating. Sam came and reminded us to shut our phones off before we go into the room. I rolled my eyes, but his glare made me do as told.

With Cleo at the head of the line we filed into the medium sized room. I looked around. It wasn't anything fancy. The interview was for a magazine's website. They were going to air it live to get people psyched for the show. There was a long couch, two end tables, a coffee table, and a comfy looking chair where the guy who'd be conducting the interview was going to be sitting.

I recognized him and smiled wide when he shook our hands.

"Hey Nick! Long time no see. How you been?" I asked him. He used to be at all the major festivals, stuck in the trenches while he attempted to get interviews from people. It was nice to see he moved on up.

"Great! No more mosh pit interviews for me," he chuckled and motioned for us to sit down on the couch. Mark took the far right, followed by Adrian and Cleo. I chose to sit on the arm of the couch. Cleo smirked but said nothing. Nick gave us a chance to get comfy and did a few more polite greetings before he announced they were going to turn on the cameras. I put on a smile as I watched the camera man count down with his fingers.

"Hello viewers, I'm Nick B for Bulletproof Magazine and I'm here with the band of the freakin' year, Maria Maria. You guys wanna give a quick wave to the fans watching this live stream today?"

I waved and my friends gave other greetings. I saw Cleo put her fingers in her mouth and spread her mouth out in a funny face, while Mark made moose antlers with his hands.

"Now that the dust has kind of settled, are we able to talk about the situation that caused you all to cancel your last show?"

All silliness left the room for a moment. My friends looked over to me. I blinked and then nodded.

"Yeah, of course. Elephant in the room and all that. I was

accused of sexually assaulting someone. We canceled the show for a few reasons. Obviously, something like that is not to be taken lightly. I was assumed guilty. It was a sticky situation and the decision was made to not perform until things were sorted out. But, it did, and we're back now to play that show. I think this one is going to be even better than the one we had planned."

"So, the band is still in tact it seems? I know there were a lot of rumors about a breakup were circulating for a bit."

Adrian sat up and addressed that one.

"A break up is the farthest thing from the truth. We are stronger than ever. Nothing is going to hold us down. Look, the woman who- "

Cleo interrupted him with a sharp slap on his thigh.

"What we all want to say is that sexual assault should never be lied about or turned into some joke. It only hurts the real victims."

"Fair enough. You make a very good point. Now, Cleo, do you have a favorite part of the tour this year?"

The conversation quickly moved on to much lighter things. Cleo talked about how she loved how big the shows were. Mark and Adrian were asked about being dads. We told the world stories from the bus and shenanigans we had gotten into behind the scenes.

"You spent a lot of time going back and forth with this pair, Fan Talk. The plan originally was for you guys to meet at the last show, is this still going to happen?"

"Of course! Derek got ahold of them and mailed them their passes to get backstage. We are going to meet them before the show tonight. We are so excited!" Cleo gushed.

"Sounds fun. I think we've all been waiting to see the faces under the masks. Whoa, hold up. Derek, are you wearing a wedding ring?"

I froze and looked down at how I was holding my hands.

My left hand was on top of my right one. I looked back up quickly and laughed.

"Yeah. Well I'm not married yet but me and my girlfriend are engaged." I raised my hand to show it off. It was a nice looking ring. Oddly enough, it matched hers perfectly.

"Whoa, that was fast. When did this happen?"

I tilted my head back and forth, trying to count the days. "Uh, Sunday."

"Oh, nice. Congrats man. You got a wedding date set?"

My friends started to chuckle. I perked up.

"Yeah, Monday. We went and got the license yesterday."

Nick swore and I laughed.

"You know what you want and you go for it. I love it. We'll be sure to send a present to the happy couple after the fact. Congrats again man."

I thanked him and we talked for a few more minutes before we ended the interview. Once the cameras were off, we all stood and began removing our microphones with sighs of relief as we stretched. I was patted on the back by a few hands as we exited the room.

"That went well! Good job guys!" Sam told us as he ushered us towards the exit. We were going to the venue already. We had to get ready for the meet and greet.

"Do they want us in our stage clothes or is this an informal thing?" Cleo asked.

"I think you can wear your street clothes. You don't want to be sitting around for a few hours in your dress and suits."

I agreed with that. I was ready for this show to be over so we could stop playing in these costumes. I wanted to play in my jeans again.

My heart started thumping furiously when we pulled into the parking lot. The line was huge. Concert goers had been lined up for hours already. The ones who were here for the meet and greet were already inside, waiting for us. I wasn't sure if I'd be able to keep a straight face when I saw my bride to be in full costume. I hoped she took her mask off sooner rather than later.

"Derek's the one who got ahold of them. Where are the group from? Did they give a real name to mail the passes to?" Mark asked me, bringing me back to earth. I shook my head.

"No. Just a P.O. Box," I lied and sent another silent prayer to the powers that be. Hurry the hell up. When the car stopped, we had to wait for security to come before we could get out. I took the earplugs Sam had given us moments before and shoved them in my ears as the door was open and the screams erupted around us.

We climbed out with grins and waves to all of the fans waiting for us. It was awesome seeing so many people. After the big mess, people still wanted to see us play music. It was a little humbling. Sam advised us not to doddle, but we all ended up separating and went to the thick, long line and hugged some fans, took some photos, and signed some shirts. Eventually, Sam whistled and insisted it was time to go. I moved away and waved apologetically at the group of girls I had been talking to.

We hurried inside and were greeted by a much smaller set of gasps and screams. I did my best to keep my smile on as I scanned the small group of people. Contrary to my face, I was a nervous wreck. There were a dozen people standing around some tables that had been filled with snacks and drinks. Security stood around them, ensuring they kept their distance and let us come to them.

I didn't see her at first. Or him, for that matter. Where the hell were they?

"Shouldn't they have had to show I.D. to get in with their badge?" Cleo whispered to me. I turned to her and bit my lip. Oh no, she was catching on. I rolled my eyes.

"Let's just go meet them so we can finally end this mystery."

When I turned back to the tables my heart stopped. There she was. To the untrained eye she looked like just another girl. My friends didn't notice how she rubbed her neck when she was nervous. Or how she always had one leg slightly bent and wrapped around the other one. I had never seen Dita in full costume, and it was intriguing. She looked surprisingly good with the dark hair, and the length was cute too. Her makeup was much darker than what she wore normally, but the red lips were sexy. It was a fantastic disguise.

She was talking excitedly with another young girl while reaching for a water bottle. The girl saw us first and froze, then nudged her to turn and look. Our eyes locked instantly. I saw her gulp. Her mouth opened and shut quickly. She didn't know what to do either. I was the first one to snap out of it. I gave her my best smile and waved.

"Hey! Who wants pictures!" I shouted to the small dozen. They all shouted back in excitement and the small party began. The speakers blasted a mix of our music with some other popular bands while we chatted with some of our biggest fans.

I took photos, signed shirts, posters, and CD's. I accepted letters, flowers, and even two shirts for Dita and I. They had our mugshots on them and on the back they both said **#CoupleGoals.** They were my favorite gifts to date. I noticed that Trigger Finger and her partner Death Wish were avoiding me. They had gone and met the other members of my band, but both blatantly skipped over me. That wasn't suspicious at all.

I tried unsuccessfully several times to catch Dita's attention, but she avoided my gaze time and time again. It was beginning to irritate me. Finally, Cleo walked over to her and I took the opportunity to go join them. I put my arm over Cleo's shoulder and smiled at Trigger Finger, demanding she finally look at me.

"Well well well, if it isn't the infamous girl who's been traveling the country with us. How does it feel to finally meet face to face?" I asked, removing myself from Cleo and crossing my arms. Dita laughed.

"You know how they say don't meet your heroes?" She said in a voice that was distinctly different from her normal voice. Cleo choked and began howling as I scowled. Touché.

"When do we get to meet the people underneath these?" I reached forward and flicked her cute spiderweb mask. She pulled away with disgust. Cleo's mouth opened in shock. I had forgotten for a split second that I had an audience. That probably didn't look good, me touching a stranger's face.

"Um, do we have to?" She asked weakly.

"Please, you can not leave this concert without telling us who you are. I will literally go insane!" Cleo pouted. Dita pressed her lips together tightly. She was nervous. I could tell she wasn't sure of this anymore.

"Okay, well why don't we get my partner and we start a video. A whole unveiling if you wish."

"That sounds amazing. I want to be in it!" Cleo said, and as if the stranger was an old friend, she hooked her arm in hers and marched away from me towards Grey. I chuckled when Dita glanced back at me and gave me a nervous smile. I replied with a quick thumbs up.

I watched from afar as they talked to her brother in his full costume, he reached into his backpack and pulled out the small yet professional looking video camera and a tripod. Once it was set up Cleo and the pair stood in front of the screen and started talking excitedly. Cleo wrapped her small arms around the pair and then screamed for the rest of us to join her.

I sauntered over and decided to stand behind Death Wish, letting Adrian and Mark be next to Trigger Finger. Once I was in place an idea popped into my head, making me move and ask Adrian to trade me spots. He gave me a weird look but did it anyways.

Cleo began loudly counting down from ten. I watched carefully as the mystery pair reached up towards their faces. They each had one hand on their mask and the other on their wigs. Just as she got to five, I leaned down to whisper in between her and Dita. I made sure it was loud enough for both of them to hear me clearly.

"Remember when I said that I was going to marry you, Trigger Finger?"

With a large gasp Cleo stopped and whipped her entire body around to glare at me and then the girl beside her.

"Dita Fiona Fox are you Trigger Finger?" She demanded loudly.

The concert went fan-fucking-tastic. After the big reveal, all hell broke loose. Dita and Grey revealed themselves for the fans and us. I pulled her in for a gigantic hug and kiss. I spun her around, holding our lips together. Once I put her down, we laced hands and I stood with her as she and her brother told the story of how they came up with the idea and how it was implemented.

"And when did you tell Derek?" Mark squinted his eyes at me accusingly.

"We didn't. He figured it out on his own. I don't actually know when. When did you figure it out?" She turned to me. I tried to remember properly but shook my head.

"I can't remember now. Sorry." I shrugged and let them continue their story for everyone. Only when we had to get ready for the show did I remove myself from her circle. I gave her one last quick peck and promised I'd see her in a bit.

I honestly couldn't remember most of the show, it went so

quickly. I couldn't focus, I was thinking about tonight, and Monday. It couldn't come quick enough. Towards the end of the concert however, Cleo decided to take a break and talk to the crowd.

"Who here has watched the latest Fan Talk video?" After a pause for screams she continued. "So now everyone knows that the girl in those videos was actually our very own Derek Turtle's girlfriend the whole time. How adorable. The things one does for love." She walked over to me and put her hand on my shoulder.

"You two are planning on getting married on Monday, right?"

I nodded. "Well, guess what sucka, you're not the only one with surprises. You told us we could plan the wedding so you're gonna get married tonight. Right after the show we're gonna need you to go get changed and be ready to get hitched!"

She bounced away like the little devil she was and signaled for us to start back up. We finished the concert a few songs later and she practically shoved me off the stage.

"Come on, you need to get moving. We all do. Get moving guys!" She shouted.

"Wait, where's Dita?" I asked, frantically looking around.

"We told her what was going on right before we went on. I made her leave so she can get ready. She'll need more time than you. Do you want to shower before you put your suit on?"

"Well yeah, are we seriously doing this now?" I asked as I continued moving.

"Yes!" My bandmates shouted in unison, and an hour later I was standing in front of a brightly lit chapel with Mark and Adrian. They gave me just enough time to shower, put deodorant on and brush my hair before I was being shoved into my tuxedo. It was maroon and black. I loved it. As I admired myself in the mirror, I wondered what my bride would look like. Absolutely beautiful. I knew it without having to see.

"Everyone else is inside. We can go in when you're ready," Mark said. They were dressed in black suits with maroon flowers in their pockets. We were having one last cigarette before heading in.

"You feeling alright?" Adrian asked me. I nodded.

"Of course. I don't want to be anywhere else right now."

"Hey, you didn't pick a best man. What's the deal?" Mark joked. I looked around.

"Where's Cleo? I thought she was going to be in a suit too," I said.

"Oh, she is. Come on, let's go in," Adrian said. I shook my head. I was slowly piecing things together. The pair stared at me expectantly. I took a step forward and hugged Mark. He swore.

"Damn it, I knew he'd choose you," he said to Adrian.

I took a step to his side and stood eye to eye with my other best friend.

"Do I have your blessing? Will you stand up there with me and be my best man?"

He licked his lips.

"I give you my blessing and will gladly stand up with you."

I hugged him tightly and once we pulled away, we entered the building. Despite already anticipating it, I cracked up when I saw Cleo at the end of the aisle in full Elvis gear, complete with hip pop. Her black wig was super high and her white, rhinestone jumpsuit was spectacular.

"Ladies and gentlemen, the groom is in the building!" She said with her best Elvis voice. I gave an awkward wave as the music was started and I walked down the aisle. People waved back and I froze when I saw my parents, my brothers, and their wives in the pews. How did they get out here on such short notice? I paused at their aisle so my parents could give me a quick hug before heading to the altar with Cleo.

My groomsmen disappeared as the music changed to something significantly peppier. I tilted my head as I listened to the lyrics. It was an older song. My eyes lit up when I finally recognized it. Dita had sang it to me in our kitchen while she made me breakfast just last week. I smiled wide at the memory. The song was "I don't know why I love you, but I do". It was perfect, just like the woman waiting in the other room for me. I pressed my lips together, but they couldn't contain my grin.

Suddenly I saw Adrian and Chase, arm in arm. They appeared and started down the aisle. I laughed as they bobbed their heads back and forth with the song. No sooner did they part and Adrian stand next to me and Chase on the bride's side did Mark and Renee start their walk. They reached the altar and took their places. Now it was the most important person's turn to come down. I stared expectantly at the doorway.

"Oh, I forgot something!" Adrian said and before I could protest, he was sprinting down the aisle.

"Ladies and Gentlemen. If you would please stand for our bride." Cleo announced.

"Wait, Adrian," I protested but stopped when I glanced back to the door and saw my best friend and my best girl arm in arm. Suddenly, everything I had ever worried about didn't matter anymore.

She was absolutely stunning. Her dress was huge and puffy, yet tight in all the right places, making her undeniable beauty shine. Her tattoo that matched mine stood front and center; exposed as she pushed her long curls behind her shoulders.

She had taken off the costume makeup and had put on lipstick the same shade as my tux. In all of my life, I had never seen anyone as beautiful as her. When our eyes met, she grinned ear to ear and her lips began moving. I tilted my head again, trying to figure out what she was saying.

With the hand holding her bouquet she used a finger to point up. My eyes followed her directions and I realized it was the music. It had changed. 'Ain't No Mountain High Enough' was playing. I laughed again as my eyes were beginning to tear up. That was the song that played right after that morning. I had sang it to her. When she reached me, she hugged Adrian and thanked him one last time before reaching for my hands and vowing to be mine forever.

Cleo's speech was a blur. I couldn't tell you what I repeated back to Dita and her to me. I couldn't take my eyes off the woman in front of me. She was my everything. Forever.

Adrian passed me a ring I had never seen before but matched her engagement ring perfectly. Dita laughed and was on the brink of sobbing when I pointed out that I was already wearing my wedding ring. We kissed and just like that, it was official.

Our reception was at the Circus Circus hotel and casino. It was hella awesome. Dita told me that she had picked it out, and I was glad they let her keep one part of her original plan. We spent the evening watching trapeze artists, eating popcorn and cotton candy, and playing carnival games. I couldn't win anything to save my life, but I didn't care. Tonight, I had already won.

Once all of our guests had left for the evening my bandmates sat with me outside to get some air. Dita had gone to the bathroom so we snuck out for a quick smoke.

"Hey, I don't mean to squish on your big day, but Ethan just got a call from another madly in love rockstar is getting married soon. He invited us all to come out to see it."

"Who?" I scanned my brain quickly, trying to figure out who she was talking about. "Wait, Emile? With the tattoo artist?"

"Cotton, yeah. Tomorrow. Want to come?"

I blinked. "I'll have to talk to the woman in charge now, but sure. We'll stop over and then head off to our honeymoon."

"Where are you guys going? Renee and I went to Hawaii. It was awesome." Mark said.

I shrugged. "I don't know yet. I think we're just gonna go to the airport and see what sounds good. I'll travel the world with her if she wants," I sighed. God, how did I end up so lucky?

There was a pause in the conversation as the three of us men smoked our cigarettes. Cleo leaned against the building and gave us a half smile.

"So, what now?" Cleo mused.

"What do you mean?" Adrian asked.

"We can turn in our tickets for prizes and head downstairs to the casino if you guys want," Mark added.

"I think another circus act is coming up," I said. Dita had been enjoying them, so I didn't want us to miss the next show.

"No. I meant with us. It's official. We're all married. We all have families, responsibilities. We're all happy. What do we do now?"

I laughed. "What do you mean? We keep doing exactly what we've been doing. We are going to keep making music, keep raising our kids to be as kick ass as we are, and we're gonna be hella famous and hella rich."

"Well as long as we're all on the same page," she winked at me.

"I think we should take some time off though. Chase and I have been talking about another kid. We've already gotten in touch with Rocky's surrogate."

"Aw, does Adrian want a little girl?" She teased. He shrugged.

"I think it'd be nice to pass my genes on, spread the wealth a little," he told her.

"I am ready for a break too. Lola is so big now. I missed so much while on tour. I just need some time to enjoy the three of us. I bought tickets to London. I'm going to surprise Renee tomorrow."

"Those two are so spoiled," Adrian chuckled.

"They deserve every single penny," Mark shot back with a smile.

"What about you, Mr. Newlywed?" Mark asked, punching me playfully. "You gonna hole up in your mega-mansion for a few months? No one in or out until you've run each other dry?"

I rolled my eyes.

"Nah. I don't know, actually. A few months off sounds fantastic though. I'm burning my suit, by the way," I joked. Adrian and Mark quickly agreed with me.

"You didn't like your suits?" Cleo asked innocently.

"You had a bunch of dresses that were made so you can move freely. We had suits. They were hot and didn't give us much freedom to move like regular clothes. Singer, your privilege is showing," I teased her. She scrunched up her nose but said nothing else.

The doors opened and we turned to see Renee and Dita looking for us. Just seeing her again, I leapt up and hurried back to my wife. *Wife.* What a simple, yet life-altering word. I had a wife. I was someone's husband. Wow, that was something I never would have expected.

We went back to the circus inside and eventually our friends took their own husbands and wives and left us. When we realized it was just the two of us, exhaustion hit. I asked her if she wanted to get out of here and she leaned against me in agreement.

A limo was ready to take us to our final destination, but Dita asked if we could get out and walk once we got a block away from our hotel. She was still in her wedding dress and her skin shone with sweat. The driver let us out and told us to call if we needed him. I thanked him and tipped him. I took her hand and we started a leisurely stroll down the sidewalk.

"I can't wait," she yawned.

"For what?" I asked.

"Everything. Our future, tomorrow, bed tonight," she giggled. I raised my eyebrows. I doubted we'd have the energy to celebrate once we reached our room, but if she was interested, I was sure I could muster up an extra wind.

"What do you want to do with our future?" I asked her.

"I have no idea. And you know what, I love that." She stopped walking and turned to face me. "I love that I am not worried about anything. For the first time in my life, I don't want to run. This is exactly where I want to be. Where I'm supposed to be. With you. I trust that whatever I do, you're gonna be there with me."

I reached for her and she put her head under my chin. I kissed the top of her head.

"We can do whatever you want. It's my turn to follow you around the world. I would love nothing more than to do so."

She let me go and hand in hand we began walking again. A moment later we were at the doors of our hotel. The casino part was still going full speed, so I led her quickly through the packed floor and into the elevator. Once we were alone again, she gave me a suspicious smile.

"Travel the world?"

I grinned. "Yeah. You said you loved photography, and the whole Fan Talk thing was great. You pulled it off. I was thinking maybe I could join you and we could do something similar. Maybe make our own little music, candid, photography business. You're the brains, I'm the muscle. What do you think?"

"Is that a real job?" She asked as the doors opened and we stepped onto our floor. We headed down the hall and as I put my key in the door I shrugged.

"I don't know. We should make it one." I swung the door open and before she could protest, I bent down and plucked her up. She squealed with delight as I carried her into the room. I gently placed her on our bed, and she giggled.

"You are crazy! You want to start a business from scratch?"

I dropped to my knees and lifted her dress to gently remove her shoes. She sighed with relief as she wiggled her toes. "Not entirely from scratch. I've got some connections. I think this could work. What do you say, do you trust me enough to run away with me?" I asked as I stood up to embrace her.

"Let's do it." She then kissed me ever so tenderly, reminding me why I loved her more than anything else in this world. A small giggle left her lips as she pulled away to look at me.

"I have never trusted anything more."

Acknowledgments

Wow! So we finally reached the end of this group of characters. It's kind of an insane thought. When I first started writing *Missing You, Missing Me* in the mid 2010's I never EVER considered that the story would go past Cleo and Ethan. I was always adamant that I'd tell their love story and then be done. But somewhere down the line it became clear that these characters weren't finished telling their stories. I am so happy I didn't stop with Cleo and Ethan.

This book in particular was the hardest to write (besides book one, but that's for another time). I went through major imposter syndrome. I was also completely emotionally drained from *Cherishing You, Cherishing Me*. The longer I put off writing the more anxious about it I grew. It was a cycle I had to drag myself out of. So, for any author suffering right now, know that you can do this and it gets better!

Now that we are at the end of this series, I want to give some shout outs to people who helped, whether directly or indirectly with these books. Thank you so much each and every one of you.

Kristen Downer, my editor. Have either of us matched a

deadline? I think we're getting better with each book! Caroline Andrus, my super patient, super kind formatter. My cover designer, H.G. Artwork. You're amazing! And of course, the reason I keep writing, my beta readers. Jodi and Sabrina. Jodi, your kind words are forever etched in my heart. Sabrina, you're the one I go to when I need validation and I love you for it.

Now to all the people I stole things from. Maybe it was your name, maybe it was some vague trait of yours. Either way, this is your shout out. In *Trusting You, Trusting Me*, Gretchen Lynch and The Turtle Family. If you read this book, you'll know where you are.

V.C. Andrews, although she will never see this, she is my biggest inspiration, and that was why I chose to name Cleo and Ethan both after her. Oh, and Christopher too, I suppose. Although that one was coincidental. S.E. Hinton, for Dallas, and Thomas Harris for Christopher's Last name. Tyler Wilson and Roger Hilyard helped name Chase, and Rita Moreno was for Adrian. Mark Lapham, Kyla Stull, The House of Yes, The Rocky Horror Picture Show, and so many rock bands that inspired me while writing.

And last but not least, thank you to my readers. My dolls. Without your kind words, we wouldn't be here. Thanks for the continued support, and I'll see you in the next book.

Check out my other books!

Missing You, Missing Me

Promising You, Promising Me

Cherishing You, Cherishing Me

Annoyingly Obvious

About the Author

With her dark eyeliner, My Chemical Romance tattoo, and the Twilight series still proudly displayed on her bookshelf, Tylor Paige is an emo girl forever. A sucker for a good love triangle and second chances, she knew the wonderful world of romance writing was where she was meant to be.

When she's not writing, Tylor enjoys watching cult films, spending time with her writer tribe- the MMRWA, and collecting everything spooky and cute.

She writes for the readers who love, obsess, and collect, like her. At the time of this publication Tylor Paige has now written and published four full length novels and one novella. Her ultimate dream is for people to write fan fiction about her stories and characters. Perhaps she'll inspire someone to write their own book boyfriend.

Find me on:
Tylorpaigebooks.com

Twitter: @TylorPaige
Instagram: @tylorpaige
Facebook: Author Tylor Paige

And join my reader group!
www.facebook.com/groups/376190999768893